Pat Marlow was born in Hartlepool and lives in Bournemouth and in France. After three years at art college, she worked in Turkey and the Sudan teaching English as a foreign language.

Having brought up her four children, Pat decided to study Law and was called to the Bar after five years of studying. After working for the Crown Prosecution Service, she practised independently as a criminal barrister. This is her first book.

JUSTICE DELAYED

Pat Marlow

JUSTICE DELAYED

Vanguard Press

A CIP catalogue record for this title is
available from the British Library.

ISBN 978 1 784656 02 7

Vanguard Press is an imprint of
Pegasus Elliot MacKenzie Publishers Ltd.
www.pegasuspublishers.com

First Published in 2019

Vanguard Press
Sheraton House Castle Park
Cambridge England

Printed & Bound in Great Britain

Dedication

For Poppy and Ava and Blakey Bee, and all the other Blakeys.

With Special thanks to Alan Lambert who encouraged me not to give up!

Chapter One

"Slow down Spike. There's no rush now. He's dead."

"What!" exclaimed Spike slamming on the brakes so that the body next to Vic shot forward and slumped onto the floor. "He can't be. Please tell me this is a sick joke."

"No honestly. I can't hear him breathing. What did you do to him for heaven's sake?"

"Nothing. I just asked him what he knew. He had terminal cancer – last stages, but a soon as he collapsed, I just wanted to get him to hospital. He'd talked for about twenty minutes. Quite enlightening. It's all on tape. He didn't kill Joey but he knew who did. That bastard priest was abusing some of the younger boys – the vulnerable ones, the ones without parents. Never mind that now. What are we going to do with him?"

"Take him to hospital as planned."

"I don't think that's a good idea. There'd be too many questions and it won't help him now. We can't go back. What the hell do we do?"

"Just keep driving. Straight ahead. I have an idea."

*****

George's last conscious view had been of a cheap purple carpet, mottled with stains, close to his eyes and nose so that he could smell its rank odour. Now, when his eyes closed, there was the smell of grass. A clean smell filling his nostrils; he knew he was close to death. He was eager to go, the last few months of his life had been depressing, the last few weeks painful, and the last few days frustrating. He had wanted to die then, but the call from Spike had made him desperately anxious to explain and apologise before it was too late. Maybe there was a God after all. He wanted absolution. He remembered talking with him hoping that Spike had believed him – believed that he was sorry. He had seemed kind, after his initial anger.

What the hell am I doing here? he wondered. How did I get here? There was a man, not Spike, but someone else. The one who had put a gentle hand on his neck and hastily pulled his arm away. George felt his heart beating very gently. Slowly he smiled then knew no more.

The allotments had been there since the end of the Second World War. Once an area of Victorian housing, they had suffered a direct hit towards the end and had never been rebuilt. From time to time they had flourished under the care of dedicated enthusiasts. It basked proudly, under organised rows of lettuce, feathery carrot tops, and sturdy beetroot. Now, it was neglected and was viewed for the most part only by passing commuters in the trains that ran into King's Cross. It was just an area of desolation.

Disordered clumps of gorse, weeds, nettles and heaps of broken bricks, played host to the old mattresses, furtively dumped at night, bags of old rubbish, old cycle wheels, soggy misshapen cardboard boxes and the rest a of kind of detritus, which makes its way to the dumping grounds that scar every big city.

In the watery golden light of a June morning, however, the ground level had a certain beauty seen at close range with the heady scent of earth. George's eyes, wide open stared at this worm's eye view but saw nothing.

That afternoon at half past two, in response to several emergency calls, garbled and distorted against the frantic background noise of King's Cross Station, several police officers in three squad cars arrived at the allotments. And within a few minutes, an area of land was enclosed within blue and white police tape. The investigation commenced.

*****

At half past two that afternoon Kate Meredith stretched her long, tanned legs and balanced her heels on the edge of a large terra cotta pot, from which a profusion of Bizzy Lizzies spilled. She leaned back against the faded canvas of her deck chair and smiled as the afternoon sun caressed her face. The garden was just about perfect. No lawns to cut. No borders to weed, just an array of flower-festooned pots, arranged around a paved terrace. A gnarled fig tree leaned comfortably against a sun-bleached wall, which extended around three sides of this sheltered paradise; its dark green leaves were a perfect foil for the tumble of scarlet geraniums at its base.

"Trollop!" exclaimed someone from the balcony above.

"Voyeur," she responded, with a smile.

"Got any cold beer?"

"In the fridge and bring me a glass of Chablis, will you?"

Within moments, Jake Scott strolled through the French windows. Clad in a pair of denim shorts that had seen better days and balancing a cold glass of wine on her bare stomach, Jake lowered himself into another garden chair. As the tenant of the flat above, they had seen little of each other when she had first arrived but had joined forces against a common enemy when the landlord had tried to lease out the two garages situated in a lane behind the property, of which the residents of flats one and two had had unlimited use, since 'time immemorial' they claimed. It was an ongoing battle.

Jake was an enigma she knew little about. She had a vague idea about what he did and even less about his background. He had claimed to be a scientist, involved in research at the university. Research into what, she had no idea. He would disappear for days, sometimes weeks, and be reticent about his whereabouts when he returned. Kate had learned to avoid asking several questions. The atmosphere would be strained and she could feel herself treading on thin ice. She grew used to his absences, due to which, she tried not to be too dependent on him. Self-preservation, she told herself, was difficult. He was important, more than she cared to admit.

Work and background aside, they had developed an easy rapport between them, which enabled them to talk sometimes into the early hours, about critical issues or mere trivia or just to settle in comforting silence. He had a sense of humour that delighted her and a gentle sincerity that moved her.

One late night he had reached out for her hand as they sat close together on her soft grey sofa; he stroked her gently at the back of her neck and slipped his fingers through her hair pulling her face towards his. Her pulse had raced as he kissed her gently and then with increasing urgency as she had responded to him. He had made love to her with extreme passion and skill, which delighted and surprised her and then he was gone. She didn't see him for three weeks. When he arrived home, nothing was said by either of them, but a bond was forged: she felt it and was sure that it would be never be broken. Words were unnecessary.

Today they sat in happy silence until they were jolted back into the real world by the shrill sound of Kate's telephone. As Kate reached for the door, he got up suddenly and blocked her way.

"Don't answer," he said and put his hand on her cheek followed by a shrug and grinned. "I have to go anyway.

Got to finish a thesis. I'll call you later." He ruffled her hair and was gone.

Kate picked up the phone and recognized the voice of her boss, Chief Inspector Charlie Knowles.

"Hi! Kate, really sorry, I know you're not due back until tomorrow, but we've got a body. Can you get down to the allotments between Kipling and Tennyson Street? SOCO is there along with the doc. I'll meet you in forty minutes, okay? It looks interesting."

"Okay, but send a car, I've had a glass of wine."

"None spare, you'll have to risk it. Unless it was a large glass you should be okay. Don't take any risks. Just be careful."

"I'm on my way." Kate took only minutes to put on her dark blue jeans and tuck in her blue cotton shirt. She grabbed her shoulder bag and climbed upstairs to get her comfortable slip-on shoes, sunglasses, warrant card, money and keys.

Dreadful really, she reflected as she carefully negotiated a right-hand turn, some poor bugger has to die before I get a kick out of the job. No, she thought, Charlie had sounded quite upbeat. The death or a severe injury to a child cast a pervasive air of grief throughout the department. The consequent investigations were distressing and traumatic. They took a long time to be forgotten. Counselling was available to all police personnel, who felt the need for it, and it helped, but there were memories that could never be erased. Kate shook off her morbid thoughts as she hurtled into a gap in the right lane and turned onto Tennyson road. At a distance, she recognised the familiar chequered stripes of two police vehicles and pulled up alongside.

"About bloody time," muttered a ruddy-faced uniformed PC, who was leaning against the side of his vehicle. "CID is always the last to arrive. It's hot hanging around here you know. For God's sake go and do what you must do, and we can all go and have a drink. 'Know all' is in the tent. It's just about big enough for him to get in."

"Why are you always such a miserable sod, Fred?"

Kate dodged as PC Laver aimed a swipe at her passing bottom and headed in the indicated direction. The allotments were surrounded by a low wall topped by metal railings. There was a gate, which was painted and locked during the initial days. At present, it hung loose from its hinges and pushed right back so that the long green grass, inside was flattened. The police tape marked out a path to the location of the body, concealed within a plastic tent.

Always alert to the danger of contaminating the evidence, she stood at a safe distance from the plastic tent erected around the body and hailed her boss, whose massive bulk she recognized, silhouetted against the tent wall. He emerged and gave her a brief smile.

"Well, the photographers have come and gone, Scenes of Crime and the pathologist are about to wind up and the ambulance is on its way. I hope to God this is a one-off and not the start of a series. It's a middle-aged male, looks as if he was killed elsewhere and dumped here. Time of death, until we can be more specific, between eight and fifteen hours ago. Cause of death – I haven't a clue, but someone has shoved a bloody great spike in his arse – something for our Black Museum. Thankfully the mutilation was post-mortem. Apart from that, and I must tell you that the thought of that is making my eyes water, I can't see any other signs of injury. Looks like vengeance killing, to me. The implications are obvious. It's homophobia gone mad, and if he gets a taste for it, there are a hell lot of potential victims out there. Here – stick these on your plates and have a butchers."

Kate took a pair of disposable plastic shoe covers from a newly opened pack, pulled them over her sneakers and walked carefully towards the tent. The body was lying with its back facing her. She saw something, which appeared to be a man of average height, the bare buttocks closest. The rusty broken end of which, seemed to be the top of a metal railing protruding from the anus; there was no bleeding. The trousers had been pulled down just far enough, once held up by a cheap plastic belt, still slotted through the waistband of cheap grey trousers. The green polyester, ribbed sweater was in place. Moving around the body she saw that its eyes were closed, and yes, the face showed no contortion. Whatever he had done or been, he was now at peace. She saw the medics approaching with a stretcher and stood aside as they went to collect their charge.

"Let's get back to base," said Knowles. "I'm interested in finding out what they can tell from his clothes. The sooner we get an ID the sooner we can get this show on the road. Fancy a quick cuppa? There's a clean little cafe up the road and around the corner, great cinnamon pastries in the window. I'm buying."

They walked in with a single file along the outskirts of the marked path, both with eyes glued to the ground looking for anything that might be significant. At the edge of an area, which had once been cultivated, nettles stood shoulder high against the fence, which marked the edge of the railway embankment, steeply rising away from them; these hadn't been disturbed at all. There was no sign of flattening or breakage. The victim and whoever had been with him came through the gate.

"But how, Kate? Did he walk? Was he carried or dragged? One thing's for sure. He wasn't alone."

"What did you find in his pockets?"

"Scenes of Crime didn't want the clothing disturbed any more than was necessary. It's the appliance of science these days. They want everything bagged up so that they can look for foreign fibres, dog hair, you know the sort of thing. The fact that there might be a good wallet full of info, which would point straight to the culprit within two hours, would spoil their fun and make them bloody redundant."

He kicked moodily at a piece of brick that lay inches from his toe.

"I refuse to believe you didn't feel in his pockets as soon as you found him," Kate said.

Taking a packet of cigarettes, from his shirt pocket, he lit one and took a long purposeful drag. He walked up to the gate and leaned against its rotting frame, gazing thoughtfully back in the direction, from which they had just walked. Kate paused to consider her boss. He was an old-school detective, close to his retirement. He was disillusioned and frustrated by developments in the law and in police work, which he considered to be restrictive and against the true course of justice. The advent of the Crown Prosecution Service, according to him had irrevocably emasculated the police service. Several months of challenging work involved in the detection of serious cases, often proved to be a waste of time and sweat, because the evidence was pronounced inadequate or unreliable, even though everyone was prepared to concede that the right man had been charged with the right offence. Defence lawyers, who would smirk with satisfaction when their clients walked, because caution had been overlooked rendering a confession inadmissible, would concede that their clients had had a lucky escape.

"Right," he pronounced suddenly and continued, "I don't know what we are hanging around here for. Get that lazy so and so Laver here to organise things. He'll know what to do. House to house, soil samples, and I don't want any bugger putting his great hoof prints here unless it is absolutely necessary. It's late to do much more today and

I have a meeting later with the commander. Assuming there is enough in his pockets to disclose his address, and I know there is because I did look but keep that to yourself, you and I will start there, tomorrow. Could you pop over to the butcher's shop first thing and see what the post-mortem turns up. Rosie wastes no time. She should have something for us by ten or so. I'll pick you up from there."

"Sure, so where did he live?"

"Stoke Newington, but you don't know that yet. You and I will go over there after I've picked you up. Well! Go on get on with it. You're not here to sunbathe."

He turned and disappeared through the gate and moments later his police Jaguar roared off down the road.

"Well, thanks for the tea," she muttered and headed for PC Laver who was sitting in his police car with the door open.

"Hi Kevin, could you get a team to do a house to house, and make sure that no one can get through that gate?"

"Already done," he affirmed, "and I'll have someone on duty here until we get the green flag."

"You're so efficient, Laver. What would I do without you!"

"You'd probably still be on traffic. I think you owe me a night out and a cuddle."

"Frankly my dear, I'd rather spend my evening cleaning dog poo from the shoes of the entire Metropolitan Police Force but, as it happens, I have a date," she lied.

She pinched his cheek and walked to her car, smiling to herself. She was aware that the invitation was a tease, and knew that if she had agreed to spend any time with him he would have behaved well. They'd been verbal sparring partners for years; despite all the coppers that she had known and worked with, he had proven to be the most reliable during a crisis. She gave him a friendly wave as she drove away and knew that the crime scene would be adequately supervised, until on-the-spot investigations were completed.

The time was close to five thirty. The sun was still warm, and the traffic had built up to the point where nothing moved more than ten miles an hour.

I wish I had a blue light, she thought. It's going to take me an hour to get to the nick at this rate. God knows when I'll be able to hit the sack.

She wondered if Jake would be there when she got back. The prospect of sitting close to him and reporting the day's events, while admiring his intense blue eyes register everything had an enormous appeal. She would have liked to be with him, to know that she was vitally important to him.

The journey back to the office was a predictable nightmare and Kate climbed out of the car hot and sweaty. Laver with the benefit of the blue light was back before her. After she'd had a glass of carrot juice and a yogurt in the police canteen she left, to head for her office, and then headed back for a plate of sausage beans and chips.

"There are times in a girl's life when a diet is simply not appropriate," she explained to Laver who arrived before her and sat opposite, polishing off the remains of a large Cornish pasty. "This is not going to be an easy investigation. I can see my private life being put on the back burner for weeks. Look at me, I'm thirty-three and still an old maid. In no time at all, I'll have bags under my eyes, boobs around my waist and a neck like a tortoise. This is no job for a woman. There's too much death and not enough life."

"You've got sauce on your chin," observed Laver, his uniform speckled with flaky pastry, "and you still look sexy," he continued. "Look," he said firmly. "You're tired out. It's six o'clock, why don't you knock off now? You were here until heaven knows what time last night. You can't do more today. If anything crops up that needs the immediate attention I'll give you a ring. I'm on nights anyway and I'm stuck in the station finishing a heap of bloody paperwork for CPS. There's a briefing at eight in the morning, you can catch up then."

Kate suddenly felt immensely weary. "There are times when you aren't such a bad bloke after all, and I love you," she said. "I'm going to take you up on that because there's someone I would really like to see. The guv and I will be back to update everyone later in the morning. I think we're going to check an address first. Thanks, Kevin."

"I'll take payment in kind," he grinned.

Kate picked up a half-eaten sausage from her plate and handed it to him with a sweet smile. "You deserve it," she said and hastily left the canteen as the sausage winged past her ear.

Kate's heart beat marginally faster when she saw Jake's Jeep parked on the other side of the road as she parked her Renault outside the front door. Be cool, she instructed herself sternly, remember the rules: be beautiful, be tantalizing, be careful and remain just out of reach. Resist the temptation to hurl yourself into his arms and beg him to love you forever. Dealing with outright rejection is not your forte. She locked the car, headed to the front door and jumped when she opened it and found Jake standing immediately inside, in the entrance hall.

"Hi, gorgeous!" he said, giving her a quick hug. "I didn't expect to see you again today. I'm meeting a couple of friends for supper... Hey! Why don't you come along?"

"Err... no thanks," she smiled, stifling the urge to accept the invitation with transparent enthusiasm. *Come on, persuade me,* she thought, but said, "It's been a gruelling day and I'm bushed. I need a shower and a drink and someone to... look, I must go. Sorry."

She hurried to her own front door and let herself in. Closing the door behind, she leaned against it, her heart heavy with disappointment. She heard the front door closing and the unmistakable sound of the Jeep's engine as it drove away. Suddenly, feeling tired and alone she slid down against the door and sat on the floor, tears trickling down her face. "Fuck!" she uttered, an expletive word she saved for special occasions because it usually made her laugh, and which didn't fail even this time. She rose to her feet and with a grin on her face went to run a bath.

How pathetic you can get, she thought to herself. All I had to say was – give me a few minutes to smarten up, and I could have been enjoying his company right now. But no! Miss Smart Ass has to obey the rules, and now she's not just out of reach, in fact, she's out of bloody sight. Oh well!

After a long soak and a couple of glasses of wine, Kate was feeling relaxed and relatively cheerful when there was a knock on the door. Clothed only in a cream silk robe, she was inclined to be 'out' but the knocking persisted.

"Who is it?" she yelled.

"It's me! Open the bloody door, I'm dropping all this stuff."

Jake was standing outside clutching a bottle of Veuve Cliquot and an untidy bunch of white and yellow daisies.

"I thought you needed cheering up, so I made my excuses. Now, let's get into this bottle and you can tell Uncle Jake all about it."

*****

"You look so lovely," said Jake sometime later when they were sitting outside in the balmy summer warmth. "How can a girl like you, ever be depressed? Great looks, great personality and your number one fan living upstairs, lusting after you every waking moment."

"Don't tease," she murmured. "I bet I never cross your mind from the moment you leave my front door until the next time you trip over me."

"You'd be surprised," he said quietly.

"Then why don't I feel it, Jake... Feel part of your life I mean? I see you for a few hours a week if I'm lucky. The rest of the time I don't know where you are or what you're doing. When we're together, I talk, I tell you about my job, my colleagues, my family, but I know nothing about you. It's like looking at the photograph of someone against a blank wall; there's no background and every time I try to fill the space, you block me, change the subject or sometimes even walk away." She paused.

Jake was silent. He stood up and leaned against the fig tree, his fingers stroking the rim of his glass. He looked miserable and Kate longed to throw his arms around him and tell him nothing mattered except the moment. She knew she loved him more than she had loved anyone before. She loved his untidy dark hair, his eyes that made her heart race when he gazed at her and his smile, that could lift her spirits up during the lowest days. He wasn't handsome but there was something irresistibly appealing about him. Something that made her instinctively trust him despite his reluctance to reveal any details of his life.

Jake suddenly turned towards her and pulled his chair up close. He put down his glass and took both of her hands in his.

"You're right and I'm sorry," he said. "It's not fair, but there are things in my life that are difficult to deal with and not easy to talk about right now. Do you think you can give me just a little more time? You'll have to know all about me one day, probably soon. Please?"

She leaned forward and put her arms around him. "Of course, take as much time as you like."

"I love you, Kate. You'd be surprised to know how much!"

"Yeah? Well, prove it! The inside of my car is filthy. Get outside and clean it."

"What! Get real. There are limits. I've seen cleaner pig sheds." And normality returned.

Chapter Two

Kate switched off the engine of her car, sat back in the driving seat and surveyed the Victorian building in front of her. There was something about the mortuary that even on a warm summer day like this, sent a chill through her. Bright sunshine cast deep shadows across the Gothic façade, glanced brilliantly off panes of glass, rippled lazily over the asphalt car park but failed to disguise a pervasive sense of death, grief and desolation. She'd been there many times before but had never developed the detachment displayed by her colleagues. Knowles was aware of her problem. That is why he had sent her there alone There was no room for ultra-sensitivity in the life of a good detective. Violent death came with the job.

She opened the car door and swung her legs out and onto the ground, squared her shoulders and set off towards the door. All I've got to do is get in here, find Wilkins, grab the report and get out. Ignore the atmosphere, ignore the smell. Think about something sane, ordinary, everyday. I must clean the cooker this weekend. No that's even more depressing. I know, I must get down to Regents Street and get myself a new bikini. Yes brilliant.

She pushed through the double doors and paused. Out of the sunlight there was familiar sense of eerie emptiness.

Just inside the door was an unmanned reception area. There was a low table, devoid of any literature as if to offer any form of light relief would be inappropriate or disrespectful. The plastic-covered bench seats were faded brown, grey plastic tiles on the floor and walls, stretched down the corridor towards the labs, and she could hear in her mind the awful muted sound the trolleys made with their rubber wheels as bodies were transported like so many carcasses of meat, for post mortem. It was a process she found abhorrent.

Two years before, she had to break the news of their daughter's sudden and inexplicable death, to a couple who lived in the leafy suburbs towards Hampstead. The girl was a music student, nineteen, and an only child. She had been found dead in her studio bedroom. There was no sign of injury, or struggle or any reason why death had arrived so suddenly. She had been an outstanding and popular student.

Kate recalled the scene in the living room as she broke the news. The mother standing motionless by the long windows staring into the garden, as if, as long as she didn't move, she could avoid being plunged into the terrible reality of grief. The father, equally mute, gazing at the cup of hot strong tea, growing cold and untouched.

At the mortuary, Kate had looked at the young body lying on a steel table. The face was beautiful, the skin flawless: long silky lashes lay against ivory cheeks, the lips then almost colourless and well defined. She was slender, long limbed and naked and Kate had fought to resist the urge to seize a sheet and cover her against the dispassionate gaze of the pathologist clad in his green overalls hand hovering over scalpel and saw. Just hours before she had been a vital and lovely young woman. The thought of what was going to happen to this lifeless and seemingly, still vulnerable child was more than she could bear. How could she explain to those parents the mutilation that would be lawfully inflicted upon all that was left of the person they had loved most in the world.

The following morning, she had been called to account in Knowles' office. He had listened in silence to her attempts to explain her feelings and then hauled himself to his feet and grabbed his jacket.

"Come on," he'd said.

They'd taken a taxi to the City and then walked along the Embankment from Temple Lane to the Tate Gallery. They'd talked about jazz, opera, politics and food. They'd exchanged office gossip and discussed the theory of evolution. They'd studied the painting of the Pre-Raphaelites, French Impressionists and Turner. They'd walked through the streets of Knightsbridge, comparing tastes, contrasting styles. They'd eaten hot dogs and drunk coffee from a stall and later sausage and mash in a pub, and gradually the haunting thoughts in Kate's mind had been almost flushed away and replaced with the images of a bustling vibrant city full of life and normality.

It wasn't until they were back at the station facing each other across his desk that Knowles referred to the previous day. "Kate," he said, "you are a beautiful, intelligent and perceptive woman. You relate to people in a way that I have never been able to do. I've seen witnesses open up to you as if you were their best friend. You are thorough, earnest and fair." He paused and considered her carefully then went on.

"I dare say that if you decided to do something completely different, you'd be equally good at it. I hope you won't. You've got to keep your heart locked up, girl. Don't let it go out to anyone, not when you're working, otherwise you'll drown in emotion. You'll lose sight of the target. There are bastards out there who kill, maim, torture, abuse and terrify. They're indiscriminate. You will see bodies of men, women, boys, girls, children and babies. Always remember what we're here for Kate. We are here to identify, catch and charge the ones who do it. Be objective, be detached but stay compassionate. It's not easy, it takes time."

He had stood up and gazed out of the window for a minute then turned and said, "Now make yourself useful and get me a cuppa my feet are killing me and I've a thirst like a guppy in a sand pit – and by the way," he continued as she turned to go, "The girl. It was a heart condition, natural causes. They didn't need to touch the head at all. The funeral is on Friday. I think you should go, and then close the file and forget it."

She had gone to the funeral and from time to time called to see the parents although she was never sure that it was for their sakes or her own. Whether each time she visited she wasn't simply hoping their grief had diminished to a level that she herself could deal with. In the end she stopped going at all, thinking that perhaps the sight of her might only resurrect painful memories.

The sudden murmur of voices along the corridor brought her back to the job in hand and she squinted her eyes in an effort to identify the source. Dr Rose Wilkins, the pathologist, was striding towards her ahead of two orderlies in white coats. She was delivering a barrage of orders without so much as a glance to see if the troops were listening or even still there. In fact, both soon peeled away and disappeared into a room on the left as the good doctor thundered on.

"Ah! DS Meredith. Just the in person. It's back in my room. Come along." She wheeled and headed purposely in the direction whence she had come, her voice rattling out a continuous barrage of information, which Kate knew would all be duplicated in the initial report. Rose Wilkins's reports were nothing if not comprehensive.

Amazing, thought Kate to herself, as she tried to keep up, that women who doggedly refuse to shave their legs, are always the ones who choose to wear sheer stockings She considered the stocky figure striding, pigeon-toed ahead of her. Clad in a green tweed skirt and long hand knitted cardigan she was the antithesis of elegance.

Big bum thought Kate unkindly, big bosom. All bum, boobs and bifocals

"Beethoven and Berlioz," Wilkins rapped out as she turned a corner.

"What!" said Kate startled.

I was saying that this place would be far less depressing if they had a bit of piped music through the corridors."

"Brahms? Or Bruch?" offered Kate.

"God no, far too sugary. We'd all be in tears. Here's your report Now tell me, my dear."

She cupped her podgy chin in her hands and leaned forward across the desk with a coquettish look. Her face was caught in a beam of sunlight and Kate gazed with fascination at a long silky hair protruding from a mole on the doctor's upper lip. It fluttered as she went on.

"How's out lovely Charlie Knowles? I haven't seen him for weeks and every time I call he seems to be on his way out. I have tickets for the Mozart at the Albert in September and I'd love him to come."

As she spoke, Kate heard her phone ring, pulled it from her pocket and held it to her ear.

"Kate, it's me," came her boss's distinctive tone. "I'm in the car park outside. For God's sake don't tell Rosy Posy. I'm on the way to Wellstead's. Came to pick you up. Are you done?"

Kate grinned at the doctor. "Well talk of the devil," she said and then addressing her phone, "Doctor Wilkins is right with me. She wants to know what you're doing on… She looked across the desk. "Date?"

"Seventeenth," hissed the doctor.

"On 17th September. She wants you to go to a concert and then a cosy dinner afterwards. Sounds wonderful, doesn't it?"

Kate settled back in her chair to enjoy to the maximum her boss's discomfort. There was an uneasy silence at the other end of the line.

"Bloody hell, Kate. How do I get out of this one? Tell her I'm tied up all that week. I'm er… cleaning the fish tank, installing central heating, painting the Albert Bridge, offering my body for medical research… no not that, she'd be the first there with a scalpel. Just get me off the hook, Kate," he implored.

"Of course, your trip to the Galapagos with Auntie Maud. I completely forget. Right through September? Yes, I'll tell her how disappointed you are."

She cut the connection quickly as Wilkins held out her hand for the phone.

"Never mind. He's an absolute Philistine really. Mozart sends him to sleep. Try suggesting a trip Ronnie Scott's for some hot jazz. I'm sure even Auntie Maud wouldn't be able to rival that."

She picked up the green folder ready to go. The doctor was already on her feet. "Interesting case this one," she said, "not as brutal as the dear chief inspector would have it. The spear shaped object fell out when the body was moved. It had been fairly gently inserted but only enough for it to stay in place while he was down. There was no muscular reflex, which would have occurred had it been alive and very little scratching or damage. It was intended as some sort of clue, I think. I would say the action had been hesitant. I dare say revulsion set in pretty quickly and the culprit beat a hasty retreat. Why he did it at all is for you people to work out but it looks as if homophobia is involved somewhere along the line. Must go. It's in drawer seven, line three – the body I mean."

It, thought Kate, at what stage do we become it? I wonder, as Rosie stomped off, no doubt eager to embark on her next physical excavation. Kate repressed a shudder, saluted and bounded down the corridor towards the sunshine outside. Lovely Charlie had selected a parking space as far as possible from the main doors and was grinding a cigarette butt under his heel as Kate approached.

"How did you know about Auntie Maud?" he greeted her.

"Hariett told me. She sounds like quite a character."

"She was, Harry loved her – they had a lot in common you see – clay and weed. Harriett made pots and Maud did sculptures. She did that buttock paperweight on my desk. Quite a lady, she died shortly after Harry. Probably exhaustion. She had dozens of lovers."

"Was she a lesbian?"

"Lord no! All her lovers had willies."

"The one on your desk hasn't."

"She probably ran out of clay."

On the way to the Wellstead's address, they discussed this rather strange case and how they should go about solving it.

"Whoever was responsible for dumping that corpse there, certainly wanted it to be found. So why? Why leave it in plain sight when, if whoever it was, and I think there must have been at least two of them, just wanted to get away with murder or theft or whatever it was. They knew it would be spotted by the passengers on a train within a few hours. They must watch enough TV to know that we can pick up shedloads of evidence these days from mere dust to DNA. There are cameras everywhere – well not actually at this site, but if they arrived by car, and they'd hardly cart him here in a taxi, chances are we'll pick 'em up somewhere. In other words, unless they are extremely thick, they must have intended us to find him fast."

"So what can possibly have been the reason? If the corpse had been a bad lad, then it's a bit late to expose him, isn't it? He couldn't give a damn now. The mutilation such as it was, clearly indicates buggery of some sort, but was it just homophobia? And again, what's the point of…?"

"Can we try and avoid the word 'point', do you think? It makes me feel uncomfortable and it's confusing. I can't think it's anti-gay. That just doesn't happen these days. Well it does, but, as you say, what's the purpose in this case. If it is retribution, why drag the police into it. Homosexuality is not a crime."

Was there anything else in his pockets when you didn't look?"

"Yes – a folded piece of paper which looked new – I mean it didn't look as if it had been there for some time, with the words 'For Joey'. I had gloves on when I found it so, if there are prints, we may be able to match them. I put it back inside the wallet. There was no money, just an old library card."

"Okay! We have his identity. We can check for previous. We can see if anyone at the library can shed any light, and we may find enough evidence at his address to help us, especially if there are details of friends and family. Someone with a grudge. Did you have any lunch?"

"Brunch. I had bacon, eggs, sausages, mushrooms and hash browns," lied Kate who had grabbed half a slice of toast on the way out.

"What! No French toast I don't know how you survive. This looks like the place and yes, there is a parking space."

Chapter Three

The address 51 Grebe Avenue was situated halfway along a row of terraced houses fronted by shallow walled gardens. Unlike its neighbouring properties, both of which gleamed with newly painted doors, shiny windows and well-tended gardens, 51 had an air of neglect, from the two or three broken tiles on its roof to the overgrown grass and weeds where once had been a garden. A climbing rose struggled to reach the sky as if to indicate that once, maybe not so long ago, it had known better times. The curtains, a dingy beige with a floral pattern were drawn across the windows. Kate banged on the front door and waited.

"'E's out, love."

Kate looked up to an upstairs window on her right to see a face, framed by a battery of pink plastic rollers and sprouting a cigarette.

"I'm a police officer," replied Kate holding up her warrant card. "Perhaps you could come down. You may be able to help us."

"Yeah right." The voice was tinged with pleasurable anticipation. "Give us a minute I'll just comb me 'air."

Knowles had by now emerged from the car and was approaching the front door. "I bet she knows more about him than his mother did," he muttered. "If we're not mistaken we've struck gold. I'll do the talking. I'll have her eating out of my hand."

Kate gave him a speculative look. "If you're going to turn on the charm, I'll concentrate on the search if you don't mind. Subtlety isn't your strong point and suppressing hysterical laughter isn't mine."

A few minutes later she turned to see an elegant woman who could have been anything between thirty and fort-five approaching from the front door of the adjacent house. She held out her hand. "It's Jill – Jill Irving."

"Erm – I spoke to your aunt, Miss Irving, from the upstairs window?" Jill Irving smiled.

"Actually it was me." The voice was almost musical. "I'm an actress. I was just getting into character. It's a sort of *My Fair Lady* scenario. I was practising the 'before' model and now I'm the educated smart one. In real life I suppose I'm somewhere in between but, quite honestly sometimes it's difficult to remember who I really am. Believe it or not, it really helps if you have the right props. Wear the rig, the curlers and the fag and it's easy to become Aggie Higgins, cleaning lady, mother of Eliza!"

"So if I handed you a glass of champagne and a cigarette holder you could become Marlene Dietrich in no time at all?"

"Falling in love again, never wanted to, what am I to do? I can't help it," sang Jill huskily with a perfect German accent

"Amazing! Brilliant," laughed Kate, you had me completely fooled. Look I'm DI Meredith and this is DCI Knowles. She turned to her boss who was standing open mouthed behind her.

"Okay, sir, do the talking."

He cleared his throat, glared at Kate and almost humbly held out his hand. "I'm delighted to meet you, Miss Irving. Can we go inside – perhaps into your place and have a chat? If you knew Mr Wellstead, I'm afraid we have some bad news."

"Oh dear! You mean he's dead, don't you? Poor George. He was desperate to die you know. So much pain, but he absolutely refused to go into a hospice. I used to go and chat but he has discouraged it lately. He was very dignified and I had to respect his wishes. I'm glad it's all over. Have they collected him? I didn't get in till late last night but the lights were on."

"You don't by any chance have a key, do you? I'm afraid George didn't die at home. In fact, the circumstances of his death are confusing. We need to go inside and take a look."

"Well yes, as a matter of fact I do. I've never used it but I think I know where it is. I'll get it."

Minutes later the two officers were inside No 51 having asked Jill to stay at home, promising to go back and have a cup of tea and a chat before they returned to headquarters.

"What a character," remarked Kate when they had left.

"Not just one, she's an actress all right and nice looking too. I could definitely…"

"Definitely what?"

"Take her out for a drink. What do you think?"

"Don't be ridiculous. She probably has a list of leading men waiting to ask her out."

"If you don't stop pouring cold water over my aspirations, you'll find yourself back on traffic. Now let's see what we can find out about poor old George."

There was a depressing aura throughout the house. A smell of uncleanliness, depression – well it would be if depression had a smell. Apart from dirty plates and heaps of unwashed laundry there was little to indicate that George had had a life at all. The bureau drawers were empty apart from some recent bills. The wardrobe held a few decent clothes smelling of mothballs. Nothing significant in the kitchen. Kate found a brown glass bottle on the mantelpiece in the living room and put it into an evidence bag, holding it carefully by the top. The label was smudged but she could just read Diamorphine. They were about to leave for the rather more exciting prospect of a cup of tea next door, when Kate spotted some activity in the back garden and was just in time to rescue a half-filled black bin bag from the refuse collectors. A quick inspection revealed a quantity on old correspondence and some photographs torn into pieces. It seemed that George wanted to take his past with him.

"Okay! We're not going to go through all this now. We need to get it back to the station. There will be stuff we have to bag and analyse and so on."

"Tempting though, I'd love to tip it all out now and get going."

"Well we can't and there'll be time enough later. Now are we absolutely sure we have found everything? There's no sign of a computer. What was under the stairs?"

"Ironing board, clothes horse and an empty suitcase and some very old Christmas decorations."

"Sounds just like mine. Okay let's go and have tea with the stars."

Settled into comfortable sofa and chairs in Jill's open plan living space with cups of coffee, they were able to put some meat on the bones of their skeletal knowledge of this sad man.

He had lived there for about ten years. Jill had moved into the house next door just six years go. They hadn't had much to do with each other really. An occasional meeting by chance at the corner shop down the road or in the front garden where George had actually spent quite a lot of time. He loved roses and was quite proud of his display. Not an unattractive man, but Jill had quickly written him off as a possible special friend. Apart from the fact that he was about ten years older, she sensed that women were of little interest to him, but no, she hadn't been aware of any male callers either.

She knew he had worked in a library. She knew he had been a teacher although he never talked about it and she realised just about a year or eighteen months ago that something was wrong. The garden was neglected. He had spent some time in hospital and just six months ago, he had told her that he had not much time left. He had asked her if she knew a good solicitor and had made a will leaving all his money and possessions to a children's charity. She had been the witness to his signature.

At first he had been grateful to her for the occasional errands, shopping, picking up prescriptions, but as time went by he relied on visits from nurses and she saw very little of him. One of the nurses had confided in her and explained that he was determined to stay at home until he died and that there was little they could do apart from provide painkillers and comfort. They had asked her to keep an eye on things as far as she could. The night before, it had been pelting with rain. She had come home and seen nothing unusual apart from the fact that his light was still on. She had not heard any activity but then it was late and she had gone straight to bed. Later that day house to house enquiries had produced no new information or evidence.

They thanked Jill for her hospitality. Kate left a card in case she remembered anything useful or saw any suspicious activity, and they left, promising to keep her informed of any developments. As they left, Kate had turned back to ask, "Did you ever see him use a computer?"

"To tell you the truth, I've never set foot in his house, but you should get in touch with the hospital staff. They would know. They called round this morning and were quite bewildered at his disappearance. I expect they will have reported it."

Back at the station the bin bag was left with officers who would examine the contents, make meticulous lists and report without delay, anything significant which might assist in the investigation.

It was just as Kate who had been up late the night before, was preparing to call it a day when Knowles walked into her office holding a paper print copy of a photograph which had been put back together like a jigsaw puzzle and a newspaper cutting.

"Have a look at this and then go home and pack your bag. We'll be travelling tomorrow and may be away for a day or two."

He held out the newspaper cutting the headlines of which read:

TRAGIC DEATH AT CHILDREN'S HOME. HEADMASTER GEORGE WELLSTEAD TO ASSIST IN POLICE ENQUIRIES.

It went on describe skimpy details of a ten-year-old child, found dead outside the building. Police had refused to give further information but all members of staff and pupils would be interviewed during the following days.

Later editions revealed that no one was in the frame but that Wellstead had been elsewhere at the time and was devastated by the event.

The dead child had been identified as Joey Jacobson. He and his brother had been residents for only a couple of weeks following the tragic death of both their parents in an accident. Little was known of the details and there were apparently no relatives available to take the boys on.

Editions several days later indicated that the coroner had decided that the death was accidental. There was to be no inquest. There was an article by a journalist who was clearly very unhappy with the verdict and very critical of the management of the home, which she described as being like a cold Victorian prison. The date of the article was ten years before.

"OK! We need everyone available here first thing tomorrow. Get a plan of action together. Sort out the urgent cases here and make sure everything is up to date with those. If CPS are waiting for any disclosure, make sure they have every last detail. When the children's home case file turns up, take a look at it. We can make notes on the train. and decide what needs to be done. Tell Laver he will be our main contact if we need anything from here while we're away. We'll let him know where we're staying.

"Call in and get as many of the team that aren't on urgent business elsewhere. We need to piece together everything we can find relating to this case and the children's home case and decide on our strategy. I've already found the name of the journalist; she still writes for the paper but she's no longer employed by them. They have her number so we can get in touch with her. Reading her column at the time you can almost feel the anger. The fact that the place closed down almost immediately is enough in itself to justify a thorough investigation. There is an indisputable link to our man so I'll get the details of the other case faxed down.

"What's the matter with those people up there? Imagine a case like that here in London. All hell would break loose – and rightly. Why aren't these bloody places regulated? I'm speechless."

"You could have fooled me. You haven't stopped ranting to breathe for at least five minutes, but you're right. It's heart breaking. Let's hope we can justify our interference into an old case, miles from home."

"Don't worry. My immediate superiors seem to trust me and we should be back in couple of days."

Chapter Four

Situated on the north-east coast, The Stables had nothing to do with horses now. Adjoining a prosperous boatyard, in a secluded bay, The Stables was, amongst other things a residential home for youngsters who had nowhere else to go. There were twenty well-furnished rooms in the former staff cottages behind the main house, a small gymnasium, a computer room, a large classroom and various workshops. Every one of the currently fifteen inmates was training. Two were trainee plumbers, two were trainee electricity engineers, one was taking A levels with a view to studying Law, another was learning how to cut and style hair at a local salon and the others were getting an all-round education until it became clear what their particular strengths were. Vic, an expert sailor was teaching them the rudiments of sailing, in the bay near the shore.

The property was owned and run by Sebastian (Spike) Jacobson who, with his assistant Victor March, and the home's manager and secretary, Philippa Hilton, were sitting in the kitchen around a large scrubbed pine farmhouse table, discussing the events of the night before.

"It was just bad luck," said Spike. "If he'd just hung on for a bit longer he'd be comfortably dead in hospital now. But there we were with a corpse in the car not knowing what the hell to do with it. We couldn't take him home; we couldn't do anything but find a nice quiet place to settle him down. I left Vic to guard him while I went back to the car to write a note so that the police would be able to identify him, and make the connection between him and The Sanctuary. I didn't want to go through his pockets, it would have seemed awful but I think there was a wallet. I didn't know that Vic had left his 'clue' until he told me later. I'm worried that they'll track me down before I'm ready."

Well what have they got right now? A body, which they will soon be able to identify from the stuff in his wallet, a note with a brief mention of Joey, which will be meaningless at this stage, and for some unknown reason, a suspiciously placed spike from the railings – er... what was the purpose of that again, Vic? Remind me."

"It seemed like a good idea at the time," said Vic miserably. I just wanted to draw their attention to the sort of abuse we know what went on there now. I couldn't get the thought of it out of my head. I lived there, for all that time and didn't realise what was happening. I suppose I wasn't pretty enough to attract the attention of the priest's customers. If only I had known, I could have told Pippa. We could have stopped it. But I'm sure that the sp... that pointy thing will make them appreciate the inference. They couldn't possibly see it as a kind of signature, could they?"

"When is a spike not a Spike. Don't worry, Vic. I know you did it with the best intentions and when I think about it, you're right. They would probably decide that he was just a sad old man who wanted to die on his own outside. They will be looking at taxi services to find out if a cab took him there and then, unless friends and relatives make a fuss, they'll just give up. Let's assume we have a day or two. I need to find some way of getting that recording to them without revealing who I am. If I just go and confess now, I may be detained for days. I don't want them to know about this place, not just yet."

Pippa stood up. "I have an idea, listen, and pick holes in it if you can. Your phone with the recording on it, could possibly be traced, but if we buy a pay as you go, from a shop in say, York, we can copy the original onto it, and send that by registered post to his address. They won't be able to trace the phone to us here. Somebody will have to sign for it, an officer or someone next door. Either way the police will get it and yes, they will be investigating the original tragedy at The Sanctuary, but it will be a miracle if they trace you. You did disappear into the mist when they tried to move you all those years ago, didn't you? Nobody could find you at the time and it will be even more difficult now. That will at least give you time, but you know you'll have to speak to them eventually."

Spike got up and stared out of the window. He had been broken hearted when, falsely accused of theft by Pious, arrangements had been made to move him to another home on the grounds that he would be a bad influence on his little brother Joey. He hadn't stolen anything. When the minibus had stopped at a filling station he had asked to go to the loo, and made his escape. On the run for two days (although he later found that no one had looked very hard), he had found The Stable buildings and taken refuge in a boat.

He was found asleep in a cabin, taken inside, offered a shower and fed and listened to by the owner of the yard, Mr Pearson, who was appalled when he heard Spike's story, trusted him immediately and took him on as a trainee. Spike was quick to learn and in no time at all was working full time for a decent wage. When Pearson became ill, Spike took over and made such a good job of managing the business, that when Pearson who had no children of his own, died five years later, he left everything to Spike.

When Spike had found out about Joey he had cried in Pearson's arms. Pearson had persuaded him to bide his time but he had vowed then to find out what had happened. What he read in the papers didn't make any sense to him. In the meantime, after Pearson died, he decided to use the space in Pearson's huge house to help other youngsters in trouble. That's what Joey and his parents would have wanted him to do. He had money in the bank and a good income from the yard, not quite sufficient to fund his project properly, but there were other ways to make money, and having a large motor yacht helped.

It was on the tenth anniversary of his parents' death that Spike decided it was time to ask questions. He turned from the window.

"Okay, we'll do that," he said. "This afternoon if you can, Pipps. First class post and they should get it tomorrow. I'm pretty sure that once they listen to what Wellstead had to say the investigation will be re-opened. If I have to disappear for a while, Pippa is in charge. Tell me the truth, Vic, have you ever, in any way been in trouble with the police?"

"You know I haven't. You've known me since I was fifteen."

"Are you absolutely sure? What about before The Sanctuary? Any juvenile convictions? I don't want you to get any comebacks because of this."

"Only a minor TWOC (Taking without owner's consent) and then I was just a passenger. I don't think they took prints. I can't remember anything like that but I was cautioned."

"Okay, let's hope for the best, and if they speak to you, Pippa, which they are bound to do, what with your outspoken columns in the local rag, at the time, can I rely on you to keep my identity secret when the time comes?"

"I won't even dignify that with a response. Are you sure that you or he didn't mention your name while you were recording?"

"I don't think I did but not absolutely sure. Let's listen one more time." He took his phone and turned up the volume and they listened. The first voice was trembling.

It's not a long story, but, to make it easier for me to

tell you, would you get me a glass of water and a couple of pills out of that bottle on the mantelpiece? They don't help the pain much, but it's better than nothing.

Then Spike's voice: *Take a couple of these. They might be better. Okay. Now just relax for ten minutes and whenever you're ready, we will start.*

Wellstead continued.

I do remember you. Damn shame you were sent away. You were no thief. Everyone knew that, but there was simply no arguing with Pious. He was an evil man. I really thought the investigation into Joey's death would be the end for him, but sadly not. Well, let me start from the beginning. You will despise me I know. But please try to control your disgust and allow me to tell you all in detail.

First of all, I swear I never ever laid a finger on Joey and never would have done. I took my job seriously. I wanted to put certain things behind me and make peace with my conscience. But I had done things in the past that would, I know, be considered despicable – although they didn't seem so to me at the time. I loved little children, little boys you see. I loved them, was kind to them, and made them love me – and they did, and then my love became physical. They didn't seem to mind, it just happened, and as soon as I suspected that they did mind, I would stop. And they would stop visiting me, and that was that. But there was always another little boy who would like trips to the pictures and meals at McDonald's or a new video game.

Are you telling me you are a paedophile! You were an abuser of children. Oh! God help me. I can't bear this. Joey...

I told you, I didn't ever hurt Joey or any of the other children there at The Sanctuary.

Didn't hurt him or didn't touch him? If you did, I will kill you now.

I swear, I didn't touch him.

You'd better carry on.

I knew that this would be considered wrong, that I would be reviled, despised. It seemed unfair. But, trust me, I never upset any child as far as I knew. It was only later, when I met one of my little friends who had then grown up, told me how much he had despised himself. And how he was filled with shame and disgust and guilt. He talked – I listened. I think sharing those innermost, deep buried feelings helped him to draw a line under the past, knowing that the fault was entirely mine.

Before I went to The Sanctuary, there was someone on the Internet who befriended me. There are websites you know where people like me can get things off their chests. His name was Frances. He seemed to understand completely how I felt. I told him so many things about my life. I told him I had resolved not go on and, in fact, wanted to get a decent job helping children, the right way. To change direction, get rid of the guilt.

A couple of days later, he mentioned to me, what turned out to be The Sanctuary job, and I applied. I had a response after a few days and to my surprise I got the job with an imminent start. There was very little in my Curriculum Vitae that was in any way similar, but I was just so happy to have the chance to right the wrongs. I hadn't heard from Frances again. I put him out of mind along with the other memories that troubled me. I couldn't of course... Paedophiles are born not made. I can understand the revulsion, the loathing, but it wasn't until The Sanctuary that I saw for myself the way children were damaged. The way they cast down their eyes, did nothing to draw attention to themselves. It was always the gentle quiet boys, the young ones. They never complained; they were too afraid. It was only after I sought the help of the embedded priest, that I became aware of what was going on. Pious had been posted to the home just a few weeks before I arrived. He was there to supervise the welfare of the boys. Hear their grievances and solve their problems.

What a horrific irony. I found one little lad crying in the corner of the playing field. He wouldn't speak to me or tell me anything. When I suggested that he should go to see Pious he recoiled. I mentioned Pious again and his reaction made me realise there was a problem. I thought about it and began to suspect that perhaps Pious may have been inflicting punishment, caning maybe, which was entirely against my principles. So, I decided to see him and have it out.

It was then that he introduced himself, not as Pious, but by his real name – Frances. He made it quite clear what would happen if I didn't do exactly what he wanted. I said I would give in my resignation – then he would say he had been watching me and said he'd show them proof that I had abused children; my own admissions in print. There would be nothing to incriminate him. The conversations had been carefully edited. He was a priest – beyond reproach. No one would ever doubt him.

I was pathetically weak. I despised myself – but I stayed and tried to close my eyes to what was going on. I think he had his claws into Matron as well, and heaven knows who else. But I did what I could to change things and indeed, I managed to a certain extent. The older boys had more freedom, were allowed out at weekends, and were able to form a football team. They were even allowed limited visits from friends outside, but only with a special permit from Pious.

When you turned up with Joey, I knew he was just the kind of victim Pious desired – beautiful, delicate and vulnerable. I couldn't bear it. I lost no time in getting in touch with other schools to arrange the transfer of you both. The matron helped; I knew she had her suspicions. I'm sure he had something on her. In the capacity of priest, he took confessions you see. He was probably blackmailing her, and who knows who else, but we never discussed it.

God help me, I tried but it took time. Then you were set up with that alleged theft, and once again I should have done something. But what a pathetic spineless creature I was.

Go on please… recriminations are pointless now.

Matron told me that Pious was visiting Joey in the sick bay too often and upsetting him. She couldn't see any reason why. She had been doing what she could to help by letting Joey sleep there, thinking that if he was being bullied, he would be safer. Ironic isn't it, she more or less served him up on a plate.

The day after you were taken away, and a couple of days before Joey was to leave, I had a visit from a young journalist. She wanted to interview me about you and Joey, other children and members of staff. There had been some complaints about the senior boys from their weekend trips to the town. At least that is what she said. She particularly wanted to speak to Joey and I had no objection at all. But somehow, Pious got wind of it and stopped it. He must have been worried. I believe he was even beginning to think of moving Joey on, but it was the next night that Joey was… when he died.

When he was killed, you mean?

I don't know, can't say. He was found outside, presumably having fallen from a window on the second floor. the window of a room next to the sick bay. The police barely investigated the matter and the coroner, based on what he was told, declared it a suicide. It might have been suicide if the poor child was being abused. He had lost his parents, and now his brother. All that was left for him was the thought of endless misery at the hands of Pious.

However, if this drove him to commit suicide, it was murder. The bastard may as well have pushed him. Find him, Spike. Find that bastard and I'll be waiting for him in hell.

There was the sound of gasping and then more faintly Spike's voice.

Vic, quick come here – he's collapsed we need to get him to hospital.

The tape ended.

"You know what," said Spike, "I never want to hear that again. You need to pop into the newspaper offices and find out whether any contact has been made yet in connection with The Sanctuary business. They can't possibly avoid sending someone up at some point and they have resources that weren't available ten years ago. They will certainly lose no time interviewing you, and if you appear still to be using your journalistic skills for the benefit of the local rag they may not look further. You can direct them away from here. Use what I told you then, when I was helping your ma with her garden. What it was that made you seek that interview when Joey was still alive. Put them in the picture, Pips. That home was an absolute disgrace. I can't bear to think about it now. Surely it was a one off. Surely someone is responsible for the welfare of orphans?"

"I just don't know. We'll have to find out, but I'm sure that's something the police will do. Presumably their first port of call will be the church to find out what the set up was."

"Who would they see, do you think? Who would be responsible for running the place? The bishop? How well did he know Pious? What checks were made? Is he still here?"

"I have no idea how Catholicism works apart from the fact that the Pope is boss, then there are cardinals and bishops. I suppose there are teams who organise stuff, like secretaries and cleaners but that is something I will research. Who is responsible for appointing significant school staff is something I will find out? At the time, my interest was aroused because of what you told me about the place, Spike. You were desperately worried and couldn't understand why they kept you apart. It seemed so cruel when he had just lost his parents. I just wanted to find out more," said Pippa. "If I had had the chance to speak to Joey I could probably have gained his trust enough to persuade him to talk. After the tragedy, I pointed them in the direction of Wellstead. I believed then that he had prevented the meeting. If anyone could have helped, he surely could – and now we know he could have done but didn't. Pious disappeared. The church did nothing to help trace him and insisted that he was whiter than white. The bishop agreed to let the police know if he turned up, but then we had the coroner's decision and that was that."

"Okay. Vic and I are going to find a way of tracing the vile priest but quite honestly, I don't know where to start. Is it still the same bishop?"

"Not sure. I'll find out. A phone call should do it. Another coffee, please." She took her phone and dialled the number of the *Whitby News*. Spike heaved a sigh and turned to Vic. "Is Griffiths here? We're due to sail in at high water. Are the boats ready?"

"Yep and the weather looks fine. Griff is settled in the cabin with a drink and looking as calm and composed as usual. He seems to have lost weight."

"Yeah, he runs a lot. Is everything loaded? Then let's get going."

An hour later with lots of yelling and hooting *Sophie* motored out, turned to starboard and headed for France with Vic at the helm.

*****

Much later, under cover of darkness, a similar boat with the name *Sophia* slipped out from a boatshed concealed behind an outcrop of rocks and headed east towards Amsterdam where it was registered to a Richard Griffiths. The same Richard Griffiths was comfortably ensconced within a cabin, downing an expensive brandy while Spike studied the charts and the weather forecast.

Within days both boats would return. Sophie, by day, loaded with wines and spirits all of which would be declared to customs who were so familiar with the routine that they rarely checked. There was, however, a water tight compartment beneath the waterline, which at the hint of trouble could be emptied into the deep sea at the touch of a button. This contained a quantity of tobacco and cigarettes, which were transferred to another hidden compartment in a diesel truck which supplied the boatyard on a regular basis. No money changed hands. Although the accounts of both showed payments made and received for a regular supply of fuel.

Sophia would come back rather more quietly, with no obvious cargo but, Spike would check for a bank transfer from Griffiths which would certainly keep The Stables going for another six months, no problem. Should the bank statements ever be checked, the lump sums would be seen to be part payments for a super motor cruiser, the plans of which were open to view and a skeleton boat was to be seen in the yard. The cost of the charter was on the books and always satisfied the accountant. The reason for the less ostentatious comings and goings of Sophia were at the request of Griffiths who liked to remain as unobtrusive as possible. Spike never asked why. He really didn't want to know.

Chapter Five

The conference room at the station was humid and quite smoky when Kate arrived. She went over, opened the window and perched herself on the sill. The teams were engaged in desultory conversation, clutching plastic cups of stewed tea and glancing impatiently toward Knowles. He with the knot of his tie pulled down almost to waist level, top buttons undone, sleeves rolled up to the elbow, was studying a report in a blue folder and seemingly, for the time being, oblivious to all around him.

Kate decided to break his reverie. "I think we're all here, Guv. Shall we get started?"

He looked up at her for a moment, frowning. "Can you believe for a moment that a ten-year-old boy would have the guts to throw himself out of a third-floor window, or be desperate enough even to consider it? Kids just don't, do they, Kate? Suicide stems from the adult mind, doesn't it? From failure, lack of hope, disgrace, self-loathing, years of misery. Kids turn to crime or bullying or drugs, not deliberate self-destruction. Tell me I'm right!"

"I don't know. No other case springs to mind." She could sense Knowles' frustration and decided to steer the conversation towards the discussion of facts. "That must be the Joey file. Are you thinking it was murder?"

"I don't know. In a way, I'd rather it was or at least an accident. That would be easier to accept." He sighed. Then he added, "Come on, let's get on with it. Find a seat somewhere, you're blocking my view."

"Right!" he shouted, slamming the file on the table and getting to his feet. "Let's sum up what we have and decide where we're going:

"George Wellstead was the principal of The Sanctuary Children's Home for two years. He was offered the job because he had qualifications and experience with accounting and had dragged one or two businesses up by the boot strings and set them well on the way to recovery. How this qualified him to take on a bunch of lost kids beats me, but apparently, he made the right impression. It's not clear why he needed to change direction but his references were okay. It was a Catholic church institution and we will, of course, be getting in touch with them for more information.

"Wellstead wasn't expected to have much to do with the kids, they already had the staff to do that. He was expected to run a tight ship, within the budget and nip in the bud the various discipline problems and disruptive behaviour. This, it appeared, he did to a certain extent. The kids, in fact, became so well behaved on the premises, that anyone with half a mind should have realised that they were being subjected to bullying and oppression."

"Outside of course it was a different story, or so it seemed. Sanctuary boys were making a significant name for themselves as petty criminals by the time the scandal broke. Well, that is the official line. Though, we have some newspaper reports that tell a completely different story.

"Joey Jacobson, aged seven, was found dead in the yard early on the morning of 9th May 2005. It is clear from the autopsy that he had fallen from a considerable height, and was later established – from a window on the third floor. My first question would be who closed it! It was also clear that he had been violently sexually assaulted before his death. This was not made public. It would be plastered all over the front pages today."

Knowles paused and took a drink from the glass on his desk.

"There was, of course, an investigation. All members of staff were interviewed because from the bruising on shoulders and upper arms, apparently, the assailant was someone of considerable strength, almost certainly an adult. All the big lads were locked up in another part of the building. No suspect was identified. There were traces of DNA, but not one member of staff, who could not provide an alibi, refused to provide a sample. There were no matches.

"We have the various transcripts of interviews. I've read them all and of course, you will have the opportunity to do so, but nothing in there clicked with me. You'll all have complete copies shortly. In short, that poor kid was abused to an extent that leaves me feeling physically sick. And fuck all was done about it. The PM was indecisive and since no suspect could be identified the case was closed. Accidental death. He fell or he jumped.

"As it is, we are investigating the death of Wellstead and reopening the investigation into the death of Joey Jacobson who may or may not have been murdered, but was certainly sexually abused. It may seem screamingly obvious to us now, that because of the circumstances of Wellstead's death, someone has taken the view that one way or another, he was responsible for Joey's demise, but that mustn't cloud the issue. Someone out there is dispensing his own kind of justice. The fact that Wellstead had cancer and was going to pop his clogs at any time is immaterial. Giving him a hefty dose of morphine most probably caused his immediate death.

"We can't afford to be sympathetic. We have to find him. This is a man with serious problems and the mind of a self-appointed executioner. What intrigues me is the spike. According to the PM report, it wasn't a vindictive thrust. It actually fell out when we moved the body. It's a mystery but it must point to something. Yeah, yeah, an unfortunate choice of words... as to his victim's culpability. There appears to be no evidence that Wellstead was involved in any way with Joey's death but we need to keep an open mind. In my view, the investigation at the time, in itself, is highly suspicious and I'm determined to find out why."

"Are there any clues as to why he waited ten years to move, Guv?" asked Kate. "Do you think it might be one of the other kids who has grown up, possibly suffered similar abuse and has decided to act?"

"Well, it's certainly a possibility. Something must have triggered this." Knowles was thrown back into the contemplative mood. "Wouldn't kids bury this sort of recollection though? Get on with their lives and not suddenly turn into callous killers after so long a period of time. Not unless something is happening now that has caused our man to divert attention from his own guilt and focus on another's – to blame someone else for his own shortcoming? Hell, I don't know! We need a criminal psychologist. Who is our local cracker? Get him here, Kate. Then you and I are going on a trip so go pack a case.

"Okay, let's split up into the usual teams. Laver, you collate and keep me informed. There are things to do. Firstly, get everything about Joey's family. Why was he there? What happened to any relatives? Get as much info as you can on the home. Who ran it? When did it close? Why did it close?"

Knowles continued without a stop. "Get a life history of Wellstead. He surely must have had a computer if he's been an accountant. Talk to people who knew him. Kate and I have already spoken to his neighbour; you needn't bother with her. I might speak to her again myself.

"Get to know the man, all traces of his history seem to have been eliminated from his home. There must be a reason why. He knew he was dying. Why did he remove all traces? There must be something nasty there. Find it."

Then, he turned to Kate. "You and I are going North. There is a train this afternoon at two. Could you meet me at King's Cross? Bring a frock and I'll take you out to dinner. It'll be too late to do much when we get there."

"A frock! What the hell is a frock? I have a dress if that's what you mean, but I'd hardly wear my Moschino for a night out in a 'fish and chip' shop. It still has green stains on it from the last time when you spilled mushy peas all over me."

"Ingrate! Those mushy peas are famous throughout the South. One of the sheiks in Saudi has them flown out regularly to go with his battered camel and fries. I suppose you'd prefer a poncy salad."

"Only because I'd prefer not to look like a walking gasometer."

"Well, I thought women like big beefy blokes."

"Only when they need a wardrobe carrying upstairs. The rest of the time they like them lean and muscular."

"Pathologists seem to like me," the banter continued unabated.

"Well, if that horn-rimmed carnivore turns you on, I have serious doubts about your mental as well as your physical health. Imagine her with no clothes on!"

"Okay, salad it is. See you at two."

Kate strolled down the corridor to her office and drank a cup of water from the dispenser behind the door. She sat at her desk and thought about Joey Jacobson, whose life had been so short and unhappy.

Or was it? What had brought him to The Sanctuary? Where had he come from? Where were his parents? Were they still alive or was it some tragedy that had caused him to end up in that cold and loveless place?

Was he so desperately hurt and unhappy that *the only* way out was to jump out of a window? Surely there was someone he could have turned to? A friend to share his misery, a relative he could have written to?

She turned to the folder that had been placed on her desk and examined the contents. There were the copies of the newspaper cuttings that she and Knowles had found in the rubbish bag at Wellstead's house, statements from staff, which revealed nothing.

The officers' observations at the time were brief, with frustration echoing through every page because of closed doors or witnesses unavailable at the time. There were photographs of the scene and photographs of the body. Joey had been a skinny little thing. The body had been found face down, arms akimbo. The skin had a bluish look and the hair, cut prison short was dark blond. His face was more or less undamaged but there was something about the expression that was forlorn and desolate as if his misery had followed him to his death. The bruises on his body stood out against the milkiness of his skin – angry blue and yellow.

Kate felt that familiar sense of pointless anger at his nakedness. She wanted to see a picture that showed Joey wrapped in a blanket with an expression of peace on his face. It was as if his misery had survived through the years and still lingered. If it was Wellstead that made you feel like this, Joey, well he's had his, but whatever happens, I promise you, we will find out.

She grabbed her bag and headed for home.

Chapter Six

Inspector Charles Knowles surveyed himself in the long mirror in his brightly lit hallway and gave a grim smile. "Look at me Harry," he said. "Not so much of the Paul Newman now. More like Mr Blobby."

He looked at the photograph on the table of a vital red-headed woman, sitting at a potter's wheel, face splashed with freckles of drying clay, laughing as she surveyed the misshapen half turned pot in front of her. Harriet had been his joy, his life, his soul, his happiness. They'd met when he was a newly appointed detective constable. He'd been sent to the local art school to take statements following a break in and theft. A large quantity of oil paints and paper had disappeared. All bought of course at the taxpayers' expense. Some rather childishly rude graffiti had provided the statue of the mayor outside with some bulging pink underpants and a bra. Not the crime of the century but a good chance for a new detective to practise his skills. His first case and he was keen.

Undaunted at first by the faintly hostile looks from some of the more unconventionally attired students and the distinct smell of cannabis, he had made enquiries feeling more and more like the caricature of a TV cop, convinced that every time he approached the building he could hear the muted sound of *The Bill* being hummed by the entire population of the college. By the time he came to speak to Harriet he had become quite aggressive in his line of questioning.

"And you are?" he fired at her as she'd taken a seat at the paint stained table allocated to him. There was silence. He looked up. "And you are?" he repeated sternly.

"I am," returned the red-head, "rather surprised at your lack of manners if you really want to know. I am also overdrawn at the bank, suffering from PMT and hungry. So shall we conclude this discussion with the minimum of delay? I know nothing, okay?"

Charles had thrown back his head and laughed, apologised and taken her out for lunch.

They married three months later and found a sun-filled studio with a flat above a parade of shops in Finsbury Park. It had been furnished by Harriet, with two deep sofas, a huge double bed, colourful curtains and cushions in russet, gold, oranges and browns. There were always flowers and Harriet's pots everywhere. Even the dullest days had seemed sunny. For more than three years Knowles had been the happiest man on earth, and then one day, Harry didn't come home. There had been a fire in a tube station.

She was the only one who had dared to call him Charlie. No one at all dared to now. That was just her name for him. He hadn't let anything change. There were still flowers. There was still clay on the wheel and all the colourful carpets and cushions were still there but it wasn't sunny in the way it used to be and in truth, things were looking just a little shabby. Harry would not approve. Charlie knew he wouldn't always feel this way but even after all these years the time hadn't come yet when he could think of moving. Not as long as he could feel her presence there. He wasn't stupid. He knew she was dead. He just couldn't let go. He was still a young man, only forty-five but he had neglected himself. His fine features had become masked by fat and he was acutely aware that to describe himself as 'a bit plump' would be grossly inaccurate. Kate was right. But hey! Salads! Yuk!

"I need to sort myself out, Harry," he said out loud, "help me." Then shrugging his shoulders, he went into the bedroom and started to throw an assortment of clothes into a small case.

*****

Surprisingly, the train at King's Cross was ready to board, fifteen minutes before it was scheduled to leave. Even more surprisingly it was clean and almost empty. Kate and Knowles had found seats on each side of a freshly cleaned table and stored their hand baggage in the overhead locker each engaged with their own thoughts.

Kate was watching the intermittent flow of travellers on the adjacent and other platforms, and musing on the absence of any typical type. Every species of age, class, ethnic origin seemed to be represented. The only common factor seemed to be a desire to get there first; her eye was suddenly caught by a little girl, with white blonde hair, running as fast as she could, two platforms away, towards the barrier. She was laughing happily and from time to time, glancing over her shoulder where Kate saw another, slightly older girl, wearing the same style red and white striped tee shirt and jeans. She too was laughing and clearly trying to catch up. A young woman with light brown hair in one long plait almost to her waist, jogged after them, hampered a little by a rucksack slung over her shoulder. She wore faded jeans and a vest top which revealed strong brown arms and shoulders.

As she strode forward she looked the picture of health and vitality. Kate found herself smiling at the picture of this happy group and craned her neck to look backwards toward the barrier. The first little girl was jumping into the arms of a man who hugged her tightly as she wound her legs around his waist and her arms around his neck. He leaned forward to embrace the second child and then looked up to grin at the young woman. Kate's heart lurched as she saw his face and then began to pound in her chest. Jake put the children down and bent forward to kiss the cheek of the woman before he turned and ushered them through the barrier. They disappeared from sight. Kate found herself staring at the place where they had been, her mind unable to take in what she had seen.

"Hallooo, is there anyone there?" she heard Knowles

speaking to her. Do you want tea or coffee and a sandwich or something? They'll be round in a minute."

"Er no thank you, I'm not hungry." She stared out of the window blindly.

"What's wrong, love? You suddenly look desolate."

"I'm okay, Guv, honestly. I just need some air. Look will you watch my stuff while I stand in the corridor for a while." She stood up and moved through the carriage door to stand in the corner by the toilet. She couldn't believe what she had just seen. How could I be so wrong about anyone? How could he have been like that with me when it was all a lie? She wanted to be anywhere but where she was. She wanted to curl up small in bed with the blankets over her head with her eyes tightly closed to hold back the tears. She took a few deep breaths and tried to take control of herself; she leaned forward against the window and felt the tears overflow onto her cheeks. Suddenly she felt hands on her shoulders turning her around.

"Come on," said Knowles. "Give me a hug and then you can tell me all about it." She leaned against him and felt his arms around her and felt comforted.

"I've made an idiot of myself, Gov. I thought something wonderful was going to happen with somebody, but I was so wrong. I saw him – just now out there, on the platform. Let's go and sit down before someone runs off with our bags. I'll tell you later."

Over a cup of tea Kate told Knowles about Jake, her feelings, her hopes and about what she'd seen on the platform. At the end of an hour she felt tired but less distressed. It was strangely comforting to unburden herself of all the suppressed feelings and unfulfilled dreams. The ache was still there but the frightening feeling of hopelessness was gone. She felt anger too that she'd been deceived so completely by someone she could have sworn was one of the most honest men she had ever known.

"But did he ever tell you he was single – unattached?" Knowles had asked.

"No but he lied by omission. He must have known I would assume he was available. We were so close. To let that happen he must have known I might get hurt, he can't have cared at all. I was just there to use."

"From the way you've spoken of him I find that very difficult to believe," said Knowles. "You are too good a judge of character. I trust you. I think there is more to this than meets the eye and you are so bloody gorgeous no man in his right mind would want to lose you. You've even got me contemplating a diet, although right now I could murder a steak and kidney pie. Come on now. We're going to put Jake out of our minds today and concentrate on the job in hand. Later, I'll tell you about my dilemma over a tasty lettuce leaf and fromage frais, this evening."

The train pulled up at their destination hours later and they descended from the carriage clutching luggage and searching for a taxi rank. "They know we're coming but it's too much to expect a welcoming committee, I suppose?"

"DCI Knowles? A distinctly northern accent behind them caused Kate to turn quickly to see an attractive woman in civvies, smiling at them.

"How could you tell?"

"It's DCI Blakey. Ava Blakey. I was in touch with your office earlier and they'd told me you'd be on this train. No one else fitted your description so I was pretty sure I had the right culprits. I am a detective after all. Come on – I have a car outside. I've booked two separate rooms at the local pub. It's not posh but the food is very good. I'll take you straight there and we can discuss the way to deal with this as we go There is one officer who wants to talk to you. He was involved at the time and has made it quite clear that he was unhappy about the way things were handled. I've told him to join you for breakfast. Is that okay?"

"Perfect," said Knowles, "we got the file faxed through but it was surprisingly thin. No one seemed to know anything. I've got a team tracing his family, Joey's that is. Why did no one do that?"

"Well it was unfortunate that we lost his brother a couple of days before the accident but as you should know from the file, his parents were involved in a fatal accident, and try as we might, we couldn't find any uncles and aunts or cousins. When I say we, I mean they. I was at university at the time."

"His brother!" exclaimed Knowles. "I remember a mention of him but no detail. What do you mean lost? Is he dead too?"

"I don't know." She sighed. "Let's save the recriminations until tomorrow, shall we? I'm as much in the dark as you are. Apparently, his brother Spike was shipped out of the home a couple of days before the event because of some misdemeanour. He slipped away on the journey to another home, and hasn't been seen since. I think a futile attempt was made to find him at the time, but Britten was so anxious to get rid of an embarrassing case, that lots of things were left undone. He seems to be very uncomfortable at the prospect of the Metropolitan Police 'nosing around' and I quote. So don't expect him to welcome you with open arms."

"Why do I get the impression that you are less than impressed with your senior officer?" remarked Knowles. "Are you a little rebel in the making?"

"Nah! I'm as meek as a lamb, do as I'm told, agree with my superiors even when they are complete idiots, bow and scrape to the Met. I am clay in anyone's hands – NOT."

"I am pleased to meet you," smiled Knowles. "Now what did you say the brother's name was? Spike? I think we need to find him fast."

*****

The hotel was old style but warm and comfortable, the rooms equipped, thankfully, with modern shower units squeezed into tiny cubicles with loos and basins. Kate, refreshed, changed into her substitute for a frock, which was a green silk shirt and black trousers and joined Knowles at the bar.

"G and T?" he asked.

"No thanks, make it a pint of Guinness, I'm dehydrated."

With a pained expression, Knowles ordered her choice of drink and another double scotch for himself. They sat down in a corner and studied the menu.

"Oh dear! No salads. Never mind we need strength. Let's start the diet tomorrow. I'm having roast beef, roast spuds and Yorkshires, since we're up here. What about you?"

"Fish pie and spinach," replied Kate, "then rhubarb crumble, followed by a large brandy. After all that, I should sleep an untroubled sleep and go for a jog before breakfast."

"Ah! Well I probably won't join you for that but I'll be waiting for you in front of a heap of bacon and eggs at eight thirty when, with a bit of luck, our local detective will join us and provide leads if not answers. I must say I like Ava Blakey. Her attitude is just right. I've the feeling that she is pleased to see us and will do everything she can to help."

"No one seems to have much respect for this Britten bloke, do they?"

"He's probably an arse licker. He's a chief

superintendent, isn't he? Drives a desk and keeps his hands clean. I'll never get that far as you know. I've upset too many people, but you know what? I've enjoyed every minute of it. I just couldn't sleep at night if I had to spend my time saying the right things and keeping the lid on trouble. What do you think, Kate? Should I be more diplomatic?"

"You know I love you just the way you are – well, twelve stone of you anyway, the rest is a bit of a pain. Are you sure you wouldn't like salad?"

Chapter Seven

In an opulent room in the Manse in York, Pippa waited for the arrival of the bishop. After about five minutes he swept in apologising for the delay.

"So sorry, my dear. Things to do and people to see; a cleric's work is never done. How can I help you?"

He sat down and brushed back his rather long grey hair and wriggled back into a comfy leather chair looking, she thought, just a little stressed.

"How do I address you… sir?"

He grinned. "'Excellence' is the accepted form of address, or 'sir' might do." He paused. "However, if you have come to give me a hard time, if you've come to criticize me in any way, it will certainly be 'Excellency'."

Pippa warmed to him and smiled back. "And how nice do I have to be before I get to call you Andrew?"

The Bishop looked aghast. "Goodness! Are you flirting with me? Nothing in my training helps me deal with something like that. Let's stick to 'sir', shall we? Now how can I help you? My secretary said you were adamant that only I would do. So what is it all about?"

"I need to know who was in charge here ten years ago when the boys' home The Sanctuary was still functioning. It closed soon after an incident involving the death of a little boy."

There was a long silence and then the bishop got up and walked over to a side table. He picked up a thin file and returned to his chair.

"So you do know why I'm here?" said Pippa.

"I do read the papers, my dear. And yesterday I read your articles about that wretched business. They are about the only things left in this file. No, I wasn't here at the time and quite honestly, what I read yesterday came as a horrible shock. The incumbent bishop at the time was James Stokes. He's dead now and I sense from his notes that he was as horrified about it all then, as I am now. There were so many questions and not enough answers. That poor little boy, he lost his parents, was clearly traumatised by their death, and yet separated from the one close member of the family who could have comforted him in those circumstances. No wonder he jumped. It is absolutely heart breaking."

Pippa could see that he was genuinely distressed at the thought of Joey's plight. "What made you think he jumped?"

"I'm not sure – did he not? But why now?" he continued. "Why is the investigation being re-opened after all this time?"

"I think as far as the police are concerned, it was never closed, but the coroner's verdict of accidental death effectively ended it prematurely, albeit with many questions unanswered. Then the OIC was killed and enquiries changed direction. What I need to find out is the whereabouts of the priest who was in charge of the home. He disappeared before they could take a statement and there are several questions I know the police would like to put to him. Do you keep records? Can you help?"

"Yes," he sighed. "I think it is quite obvious that Stokes wanted to speak to him. The fact that he cut out and kept your articles prove that, but the day after Joey's death, Pious phoned to say he had to leave immediately for France as his mother had been taken ill. The infuriating thing is that there is so little in the file about him at all. Where did he come from? Where did he train? Where was he born, where was he ordained? Who is his next of kin? It is as if someone had removed every piece of information about him."

"Perhaps they did. So how does one become a priest?"

"Well a degree is usually required these days, then a period in a seminary, about four years, and once one is confident that one has made the right choices, one applies for a position like in any other post only he would have been a deacon first."

"What about those who are clearly unsuitable, do they get the push?"

"I suppose it would be suggested to them gently and tactfully that they would not be happy in the job. That they should consider other options."

"So to be accepted as a priest in charge at a school full of vulnerable children, he would have needed to be able to show proof that he had had the appropriate training…"

"Indeed."

"And all that paperwork, those checks, should be in the file that you are holding, but are not."

"No, but I did see a note scribbled inside the cover." He passed over the file and Pippa saw scribbled faintly in pencil inside the back cover: *File missing? Enquiries re. Mother? Did she not die some time ago? Where are the other papers?*

"What about the staff? I mean do all the people you employ have to be Catholic?"

"Of course not. We have to have lawyers, accountants, cleaning staff and so on. They can be anything: Jews, Muslims, heathens whatever, as long as they can do the job. It's just that the church itself requires some sort of unity. I met James before he died. I sense that he was struggling with his beliefs, it's difficult sometimes in this world."

"You mean with all those thousands of starving children and the billions of prayers that are never answered?"

"My dear girl, can you imagine what this world would be like if all our prayers were answered, we'd all be beautiful and no one would ever die, unless of course someone prayed that we would."

"And I would be able to gorge chocolate without losing my waistline and get to shoot the person who keyed my car. Maybe that's what happened billions of years ago, so he swept us all through a black hole and decided to start again and let us get on with it."

"Well that makes as much sense as evolution. But seriously, I think James was very uncomfortable about the way Pious had managed the place. I believe he did his best to trace him but when the case was closed, he was probably greatly relieved. It was he who was instrumental in the home's closure. His was a position of great responsibility you know and it would bring the entire religion into disrepute, if indeed Pious had failed in his duty of care."

"So he just closed the door on it and threw away the key? I think, sir, that it maybe something much more serious than that, and the police will certainly want to see that file even as it is, so please take care of it. What sort of records do you keep? Should we expect the files to be complete after ten years? Who would have access to them?"

"Almost anyone who works here. There seemed to be no reason to keep them under lock and key."

"Do you know whether any of your staff may have known Pious at the time?"

"I will make immediate enquiries, I promise, and if the police come to interview me I shall do my utmost to help."

"Well you know what I do, sir, I'm a journalist, and the time may come when information comes to light that does the Catholic church no favours. It will be published when the facts are established, and you are going to have to find the strength to face up to a lot of criticism. Not you personally of course, but in so far as you are the representative here, it may be extremely distressing for you… Your Excellency."

"My dear girl. If I have not the strength of character, not only to face up to what may be coming, but to do everything I can to expose any historical horrors that involve our Catholic brothers, then I am not a fit person for this job."

. He held out his hand. "God bless you, my dear." Pippa left with a promise to return as soon as she needed to.

He had seemed like a thoroughly decent chap, she thought, and why shouldn't he be. She had interviewed him without disclosing too much of her own involvement and, would, when the time came, go back and enlighten him, but not while Spike was vulnerable. She knew that it was inevitable that they would trace him, probably soon, but if there was any justice in the world, he shouldn't be charged with offences regarding Wellstead. As for any other activities – well fingers crossed.

She was about to leave when the bishop called her back. "I know that the police will be here before too long, and of course I shall do all I can to assist them in their enquiries, but you have been straight with me and I can't see how it would do any harm if I introduced you to one of the monks who has been here for years. He might be more inclined to talk to you than to anyone connected to the law. I won't go into it but he did some foolish things as a young man, and has spent the rest of his life here trying to make up for it. Nothing that involved violence I hasten to add. He's in the garden right now. Maybe you can pop over and say hello. Tell him I suggested that he might be able to help."

"Thank you, sir. I promise to be tactful, and if I can help him to avoid a direct confrontation with the law, I will, but I can't promise."

"Understood. Good luck."

In the garden, which was an absolute frenzy of colours, displayed in borders and clumps of shrubs, she found an elderly man, dressed for gardening in shabby trousers and a shirt. "Hey!" she called out. "So you lot don't always wear tasselled robes."

He looked up and smiled. "Sorry to disappoint you, miss. I can go in and change if you like but I keep tripping over when I wear them out here, and anyway it's too hot."

"You look fine. Can we have a chat? The bishop said it would be okay, that you may be able to help me. I'm Pippa by the way and I work for a newspaper but I promise not to share with the editor, anything about you. Not your name or where you are or what you do."

She sat down on an ornamental bench and patted it inviting him to join her. "It's about an investigation into something that occurred a long time ago. The police are re-opening a case, which may involve a priest from here, known as Pious. If you can tell me anything about him, it might help and I may be able to pass that information on without disclosing my source. I can't promise of course. It depends on what you know, if anything. Perhaps you could let me know your name?"

"Peter – call me Peter for now. Yes I do remember Pious. He was a strange bloke. I didn't really take to him. He seemed to look down on me. I did try to talk to him but always got the brush off. He just disappeared. Dunno why. I got his room when he didn't come back. They kept it for him for a couple of months but he never got in touch as far as I know."

"And was there anything left in his room, anything that might point to where he went?"

"No, not really" He left a few clothes and books, nothing worth having. It all got chucked out. There was a postcard tucked into the pages of one of his books. I kept it as a bookmark for a while – somewhere in France; a picture of a castle. Began with Fou… something. I didn't take much notice, but he did speak French. I heard him on the phone in the corridor once. He was speaking quickly and I remembered enough from school to recognize the language. He seemed to be fluent. He didn't see me. I just forgot about it but I was quite impressed at the time."

"That's great, Peter, thank you so much. If I give you my card, could you call me if you remember anything else? And if you're ever in town, I owe you a lunch. Thanks again."

And with that she left.

Chapter Eight

Thursday morning, Kate sat at a small table in a café halfway along Silver Street staring into space and seeing in her mind's eye, Jake and the children and the woman – his wife? cousin? fiancée? girlfriend? She certainly wasn't just a casual acquaintance but Knowles was right. Jake wasn't a cheat, he was – he had to be as trustworthy as she thought him to be but why the mystery? What on earth could he be hiding? What could it be that he couldn't trust her with?

Her thoughts were interrupted when an attractive woman pulled up a chair opposite and sat down.

"DI Meredith?"

"Kate – yes, and you must be Philippa Hilton. Hello."

"Pippa please. Yes, you wanted to see me."

"You must know why. I've read the articles you wrote a few years back about The Sanctuary. You covered the tragedy, and I guess you know a hell of a lot more about the place than we do at the moment. You've no doubt been informed that the body of the headmaster at the time was found in rather strange circumstances a couple of days ago, and our enquiries seem to have opened a hornet's nest."

"Yes, I can imagine. It's a pity that more wasn't done at the time and to tell you the truth I'm glad that the case has been re-opened. That home was my bête noir. I was involved enough to realise that there was a lot wrong with that place, but every time I tried to cast light on what was going on there I was side-tracked. It was only after Wellstead arrived that I made some progress."

"What changed?"

"Well before he came, it was more like a prison. Some of the older boys would break out from time to time for the sheer hell of it and cause a bit of a rumpus. I think they were so strictly controlled at the time, that they would risk anything for a bit of freedom. When Wellstead arrived, he actually managed to persuade that complete tyrant Pious, that the kids would respond to a bit of kindness. He organised passes for the lads, as long as they had appointments to do some work, to help old people, cut grass, go shopping etc. Some of them even managed to get Saturday jobs working with the council, tidying up the parks, cleaning graffiti, – lots of which they had planted themselves, stuff like that. I know they were all discouraged from talking to outsiders about conditions in the home and rather than risk losing this new privilege, most of them kept quiet."

"Did you get to know any of them?"

"Yes one. A lad called Sebastian. He came to us a couple of times. He was lovely – polite, intelligent and helpful. He transformed our garden in a couple of hours."

"So come on, what did you find out about him, about the place?"

"It was such a sad story. Sp… Sebastian's parents had died in a terrible accident on the motorway. There were no grandparents, no relatives that could be traced and so the kids were both placed in the home until another solution could be found. They were immediately separated. The older boys were allowed no contact with the younger ones. Can you imagine?

"Spike was desperately worried about his little brother Joey. He begged for a special privilege just to help his brother through such a difficult time. He was just a little boy and after the death of his parents, completely traumatised. He begged me to try to find out how Joey was and so I contacted Wellstead, who was willing, in fact he seemed eager for me to go in and see the place. I made an appointment, met him on the day in his office and was waiting for Joey to arrive. I sensed that Wellstead was clearly uneasy. He was fidgeting and kept getting up to look into the corridor. The next thing I knew was that Pious swept in, full of a transparently false charm, to tell me that Joey was unwell and had been taken to the sick bay. He would let me know when he was well enough to see anyone. He left after giving Wellstead a rather menacing look and I have to say that Wellstead looked devastated. He apologized of course and suggested that we should meet up in town sometime. Not in a flirty sort of way. I think he wanted to talk, but it was quite clear to me then that he was head in name only."

"You said Spike – that was the name of Joey's

brother?"

"Yes. When he didn't turn up for his next gardening session, I rang the home, only to find that he had been transferred to another home somewhere else."

"Who did you speak to?"

"I think it was the woman referred to as matron. She also seemed reluctant to divulge anything. I asked her about Joey but she fobbed me off with some excuse, apologized and said she had to go. I found out later that Spike had been accused of taking money from Pious's office. I refused to believe it. Spike is no thief."

"And that was shortly before the death of Joey?"

"Yes."

"And what happened to Spike?"

"I don't know. He called once to see if I had seen Joey. I had to tell him what had happened. He didn't know you see. He'd been in hiding." She paused. "It was the worst moment of my life."

"I can imagine. That poor boy. And is he still in touch? We really need to speak to him."

"No, sadly I haven't heard from him since. I just hope he recovered and made something of his life. He was a clever lad. I'm – I was very fond of him."

"How old would he be now do you think?"

"Twenty-six, well about twenty-six. He was sixteen when he was here. I think that's why, when he disappeared, there was very little effort to find him. The police tried for a day or two, and then of course they shelved it after the OIC was killed in an horrific crash and the coroner's verdict on Joey, which was so clearly indecisive. It was effectively an open verdict and soon forgotten. Had Joey not been in that home –if it had been a boy living with a family, the police would have moved heaven and earth to find out what had happened, but these kids don't matter. It infuriates me."

"What precisely happened to the OIC. The officer in the case?"

"Please don't quote me, but I have my suspicions about that – another hush job. He was alone in the car, but there was another officer working with him – Sam Cartwright. He was very unhappy about the whole investigation. The OIC, Crowther, had been found to have been driving over the alcohol limit. Sam had been shocked by that because he had been with him for most of the afternoon. Admittedly Simon had gone off on his own and could have stopped for a drink but as far as Sam knew there was nothing to suggest he'd gone off to get bladdered. Sam decided to make his own enquiries and went from pub to pub in the area, with a photo of Simon and found one place where the landlord did recall seeing him but couldn't remember when. It wasn't one of their usual haunts. By the time he'd been to every possible pub he was no further forward. He did express his views to the DCI weeks later. The funeral was long over. The wreck of the car had disappeared and he was told not to make waves. The alcohol level had not been made public so Crowther's wife had not had to face a critical press. There was little point in re-opening the investigation and it was better just to let the matter rest. By this time Sam was so thoroughly disillusioned by the service that he agreed to take early retirement on a full pension. Even that seemed suspicious. He'd had years to go, it was as if they were happy to get rid of him."

"Do you still have the same coroner? His conclusions in the Joey case seem to have fallen far short of competent."

"No, it's a different one now, and yes you're right. Why is it that we assume these austere professionals are always reliable or even honourable?"

"You think that his decision was unacceptable? That he manipulated the facts? Or that he was incompetent? What did he have to gain?"

"I don't know. I had such a bad feeling about that place, I just felt uncomfortable with it, not to mention the fact that a little boy had died. I thought they should have taken the place apart. Instead it was tied up with indecent haste. I do feel though that Sam Cartwright wanted to tell me more, but then he remembered what I did, well do for a living and clammed up."

"We'll be speaking to Sam very soon and I'll add the previous coroner to the list of people to interview if we can find him. Look, Pippa, you've been very helpful. Give me your card. We have to get home to London today or tomorrow but we will certainly be back before long. There are lots of questions to ask and lots of people to see. Can I ask you please to keep this discussion absolutely private for now? Discuss it with no one We don't want to scare anyone off, and I promise that when anything breaks you'll be the first to know."

*****

Knowles was drinking tea when Kate returned to the pub. "Come on tell me all. Where is this Spike and why did he do it?"

"I haven't a clue and Miss Hilton insists that she has no idea where he is. I'm not so sure about that though. I think she does – she refers to him in the present tense from time to time and was, or is very fond of him."

She reported all the salient facts and ordered a ham salad from the luncheon menu. "Don't bother to order a pud. We're heading back on the two o'clock. Kevin has just phoned. There have been developments. Our lovely lady next door to Wellstead, Jill Irving, has just signed for a packet addressed to Wellstead and the postmark is York!"

Chapter Nine

It was late when Kate arrived home but still light and warm. She had arranged to be meet Knowles back at the station in the morning 'as early as you like' he'd said.

She was surprised to hear young voices somewhere in the building and even more surprised, when opening her own door, she could see two girls with familiar faces trying to launch a kite into the air in her garden. When they saw her, the older of the two ran up.

"Hello, I'm Poppy. Uncle Jake said he thought you wouldn't mind if we played out here, as long as we don't go into your house. We had to go in for a moment of course but just to get out here."

Resisting the urge to seize and hug her, Kate smiled. "It's absolutely fine Poppy – and your sister's name?"

"It's Amy," said a voice from the balcony above. "Thank you for not minding. Jake does tend to take liberties but they were so keen to get out with that kite that I took him at his word. I'm Sarah by the way, his sister."

"I'm so happy to meet you, Sarah, I was beginning to think Jake was an orphan."

Sarah head disappeared and moments later she was knocking at the front door.

"Hi. It's good to meet you at last. I haven't been here

for years but I did notice that he mentioned you at least three times during any telephone conversation. Do you have a key to his?"

"Actually no! He kept saying he would get one cut for me but never got round to it. Anyway, why would I need one? He had mine so that he can throw some water on my plants from time to time. I don't think he had even a cactus."

"I think there was a shrivelled one last time I was here. Trouble is, his work can take him to any place at any time so he can't really risk plants, but I'll leave him to tell you all about that. He's just popped out to pick up some papers. He'll be back soon. I'll see you later and we can have a drink. Must get those girls to bed now though." She swept the children in front of her and the three disappeared up the stairs to the flat above.

"Has Uncle Jake gone to the River Shop?" she heard Amy ask? "Do we need some more spice?"

The reply was inaudible. She heard Jake's car pull up outside about half an hour later and he was soon ensconced on her comfortable sofa having greeted her with a hug and a kiss."

"Isn't Sarah coming down for a drink?" she asked.

"Yeah sure, I told her to give us half an hour. She's given me strict instructions to come clean. She's here for about a week – they've come from Sweden. Her husband couldn't come and she needed a break. He's a nice chap. I met him at work and introduced them several years ago."

"So work then?" she asked.

He sighed. "It's going to be a lot less exciting than it sounds. I work at Thames House. More commonly known as the MI5 building. We call it River House at home and as far as the girls are concerned I manage a shop that sells spices from all over the world. They overheard something Sarah said once about spies. She was being sarcastic about what I did. So we had to make up a silly tale on the spot. I also occasionally get involved in an MI6 job. The Circus as they call it.

"Before you get the wrongs idea. I am no James Bond and I haven't got a gun in my pocket. I'm just pleased to see you." He grinned. "My specialty is computer work. I spend my time in cyber space mostly but quite often the job requires me to travel abroad. You must understand why I haven't told you this before. We are not encouraged to blab about what we do. I needed to be quite sure that we were serious. I hope I'm not wrong about that? And it is quite possible that they will look into your background, because you will from now on feature in my personal file. If you object to that we'll have to part here and now."

There was a long pause while Kate digested what she had heard. "So, all that stuff about lecturing and marking papers was made up?"

"Yes it was necessary. No excuses. I can't guarantee that I won't lie to you again. But only if it is vital that you don't know where I am or what I'm doing. It probably won't ever happen, but I'm being honest with you. Can you cope with it?"

"Well you've told me now, so I'll have to, won't I?"

"No. I know you well enough to trust you. If this relationship ends now, I'm quite sure that you wouldn't risk my safety, but I might have to move. Well I would move. I couldn't bear to see you and not be able to give you a cuddle."

"I love you, Jake, and the thought of not being part of your life is well – unthinkable. So one way or the other, we'll have to work out how to handle this. As far as it goes, the sticking point is that your lot will know all about me, but I won't be able to tell my lot anything about you."

"Don't be daft. I'm a computer geek who lives upstairs with whom you are having a torrid affair whatever torrid means. You can tell them what I look like: how brilliant and hilariously funny I am; where we go for posh meals; what I'm like me in bed – well perhaps not that far. Just not where I work."

"Yes. Okay. But just suppose, I needed you to examine a computer for me. Would you do it?"

"Naturally, and no one could do it better. Do you have one?"

"Sadly no. There are two that I would very much like to investigate but there's not much hope of finding them."

She told him about the events of the last two days. "Computers are rarely destroyed, you know. Both your corpse and the suspect priest both had one. Keep looking. Second-hand shops near his home. What about the priest chap? Have you any idea where he is?"

"Not yet. But we'll have to go back North in a day or two and the police up there are making enquiries. I'll waste no time in telling you if you can help, but the info we want is years old and I don't know whether there is the faintest chance of anything useful surviving now. Why don't you shout for Sarah and we can have that drink?"

*****

Kate was at her desk early next morning with a slight hangover, which hopefully the two painkillers she had swallowed minutes ago would soon dispel. Knowles had not yet made an appearance and she was eager to know what had turned up. Still it gave her time to grab a strong cup of coffee and she was still drinking it when the guv appeared and yelled for everyone to go into the conference room.

Once everyone was settled he switched on a machine. "This arrived at Wellstead's address a couple of days ago, as you know. It is a recording of a recording I think and we've had to try to sharpen it up a bit, but it more or less tells us what happened a short time before Wellstead died, so listen up."

The tape began and they heard: *"It's not a long story – but to make it easier to tell you, would you get me a glass of water and a couple of those white pills, the bottle on the mantelpiece. They don't help much but better than nothing."*

A different voice was heard after a pause: *"Take a couple of these. They might be better."*

They listened and the tape continued until there was a cry of pain and the noise it seemed of somebody falling, gasping and after a minute or two, the second voice, fainter, as if he'd moved away:

"He's collapsed! I need a hand to get him into the car, Vic. We've got to get him to hospital. The tape ended. There was complete silence in the room as the group considered what they had heard.

Knowles broke the silence. "So we know how and why he left home, but not why he ended up by the rail tracks, but if he died on the way, I guess they didn't see the point of going to the hospital or the police – and didn't want to have to explain the whys and wherefores."

"Well we know at least that Wellstead himself took the morphine."

"I'm not so sure about that. What Spike said was: *'Take these, they may be better'* better than the ones in the bottle presumably, so if they were given him by Spike, stronger ones. Where did he get them? It's still supply if the postmortem indicates that the amount in his body was greater than his own tablets could have explained. Certainly Wellstead took them willingly. We may never know. The significant thing is that this tape strongly indicates that a nasty piece of work, posing as a priest was brutalising small children in that awful place that described itself as home, and because I intend to catch the bastard, we're going to hang on to this link and follow up this investigation till we catch him wherever it takes us."

"Did you find out anything more? Has Jill Irving remembered anything useful?" asked Kate.

"Well I was thinking, Kate. We didn't find any bank statements anywhere, did we? He must have been paying bills, so I guess he was doing stuff online, day to day stuff. Therefore, he must have disposed of his computer elsewhere and fairly recently. Jill did remember seeing it, but he didn't go out so we need to speak to the team that visited daily to check him out. I'm on to that already. No doubt he has erased all the old stuff: the chats with Frances, but I know that the hard drive might still have some evidence. I need someone to get onto that today, please, lads, and let me know as soon as you get a trace."

"Now, Kate, if you could just update the lads on what you found out from the reporter. I don't think you can add much, but we'll see her again when we go back. We need to be able to identify 'Vic' if we can. We need information on anyone who was involved in any way with the home and we need to analyse the tablets you seized from Glebe Avenue – how long he'd had them, whether there were enough to polish him off. Also, get onto traffic and see if we can see a car near the crime scene that we could possibly follow back to Glebe Ave. It's a long shot but try it anyway."

Having rattled off a few more instructions to the

teams, he grabbed Kate's shoulder. "We have to go back, Kate. Liaise with DC Blakey and ask her to set up a squad ready for tomorrow. When she's heard this, she'll be as keen as we are to find this chap. I know they were going to find out as much about the place as possible. I spoke to her this morning and the indications were, that the priest has French connections. How is your French? We may need to get Interpol onto this and sort out a European Arrest Warrant."

"I love you when you're excited," said Kate "Why don't we drive up? It'll be quicker than hanging around for trains and we'll get about more easily under our own steam when we're there, and on the way you can tell me how it went with our character actress. Is that a smudge of lipstick on your shirt collar?"

Chapter Ten

At The Stables, all was being prepared for the return of Sophie. Most of the cargo would be unloaded and stored straight away; all the residents ready and happily willing to help. Sophia had slipped home before dawn and Griffiths had gone to engage in whatever nefarious business that involved him. He never talked about it and Spike never asked. He didn't want to know. As long as the generous fees were paid he was satisfied.

The diesel truck was due at around dusk and the various tanks would be filled. The driver of the truck, as arranged, was entirely responsible for the second cargo, which would be transferred while the students and other staff were enjoying an excellent dinner.

The skipper and first mate on Sophie were of course trusted employees. Should any unofficial cargo ever be at risk, they had orders to press the release button immediately, but so far there had been no trouble.

There were, however, on most return trips, a couple of extra passengers, usually young. They would come on board off the French western coast, looking dirty, hungry and lost but after two or three days at sea, they looked cleaner and happier and full of hope when they left the ship at the boatyard to be greeted with joy, love and relief, by relatives from Syria or North Africa who had made UK their home. They were soon equipped with all necessary papers. Once they left, they were instructed never to contact the boatyard again. Sometimes Spike received payment for this service, sometimes the beaming smiles and tears of joy on the faces of his passengers were reward enough. Whenever the boat had been stopped for a routine check on cargo, it had been accepted that all the crew and passengers were from The Stables but should passports or papers be inspected, Spike was confident that offshore, the inspection would be cursory. Once they reached the boatyard there was no more help. The families were on their own. All Spike could do was to wish them luck.

It was Vic who had organised this venture but Spike had taken little persuasion. Anything to help these desperate kids who had travelled for weeks, only to find themselves stuck in terrible conditions at Calais or Marseilles with no hope of rescue.

The boat and crew were familiar visitors to France, they spoke the language very well and had friends there. From time to time they took students with them. French lessons were popular at home (it was always referred to as home never The Home) and some of the students were fluent. They would stay for a couple of days and help with the shopping. Pippa was never without her perfume and fillet steak wasn't anything special at home and Pippa was a first-rate cook.

It had taken some years and a lot of hard work to be

able to provide this kind of lifestyle to his lads, but something in Spike made him determined to make up for the horrors he experienced during his brief stay at The Sanctuary. From the care and love of the best parents in the world, he had found himself in a kind of hell, and his brother had died there. It still caused him pain. Had it not been for Pippa, who had held him and comforted him night after night, and his patron Stephen Pearson who had found him and looked after him like his own son, Spike might have followed Joey and his parents. He had been tempted. Now all he wanted to do was keep his new family safe, give the lads the right start in life, make them self-sufficient and able to look after themselves. Not one of them was discharged until Spike was satisfied that they could be independent, confident and loyal. He knew that none of them would betray him, although as far as it was possible to do so, he kept them separate from any activities that weren't completely above board!

Now, sitting with Vic and Pippa around the table, he needed an update on everything that had happened while he was away.

"Well done with the bishop, Pips. So we might have to investigate the French connection."

"Well presumably the police will be talking to him soon. I didn't tell DCI Meredith about our little interview, but I expect she'll want to see me again. As far as she is concerned, I have no idea where you are now, although I'm not convinced she believes me. I've asked the newspaper staff and the other journalist not to give them my address here. I don't think they even know it anyway. They always contact me by mobile, but if they do have any way of tracing me here, they'll find you. We can't ask the boys to lie, and if they do a land search, they'll have you."

"Well not too soon I hope, but they will certainly have the tape by now so I'll be a person of interest. If I am arrested, it depends on what and if they decide to charge me with, but you two can manage for a while, and anyway, I should get bail. Their main concern must be to find Pious, if they get their priorities right. I will of course do everything I can to help."

"Surely they'll get Interpol involved, won't they?"

"Not necessarily. Just because he speaks French, and they don't know that do they? Not unless they've spoken to the gardener chap. You need to tell them ASAP, Pippa."

"If they share info with us, we could pop over and do some digging ourselves."

"What? And where would we start, Vic? Calais? and then work our way south?"

"Well we have a lead. We have the postcard with a castle. Fou or somewhere. Get an atlas. Get the charts. Let's whittle it down." Vic seated himself in front of the computer and within seconds was grinning. "Okay, we have Fougères, Fouras and Fourcès. Only Fougères has a castle according to these pics. Tell me I'm brilliant."

"You certainly have your moments," said Spike with a smile, "but some of your good ideas leave a lot to be desired – okay Google Fougères and let's see where it is."

"I'm on it. It's in Normany How good is that? About three hours' drive from Cherbourg depending on who's at the wheel. When do we start?"

"Look," observed Spike, "we need to get help with this. I'm going to have to come clean and speak to whoever is dealing with this case so that they know everything we know. They must have worked out who I am – my full name I mean. They know Joey had a brother. They'll search every record. I'm the registered owner of this place and I have a passport in my own name. Pippa, you had better get in touch with that DI woman and arrange another meeting. Tell them I will meet them on condition that I am not put out of action. Make sure they get the right message. I did what I did because I needed to know what happened to Joey.

"Until now I didn't have the resources. It was the anniversary of my parents' death and I felt that I'd let them down. I have no previous convictions as and far as I know, no one is going to betray me now. If at all possible, I want to be able to carry on with what we do, because we don't really hurt anyone, do we? We just redress the balance a little bit. There are nasty sods in this world – all over the place. It's difficult to understand how they function. Is it just chemistry? Something in their brains that makes it impossible for them to comprehend the pain and distress they cause? I don't think so. They know what pain feels like. They wouldn't want to change places with their victims. They need to pay – and Pious is going to pay if it's the last thing I do – and heaven knows, it just might be.

I accept that."

"Okay, Spike, I'll try to get that message over. I'll tell them they must guarantee your freedom at least until we've found him, and then all we can hope for is the right kind of justice. What we will need to do is protect this place at all costs. I would rather meet them elsewhere but if they do make a surprise visit, so what. It's a prosperous business and you are the legitimate owner. No problem!"

"Yeah," muttered Vic. "Let's hope you're right, but I think we'd better get in touch with Pierre and tell him to hold fire over there for a week or two. We have two little lads on the way from Calais right now but let's postpone any further rescues until we feel it's safe to carry on."

"Okay – well I'm not going to destroy their hopes, but once they're here we'll hold off for a couple of months, or however long it takes. Can you sort it in a couple of days? You could go over tomorrow. Even pop down to Fougères maybe. Do some digging."

Chapter Eleven

Vic wasted no time and was busy arranging the imminent trip to collect the two boys. The paperwork was ready in advance due to his meticulous arrangements, and it was now simply a matter of getting over there, picking them up from the kindly Pierre, who never let them down, turning round and heading home. He knew Spike depended on him to make sure there were no mistakes, or avoidable hold ups and no information leaks. Few were aware of this scheme and the three that were the prime movers, were cautious. It was risky, but to the men involved, compassion eclipsed any feelings of guilt.

Since his first meeting with Spike, Vic's entire life had been transformed and he would do nothing to risk damaging this close friendship. He loved Pippa too of course but not in the same way. He'd never had a girlfriend. Didn't even bother to try, he thought it was pointless. He was not a handsome man; he had a harelip and a large scar across his left eye where one of his stepfathers had slashed at him with a knife. He was told by his mother, who was unable to identify his blood father among the numerous men she had slept with, that no one loved an ugly baby. He was neglected, cold hungry and miserable but was kept because the child allowance came in handy. When social services became aware of his plight, he was taken into care, and, while the home that took him was far from perfect by today's standards, to Vic it was paradise; a warm, clean bed and three meals a day were things he had not experienced before. The fact that no one talked to him much and the other kids shunned him and called him names, didn't really bother him. He was inured to that. No one loved an ugly little boy but at least nobody beat him.

He had been passed from one home to another and had been at The Sanctuary for three years when Spike and Joey arrived. Joey had been immediately removed to 'the kiddies' wing' as it was known, leaving a grief-stricken Spike in tears in the corner of the common room. Wellstead had tried to communicate, but failed and had called Vic to show the new boy round when he felt up to it.

Vic had talked gently to Spike, not about the home but about the good things in his life: the squirrels that raced up the tree trunks and the underground shelter he'd found in the grounds and the gardener who sometimes gave him wild strawberries if he dug the vegetable garden while the gardener had a fag. He had a gentle voice. When Spike looked up, he didn't notice an ugly face, he saw a teenager with kind eyes who was trying to make him feel at home. They had developed a firm friendship in a very short time, a dependence on one another, and both felt stronger for it. It was Vic, who had introduced him to Pippa. He had been allowed out to do useful work in the community and had been allocated a gardening job at the home of a local newspaper reporter. She was barely out of her teens and lived with her parents but was already attracting attention by addressing local issues. She liked Vic and was already enraged by the insensitive way he was treated at the home. When he brought Spike along she promised to do her best to visit the place and try to see Joey. She had given Spike a mobile phone and told him to call her whenever he needed help or just to talk. When he was removed and then absconded, he kept in touch so that she and Vic always knew where he was.

When The Sanctuary had closed Vic had simply walked away leaving everything behind him. He went straight to Pippa's and together they went to The Stables. Pippa had the ordeal of breaking the news of Joey's death and had been able to comfort him in a way that only a woman could, had held him and talked to him and promised that the pain would ease with time.

When Vic arrived, he was introduced to Pearson who took him on as a handyman. Over the years Vic had grown in confidence and learned skills and was now a seasoned sailor and skilled boat builder. Together the three ran a tight ship. There were rules of course. Girlfriends were not allowed to stay the night, smoking was not permitted, any other kind of drug was absolutely forbidden and bullying of any description was unacceptable. In fact, there were few occasions when the harmony was disrupted as disputes were discussed and dealt with in the fairest way possible.

In the library, Vic sorted out the appropriate charts and planned the best way to travel to Fougères when the time came, but first, they had to collect and safely deliver the two children – that meant two trips. Once they had handed over the children, possibly to Poole, he could be back in France a couple of days from now. They had friends in Mont-Saint-Michel, whom he knew would provide them with transport. From where he usually docked, it was about an hour's drive to Fougères. Once there he had no idea what he would be looking for, but somebody at some point in time had visited there and knew Brother P. Where to go from that point was an absolute mystery. He was totally stumped, but once the police were involved, surely something would guide them.

Pippa meantime was in touch with the local police station to find out when the Met would be back. No one seemed to know, or perhaps were unwilling to disclose information to someone who had in the past slated them for failing to investigate matters with sufficient application, so she found the card that DI Meredith had given her a few days ago. Kate answered on the third ring. "DI Kate Meredith, Hello."

"Hello it's Phillipa Hilton, we met in Silver Street the other day. Are you likely to be back soon?"

"I'm on the way – should be arriving about three this afternoon. Have you anything for me?"

"Yes. I think we need to exchange some information. I spoke to someone at the church offices just yesterday but I would rather speak to you in person than over the phone, can we meet up?"

"How about this evening? We're staying at the King's Head – say seven p.m.?"

"I'll be there. See you then."

It was about half an hour before her appointment with DI Meredith that Pippa received a call from a number she didn't recognize and was quite excited when the caller identified himself as Peter the gardener.

"Hello," he said hesitantly. "Is that the lady from the newspaper that spoke to me yesterday?"

"Yes, Peter. It is me, Pippa. Can I help you?"

"Well the bishop had a word with me, told me why you had wanted to talk to me like, and asked what I had said to you. I told him about the postcard and he said I should go and look in the cellars to see if there was anything else that might help. He said I must tell him before I spoke to you again, but he's away somewhere so I couldn't. I did find something though. It's his old computer. I think it's broken but it does light up when I plug it in, but there's nothing on it. There were a couple of letters too in the pocket of an old jacket."

Pippa's heart was pounding and she tried to keep her voice steady. "That is brilliant, Peter. Where are you now?"

"I'm back in the garden I'll be here for another hour

or so."

"If I come over, could you let me have a look at this stuff? It's really important, Peter."

"Yes, I see no harm in that but you can't take them until I show them to the bishop, okay?"

"Absolutely fine, Peter. I'll be right over."

Pippa could barely contain her excitement and rushed out after telling Spike the news.

"Don't rush take it easy, and if he won't part with the stuff, take pictures."

Peter was raking up leaves just inside a side gate in the walled garden, which led into a narrow lane. Near him on a garden seat was a laptop with a damaged lid, and a transparent bag containing what looked like two handwritten envelopes. He grinned when she arrived. "Bloody hell! That was quick."

Taken aback by the language which was more suited to the inside of the local rag's print shop, she couldn't help laughing. "Hey I thought you guys were forbidden to blaspheme."

"That's what's so good about working out here. Only God can hear me and He doesn't mind. In fact, I think He likes it. He hates hypocrites who go to church every Sunday and spend the rest of the week lying and cheating. We've come to an understanding Him and me. Words is just words. It's actions that count."

"Too right, Peter. Now can I have a look at this stuff?" She sat down on the seat and lifted the lid of the laptop.

Nothing to see of course. The letters would much more rewarding, and she was just about to remove them from the bag when a voice hailed them from the other side of the lawn.

"Good afternoon." The bishop was approaching from the back of the Manse and she had no time to examine them further.

"Damn."

"Sit on them," muttered Peter.

"What?" she said startled, then sat down, immediately spreading her coat across the plastic bag and smiling as the bishop approached.

"Well how nice to see you again, Miss Hilton. Have you come to do some weeding or are you here looking for a scoop?"

"It was me that invited her, sir," intervened Peter. "I told her I had found this old computer in the cellar which I thought I'd seen Pious using, but there's nothing on it at all."

"Well, Peter, I did tell you to let me know first because of course it is the police who must have this. Not that there will anything useful on it now. I'll put it in a safe place until tomorrow when I think one of them is coming to see me." He turned to Pippa. "Would you care to come in and have a sherry?"

"Sorry no. I have an appointment with the cops myself. And I'll be late if I don't go right now. Good to see you again, sir." She carefully gathered up her coat, smiled and headed for the gate. "Enjoy your drink. Bye, Peter."

On the way to the designated pub, Pippa pondered on the events in the garden of the Manse. Why had Peter decided to help her to leave with the evidence? It had been so unexpected that she had almost failed to act in time. Was there more to Peter than met the eye? What did he know? Had he remembered stuff about Pious or did he have his doubts about the bishop? All very interesting, and she decided she must see him again – perhaps lure him away from the Manse to a place where he could speak freely.

She shelved the thought for the time being and concentrated on her next rendezvous. It would be interesting.

Arriving twenty minutes late for the meeting with Kate, she had to resist the temptation to examine the contents of the bag and took it with her into the pub. Kate and DCI Knowles were sitting in the garden outside and after the introductions were made and apologies for lateness were dealt with, they sat for a minute or two in the warm sun with cold beers.

"Okay, Philippa, what have you got for us?" Kate broke the silence.

"Well before I start, can I assume that a tape which was posted here, and which is relevant to your investigation, is now in your possession?"

"You can," replied Kate, "and since you are aware of

its existence, can I assume that you know full well what was on it, and consequently where Spike is right now?"

"Yes, I know what was on it, and no I can't tell you where Spike is at this precise moment, but I can help you with where he will be, and assure you that he is willing to talk to you, in certain circumstances."

"Go on."

"I'm sure your investigation so far will have established that Spike is Joey's brother. You may also have discovered that their parents were killed just a week or two before Joey's death and that Spike was expelled as a result of trumped up theft charges. Can you imagine what sort of state he must have been in? Yes, we did keep in touch, and I can assure you that he is one of the most decent people I know.

"On the tenth anniversary of his parents' death, Spike felt he had to find out more about the incident at The Sanctuary. He had always felt guilty because he hadn't managed to keep his brother safe. The coroner's report was a disgrace. How could it have been accidental death when the window from which he had fallen, was found to be closed the next morning? Yes, it could have been closed by someone who had no idea that there was a child lying dead outside, but no one remembered doing it. The police investigation was shamefully shallow, and then of course once the investigating officer died everything fell apart. Accidental death. End of investigation."

"Hm," muttered Knowles. "Well let's see what turns up now. Tell me about the officer who was killed –

Crowther wasn't it? There seems to be very little available info on that."

"You need to speak to his sidekick. He was fuming. In fact, he left the force after he got on the wrong side of the wrong people."

"Are you in contact?"

"I know where he did live. I'll make enquiries."

"Thank you, and we need to speak to Spike as soon as possible. I know that there are questions we should be asking about how Wellstead ended up where he did, but quite honestly that is a side issue. It will eventually have to be sorted out even if only to be able to explain it to his relatives, if we find any, but when and where do we speak to Spike? If you are worried, let me assure you that we are going to assume that Wellstead died from natural causes, possibly accelerated by the ingestion of a rather large dose of diamorphine, but there is sufficient doubt as to whether or not it was his own medicine or something provided to him by someone else, to push it way down the priority list. It's quite clear that the man had had enough of this world, and I think to rake up his past would be insensitive. I do need to know who Spike was with on the day though. We will have to have his account."

"Of course." Pippa paused and gulped some of her drink. "Okay, may I take it for granted that the top of your wanted list is the priest – if indeed he really was one?"

Pippa gave a detailed account of her chat with the bishop and then took the envelopes from her coat pocket and told them about Peter and his rather strange behaviour only a short time ago. "Peter is a strange character. I understand that he is no great friend of the police but I can't imagine him being a gun runner or international hit man. In any case, he's been doing the bishop's garden for years so it would be a waste of time examining his past."

"Say no more;" interrupted Knowles. "We are certainly not here to rake up minor offences of any of the locals. I won't even mention him to the bishop. You seem to have gathered all the useful information he has anyway but I suppose I'll have to see him myself even if it's just to pick up the computer."

"Good but look I've resisted opening those letters since I smuggled them out. Surely you're not going to wait till I've gone before you have a look. I'm consumed with curiosity."

"Let's do it now, shall we? We'll go and sit in Kate's room so that we can discuss whatever they contain in private but be prepared to be disappointed." But they weren't.

Chapter Twelve

The letters were addressed to a M Francois Tellier and dated some twenty years before. Slightly grubby and faded they were still readable, and surprisingly, in English, with UK stamps.

Rue de les Arbres Fougerolles-du-Plessis 53195 France

Dear Frances

It is such a long time since I heard from you. I hope you are well. Your aunt tells me that you are still not communicating with her very much and are desperately frightened that your father will be able to trace you. As I have said so many times before, the safest place for you would be here in England with me and I implore you to come here. There are so many good opportunities for bilingual people. You may even be able to get a job at the foreign office. I have a contact there and he would be interested to meet you.

"Well maybe that's something we could investigate – a friend at the Foreign Office."

"Read on, please, Guv."

The doctor tells me that I should be able to walk normally soon. The bones have aligned properly and I feel very little pain now. I don't know how Marcel found us, but he was in such a fury that I'm glad you ran. The police have told me that I should have reported the attack immediately. I spent so much time wondering where you were. It wasn't until I realised that your passport was missing that I guessed you had gone back to Fougères.

She was never right for you, Frances, but if you have reunited I am happy for you.

"So presumably his father was Marcel Tellier – and at one time he had a girlfriend who is nameless. Not good."

Please get in touch soon. I am at the old address in Dorset. I worry about you. I feel guilty that you suffered so much at the hands of that beast that I married but I will make it up to you if you will only come home. If you stay in France, I fear that he will find you.

Your loving mother

There was no date on either letter, which was frustrating but the tone of it suggested that the second one was a lot later.

My dear Francois

I am glad to hear you are coming home. It would have been nice to hear it from you. Maybe I am assuming too much and that home is elsewhere as far as you are concerned. Edith doesn't give me any clues but I can only hope. There is a place at the college ready for you in September if you want to take it up. It depends of course on your attendance at interview and verification of the exam results that Edith reported to me and you would be able to stay as a resident at the college if you wanted to.

But Frances, if you genuinely want to be a priest, you must try to forget the past and set aside your anger. I wish you would talk to me. I worry that you blame me for all our misfortunes but how could I know that the man I married could turn into such a demon. I should have waited till I knew him better but he seemed so nice. The worst thing is knowing that when necessary, he could control his temper and he did, until I was in his power and he had control over everything that was mine.

You must try to contain your hatred for him. You never talked to me. It would have helped I'm sure. If I had known more about the abuse, I think I would have gone to the police so much earlier. His legacy must not be hatred. It is not the kind of emotion that would be welcome in a college like this. I am worried sometimes about you. You seem to have little sympathy for others. Compassion is a not weakness. It is strength. I should have protected you more than I did but I was a coward. Better to be a coward, Frances, than a monster. Sometimes I dreamed about killing him, pushing him in front of a train, or just hoping he would die in some horrible accident. It wasn't revenge, just a longing to know that he no longer existed, but you, Francois, seem to feel that you can transfer your pain by hurting others. Vulnerable others. Can you not see that you are assuming his robes, being him? How does that help you? Does seeing pain suffered by others not remind you of your own suffering or do you feel you can somehow exorcize your pain by transferring it to them. What has happened to you?

I'm sorry, Frances, I've let my feelings run away with me, but please think on what I've said and let me know when it is that you'll be coming home. I will have your room ready for you. I can't bear to think I have lost you for ever.

From your loving mother.

The second letter was crossed by an angry red line from corner to corner and looked as if it had been crumpled up at some stage and then smoothed out again. The address on both envelopes was the same. The three readers having passed it round sat in silence for a while.

"Well that is very depressing but quite enlightening," observed Knowles, "and it certainly gives us some leads. If Edith is still alive, we can probably get an address for him, but it looks as if he was not in a hurry to get in touch."

"We have an address in France. That has to be the first port of call," said Kate. "What about Interpol?"

"Can I say something?" interrupted Pippa. "It is only fair that we keep Spike in the loop. Apart from anything else, he wants to talk to you, and we make frequent trips to France. It's part of what we do."

"And precisely what do you do?" asked Kate.

"I'm going to let Spike tell you that," said Pippa not knowing just how much she should reveal. She needed to discuss the developments with the other two before she said more. "If we can both come over tomorrow morning?"

"By all means, but please make it early. Can we say eight thirty? You can have breakfast and then we'll decide who does what and how and when. It's all getting a bit complicated and while the full picture is far from complete, we should have some idea of where the gaps are and who's the best person to fill them."

"Can you give me an absolute assurance that if I bring Spike here tomorrow, that he will not be arrested for any offence involving Wellstead?"

"Yes. I give you my word, as long as he is straight with me. I need to know who was helping him that night, presumably it wasn't you, and I'll need a statement from him too. If at the end of all this, if I feel bound to register a misdemeanour of any kind, it will almost certainly result in a caution, unless something is disclosed which would render that entirely inappropriate."

"Okay, well I'll have to be satisfied with that."

"It doesn't apply to anything which follows from here of course. If I find the priest with part of his head missing, that will require further investigation."

"He's not usually so pompous," grinned Kate. "He's just covering his back. Don't worry. We're all on the same side."

*****

Back at The Stables, Vic had already left and Spike was drinking a cup of builder's tea at the large kitchen table.

He got up as soon as she entered and gave her a hug. "You look pleased with yourself," he observed. "How did it go? Should I get ready to scarper?"

"Not until you hear police sirens. You should have about ten minutes to pack. Just kidding."

"I could tell. Now sit down, here's a coffee, and tell me about it."

She began by describing how she had come into possession of the two letters.

"The priest's name is Francois Tellier. He may be in the UK. He has connections here, but he is much more likely to be in France now. He has or perhaps had an aunt there. It sounds as if he was an abused child. His father was a right bastard who, it seems brutally assaulted his mother. She refers to it in her letter to him which you will be able to read tomorrow, but she gives the impression that Francois is a chip off the old block."

"Really? It seems to be a common occurrence. The abused becomes an abuser, which is something I fail to understand."

"You're not alone. It's something which his mother seems to have picked up and is equally bemused by it. Perhaps a psychiatrist could explain, but the thing is, we have leads and a reasonably sympathetic police crew. We're meeting them tomorrow at breakfast and I have a guarantee that you will not be arrested. Not yet anyway."

She gave a detailed account of the earlier conversation. Spike looked relieved and exhausted at the same time.

"Well it worked, didn't it? and maybe that's thanks to Vic after all. His rather distasteful clue has helped send them up here, but it's Peter that we really need to thank. I'd like to meet him. I like his style."

"Well that could be arranged, but whether I need to do it behind the bishop's back is the question. There was something about the way he gently chastised the guy for letting me see the computer first, and why did Peter suddenly decide that I should have the letters? Did he doubt that they would be handed over to the police, I wonder?"

"Well look at it this way. The guy probably hasn't been near a woman for weeks, and then suddenly this gorgeous bird is paying him attention. Here is a chance to get into her good books, to please her. Maybe it's just as simple as that."

"True, I am gorgeous." Pippa smiled. "So introducing him to you would only make him jealous, so better not risk it."

"You're not that gorgeous! How about another visit through the back door? Was that gate locked? It's a lovely evening, he could well be in the garden."

"Yes, but we'd better get tomorrow's breakfast over first. Shall we let them know the plan? Knowles might want to get at him first."

"Did you tell him about the gate"

"No I just said I left, but not how. Let's get some

sleep. I'll set the alarm."

*****

When they arrived at the pub, Kate was waiting to meet them and ushered them into the breakfast room where Knowles was seated in front of a plate of bacon and scrambled egg.

"Looks good," remarked Spike after introductions had been made. "Is that bacon thin and crispy or just thin and bendy? I like it to shatter into delicious fragments as soon as I bite it."

"Ah! A man who appreciates good food. I absolutely agree," said Knowles. "Sadly this is the bendy kind, but the scrambled eggs are perfect."

Kate had two boiled eggs, Pippa went for the same and Spike opted for croissants and honey. The coffee was excellent and it was only when they were settled in the snug with second or third cups that they got down to business. Spike knew it was time to describe in as much detail as possible the series of events that had led to Wellstead's final resting place. Kate found it difficult at times to hide her amusement although she had to wince when it came to Vic's decision to plant a 'clue'.

"You know what," she said, "he was probably right. Revolting as his idea was – it got us going. I can't wait to meet him."

"Vic is one of a kind," said Spike. "He just about kept

me sane in the really bad times. Please be gentle with him."

"We're reserving judgement," said Knowles, "but he's certainly resourceful and Kate's right – enough of him for now. Let's discuss what we know so far."

The evening before Pippa had described in detail, her conversations with the bishop and meetings with Peter.

"Well I'm meeting with him in about an hour," said Knowles. "Kate has the address of the matron who is getting on a bit and probably won't help much but you never know, and this evening we're meeting up with an ex DI who was involved with the original case. Maybe you two would like to come along, although that could be quite painful for you, Spike."

"I've lived with this for so long," said Spike thoughtfully, "and I thought I could cope with it now, but to tell you the truth, it's beginning to upset me. It's like we're bringing it all back, as if it happened yesterday. There are waves of pain and sometimes I want to cry." He paused and sighed. "But the only way I can really let go of those terrible memories, is to clean up, if you see what I mean. Pick up all the broken pieces and put them together – I can't say make sense of it, because there is none, but I don't want to live in a world where my particular monster walks free. So yes, I'll deal with it, and talking to you all now is actually helping because I know you're on my side."

There was a moment of silence. Knowles cleared his throat. "Right then, we'll work as a team. Kate and I will have to go back to London tomorrow morning so can I suggest drinks at the bar at about seven this evening to compare notes? We'll do what we have to do. If Pippa gets the chance to see Peter again and do some probing, that would be good, but don't frighten him off. We don't know what you two get up to. Presumably you are both gainfully employed, perhaps we can hear more about that some other time. One thing I need to do is talk to Vic before I go. Can you arrange that soon?"

"The only reason he isn't here right now, is that he is away for two or three days on business. His name is Victor March."

"That rings no bells," said Knowles, "but I'll look up the records."

"You might find that he was cautioned if the records go back that far. Taking without consent or something. Certainly more than ten years ago."

"Then I won't waste time on it."

And with that, they all went their separate ways.

Outside Kate saw the two climb into a very new looking BMW and wondered exactly what they did do. Self-employed clearly. Pippa's shoes were far from cheap and her handbag must have cost about £250. Knowles wouldn't have noticed that of course. She liked them both and decided that unless it was absolutely necessary, and she could see no reason why it should be, their business was not something of interest to the police. Not the Met anyway.

It was on the way to visit Matron that she suddenly realised that she hadn't thought about Jake at all since last night, but the computer that Peter had found would be of interest to him. Hopefully he would be able to extract useful stuff from the hard drive.

Chapter Thirteen

Spike was quiet on the way back to The Stables. Pippa knew he was struggling with demons, trying to rationalise.

"This is what you wanted, Spike. You didn't think it was going to be easy, did you?"

"I didn't really think about the process at all. I don't think I even thought it would happen. When I went to see Wellstead, I just wanted answers. I wasn't expecting this. I thought in my own mind, it would be him. I hadn't thought beyond that, but he wasn't at all what I expected. There was nothing evil about him. When he started to tell me about his past it was what I anticipated I suppose and I actually tried to be angry. To work myself up so that I could deal with him, and yet, I hadn't a clue what I was going to do. Then when he was such an obvious wreck. What kind of man would have hurt him further? It would have taken a hard, cruel, thick-skinned monster and that's just not me. It was almost a relief to find out it was someone else. After that, events took over, he collapsed. My first instinct was to get help, get him straight to hospital. And you know what happened after that – some sort of nightmare. But, suppose we had left him with just the Joey note in his pocket. I think Vic was right. They might just have thought he was an old drunk, or, if they looked at his medical records, assumed that he'd – I don't know, somehow found a place to die in peace. The Met are so busy, why would they take it further when a dying man died. It was that pointed object thing with which Vic somehow had the stomach to do what he did, that's what made them investigate further, because it was something he couldn't have done himself. The spike was introduced postmortem."

Pippa was silent.

"So suppose we find the priest, a man who was abused as a child. How will you deal with that?"

"I'm not sure. Right now, I feel an all-consuming loathing for him. To inflict pain and misery on a skinny, vulnerable little boy whose world had just about collapsed around him, takes something beyond evil and I think I could kill him. But it will do to have him tried and punished in a civilised way I suppose."

"I've been reading it up. Apparently twenty-two per cent of children who are abused by parents grow up to be abusers. The reason being, that they confuse parental love, and abuse. That's the way they were 'loved' so that's how they demonstrate their love to their victims. I have to confess that it doesn't make much sense to me. I suppose if they were sexually abused in a gentle loving way, it could be confusing."

"Yes, but it wasn't like that, was it? This man was a cruel bully. He knew what it was like to be beaten and hurt. How could he possibly confuse that with love? Look what are we going to do today? Remind me. Let's get on with it. Maybe we'll find that he's dead and as long as it was a long and agonising death, I'll be able to put this all behind me and concentrate on what we seem to be very good at doing and that's looking after our lads. Making sure they grow up well balanced and happy."

Breakfast was long over at The Stables. The boys were in three teams and took turns on kitchen duty, house duty and boatyard tidying, all to be finished by ten o'clock when lessons and lectures started. Spike did his daily check at ten thirty and everything was going well. Mathematics was in full swing in the lecture hall and in the workshops, three boys were taking an old mini apart and another three were discussing the workings of a gas central heating system.

In the kitchen the day's menu was on a chalkboard and the beginnings of a light lunch were evident – salad and Quiche Lorraine followed by cheese biscuits and coffee. Dinner would be much more exotic.

"We're expecting a delivery of local produce any minute," said Pippa, "and we'll be able to stock up on stuff when Vic gets back. He was in touch earlier and suggested docking at Poole in the circumstances. It'll be much quicker and safer and he can hand over his charges to the families there, then head back here."

"No more residents till this is all sorted, Pippa. When it is, we can concentrate on enlarging our intake. Promise me one thing. If all this goes tits up, and we're on our uppers, keep it going somehow: At least until our last student is launched. Hopefully, unless I'm locked up for assisting illegal immigrants, we should be fine, even if Griffiths is off the scene. I've got a feeling that whatever he does, it's not lawful and possibly dangerous. I think it's diamonds, probably stolen but I'm not asking. The police have been known to catch them at it though, and if it happens on my boat, I might have a problem convincing them that I know nothing, especially as Sophie is registered to him and anchors here."

"Could we manage without him? I mean could we tell him we need the space and that we're a bit worried about things?"

"Quite honestly no. We couldn't. Not at the pace and the standard we have now. It's so perfect. I don't want it to change. These kids are transformed. They're decent, sophisticated, well-educated lads and I'm proud of them all. They'll go places. And look at Vic, remember what he was like, a humble frightened lad who avoided looking at anyone because he was ugly. He's fine now, confident and poised. All we have to do now is find him a girl, but he's convinced that it's impossible."

"I wonder if he would benefit from plastic surgery?"

"No, Vic is fine. He needs confidence. If you mentioned that, he would regress, think he needed it, and he doesn't. He has an attractive personality and, quite a nice body, I think you observed the other day."

"Yes he does actually. He's tall, lean and muscular,

pity about the mermaid tattoo though. How do you think he will stand up to interrogation by Knowles?"

"He'll be fine, why shouldn't he be, apart from mutilating a corpse he's done nothing wrong and the corpse isn't going to complain. I'm going to leave him to explain that. I wouldn't know where to start. I'm just hoping they're not going to quiz me about the drug. 'Take this, it will be better' is open to all sorts of interpretations."

"Well I keep meaning to ask, Spike. What was it and where did you get it?"

"You're going to have to trust me, Pip. You know me well enough. I would have nothing to do with drugs. It should have been destroyed a while ago. I just felt it in my pocket when I got out of the car and it seemed like fate. I knew it was a painkiller and Wellstead was dying and in pain. It helped him. I don't think he would have talked as he did without it."

"Did it come from here – from one of the boys?"

"It was one of the boys who gave it to me. Its source was outside these premises and has been dealt with, I promise you. Okay that's enough small talk. Get me a beer, please. I need strength for this meeting tonight."

"You do realise that tonight we can hardly avoid disclosing our address and what we do. I noticed eagle-eyed Kate was clocking my handbag. She probably thought it was a genuine Mulberry, but let's face it, we look prosperous and if we don't talk about it, they're going to think we have something to hide."

"Yes and we do, don't we? but you know I think the dodgy stuff is far from obvious. We can be proud of what we do. The boatyard pulls in a lot of legitimate money, the bungalows are tasteful and functional, but not extravagant. The store-room is stuffed but they needn't see that, and there are two boats under construction that show we're doing good business. To be honest, the work sheds are beginning to bring in some cash for good work carried out by the boys under the supervision of their expert tutors, and I'm quite optimistic when I think about it. Maybe one day we'll be self-sufficient and not have to rely so much on Griffiths and his shady deals."

"Are you absolutely sure he isn't into drugs?"

"I've told you. I'm one hundred per cent sure. He's a decent sort of chap and there is no evidence at all that he uses our services for anything like that. It's diamonds. That's what he's into. And the only people he could hurt are rich ones, so good luck to him. For heaven's sake though, never accept a shiny gift from him. Receiving would look bad on your record."

"What record – I haven't got one. My only vice is vanity, and who can blame me? Shall we invite them to lunch then? The weather is good. We could eat outside."

"Well if Vic isn't going to come steaming in sporting a boatload of illegals, it's a good idea. Get in touch. Get him to confirm that he's going into Poole and to let us know when he's likely to arrive here. Lock the filing cabinet and we'll try to look innocent."

"Well Kate said they are heading back to London tomorrow anyway so we've time to organise things. It's beginning to get exciting, isn't it? something new every day. I wonder if Matron will reveal any nasty secrets?"

*****

Kate was wondering exactly the same thing as she pulled up outside the given address. It was sparkling clean and the front step had recently been white washed. She rang the bell and waited until a rosy faced middle-aged, slightly plump lady opened the door.

"Hello," began Kate. "I'm…"

"You must be Detective Inspector Meredith, yes? I was told you'd be here about now. Do come in."

Kate stepped over the threshold and began to take off her shoes. "No, don't worry, just come in and sit down."

"Thank you," said Kate. "You must be Mrs Marsh. Matron's sister?"

"Yes. I'm afraid Elsie is suffering from advanced Alzheimers. I'm afraid she won't be able to help much, but do come and say hello." Kate followed her into the small living room where Elsie was sitting in an armchair gazing out of the window. Silvia turned the chair around so that she was facing into the room.

"Can I call her Elsie or should it be Matron?"

"Matron." The response had come from the hunched figure in the chair.

"Well hello, Matron, my name is Kate and I came to see you. I wanted to talk about The Sanctuary."

"Matron," replied the figure in the chair gazing at the ceiling.

Kate turned to Silvia. "Do you think we could all have a cup of tea. Maybe if we chat about it, something may ring a bell."

While Silvia was in the kitchen, Kate tried make eye contact with the sad little figure in the chair but there was not a flicker of a response. When they were all seated, Kate asked Silvia what she knew about The Sanctuary affair, and why the place had closed.

"Everyone local knew about it. It was a horrible affair. I didn't see much of my sister at the time. She spent quite a lot of time anyway at the place. Quite often overnight and I was working as a secretary miles away myself. I did sense though, when we did meet that there was something wrong. Elsie seemed unhappy about something. I tried to get her to talk but she said she couldn't discuss whatever it was that was bothering her. She said once that she had done something very silly and regretted it afterwards, something that could get her into trouble. I confess I did try to get her to confide in me. I became quite cross and we fell out. I didn't see her for a while. After the place closed, I came down and she seemed a little more relaxed. She said she'd come to terms with the problem. She'd made mistakes but needed to put them behind her."

"Did she ever mention the priest – Brother Pious?"

"No!" shouted Elsie suddenly. "No go away, I didn't. I had to." She was crying now and Silvis rushed to comfort her.

"It's all over, dear. He's gone now, don't worry it's all right. Best not to ask her any more if you don't mind. I'm really sorry. I wish I could do more, but whatever it is that happened, it's best if she's allowed to forget it. Let's leave her, she's calm now and I'll try to think of anything that might be useful."

They moved into the kitchen out of the hearing of Elsie who had calmed down and was drinking her tea.

"When the place was closed down and I came to see her, I could sense a feeling of relief in her – as if some awful episode was over and done with. I remember asking if Wellstead had been a decent man or could he possibly have been responsible for what happened? She leapt to his defence. She had seen him in his office after they had taken the little boy away. Wellstead had been sobbing, and asked her if she had seen anything of the boy that day. She hadn't because she was at home that night but seemed to feel that somehow it wouldn't have happened if she'd been there. I remember her saying something like, 'That poor little boy, I tried to protect him. If only I'd been there, but it's all over for him now and that's a good thing.' I simply could not understand what she meant, but I could never get anything more from her and from that moment, the ghosts that haunted her gradually disappeared – then dementia set in."

"It was the name Pious that upset her, wasn't it?" said

Kate. "If only she could tell us what she knew, but you're right. I won't trouble her any more. If we ever catch up with the priest, things may become clearer and I promise that I'll let you know anything that I find that might have distressed her but it's probably better never to bother her with it again. I'll keep in touch."

*****

At the Manse, the bishop was proving to be as little help as Elsie but with rather more deliberation, Knowles felt. Each avenue was proving to be a dead end and he was getting more and more frustrated.

It had all started well. Knowles had been on time. The bishop greeted him politely and they had both been skirting round the business, each wanting the other to put his cards on the table first. Almost as if he had something to hide, thought Knowles.

"Well enough about the spread of religious differences and the Middle East, your Excellency. Let's get down to business. You know why I'm here, I'm sure, and I have to be back in London by five so can we get on with it?"

"I'm sorry, Inspector, if I seem reluctant. I feel I am skating on very thin ice. Of course I know why you're here. You're not the first person this week to rake up old ghosts, that everyone would prefer to stay buried. As you say, let's get on with it. What can I do to help you?"

"Well let's cut to the chase, shall we? I have spoken to Philippa Hilton. She has been here and reported to me that in fact you claim to know very little that could help us. The file on Pious has either been plundered since or was never completed in the first place. If the first, then, we need to know why and to whose advantage it would be to remove evidence. If the second, how could it possibly be acceptable for someone in such a position of responsibility to be let lose without any checks being made? Either way, some child was molested and killed or died, and very little effort had been made to discover who, why and how. I have to tell you that I am becoming more disgusted as this investigation progresses, day by day."

"Is not your investigation limited to the nature of George Wellstead's death, Inspector? I would have thought that officers of the Metropolitan Police Force would not be expected, nor have the resources to travel North to unravel a matter ten or so years old and completely outside their jurisdiction."

"The death of Wellstead and the situation of his corpse have distinct links to this part of the world, sir, and until I have the complete picture, I shall go wherever my investigation leads me and ruffle as many feathers as it takes."

"Right. Let me tell you first that I was in another country when all this happened but I will do everything I can to help you. This is the file I have, and you are quite right, it is uncomfortably thin. I cannot explain that. If I showed you the files of other members of this organisation they would be thick and comprehensive."

He got up and collected a thick file from a shelf.

"This for example is mine. Read it if you will. Everything about me is there, even my faults and misdemeanours. I have nothing to hide."

"It didn't occur to me for a moment that you have," replied Knowles, "but I suspect that you are concerned that information will be revealed as a result of this investigation that reflects badly on the entire Catholic... family. That is something that you must accept. The trouble is with historic cases like this, witnesses' memories are clouded. Other witnesses are dead, there is a mass of evidence that is useless because it's second hand – hearsay or rumour, but sometimes, even when justice cannot possibly follow, at least clarification can assist those who have been left in the dark, who have lost loved ones, so please – consider your priorities. A revelation that will assist a bereaved relative to find closure, and weigh that against the discomfort of an organisation that places so much emphasis on the Confessional."

The bishop stared at him for a moment. Knowles surveyed him and noticed the manicured nails, the slightly long hair, his immaculate attire and the very faint smell of aftershave. He's gay, he decided. I wonder if that's in his file? Presumably that's irrelevant.

"I suppose Miss Hilton told you about the computer. I have it here. Experts can find all sorts of information from the hard drive I believe, but Pious wasn't stupid. He will know that. Perhaps he left it on purpose, to mislead you. I think he was clever enough. There is something that might help you. I saw and spoke to James Stokes before he died. He believed something unwholesome was going on. That's the word he used anyway. 'Pious is not the man we think he is', he'd said. He told me that I must be careful. That Pious was dangerous and he was taking steps to expose him, but that it was difficult. There were others involved, important enough to do huge damage to the church; people who would challenge him, who were in positions of power and authority and would stop at nothing to silence him. We were going to meet again, but he kept putting it off. I think he lost heart. His death was absolutely natural, there was no foul play. The coroner's report was quite clear. It was a heart attack."

"It's a pity the coroner wasn't so clear when he dealt with the case of Joey Jacobson. That was a travesty. Are you sure about him? Did Stokes ever hint as to who these people were?"

"No never, but if you could identify Pious' associates somehow?"

"Yes, well I'll certainly be doing my best. Thank you for telling me this, Bishop. We have resources that are not available to you, and a lot less to lose. No doubt we'll meet again. I'll send someone for your fingerprints, if you don't mind, since you've handled this device."

They shook hands and Knowles left with the battered old computer under his arm.

Chapter Fourteen

Seven o'clock arrived very slowly. Pippa and Spike were sitting in the bar waiting for the detectives. There was no sign of Sam Cartwright yet, but there was a man with his elbows on the bar staring into a glass of lager. Spike nudged Pippa and nodded towards his back.

"It's not him," murmured Pippa. "I'll recognize him when he arrives. I tried to interview him at the time so I know what he looks like."

She suddenly got to her feet and held out her hand to a balding middle-aged man who had just entered the bar. "Hi! It's Sam, isn't it? Remember me? Pippa Hilton. I wrote for *The Gazette*."

"Yes of course. Hi. Nice to see you again. I used to read your column. It was good stuff. No holds barred. I liked it. Why did you stop?"

She shrugged. "Thanks, I just got fed up and found more rewarding things to do. I still send in the odd article, people like a rant! I think you're meeting up with DCI Knowles?"

"So, you too, eh? This should be interesting. I was hoping that one day someone would re-open this case. I spent some time on it myself, but things became uncomfortable and I reluctantly gave up, I just got the feeling that all avenues were closed to the likes of me."

"Infuriating, isn't it? I've been there. Got tired of banging my head against a brick wall. It was quite satisfying though. I know I got under the skin of some people and it was nice to see them squirm. Anyway, the Met should be here soon. Let me introduce my friend, Sebastian Jacobson."

"Spike stood up and Sam grasped his hand. "I so wanted to talk to you at the time, Sebastian. It was terrible for you, but you disappeared and everyone was focusing on other issues. You look well and I'm glad to see it. I hope we can all find out what happened all those years ago and put things right if that is at all possible. Too late for Simon Crowther, but justice for him and Joey would go a long way towards healing the wounds."

At that moment, Knowles and Kate made an appearance. Kate looked at the man leaning on the bar for a moment and then said, "It's a lovely evening, why don't we talk outside."

Once settled around the wooden table Kate looked towards the door for a while, and then remarked, "I know it's a small world, but that bloke shows up rather more often than is just coincidence. He makes a point of not looking at me but always seems to be close enough to hear what I'm saying. He moved to the table next to us at breakfast and I'm sure he followed my car for a while when I was on the way to Matron's." She shrugged. "There was nothing much useful from that visit I'm afraid." She turned to Pippa and Spike. "But there was a definite adverse reaction when I mentioned Pious. Her sister gave me something to chew on but we'd need to find an instant cure for dementia before we'd get anything enlightening from Elsie."

"I think we'd need to send the bishop to Guantanamo for recall lessons too," added Knowles. "I don't think he's a bad bloke, and he did indicate something nasty in the woodshed but I'm leaving him struggling with his conscience for a day or two. I did get the laptop, which may reveal something, but the bishop thought Pious may have left it behind to create a false trail. I don't think so myself. I think he scarpered in haste. We are talking about ten years ago. If he wanted to beat a hasty retreat, he wouldn't have had the time to fiddle about planting lies onto a computer. It appears to have been wiped anyway. Maybe he just forgot to pick it up."

"I understand that the technology exists to recover stuff from hard drives," Spike said.

"Yes, and we know just the chap to do it." Knowles smiled. "Kate has a best friend to whom exploring the heart of a machine like this is no more challenging than the easy crossword in *The Daily Mail*. He'll have it by tomorrow evening." He checked to see that there were no unwanted observers within shouting distance and then turned to Cartwright. "Do you feel up to filling us in on the history then, Sam? Let's start with the first alert. How did it all start?"

"We were called out at about six in the morning. Simon came and picked me up and I was waiting at the gate. He didn't say much, just 'it's a kid that's all I know', so we got there as quickly as we could. It was a caretaker who'd called – he was very upset... You can imagine the effect on us. I'm sure I don't have to tell you. The little boy was on the ground about three feet from the wall and below a window on the second floor."

"Joey," interrupted Spike. "His name was Joey."

"Yes, mate, I'm sorry. Sometimes it's easier to deal with things like this if you don't give them an identity. Keep the fact that he was a living little person out of your mind.

"Soco were there already," he continued. "There was a tape around the scene. We went inside and upstairs. The relevant window, in fact all the windows were closed from the inside. The kids were assembled in the hall. We took statements from all the boys who had been in the dormitory, which was adjacent to the sickbay, from which the boy had fallen. Not one admitted to closing the window or seeing anyone else do so. There was one kid who seemed quite traumatised. I couldn't get a word out of him and he said he felt sick. I did check him later but he had nothing helpful to say.

"Matron wasn't there which seemed strange to me. I mean surely when kids sleep in a dormitory there should be someone close at hand. These were all youngsters. There was a male teacher down in the staff room who'd been on duty but he had heard nothing. He was under the impression that Matron was on the premises. He had seen her at seven the night before and said she would be there."

"Did he say why he was there?" interrupted Kate.

"He was supposed to be supervising the older boys' wing. Said he'd come over to watch the early morning news. We did check with Matron of course and she said she should have been there but was sent home by Pious because she had complained of a headache and nausea. I must say she was absolutely devastated by what had happened. She felt she was to blame. She should have stayed but Pious had insisted that she left. 'Make him explain', she had said. 'Just make him explain'."

Pious had left, he thought, before the body was found. They had gone straight to the Manse to ascertain his whereabouts as soon as it became clear that he had questions to answer, but the idea that he may have been responsible didn't occur to anyone. "He was just a possible witness. When the bishop said that his mother had suddenly been taken ill and he'd gone immediately to see her, it was accepted. When there had been no contact from him after a few days, suspicions were aroused and I was told the ferry ports were contacted, but there was no record of his journey. Even then, no one seriously considered him to be guilty of anything. He was just a person of interest.

"But there was one exception. Simon Crowther was suspicious. He had been to the Chief Superintendent, intent upon getting in touch with Interpol. The chief said he would but with the caveat that there was no reason at all to believe that the priest was guilty of such a terrible crime. He was simply needed to assist in the investigation. They tried to isolate his prints from the number they took in his office, by concentrating on his desk drawers and certain book covers, but none that they took were found on the inside of the window. Personally, I found it suspicious that his prints weren't there. Surely in the normal course of events, during the summer, he would have opened or shut the window at some time. He could have wiped them."

"Were Joey's prints there?"

"Yes they were, but on the inside of a pane of the adjacent window. Not on the handle. Three days later Interpol came back to report that they'd come up with nothing. They needed more than we'd given them. All they could say was that he had travelled to the UK some years before, and that they believed his mother was dead."

"So what we have in the way of evidence is bugger all," remarked Knowles. "Witnesses are either dead, demented or departed without trace."

"Not quite," said Sam. "The next day Simon Crowther got a phone call. The body was with the coroner by then and Simon believes the caller was his secretary, but she wouldn't give a name. She had said quickly, 'They're going to say it was an accident. I don't think it was. There was a struggle. He had scratched someone.' She had started to say something more but then stopped." Sam got the impression that she was speaking to someone else. "Her voice was muffled. When she came back on line, she said, 'Yes, of course, Mrs Gould, I'll see to it straight away' and put the phone down. Simon rang the number back and the coroner answered. He made an appointment to see him the next day but when he went, the coroner said he had read the statements of several witnesses and was satisfied that Joey's death was a tragic accident. His secretary was there and he said she was staring at him begging him not to say anything about her call. He had asked if the forensic report had revealed any signs of a struggle and the coroner said no but there were significant signs of abuse. He could hardly say otherwise. The area of bruising spoke volumes, but he didn't order a full inquest. Accidental death. Nobody questioned it. No family to make a fuss."

Spike suddenly got up and walked away from the table into the garden Pippa followed him.

"Did you see the pathologist's report? We have it," said Kate. "There's nothing about skin under the fingernails. It would be the first thing they'd look for. Could it have been redacted?"

"Easily I imagine," said Knowles, "but there should be a paper copy of the original if proper records are kept. Okay! Let's take a break. What do we have? Wellstead is dead, but we have a sort of dying declaration which let's face it is nothing more than 'It wasn't me it was him'. Recorded hearsay. Matron has nothing sensible to offer.

The coroner, however, useless he was, as a coroner, wasn't there, but we need to check him out. Do we know where he is? If not find out. None of the boys apparently saw anything. The teacher on the premises saw nothing and the man who is clearly guilty of serious abuse and possibly murder is out of the country. Furthermore, my investigation into the mysterious circumstances into the death of George Wellstead is just about solved. All I need is a statement from Vic and I'll have to tie it up. I have to go back. Have you any leave due, Kate? Would you be willing to spend a week up here if necessary and give Sam a hand? Find the guy who did the autopsy?"

"Let's hear the rest of the story and I'll think about it," replied Kate. "I must say I'm reluctant to walk away and leave it hanging but what authority do I have up here?"

Spike had come back to the table and was sitting down. "Sorry," he said, "some things are difficult to hear, but let's get on with it, Sam."

"The next bit is going to be difficult for me. I was with Simon all the next day. He had found it difficult to bite his tongue at the coroner's but he couldn't let the secretary down. He was determined, however, to get to the bottom of this. When he left to go home that afternoon, he gave me his pocket book, entirely against the rules of course but he had an appointment to meet his wife for a game of tennis and he wanted me to read his notes and see if I had any ideas. Now he may have stopped for a drink or three on the way home but I doubt it and no landlord has been able to confirm it. He never made the tennis. He was in a head on collision with a petrol tanker on the way home. It was a sharp bend, no skid marks, no evidence that he had tried to stop. The petrol tanker was over the central line. No skid marks there either. Driver didn't see anything coming until it appeared in front of him and smashed straight in. He was unhurt. The car was a right off and was crushed. I was told it had been examined and they couldn't find a fault. Then, the story that Simon was over the limit. I just don't believe it.

"I know he wasn't and I know he was an excellent driver. Try as I might, I cannot find the examiner who checked the wreck of the car. Quite honestly there are so many closed doors here that sometimes I think the whole bloody force and everyone connected are lying hypocrites."

"Sam," said Knowles. "This is getting silly. The accident investigators are thorough and certainly not bent. I'd stake my life on it. If you're thinking that the accident was somehow arranged, quite honestly that is fanciful and daft. It would have been nigh on impossible to stage. He must have been distracted or... I don't know."

"What about his phone? Did they find it?" asked Kate.

"It was on the back seat."

"Well just suppose he had a call and needed to take it," she said thoughtfully. "Suppose it was as he neared that bend. If he had picked up the phone to glance at it, saw that it was a significant call, and looked just a second too long, because it was really getting to him, then looked up to see the truck very close, his instinct would be to throw up his hand to grab the wheel; the phone could have gone flying over his shoulder to the back seat and then bang. No time to brake. It could have been like that."

"Yes, that is possible, I suppose. I've nearly had a prang myself doing the same thing. I did get hold of the phone. The sim card was gone. Another dead end."

"Not entirely," said Knowles thoughtfully. "The data for the history of calls is stored in the phone, not the sim. Can you get hold of it? All the physical evidence from that case should still be in storage, strange that the sim card had gone though."

"Not really. It will have been taken out to examine. It's probably in an envelope somewhere. If you can't get it I guess I can," said Kate. "I'm coming back in a couple of days. I'll be taking a statement from Spike's friend Vic. I can make an official request. I'll take your number and arrange a meet. Probably at Pippa's place if that's okay with her?"

"Absolutely fine as long as we can be in on all discussions. Don't book in here, Kate," ignoring a glare from Spike. "We'll be able to put you up for a day or two if you like."

"Count me in – great. That's kind of you."

Kate and Knowles said their goodbyes and headed home. Kate exchanged phone numbers with Sam Cartwright and they each promised to keep the other in the loop.

Spike was silent in the car on the way back to The Stables.

"I'm sorry, I should have consulted you before handing out invitations but it seemed the natural thing to do. We are far from their area of interest, Spike, and the sooner we get this over the better. Everything will be fine I promise."

"Yes, I know. It's just been a hard day and I need a drink of some very good wine."

Chapter Fifteen

On the way back to London, Kate and Knowles chewed over the progress of the case. As far as Wellstead was concerned, they decided that to take any action against Spike would not be in the public interest and if they did proceed, it would never get past the CPS anyway. As for Vic, unless his account was substantially different from that given by Spike, his contribution had served its purpose and to take it further would be pointless – 'forgive the pun'.

"There are certainly question marks over the coroner, and, I'm afraid to say, the chief superintendent, whom I feel, should have been as anxious as Crowther to seek out Pious. The dead bishop could have helped if he'd had the decency but I suspect that he was aware of something very nasty and had no idea how to deal with it. The current one has his suspicions too but is reluctant to face up to what possible horrors could emerge. We need to work on him. I think we're just scraping the surface, Kate. There was a nest of vipers there somewhere and the fact that the home was closed so quickly after Joey's death, begs the question – why the speed? Who made that decision and organised it? They had to relocate nigh on a hundred kids. It will be a nightmare tracing them, the young ones, but I'm going to get a team onto it."

"Do you honestly think it would be right to drag all that up? If more little boys were abused, the last thing they will want to do is talk about it."

"I know, but I think we should at least give them the chance."

At the station there were other matters to see to. Kate checked her desk and decided to head for home. She was tired. Jake had texted to say he was there, longing to see her and was poised to rush out and buy fish and chips so she sought out Knowles. She found him smiling as he chatted to someone on the phone. He motioned her to sit down and after couple of minutes, hung up with a 'Yes look forward to it. Till tomorrow then.' He looked up with a grin. "You'll never guess who that was."

"Judy Dench?"

"Almost. It was Jill Irving. She wants to meet me tomorrow because she has managed to find George's computer. He had given it to one of the medics a few weeks ago. The guy had thanked him, but wanted something that actually worked so had taken it to a charity shop. Amazing isn't it. We've got them both. Your Jake is going to be busy. Off you go now. Keep in touch and I'll see you tomorrow afternoon."

*****

Jake greeted her with a pleased smile and a breath-restricting hug. "You look almost edible," he said, but fish and chips would be easier to digest. Sit down, have a glass of white and tell me all about it. She did, and pointed to the laptop on the table. "Get to work. It might not have anything useful on it but we need all we can get. Are the girls still around? Maybe it'll be better to work down here."

"They've gone to the Natural History Museum. I need to do it in my study anyway. Look I'll go and get some grub. You relax with your drink. I'll be back ASAP."

Kate had a shower, put on fresh jeans and T-shirt and thought about her impending visit to Spike's place. She had been given the postcode and name, but had no idea what she'd find. She knew Vic had the same address and had picked up on Spike's lack of enthusiasm when Pippa had offered the invitation to stay. She took out her own laptop and googled the postcode. An aerial view came up and revealed a large expanse of the coast. She could see a very large house surrounded by a number of small buildings, and what looked like several moorings. She Googled 'The Stables', but there was nothing that could be connected to her imminent destination. So, she thought, very private people then. When she looked up boatyards in the area, it was much more rewarding and detailed a yard which had been owned by a Stephen Pearson now

deceased, now registered to Sebastian Jacobson with no moorings available at this time.

Jake was soon back with super and they enjoyed

eating together and an early night. Kate felt happy and relaxed. Better than she had for months and absolutely determined to make some progress with the case. She had told Jake as much as they knew. He had decided to take some time off and they both considered the possibility of going North together.

"It would be great. Two heads are better than one and as long as you don't distract me, which you have a tendency to do, it might just help the case along. I'll call Pippa first thing and see if it's okay for you to stay there – she said they had plenty of room. If not, we can both stay at the pub."

*****

The next morning Pippa assured her that they would be very welcome and assumed they would be happy to share a room. Kate gave her an ETA for between two p.m. and three p.m. the following day.

Jake had disappeared with the computer and Kate didn't see him before she went to meet up with Knowles at lunchtime. The guv was looking quite smug and Kate felt pleased that something or someone in his life was attracting his interest. He had certainly made efforts recently to lose weight and she did recognise the fact that a slimmer Charlie Knowles could be quite attractive. She'd seen photos of him with Harriet who had been gorgeous. They'd made a very handsome couple.

"Well," said Kate. "Tell me all about it."

"A gentleman never tells."

"I was talking about the computer."

"Ah yes well here it is, a complete wreck by the look of it. It won't power up so I hope whatshisname can find something."

"Jake. His name is Jake – and he's working on Pious's right now. I'll keep you informed. Actually, I didn't mean the computer, I mean, how was it was with Jill? What sort of character was she portraying last night? Mata Hari? Cleopatra?"

"I'm not sure. It's disconcerting really. I think she was just Jill. Anyway, we had a drink in a nice bar and she told me about herself and I told her a little bit about me. That was quite hard actually but it got easier with each drink. I think we'll meet again; well I hope we'll meet again. She did say how gorgeous I would be if I lost a couple of stone and I said I'd try."

"Excellent, Charlie. Did you let her call you Charlie?"

"Yes, and that was hard too, but by the end of the evening I'd got used to it. That doesn't mean that you can though."

"Don't worry, Guv. I wouldn't dream of it."

She told him of the plan to take Jake with her the next day and he was visibly relieved. "I'm glad, Kate. I was a little concerned about the guy who seemed to be following you. Probably nothing, but heaven knows what's going to creep out of the woodwork up there. Some folk are going to be worried I think and although I know you're tough, I would hate anything to happen to you."

"I'll be fine, but thanks for caring. Are we having a conference with the teams today?"

"Yes, they've done some digging into Wellstead's history so let's go and see if there is anything we can use."

It seemed like an age since they had gathered in the conference room but there they were again. All the windows were open and the officers who refused to give up smoking were sitting on the sills and holding their cigarettes outside.

"Right, teams. Let's have what you got. Robs, you first."

"Okay, Guv, not a lot really. He was a librarian until he became ill. Didn't form any friendships… Was always polite and helpful to customers. Left when the cancer became too much for him to cope with, earned miserable salary and left all his savings to a children's charity. Executors are his neighbour Miss Irving and a sister. That's about all I can tell you. His life after he came down here was mega ordinary. There are no listed previous. He had a driving licence but no car and has never claimed any benefits."

"Steve."

"I managed to trace his original family address. Lived in Liverpool. Father unknown, one sister and a nephew. Mother dead. The sister used to visit him with her boy but stopped years ago. I managed to trace her but she was reticent. Said she stopped visiting him because the kid didn't want to go. Wouldn't say why. All she was interested in was his will really. I said I had no idea about the beneficiaries, but that I was sure she would be notified if she had been left anything. Nobody recalls girlfriend, or boyfriend for that matter. Sorry but that's about it."

"Anything else?"

"Guv."

"Tom."

"I went to interview the hospital staff. They got to know him quite well in the last few weeks. He talked about this life from time to time to one of the blokes in particular. Said that in a way he was lucky to know that this was the end because he had time to look back and consider his past. To face up to death and show how ashamed and sorry he was about some of the things he had done. If there was a God, he hoped he would understand the person that he was. He said he couldn't help being what he was, but it had taken him a long time to realise that he had to try to be different and what a terrible struggle that was. He had remarked on many occasions that it was difficult to live a lie. He was born with these natural tendencies and had to fight them, which seemed so unfair. The guy he talked to said that he would sob uncontrollably sometimes, and he genuinely felt sorry for him. He realised what the problem was of course. He wasn't gay himself but he certainly felt sympathetic."

"Being gay was not the problem, Tom. I think he was

misleading you, or at least the guy he talked to. Wellstead was a paedophile with a preference for young boys. Maybe this chap didn't realise what he was talking about, but to give George his due, he stopped. It came home to him, and all this sobbing was regret for the damage he had done in the past. But he had the strength of character to stop and I'm inclined to feel that if we can avoid blackening his name now, we will. Keep his history out of the press in recognition of the fact that he did successfully fight his instincts. We have much bigger fish to fry," and he gave them a summary of what he and Kate had discovered and how they were going to take it further.

"Guv, we've got a hell of a lot on at the moment. There are God knows how many terror alerts on: a pretty serious one in London. We could be called out at any time of night or day to a serious incident. In fairness, couldn't we leave the cops up there to take care of their own cases. This sounds like a historic abuse case. We'd be digging into all sorts of stuff and we need every man we have to be on call here."

"Yes. You're absolutely right, but Kate here is due some leave and she's going to take a busman's holiday."

"Don't worry," interrupted Kate. "If you need me I'll be back, I promise. I'll only be a few hours away. I agree with you. This is an old case, but it was the horrible, cruel, despicable abuse of a vulnerable little boy whose parents had just been killed and I would so like the man responsible to pay for it. This kind of offence doesn't die with time, it festers. Time for payment, don't you agree?"

"Yes, one hundred per cent. Good luck, Kate. We'll expect bulletins. Let us know if there is anything we can do to help and if I get any time off and can help, you can rely on me."

*****

Kate was home and sorting out her small suitcase when Jake came downstairs holding the hard drive of the laptop and a piece of a sheet of paper, which he waved at her. "Read and inwardly digest."

"What is it?"

"It's a list of names and dates. You may recognise some of them."

Kate took the list and skimmed down. Then she sat down quickly. "Well I know one of these and another sounds familiar."

"Well one is an MP and another is a sports reporter. You'd know it if you watched the right programmes."

"I didn't see either of those. The one I recognise is a police superintendent and I'm expecting to get an appointment with him the day after tomorrow. What do you think this list is?"

"Well there are dates alongside and numbers. All of the numbers are the same, forty, except for one name which features four times and the number in that case is twenty. The dates seem to be about two weeks apart. Could be sums of money. I have no idea. Could they be charitable donations?"

"What! Nearly all the same amount. I hardly think so."

"This superintendent guy you're due to see, is he the same one that was there at the time?"

"Yes, but he was a lower rank then. He's due to retire soon, I think. I've never met him but he is not popular. What about the dates? Can we deduce anything from them?"

"Well there are more than one date against certain of the names. So whatever they signify, it happened more than once and four in one case. I don't recognise that name."

"I suppose there are no bank statements on there?"

"Sadly no, and if it's something very unpleasant, he'd probably insist on cash."

"Horrible thoughts are invading my mind, Jake. If this is money changing hands, could it be some sort of paedophile ring. Pious had the goods, the boys and that's a list of his customers."

"I think that conclusion has legs certainly. What are we going to do, Kate? This is as serious as it gets. We will be exposing very high-profile individuals and possibly ruin their lives. If we're wrong, we'll have massive consequences to face ourselves."

"Yes I know, so we say nothing, do nothing until we are absolutely sure and have proof. I'll talk to Knowles of course. I know he'll feel the same way as we do. In the meantime, we have to go and see Spike and talk to Vic. He was at the home for a year or two, I think. Maybe he noticed something, but we must avoid suggesting anything sordid."

"Kate this entire thing is looking sordid with a capital S. If this Vic can make any contribution at all, he needs to be quite clear as to what might be involved. From what you've told me up to now, the guys you met up there and talked to are all singing from the same hymn sheet, only hymns are clearly not involved. Something unspeakable happened at that children's home, and anyone who might have the slightest idea what it was, is going to have to speak up now. We might be completely wrong, of course, but this kind of situation needs to be shaken up and turned inside out so that nothing remains hidden."

"Yes I know, you're right. I haven't met Vic but Spike clearly thinks the world of him. Let's get an early start. I've got two weeks. We should be able to close the investigation by then, and there's always the chance that I'll be recalled anyway. There are rumours that there's some nasty bomb plot looming."

Jake nodded and glanced at his phone. "Yes, I've heard the same thing. Don't worry! It's not an immediate threat. Did you say there was a French connection to this case?"

"It's possible I'll have to go over at some stage. Come on let's pack."

Chapter Sixteen

They found The Stables with some difficulty in spite of the satnav. The house itself was surrounded by a high brick wall at the front, and a copse, which spread around the sides and back. 'The Stables' was etched into a small brass plate outside the electric double gate and, another small sign invited visitors to ring the bell. They did so and a voice asked for identification before the gates silently opened.

"It's easier getting into The River House," remarked Jake sticking his head out of the window.

"Would you like to borrow my comb; you look a bit tousled?"

"No! this is how I wear my hair and I'm not changing it for anybody. I don't do neat and smart. I just do brilliant, okay?"

"Okay I knew that. Hey just look at that view."

From the house, which was Georgian style, a cobbled slope led to the water where a number of boats were moored. At the side of the house were what presumably had been the original stables – three workshops – and looking further up the slope, behind the house were a number of single storeyed, stone bungalows. Three of them were wholly visible and Kate suspected there were at least two more behind. Steps were cut into the grass slope leading to a brick edged path that ran along the front of them. They made their way up to the front door, admiring the window boxes that adorned each of the three windows either side.

"Phew!" said Jake. "Makes our place look a bit third rate, although where we live would probably cost as much these days."

Pippa came out to meet them and gave Kate a hug. Then: "You must be Jake. Great to meet you. Come in and have a late lunch."

A large pine table was set with various salads, cold meats, cheeses and crusty bread. Spike was already munching a crusty roll stuffed with salami and spring onions.

"Beer or wine?" Pippa asked Jake.

Kate was already holding a wine glass looking expectantly at a bottle of chilled Prosecco. "This is fabulous," she said, "and I'm starving."

"The whole place is fabulous," added Jake. "How did you find it, dare I ask?"

"I found it when I was running away after I was booted out of The Sanctuary. Fool that I was, I imagined the entire Shire police force would be hunting for me. I later found that as soon as my escorts realised that I'd climbed out of the service station loo window, they just went home. I ran, climbed over a fence that led into the woods up there." He nodded towards the copse. "It was dark and I worked my way down to the boats. I climbed into a big one and went to sleep in one of the cabins. I was starving but there was nothing to eat. That was where Stephen Pearson, the previous owner found me. I was in a terrible state and he was so kind. I told him everything. He was quite angry but I begged him not to do anything about it. He let me stay and said he'd try to find out if Joey was okay, maybe bring him here." He paused. "What he did find out was very difficult for him to tell me. Then Pippa came with Vic. Pearson, had phoned her to tell her I was safe. I think Vic had told him a lot more about The Sanctuary. He'd been there for years. Well, to cut a long story short, he kept us on, Vic and me, and we did everything we could to repay him. We worked hard. His wife had died before I came. He had no children, just a brother I think who had gone to the States and made a fortune. When Stephen died, he left everything to me as long as I kept it going and looked after the staff that were already there. I did of course. They're a good crew. We all work hard and we do well. We have eight moorings which are permanently rented and of course we build boats too."

"What about the bungalows?" enquired Kate. "Are they for staff?"

"Er no. The staff all have their homes and families in town. We've spent time modernising the bungalows, which were for staff originally but now we run a sort of college. It's a private college for boys only, boys like me, and Joey and Vic, that have nowhere to go. We run the college. We have fifteen students at the moment, there are no fees. We keep them and we educate them and try to identify their strengths, their skills their ambitions. We have teachers who see to the academic side and skilled craftsmen who train them in their chosen fields. We are training electricians, motor mechanics, a hairdresser and a draughtsman. We even have a budding lawyer doing his A levels. The rest are happy just to work here. Once they're self-sufficient they will move on and make a place for others."

There was silence for a minute. Kate felt herself almost moved to tears.

"Spike, that is absolutely breathtakingly amazing. I am so impressed. Will we meet any of them? Can we talk to them?"

"Why not? They're just ordinary kids. Happy ones I'm glad to say. As long as it is not in the course of your duty though, at least I hope not. So far we haven't had any trouble from any of them."

"God no," said Kate. "It's just such a contrast from the other place. I can understand now why you keep such a low profile. There must be parents who would pay a fortune to send their kids to a place like this and I think I can understand why you want to keep them out."

"Yes, well things do get a bit tight sometimes and I have thought about taking a couple of outsiders, but it would spoil things. These kids take nothing for granted. They see Pips and me as parents, I think, and Vic as an uncle. Children from established families would confuse things. Come on, let me show you around."

"Talking of Vic," Kate said as they strolled up towards the workshops, "will we meet him soon?"

"He's on the way from Poole. He may arrive late tonight but you'll certainly see him at breakfast."

They had already been very impressed by the functional and well-run workshops. The boys working there seemed cheerful and were concentrating on the work. Pop music was playing in the background and a drinks machine and half eaten sandwiches were evidence of a light lunch.

The bungalows were clean and well-designed inside with wet rooms, mini kitchens, a living space and twin bedrooms. "We have two lads in each of these and the younger ones live in the main house. Down there we have a dining room large enough for all of us, but they don't have to eat there. Most of them do though. We serve very good dinners. You'll see."

Kate and Jake had already taken their overnight bags up to a room on the first floor. It had many of its original features and a lovely view over the bay.

"This doesn't feel a bit like work. I could stay here for a week just relaxing, except at the back of my mind I have the feeling that we've hit upon the awful truth about The Sanctuary. It's not going to help Spike if we're right, but I suppose he'll have the satisfaction of knowing that with a lot of luck we'll bag more than just Pious."

"It depends on what he's like," said Jake thoughtfully. "It might be a good idea to involve Vic – I mean tell him what we think went on. He was there for years, of course, but if he knows what we're looking for, he's more likely to have noticed things, unusual things."

"Like what?"

"Like visitors arriving late at night – going to parts of the building where there was no need for them to be."

"And what if he was abused himself?"

"Well if he was prepared to talk about it – bingo!"

"If he was prepared to talk about it I think he would have done so already."

"Not if he thought Joey was a victim. He just wouldn't do that to Spike but he may do for us."

"Are you ready to go down? It's nearly dinner time."

The sound of a gong ringing through the house confirmed this and they made their way down to the impressive dining room where most of the seats were taken by boys and young men, all chatting and laughing happily. They stood up when Pippa walked in followed by Spike and the two visitors.

'Well done, boys, you can sit now." She grinned at Kate. "We made them practise before you came down. Here's the menu; only two choices I'm afraid, but I can recommend the fillet steak."

The four of them sat at the top table and Kate was soon chatting to a boy on her left who was excited to be able to talk to a real live detective and quizzed her remorselessly about the cases she had been involved in. On the other side of the table, Jake was equally involved in a discussion about hard drives

"If you have access to another computer," she heard him explaining, "remove the failed hard drive from the old PC and hook it up as a secondary drive to the alternate computer through a USB universal drive adapter. It's not too expensive but to recover stuff from a badly damaged drive can be, so back up is important."

The meal was delicious but there was no sign of Vic until coffee was served and he walked in clutching two bottles of wine. "Sorry I'm late, folks", he said, "unavoidably detained at Poole. Is this the wine you wanted, Spike?"

"Yes, Vic, just put it on the table. You must be starving. I'll go and get you a plate full. You go shower and change, you look salty, and we'll see you in the living room when you're ready."

Kate studied the youngish man who had arrived on the scene and knew immediately that he would not have been a victim. His face, tanned and full of character now, was scarred and in a way very attractive, but as a child, he would not have been picked out as a target for a paedophile. He looked across and smiled at her as Pippa introduced them. Waving the bottle of wine at her, he said, "I'll pour you a glass later. This is a rare and beautiful wine."

"Can't wait," Kate smiled back. She noticed Jake

looking at her with a raised eyebrow. "Trollop," he mouthed. She laughed to herself and was so pleased to have him with her.

They both followed Pippa into the living room and waited for Vic. They had settled into comfortable armchairs when Kate had a call from Knowles. "Any developments?" he asked.

"Yes, but I can't talk now. The priest's laptop has come up with something rather troubling though so I'll give you a call before I go to bed. Keep your phone with you."

"Yes I will."

"Do you have the appointment with the Super fixed yet? If not, wait until we've talked tomorrow, there's something you should know."

It was half an hour before Vic came in with Spike. They had been in deep conversation in the hall. The relatives of the young Syrian boys had been late, having found it difficult to locate the rendezvous in Bournemouth but everything had gone well and there was a loving reunion. Spike was always on the alert for some kind of racket. He was adamant about not taking girls, having heard spine chilling stories of slavery and prostitution. He vetted the receiving families ruthlessly.

The payment for this latest reunion had barely covered the cost of the exercise, but there were two fewer children in desperate straits in Cherbourg and Spike would go on with his mission till there were none.

Kate decided she would like to speak to Vic alone so they retired with glasses of wine to the kitchen.

"Just to let you know where we're at. I expect Spike filled you in to a large extent to what we've been discussing. We've spoken at length to Sam Crowther, who was involved in the investigation into the tragedy at the home, but for the record, could you run through what happened last week with Wellstead?"

Vic's version reflected Spike's and the episode with the pointed object was described with acute embarrassment. "I just thought that with all the drunken corpses that litter the streets of London at night, that this one had to be different."

"And it was, and it worked, and I'm here to prove it so don't beat yourself up about it. I don't think there'll be any repercussions. I think you might have to revise your opinion of London though. It ain't all that bad."

"Phew!" He gulped some wine. "So how can I help you?"

"Let's talk about The Sanctuary."

"If we must. It was hell on earth – not so much for me, they tended to leave me alone but there were some very unhappy little boys. I'd see them crying in corners, some of them – mainly, the little ones, the quiet ones. Some of the others were nasty little sods, bullies, bad-mouthing the others. I was left alone most of the time. I could look after myself. If they came at me, I let 'em have it. I was bullied as a child, bullied and abused by grown men, so I was used to it. Being attacked by someone my own size was a novelty. I gave as good as I got."

"What about the teachers – were they rough?"

"No not really. Strict some of them, others were nice, funny. I loved lessons."

"What about Pious?"

Vic looked thoughtful. "There was something about him that seemed… evil. He was never kind. He would walk past a kid who was crying without a second look. I saw kids trying to hide from him. One night he came storming into our dorm demanding to know if we'd seen some kid or other. He was in a rage."

"Did you ever see men who weren't teachers turn up in the evenings?"

"No, but I wouldn't have. We were in a separate wing. Visitors came in at the other end of the building through a back door. I saw cars in the car park at night that weren't there during the day though."

"The night Joey fell did you see Pious that evening or the next morning at all, before or after the police arrived?"

"Everybody was looking for him. Police were all over the place. Wellstead stayed in his office. When he did come out, he'd been crying. His eyes were red. A couple of days after that, buses arrived to take us all away. I legged it, went to Pippa's. She'd had a call from Pearson about Spike and she drove us straight there."

Chapter Seventeen

"Is there anything else at all on that laptop that may be related to this business?" Kate, propped by pillows asked Jake who, with a towel around his waist, was making cups of tea.

He sneezed. "I must tell Pippa I'm allergic to feathers. I'm going for a run to clear my head. Well I'm working on it but I can see there are lots of brief emails with times and dates that might tie up with the other dates. Trouble is they all have strange addresses. Probably accounts they use for a specific purpose, like getting in touch with this guy."

"All the more reason to suspect something nasty."

"You need to get in touch with Knowles. Send him the list. He can get them traced. If what we suspect is correct, they'll all be local."

Kate jumped out of bed and dressed quickly after a hasty shower. "I need to eat. I'll see you later."

*****

"Well what have you got for me?" Knowles asked. "Has wonder boy found anything yet?"

"Yes, an interesting list of names. I tried to call you yesterday. I've scanned it and attached to an email. Any developments at your end?"

"Yes. You know that bloke at the pub that you didn't like? I phoned the manager. I remembered he said they only had three rooms. We had two of them, and that guy had the other. He paid by debit card. I have a name, not an address yet but that's just a matter of time. He's called Mike Gambler."

Kate stood up quickly. "Have you got that list yet?"

"Yes I have it. Hang on." He was back within seconds. "Gambler, he's on the list, Kate. Along with three other names I know, including one we both know very well. I'm coming up, Kate. I need to deal with our mutual friend myself. It needs someone of a higher rank than you, my love. In the meantime, do nothing. We'll start with the other guy. I'll put a trace on him. Hopefully, this list is just a cricket team or something."

"In your dreams"

"Nightmares! I need to think. I'll see you tomorrow."

Kate looked up as Pippa made an appearance. "Pippa – I promised to let you know how things are going. Are Vic and Spike about?"

"They're either in the sheds or checking the progress of the new boat, I think."

"Well when Jake gets back from his run, he'd hate to miss this breakfast, but can we meet up in about half an hour? Here would be fine."

"Should be possible, and thanks by the way. I know Spike feels so much better knowing that something is being done and he does appreciate the fact that you are including him."

When they were all assembled Kate brought them up to date leaving nothing out. Vic was the first to speak. "You think that something unspeakably nasty was going on, don't you?"

"Well taking everything into account – Joey, the speedy closure of the place, frightened kids, Wellstead's allegations and the list of names, dates and presumed payments on the laptop belonging to someone in control of the place – it's difficult to think otherwise. Sorry, Spike, this must be a nightmare for you but we mustn't jump to conclusions. In any case historic abuse is very difficult to prove. We need witnesses, and quite often victims are too ashamed or too embarrassed to come forward. They just want to forget and who can blame them. The good thing is that more of these cases are now being investigated and more and more survivors are realising that they are not alone."

"Joey wasn't a survivor."

"No, which makes it essential that we find everyone involved. What else can I say, Spike. I hate what we are unearthing, for your sake, but there's nothing I can say to make it better. If we expose all this, you'd hear it anyway. Hang on in there. Whatever went on, it may be some comfort for you to know that Joey wasn't there for long and it's possible that he put up a very good fight. Had it not been for him this could have gone on for years."

"Yes I know. Sorry, Kate. Just let me help however I can."

"Depend on it."

Vic stood up. You know that ever since Pippa told me about those letters that were found, I've been thinking of popping over and having a nose round Fougères. This guy must realise that we'll be hunting for him now. He'll keep up to date with news in the UK. He probably still has contacts here, and I think there was a brief report on BBC news after Wellstead was discovered. I suppose there's a slight chance that he is blissfully unaware that he is the object of a manhunt, but if so, all the better. We'll give him a nice surprise."

"We'll come with you. How about it, Jake? How's your French?"

"Not bad," said Jake modestly. "I got a first at uni, but it was French literature really."

"Mon Dieu! is there no end to your talents?"

"I haven't actually found anything that I'm not good at yet."

Kate wracked her brains for a scathing response but couldn't come up with anything clever enough. "Do you have your passport with you?"

"I'm never without it. Best form of identification."

"Knowles will be up later, or maybe tomorrow. When do you propose to go, Vic?"

"I'll be sailing there and it'll take a day or two, but I don't mind waiting till tomorrow. We could even set off in the evening if that helps. If we have a boat, we'll have a base. I have a mate over there who will lend us a car, and he knows people who know people if you see what I mean. The alternative is for me to get going today and you two could fly over when you're ready. Rennes is about fifty kilometres away or Dinard about ninety I think but the roads are good."

"I thought it would be impossible to moor there – at Mont-Saint-Michel I mean?"

"You have to know the tides. The waters are incredibly deep at high tide, deep enough to get close in, but stay there too long and you'd be beached. What we do, is moor a few miles away, in one of three small marinas and leave one of the lads on board. They're all very good at sailing and navigating."

"Great, one way or another we'll be there. We are meant to be on holiday after all. Right now, I'm waiting for the guv to find an address here for me. Actually the guy who lives there knows I'm a cop so he's going to get the wind up if he sees me, but he's never seen Jake as far as I know. I thought we could stroll past without looking too furtive and check that he's at home. At some stage we need to interview him under caution but his name on the list, on the computer of the dodgy priest, I hardly have grounds for arrest. There's always the chance that he could volunteer a statement but we're going to have to rely on Knowles to persuade him to do that."

"So is there any point in gong there at all?" asked

Jake. "If he does see you, and he might have already overheard what you're working on, he'll definitely get the wind up."

"I'll be heavily disguised in a hat and sunglasses. You'd be surprised what you can pick up from where and how a person lives. Is he happily married? Does he have kids? Do the neighbours like him? What's his job?"

"Does he have fangs and only come out at night?" continued Jake. "Are there spots of blood up and down his drive?"

"Exactly, so let's get going. Bring the camera."

*****

Knowles arrived in town late afternoon and checked into the same pub. Kate met him at the bar and introduced him to Jake, then left them chatting while she went to speak to reception. "You were here the other night when we stayed, I think. Do you remember anyone asking about us at all, after we got here?"

"Well, let me think. Your booking was arranged by DC Blakey around lunchtime. I think there was a bit of excitement locally when she said the Met would be here. One or two people at the bar heard and were curious."

"Were they all locals?"

"I'm not sure. Have a word with the barman. He was definitely on duty that afternoon."

"No one can confirm that he was there the afternoon

before we came," Kate reported, "but they get a lot of passing trade. He could have been. He did check in after we did though. He doesn't live near, but why on earth would he need to stay here when he has an address in town. If he turns up tonight, I'll have a chat to him."

"If he turns up tonight, I'll have more than a chat to him," said Knowles. "I'll make an appointment to interview him at home or at work and let him know exactly what this is all about. I'm going to take DI Blakey with me. If his answers aren't completely satisfactory she can arrest him. Let him explain why his name is on that list four times."

"We're on thin ice though, Guv. I know what we're all thinking, but let's face it, a name on a list is flimsy evidence and the numbers have no £ signs beside them."

"Yes I know. I think we need to do the Super first. I've tried to keep this visit quiet; I'm just going to turn up at his office and catch him unprepared. No one knows I'm here yet. I can't say I'm looking forward to it."

"Look, if he's a half decent bloke and totally innocent, he will understand your reasons. You would be a pretty useless cop if you didn't follow this up. If he does get angry he's guilty."

"Yes, your honour, the defendant spluttered and went red in the face with rage. This was irrefutable evidence and I arrested him. I rest my case."

"Did you want me to come with you? Only Jake and I planned to go over to France tomorrow and look up the address Pious's mother used to contact him, if that's okay with you. We're both officially on leave but we can do some groundwork. Vic has contacts over there. I promise not to do anything without speaking to you first but we thought we could nose around, see if anyone remembers him, or her, or the father even. There's the aunt too and there's a chance that the father had a record for assault, but getting permission to examine old police records is a matter for you."

"Yes, go for it. And don't worry. I'll make sure this is paid leave. If you can't get in touch with me, contact Laver. He'll know where I am. Hopefully that won't be under this superintendent's lawn pushing up daisies."

They finished their drinks and climbed into Jake's Jeep. Knowles wanted a quick look at Gambler's house so they drove by. There was a shabby Ford Fiesta parked outside. Neither Kate nor Knowles had time to avert their faces when Gambler climbed out of the driver's seat and stared straight at them.

"Blast – he clocked us. Keep going, Jake, there's no point in stopping now. Maybe it's a good thing to get him worried." Then: "Hang on. On second thoughts, stop round the corner. Have you got your warrant card with you, Kate? Yes, good. Let's do this now, while he's worried. Jake we might be a while, hopefully not but wait here for us, will you?"

"Sure, I'll turn round and wait outside. Be careful. If I hear screams, I'll beat it!"

"It took a while for Gambler to answer the door."

"Yes, I know who you are," he said when Kate showed her card. "I suppose you want to come in." He held open the door and they went inside. He motioned them to go into the living room and invited them to sit down.

Knowles spoke first. "You don't seem too surprised to see us, Mr Gambler, why is that?"

"It's no secret that The Sanctuary is under investigation. Everyone round here is aware of that, and I worked there for a while."

"Really? Then I'm sure you will be able to help us."

"You mean you didn't know I worked there? So why are you interested in me?"

"Tell me, Mr Gambler, what do you know about this investigation? What is the local gossip?"

"I thought it must be the death of the boy. No one swallowed the inquest finding. It was all very fishy. I knew Joey actually; he was a sad little kid. I was sorry for him."

"How well did you know him?"

"What do you mean? I just knew who he was. He hadn't been there long, I let him help me in the garden and we did some bird watching."

"So what precisely was your connection with the place? Teacher?"

"No, I was sort of an odd job man. Fixed fences, oiled hinges, mowed the lawns."

"Were you full time? How was your salary paid?"

"By the church. It went straight into my account."

"How well did you know the priest, Pious?"

"He used to tell me what to do."

"Was there any reason for you to pay him money?"

"What do you mean?"

"Did you ever pay him money?"

"What kind of money?"

"Come on now, what kind of money do you think. Monopoly money? The kind of money you use to buy food and fags and favours. Did you ever pay him £20, once or twice or four times?"

There was a long silence.

"Mr Gambler, this has not been a formal interview. You are not saying anything under caution at this time, but I am arresting you on suspicion of committing an offence, that of having sex with a minor. You do not have to say anything, but it may harm your defence if you do not mention when questioned, something which you later rely on in court. Anything you do say may be taken down and given in evidence."

"What! Sex with a… what are you talking about? I want a solicitor." He was ashen faced.

"Don't worry. You will most certainly have one."

Chapter Eighteen

At the station, the duty solicitor advised Gambler to make no comment, which was exactly what was expected. He was released on bail.

The superintendent arrived at four p.m. Knowles was waiting and desperately trying to plan his approach. He decided that Gambler had helped him in a way. He greeted Superintendent Britten politely and there was a brief discussion regarding the purpose of the visit. Knowles began by explaining why Gambler had been arrested.

"From what we have by way of evidence so far, it seems that the priest Pious had complete control of the home in spite of the fact that there was a nominal head, – Wellstead whose death has given us reason to have another look at the case."

"Yes," said Britten. "Unfortunately the man disappeared without trace before we could question him. I don't think there's any reason to suspect him of anything untoward though. He left due to the deteriorating condition of his mother. He was probably completely unaware of what was going on over here. I understand that his mother did die in fact."

"So I've heard. It's all rather vague though. When did she die exactly? The man who could have helped us, that is the late bishop, has also passed away. In fact since the tragic death of the child, the case seems to have been dormant."

"I think closed is the word, not dormant, Chief Inspector. The usual procedures were followed and the coroner found accidental death."

"With absolutely no evidence of an accident, no witnesses and if I may suggest it, no thorough investigation."

"Just a minute. Were you here at the time? How dare you come up here and question the competence of this division. Who the hell do you think you are?"

"I'm the man who is sitting here suggesting that the original investigation was suspiciously inadequate. Evidence has emerged recently which suggests that there may have been serious incidents of abuse at The Sanctuary involving a number of visitors to the place after visiting hours. Do you have any contact with the current bishop, if so, he may have told you that the computer which belonged to Pious has been recovered and, as we speak, information is being recovered from that computer, which has sinister implications."

The chief superintendent was silent, then he replied, "What kind of information? What form does it take?"

"There is a list of names."

"Is that all?"

"No, sir. There are dates and numbers which we think refer to sums of money, beside the names."

"So what – patrons, bills to pay, prospective charitable donations. They could mean anything."

"Then I have to ask you, sir, did you make any charitable donations to the home?"

There was a long pause. "I may have done. I can't remember."

"But, sir, the Catholic church has massive reserves. You must know that. Certainly enough to fund the home. Surely there were more worthy causes that you should have considered. There are people sleeping in shop doorways right here in this town. What did you do for them? The strange thing about the list," he went on, "is that all the names except one, have put exactly the same amount of money in. Strange, isn't it? but I'm sure there's a reasonable explanation as far as you're concerned, sir. I wonder if you could help me with some of the other names. Gambler is one, he was a regular but paid a lot less. Maybe mates' rates for people who worked there?"

He handed over a copy of the list. The superintendent was quiet for what seemed like an eternity but was in fact about three minutes.

"Was there anything else on the computer?"

"I'm sure there will be."

"Leave it with me and I'll go through this and see if I can identify anyone, and I'll try to remember what my contribution was for."

"Yes of course, sir. I'll call in tomorrow. I have colleagues who will be in France for a couple of days.

They'll be visiting the priest's last known address. I'm sure we'll clear all this up when we find him."

Britten cleared his throat. "Do you have any leads yet?"

"Yes, sir, I'm pretty sure we'll have him in a day or two."

On the way out Knowles called in on Ava Blakey. He had decided not to disclose his suspicions at this stage: it would be embarrassing for her. It was not too much of a surprise, however, to learn that she had already received a call from Britten, who had told her to assist him in every way that she could but that he was to be kept informed at every stage. She was told that she would be shortly given a list upon which she may be surprised to see his own name and that she should not draw any conclusions from it. He would explain in due course, but the other names should be traced and communicated to him, before anyone else. Emphasis on anyone!"

Knowles smiled but made no comment. Ava raised her eyebrows. "Your silence speaks volumes."

"I'm sure he'll come up with a reasonable explanation for his name being on the list, to think otherwise would be unfair. Let's wait and see. Has he left?"

"Yes his Mercedes shot off minutes ago."

"Well any speculation on our part would be outrageous. He is a pillar of society. A man with a spotless record, not even a point on his licence. One can sense the halo if not see it."

"The only reason that he has no points is that we all know his car and daren't stop him, and he knows every speed camera in the area. I can't stand him myself. When he talks to me he stares at my tits."

"Well that's definitely a point in his favour then. He's a good healthy male with all the right instincts."

"Probably a decoy, and he has terrible BO. No nice female would want him."

"I sense a degree of revulsion here which makes me feel that I can confide in you. Have you had lunch?"

"It's nearly five o'clock, but a coffee somewhere would be nice. We can safely plan a strategy. If he's going to edit any information before I refer it to you, we need to have a system in place."

"Right. I was hoping you would assist me with that. Don't use your official mobile phone, use your own. We could have a daily update and agree what I officially know, and what officially I shouldn't know. I'll promise to protect you as much as possible but the time may come when I'll have to come clean. Hopefully by then he'll realise his number's up and shoot himself, scarper abroad or face up to a very long and uncomfortable spell in jail."

"So you do think he's involved then?" Knowles had given her a brief rundown earlier thinking that she would probably be involved in the name search.

"Yes. I think the bastard was abusing young boys and paying Pious. If he'd been innocent, he would have been much more anxious to make progress and excited at the thought. He probably turned up there in his jeans and a sweatshirt looking all the world like any ordinary bloke, but Pious would know exactly who he was and he was probably planning to retire with a substantial income from blackmail. If we never find him, I wouldn't put it past Britten to have bumped him off – don't quote me."

"Hang on though. I mean it was a two-way thing, wasn't it? If Pious fingered Britten, he would have landed himself right in it, wouldn't he?"

"Hmm. Yes, I suppose you're right. Anyway, we're making progress. Let's drink to that. You've already met Kate. She's up here with her bloke and they're staying with Joey's big brother Spike. He runs some sort of boatyard."

"Not The Stables?"

"Yes I believe that's what it's called. Is that a problem?"

"Difficult to say, but there is one visitor there, possibly a customer who is of interest. Nothing to suggest that anyone there is involved, but this guy operates below the radar and seems to make some pretty pointless trips by boat from there."

"Pointless? What do you mean?"

"Well in the dark, no luggage, to Amsterdam. And back in a couple of days. I don't know how much it costs to charter a boat for two or three days, but it certainly isn't peanuts."

"Does he come back through customs control?"

"Yes, nothing on him, but then he pops into the yard

a couple of days later and talks to the owner. Pays his bill we think."

"And picks something up you think – drugs?"

"Well he has been watched for months, there's absolutely nothing that suggests he's supplying. We stopped once and asked him if he minded being searched. He laughed and offered to strip. He's as clean as a whistle so we have no grounds to raid the premises. It's just a bit odd. He seemed to appear out of nowhere. Then we were asked by one of the security services to keep an eye on him, but not to interfere in any way with what he does but to report for example if a boat comes back without him or if somebody came with him. Almost as if they were watching his back No clues as to why, well not as far as I know. But quite honestly we have enough to do without babysitting"

"It's unlikely to be drugs then. That's not in their remit. Where does he live?"

"In the shadows. He always manages to give us the slip. Anyway, I'm off duty now. Must go home and feed the cat. A mate is coming round later so I'll have to find something for supper. I hope to see you again soon, and of course I'll keep in touch."

She tapped the side of her nose with two fingers, kissed him lightly on the cheek and left.

*****

At The Stables, Kate and Jake had packed their bags and were ready for an early morning trip to Manchester Airport to catch the midday flight to Rennes. Kate was luxuriating in a hot bath and Jake was sitting on the window watching Spike outside talking to someone he hadn't seen there before – a tallish man wearing dark glasses. There was something familiar about the man, the way he stood. It was what Jake thought of as 'the marine stance' – ready for trouble although the conversation seemed quite amicable. He decided to take a stroll down to the water. As he approached the pair, the man looked up at him and Spike saw who it was. He put his hand up to his left earlobe and gently pulled. The man gave a slight nod as Spike turned.

"Hi, Jake. You all okay? Let me introduce you to one of my customers. This is Mr Griffiths, usually referred to as just Griff. I have no idea what his first name is although I should, because he has commissioned the construction of this beautiful boat."

Griffiths smiled and held out his hand to Jake. "Yes, she really is beautiful and it won't be long before we put her in the water."

"Is it just for pleasure or part of your business?"

"Well, that's none of yours," laughed Griffiths.

Spike intervened. "Look, Griff, I'm really sorry I can't leave here for at least a week. Vic is away and it would leave the place unsupervised. Pippa is great at admin but she couldn't deal with any practical problems. Can it wait a few days? I'll catch you later. I've left my phone in the kitchen and I'm waiting for a call. I'll be right back – are you coming Jake?"

"I'll be right behind you," lied Jake.

When he was out of earshot he turned to Griffiths. "What the hell are you doing here? Please don't tell me these people are involved in anything nasty."

"Absolutely not. On the contrary, I think they might be involved in something rather nice and I have no intention of interfering in it. I'm into something offshore. Spike has no idea. He's not involved in any way. I think he has his suspicions about me, but he never pries. He's a good bloke. He just helps me to get to places without leaving a trail. How about you? What are you doing here?"

"I'm with my girl, she's a cop – a detective. We're investigating an old, very unpleasant case, the death ten years ago of Spike's young brother. Horrible things are creeping out of the woodwork. Do you have contacts in France by any chance?" He explained briefly what their mission over there would be.

Griffiths took his mobile number and promised to get him the details of a couple of guys he knew there. He needed to speak to them first but he was pretty sure they could help.

"As it happens, chances are I'm going over myself. Information that the guy I'm after was coming through Holland proved false and I'm damned sure he'll be coming from Calais, strangely enough, possibly with the help of our friends here although they have no idea at all."

They changed the subject as Spike approached looking slightly anxious, and they walked together back to the house. Griffiths politely turned down an invitation to dinner and said he must go. Jake noted that he left via the copse at the back of the house and smiled to himself. He and Griffiths had met two or three times at the River House, both of them completely enamoured with their headquarters designed by Sir Terry Farrell and definitely one of the most beautiful buildings in London. Griffiths had been a marine and was just the kind of guy to have on your team. To disclose to Kate his identity was unthinkable and the fact that the local police were wasting time trying to work out what he was up to, was just too bad. He himself didn't know, but whatever it was, it would be on the right side of good if not the right side of legal. If Griffiths was going to France and happened to be in the same area, he could be a great help. The European Services worked closely together, exchanging information and these days that exchange was vital to the safety of the entire continent.

Chapter Nineteen

"Who was that chap?" asked Kate who had come to the front door to drag Jake in for a pre-dinner drink.

"Just a customer, I think," replied Jake. "Seemed like a nice enough chap. Anything from Knowles? How did the chat with the Super go? I'd love to have been a fly on the wall."

"More or less as expected really. He knows he's on a hook and is wriggling like crazy. He has to come up with an explanation for his name being on that list. I've been trying to put myself in his place. What would I say if I was an Olympian liar with so much to lose? He's already struggling. If he'd been innocent, he would have given an immediate and convincing explanation. In the circumstances of Joey's death, he could not possibly have failed to appreciate the inferences."

"Well just suppose it is so trivial and innocent, that he really has forgotten all about it. It's a long time ago, and to a guy with his salary, forty pounds is nothing. Suppose he remembers that Pious had some sort of scheme in mind to improve the home: a football pitch, a gymnasium, a better heating system, and was collecting contributions?"

"That sort of scheme costs thousands, and there wouldn't have been a set sum and how come the odd job man makes four contributions when he's on a tight budget. Gambler would have explained straight away. A fund like that would have been publicised too."

"OK well…"

"And you can't avoid the Super's reticence," she continued. "If it had been anything like that he would have remembered and if not immediately, he would have lost no time in letting us know as soon as he had. Gambler is the weak link. He was the most frequent donor and is obviously as guilty as hell. Maybe we could offer some sort of inducement?"

"It wouldn't work. The others would expose him. The original list has to go in as evidence, won't it? and he's on it – four times."

"Hopefully we'll get the addresses of at least some of the others. Maybe someone will talk, although I doubt they can name each other. I reckon they would have been kept totally separate and in the dark. If you look at the dates, there are no two on the same day. If we can just get one to talk, the others will be implicated by virtue of the fact that they're on there, and each one will have to come up with an explanation. Knowles wants us not to approach any of them until we get back from France."

"What do we do if we find Pious?"

"When, you mean. Let's go in with a positive outlook. When we find him we will execute an International Arrest Warrant and bring him back. Quite honestly I don't know where we're going to start though. Vic might have something, but I'm going to have to rely on your impeccable French to make enquiries."

"I may be able to help. I got in touch with the office and should have a couple of names – contacts, who should be able to persuade French officers to do a search. They have the means."

"Officers? What kind of officers?"

"Don't ask, okay? Just trust me. Give me all the information you have."

"That's not much though is it? I'm going to get in touch with the bishop this evening if I can and see if anything else has turned up. But I haven't been introduced. Pippa is the one who approached him first but it was the gardener Peter who gave her most. It might be worth having a chat to him. Come on, I'm starving. I can smell roast pork and I saw the most amazing looking pudding earlier. French food is not all it's cracked up to be, so let's feast while we have the chance. It might be snails and frites tomorrow."

"Rubbish! I know the most amazing restaurant in the area. It's called Le Moulin de Jean."

"Ah yes, I've heard of it. The chef trained in England so it's bound to be good."

"You are a bit of a Philistine, aren't you?"

"On the contrary, I am the very essence of culture and sophistication, you just haven't seen me in my element."

"I'd rather see you in the nude."

"Well take a shower with me."

"I'm going to have to – you sleep with your clothes on."

"It's called a nightie."

"Well it was *so* difficult to get it off over your head last night that the honourable member began to lose interest."

"Well you managed okay in the end."

"It wasn't all that hard."

"Felt okay to me."

Any further smutty conversation was interrupted by Pippa at the door. "Dinner in five, but I wanted to run something past you. I thought it might be time to put something in the paper. It's all been pretty hush hush up to now but what with rumours about a Met investigation drifting up here, I thought it might be time to give them something."

She handed Kate a printout from her computer:

TIME FOR AN OUTING!

There is a cavernous gulf between making love and rape, but essentially, the physical act is the same. There may be violent blows instead of caresses, loving endearments rather than insults and the aftermath may be a feeling of cosy satisfaction, or revulsion at the thought of it for the rest of a life. Cases of rape are rarely prosecuted because survivors are too embarrassed, or have no confidence that they would be believed if they did come forward.

Every day we are bombarded with so many reports of children being orphaned, starved, abused, wounded and killed in places so far away, that we try to obliterate the thoughts from our minds because we're helpless. We can't do anything about it. But we are all aware that terrible things happen here too. If we stand by, knowing that such damaging acts are occurring in this very country we are culpable. We are accessories. Is there anyone out there who has the moral stature to stand up and say, "It happened to me when I was a child and I want to help to stop it happening again." If you are, or have been a victim of abuse and are willing to provide information, neither your name, nor anything that could identify you will be published in this or any other newspaper. All relevant information will be conveyed immediately to the police department, which is handling the matter. Be brave. Show that anyone who abuses a child, will now be looking over his shoulder until he's caught, even if it does take ten years!

If you are a victim of rape, woman or man, give the police a chance.

If you are or have been a perpetrator of such vile offences, then upon conviction your name will be headlines. You can rely upon it. If on the other hand, you truly regret what you have done, any help you can offer will be taken into account.

Kate read the article and handed it to Jake. "Yes. It's good.

It's an appeal to victims and in itself will put the wind up the perpetrators. All we need are a couple of survivors, filled with resentment and a longing to get even. You'd think they'd be queuing up, wouldn't you?"

"No, not really," said Jake. "I think it's the sympathy they'll want to avoid if their names get out, and they will, if it comes to court. They've learned to live with it. The last thing they want is people coming up with comforting comments. Somehow, we have to get that over to the public. Just get one brave soul to come forward, head held high and say, 'Please leave me alone now. I am fine. I am not a victim. I am not damaged goods. I like my life. The nightmare is over and these guys will get what's coming to them. That is why I told my story'."

"Yes, Jake, I can see you're right, I think that's how I'd feel too but maybe they won't all be like you and me. Some will feel blighted for life. We need to offer counselling or compensation. We'll just have to hope they come forward so that maybe we can help at all."

"Before it goes to print I need to run it past Knowles. If that's okay, Pips?"

"Sure – absolutely. Let's eat."

"I remember Vic talking about the gardener," said Spike thoughtfully, during dinner. "I think he liked the guy. I wonder if it was the same odd job man? I can't recall his name and I wasn't really there long enough to make his acquaintance."

"Can we get in touch with Vic? I know we'll probably

see him in France tomorrow or the next day but anything that might help Knowles while he's up here would be good."

"We have ship to shore. I'll try to get him in a minute."

"Yes, if you could just ask him if he remembers the name or anything else."

Spike came back from the office while they were enjoying coffee. "Spoke to him, and yes he remembers. The guy was called Mike. He is quite sure that he would not have abused the boys. Vic liked him. Whenever he saw one of the kids in trouble, he was concerned. He looked after Vic because he was a funny looking kid with no friends. If his name was on the list, it was for another reason, Vic got quite angry. He would stake his life on 'Mike' not being an abuser." There was a long silence.

"Well that puts the whole bloody list in doubt, doesn't it? I'll tell Knowles. He'll want to speak to him again, find out what the payments were for."

"We've been working on the assumption that they were payments to and not from Pious, haven't we? Could it possibly be the other way round?"

"I don't know. I'm totally confused now. I'm going to ring the boss. We need to get to the bottom of this before we go."

She left the room looking thoroughly fed up and confused. Fifteen minutes later she was back. "Gambler has been in touch, he asked to speak to Knowles again. I think his solicitor has spoken to Charlie, or sussed what the case is likely to be about, and is insisting that Gambler sees an officer without delay. Hopefully we'll get a report later this evening. Knowles doesn't want him interviewed at the police station so he's going to the house to take another statement."

It was another two hours before Kate's phone rang and she retired to the corner of the room to take what turned out to be a rather long call. The others were silent. When she came back, there was a look of relief on her face.

"It was the same chap. He remembers Vic. He was paying regular sums to Pious. It was blackmail. He had been in charge of ordering supplies for the kitchen and just about everything else really. Pious found that he was filtering stuff out, filling his own larder and getting odd bits of other stuff: duvets, sheets, pillows and things like that. He threatened immediate dismissal. Gambler actually loved the job, liked the kids, he had none of his own. With a criminal record he would never get another job like that or at all so he complied."

"So why didn't Pious just take it from his salary?"

"He had nothing to do with salaries. He just kept the money and relied on Gambler to keep his mouth shut. Gambler turned a blind eye to things that went on although he claims he had no idea about any sexual abuse. He's going to the station to make a formal statement tomorrow. Hopefully he will be able to give us something useful. At least it shows that the payments were to and not from.

Phew I feel better. I'm going to get an early night." She and Jake disappeared upstairs.

Pippa and Spike talked about their friend who had had such a terrible start in life himself and who had matured into a reliable, self-sufficient, attractive man.

"He could be so different, Spike, with a start like that he could have turned into a monster. I can't imagine life without him."

"No. Me neither. And I trust his judgement. You know all the youngsters we've brought into this country. They all found it difficult to say goodbye to Vic. I wonder if he did suspect what was going on. He's an intelligent bloke and he must have sensed something evil, don't you think? His childhood was horrendous. He was familiar with acts of violence. He has never said that he was sexually abused. I hope he wasn't, but would he have recognised the distress of the other little ones if he saw signs of it? He was so kind to you when you arrived."

"The little ones avoided him. He had a scary face. He knew that, so he kept away from them. He said once that he had tried to talk to a little kid crying in a corner once and the kid had run away terrified. He didn't try again."

"Well he got over it thank goodness. He's always fine with the young ones."

"Yes but the scars are old now. No one even notices them. He's grown into them somehow. And as you said the other day, there's something very attractive about him."

*****

Handsome Vic was at that very moment approaching the Channel. He reluctantly cast his mind back to The Sanctuary days. Mike the gardener odd job man had been one of the first people to show any interest in him. He had asked about the scars, from which most people turned with embarrassment. It was much easier just to ignore him. Mike had listened with sympathy and outrage. It had been a cathartic experience for Vic. to tell someone all about his unhappy childhood. To see the disgust and outrage on Mike's face. After he'd got it all off his chest, they never spoke of it again.

Mike loved nature. He knew the names of every bird and flower, and kept a diary through the year of first sightings. The most beautiful bird they saw was a tiny goldcrest perched on a columbine. They hardly dared to breathe as it chirped its happy little song and then flew away. He had been upset when Spike had enquired about their relationship, but, he supposed, Spike had had to ask, just to set the record straight. There had been times when he had seen strange comings and goings during the evenings, usually after Mike had gone home. He had mentioned a couple of times seeing men, who looked distinctively furtive, going upstairs with Pious, but Mike had told him to forget it, said that Pious was not a nice man and to keep as far away from him as possible. Vic had been only too happy to do so.

Something had warned Vic that Pious was not a kind man, but looking back, and thinking about what he had recently been told by Kate, he wondered how he could have been so naïve. He had suffered at the hands of men without education or standards or compassion. Something should have told him that Pious was the same; – well read, well-spoken but just the same cruel unscrupulous individual that Vic had lived his childhood alongside. Beside him, Mike was a saint. He needed to make sure Kate knew that.

Chapter Twenty

The airport at Rennes was small but busy as they headed for the car hire offices. They were well on the way to Fougères when they had a message from Vic to say he wouldn't be able to anchor till late that evening. He gave them the names of a couple of hotels. Brit Hotel sounded pretty mundane so they decided on Chateau Montbrault at twice the price. It turned out to be an absolute delight – a unique marriage of history and all mod cons. After a lunch which, Kate had to admit, supported France's claim to be the home of 'cuisine superbe', and coffee, which actually tasted like coffee, they left to begin their search for the odious priest.

The address was quite easy to find. A street of three storeyed houses many with closed green shutters, most looking run down, some with shop fronts and others clearly divided into separate apartments. Seventeen proved to comprise 17A, 17B and 17C, C being at the top of the building. There were names beside the numbers. None was Tellier. "How the hell do we get in?" wondered Kate.

"Try pressing one of the bells," said Jake doing just that himself.

"Oui," responded a male voice

"Bonjour Monsieur. Je suis Monsieur Scott. Je cherche un ami, Francois Tellier, ou sa tante qui, je crois, habitent ici, il y a dix ans."

"Désolé! Je ne les connaissais pas. Ils n'habitent pas ici maintenant. Au revoir."

There were similar responses from the two other apartments and the neighbouring ones.

"This is hopeless," observed Kate. "What about the town hall or local doctors perhaps?"

"I have an idea," replied Jake. "At the end of the road there was a shop which looks as if it's been here for decades. It might have been here at the right time. The woman inside looked about a hundred. Let's go and see."

There was an elderly lady arranging loaves of French bread behind the counter and an impressive display of pastries, eggs and fresh vegetables in a glass fronted case. Bottles of wine were on shelves at the back of the shop and there was a cosy glow from two wall lamps and another hanging above them with an art nouveau shade. So much nicer than strip lighting, thought Kate.

"Bonjour Mademoiselle, Monsieur."

Jake gave her a winning smile and in what sounded like impeccable French, introduced them both, complimented her on her shop, picked up the most expensive bottle of wine that he could see, and explained their mission.

There followed a long conversation between them which was too fast for Kate to follow but she did get the impression from the frowns, other facial expressions, and the occasional gasp and 'Mon Dieu' as the lady held her hand to her mouth in apparent horror.

"What on earth are you telling her?" she muttered.

"Don't worry. I'll tell you later but I think we're getting somewhere. She remembers the aunt."

The lady had shuffled out to a door at the back of the shop, but came back when the shop bell rang. A young boy came in and left with a bag of croissants and some honey.

There was a further conversation between her and Jake before he ushered Kate out of the shop with a smile and a handshake with the lady. "A ce soir, madame, et merci beaucoup."

"Well I understood that bit. Why are we going back ce soir?"

"Somewhere she has a newspaper cutting with a picture of Frances and his ma. The father was a bit of a bastard and a drunk apparently. The police were there every five minutes but they did arrest him when he punched the kid and laid him out. That's when the press came round and took pics. After that, he and his mother fled. The aunt moved not too far away, but she doesn't have the address. She was his sister so she could be a Tellier too unless she married."

"So what did you say that made her react with horror?"

"I told her the police in UK needed to speak to him in connection with something very serious. I didn't go into any details. I let her imagination do the rest."

"You didn't pay for the wine."

"No there was no point in offering a cash card. I said I would go back this evening and pay for a case of the same with cash. Can you remind me? It'll be heavy but we can park outside."

"And she trusted you?"

"She loved me. I have a way with old ladies. It's my eyes."

"Well your irresistible charm has its uses, I suppose, but it does wear thin after a while."

"So how do we find the address of Auntie Pious?"

"Bear with me, this is where good contacts come in." He took out his phone and there was another lengthy conversation which made Kate determined to register for French lessons as soon as she got home.

"Oui, je t'attend. Merci." He turned to Kate. That was one of my contacts. He can check the name against all sorts of registers and if there's no joy there, he'll check the marriage register in this area but we'll need her first name and approximate age in any case. If she has a married name, he'll start the search again and get back to us as soon as he's got something. I told him about the newspaper report which he'll need to have. I can send him the details and a picture but I don't want to pester Madam too much right now. I think she's interested enough to turn the house upside down to find it, but she doesn't close until about ten tonight so we'll have to stay another night."

"Oh no," said Kate cheerfully. "I'll get in touch with Vic. We need a meeting point…"

"Well he knows the hotel. Tell him to meet us there. Let us know the time and I'll book him a room, for tomorrow night. I think he said he could leave the boat in the hands of the crew – of one."

"Excellent! This is turning out to be a pretty good holiday after all."

"Hm any news from Charlie?"

"Don't ever call him that to his face. It was his wife's name for him. She was lovely but she died, and he said he couldn't bear to hear it from anyone else. Actually, I think there maybe someone on the horizon now. He's started to diet. He was quite dishy when he was younger and skinnier."

"Yes, he has good bones. I really like him. Why not give him a call? Surely they have traced the coroner's secretary by now and the original forensic report. It is quite staggering to think how that inquest was rushed through. It shows how much a family counts, doesn't it? I imagine there would have been people banging on the door demanding answers if there had been parents or any other relatives. It was an absolute travesty and now we know that information was suppressed, don't we? I'm surprised Philippa didn't kick up more fuss at the time."

"She was young and new to the job I suppose, and for heaven's sake, you have to have faith in your own justice system. How could she question the coroner? I think she tried to ask a few questions in her column but she was discouraged by the editor."

"Well maybe he's another person with questions to answer."

"Watch this space. I think she's on to that. She's quite sure the editor was a decent bloke – it's a different one now. The old one just thought it would be wrong to question the decision of a man with a reputation that was whiter than white. Said that in such a tragic case it wouldn't be good for the paper if she tried to make a story of it. I think he's regretting it now. Making a fuss then might have got him a huge scoop."

"Hindsight is a frustrating thing!"

They were having croque monsieurs when Knowles called to tell them that he had indeed traced the secretary, Helen Paton, and no – she didn't have dementia, she was delighted to talk. He'd taken Sam Cartwright with him, since he was able to remind her of the telephone call from Simon Crowther. It had gone well. Helen Paton had been nursing a sense of guilt for ten years, knowing that she should have spoken up at the time but had been worried about the consequences. It was easy to understand why.

She said that one evening at the time, she had gone back to the office to pick up her phone. She was surprised when she found the door unlocked. She went quietly into the outer office and heard voices in the next room. It was the coroner speaking. He had sounded angry and said something like 'I absolutely refuse to do that. This is an official document and the fact that there was skin under this child's nails, as I told you on the phone, is significant. It was fresh skin!' He might have said new skin she can't remember. She wasn't sure what the other person had said and decided to get out fast rather than reveal her presence. She sat in her car in the car park outside and waited. A police officer came out. She remembers he had a file in his hand.

The next day she had a chance to look at the statement from the pathologist but she strongly believes that it was not the original. There was no mention of skin under the nails, just a description of the bruises.

Knowles had managed to examine the original evidence. "The pathologist's statement was missing. Anyone who has access and examines evidence in the files has to sign for it. Guess who signed the book before the hearing – Britten. He must have taken the original statement away. No one would think of questioning him.

"The phone still had the call from Mrs Paton registered in it. It was just a request for an urgent meeting. She told us that she had tried to get in touch with Crowther again, but then heard about the accident. That's when she gave up. She decided not to mention it to the coroner. He had clearly been upset by the officer's visit, but pronounced accidental death. He had retired a couple of years later." Knowles was trying to find and interview him. He was also looking for the pathologist and planning another chat with the superintendent. Mrs Paton wasn't at all sure that she would recognize him again but he was going to try a few police ID photos.

"The days of police line ups are long gone which is just as well," he'd said. "We'd never get a row of ugly enough blokes to stand beside him and I would probably get early retirement with no pension if it went wrong. He is very good at telling convincing lies. I want a cast iron case before I go near him again, Kate, so keep shtum."

Kate updated Knowles with the details of the Fougères trip and they arranged another update for the next day

*****

One thing really irritated Kate. Jake kept getting furtive phone calls, turning away from her as he spoke. Sometimes he explained what it was about, anything to do with their own enquires. Other times he would say, 'It's nothing important. Just business.' She got fed up with it after the third or fourth call.

"For God's sake, Jake, you're going to have to trust me. If I'm going to be left out in the cold every time we're together this just isn't going to work. For all I know you're talking to one of the three hundred virgins you boast about."

"Well don't worry – you wouldn't qualify to be the three hundred and first," he laughed. "I'm sorry it must be infuriating. Let's go and find a bar and I'll reveal as much as I can. It's just habit. I'm watching my back and yours too, but there is something I think I had better tell you."

They found a cosy bar, ordered two glasses of wine and sat in a quiet corner. "You remember the bloke you saw me talking to at The Stables?"

"Yes, just a customer you said."

"Well yes and I think he was essentially; he and Spike were discussing the boat that was being constructed for him, but I actually have met him before, at the office."

"What! Are you saying he's a spy?"

"We are not bloody spies. Will you stop saying that. We are simply investigating agents in several fields, most of which involve the security of our country."

"So why are you telling me that now?"

"Because I've just had a message or two from him. He's over here."

"Doing what?"

"This is difficult and I'm swearing you to secrecy. It might just involve Spike, and we wouldn't want any harm to come to him, would we? That's a rhetorical question by the way. No response required."

Kate was quiet then. "You need to tell me. I might need to help. Please tell all."

"Okay. Stand by."

Jake motioned the barman to bring two more glasses of wine and put his elbows on the table. "Let me tell you what I know about Griff. He was a marine and he works for '6' you know that. His father was in the army and as a kid he spent a lot of time in other countries. It wasn't long before it was noticed that he had a certain skill. He picked up languages very quickly and as a teenager he worked on that. I know he is fluent in French, German, Swedish and Arabic. There are probably others. His pronunciation is flawless and he can switch dialects. That made him very useful to the intelligence services. At the moment being fluent in Arabic is vital to our security. Most terrorist plots these days are born in Arab speaking countries and he knows them all. He has already taken the sting out of six potentially deadly hits. He never stops.

"You've heard rumours of a threat to our capital? He's onto that. The reason he's spending time at The Stables is because intelligence pointed out Amsterdam as the place where it was being planned. No threats from the Dutch, but there was a gathering of known individuals mainly from Syria. Griff set himself up there for a couple of months as a rich boat owner with one of Spike's boats. He even registered it there in case anyone checked, with Spike's permission of course. The Stables got a hefty fee for that. He lived there, heavily disguised as a drunken idiot with more money than sense. If you'd met him in Amsterdam, you wouldn't have wanted to know him. Most people tried to ignore him. It paid off. He did unearth enough info to know that the plot has moved to stage two and they've moved to France with a view to getting from there to the south coast of England. What bothers all of us is that they have shown an interest in the trips Spike's boat makes to and from France. It is whispered that Vic picks up the odd passenger, one that hasn't a passport. That's what caused Griff to go there in the first place."

I just refuse to believe that Spike or Vic would do anything like that."

"No, they wouldn't knowingly, what they are doing is helping children to get to families in England. They only take refugee children one or two at a time. Helping kids is Spike's mission – always will be and Griff understands and approves of that. He is very concerned for their future right now though. That is why he's here. Anyway, you know nothing of this – understand?"

"Yes, I totally understand, Jake. Of course I do and I don't believe Vic would be involved with anything like that either. He's lovely."

"Yes I like him too. And he's kind, and kind people can be manipulated. Anyway, that's all I can tell you at the moment. I don't think Griffiths has seen you, has he? If we meet up here, just be straightforward about what we're doing but don't go calling him James Bond or asking him when the next terrorist attack on London is going to be. He's just a business man, okay?"

"I promise. It's quite exciting though, and thanks, Jake. Thanks for trusting me. Does he know where we are? Are we just going to bump into him by accident? Are we going to tell him where the boat is mooring?"

"No. He will call me this evening. He was at the boatyard enquiring about Vic's whereabouts, asked where he was likely to park up. Spike said he was never sure but he'd let him know. Griff said he happened to have business over here and maybe could hitch a lift back. Spike again wasn't sure but did say we were in the area too, and would let us know."

"So Spike was fairly evasive then, maybe he is beginning to wonder about Griff."

"I don't know but he's not daft. He probably realises that people could take advantage and has warned Vic. I dare say we'll find out. We're supposed to be sailing back with him when we're through here. It would be great if we could take Pious back with us. We could draw lots for the honour of shoving him overboard."

"No it has to be a prolonged and painful death – or we could just take him back and let Spike decide. I don't think keel hauling would work on a small boat though. Anyway, we have to catch him first, hopefully Auntie will help. Does Griff know I'm a cop?"

"Yes – I mentioned it when I met him at the yard."

"I may be able to put his mind at rest about Vic, although, come to think of it, the local constabulary are a bit suspicious of Griffiths already. Ava Blakey at the station was telling Knowles about this furtive bloke who kept turning up there, and asked him to try to find out what he's up to. Somebody had said something that aroused their suspicions."

"Now she tells me," said Jake taking out his mobile. "I'd better have a word with him." He spoke for a few minutes, laughed and turned to Kate. "He's already at our hotel and looking forward to seeing us. He knows about Ava Blakey's. 'furtive bloke'. He set that up himself, just in case anything went wrong and he needed police support in a hurry. Come on, let's go."

Chapter Twenty-one

Kate was watching through the hotel window when Jake went out to meet Griffiths. They shook hands, there was a brief conversation and then they both laughed and walked toward the hotel.

Griffiths smiled at Kate and held out his hand. "Definitely the best-looking detective inspector I've ever seen – apart from the ones on telly, but they all have those daft hairstyles – begging for an arrestee to grab and strangle them. Look let me get you both a drink. I believe Vic is on the way too, I know his tipple but what about you two. Wine?"

"White for Kate and red for me please. The house wine is excellent."

"You certainly get around, Mr Griffiths. I saw you briefly from my bedroom window at The Stables," said Kate when he came back followed by a waiter carrying a tray of drinks."

"Small world, isn't it? Please call me Dick. Yes, Jake has probably told you about my half-built boat. I hope it'll be finished by the end of the year. I'm paying in instalments, so there have been delays. I'm just looking forward to the time when I can sail down here. I hate flying. I usually hitch a lift from Vic and he drops me off near Cherbourg but I missed him this time."

"Pretty time consuming though," said Jake. "We're on leave so if it takes two days to get home it doesn't matter. The guest cabin has already gone by the way."

"Well if I do travel back that way, I'll sleep in the galley on the floor, or on deck if the weather holds out. It all depends on where he's moored, I've yet to find out. I usually just catch the Cherbourg–Poole ferry back. It's less complicated and I can get a decent breakfast."

"I was under the impression that he dropped anchor behind Le Mont-Saint-Michel. His friend lives nearby and he has a truck, but I now understand that it is nigh on impossible without getting stuck," said Kate. "Vic told me that there are three possible marinas and it depends which is the most convenient."

I imagine it's somewhere nearer St Malo. Do you know his name; the friend I mean?"

"Pierre I think, why?"

"No reason. Just wondered. How's the wine?"

At that moment, Vic hailed them from the door of the bar. "Be with you in a mo. I just have to say goodbye to Pierre and arrange the pickup."

Griffiths hurried to the door and followed Vic outside. "I've left my wallet in the glove box, and I've just ordered a round of drinks," he explained, as he walked towards a sporty looking Renault. He watched carefully as Vic went over to a white high-sided van. He noted the number and waved when Vic made his way back to the hotel entrance.

The van was still there and had just started up when Griff waved it to stop. He went to the passenger door and then motioned to the driver to open it, which the driver did with some impatience."

"Monsieur, you seem to have a flat tyre." Griffiths crouched down and put his hand under the wheel arch. The driver was about to get out when Griffiths stood up. "A thousand pardons, Monsieur, I was wrong, it must have been another vehicle. This is fine, au revoir, Monsieur." He followed Vic into the hotel, spoke briefly to the man behind the bar and went to join the others. "Look, guys, I'm really sorry. I have to go, something's come up I'll be in touch tomorrow." He waved and was gone. Kate shrugged and smiled at Vic.

"Weird bloke. Come on, sit down and tell us the plan. Jake and I have a meeting with a little old lady later this evening and hopefully a visit to make tomorrow morning, if she provides us with an address. If that doesn't fit in with your return trip we'll book a flight. I've got to get back soon. There are things I have to see to."

"Well I can't get back to the boat till later so I'll be here till tomorrow. If we keep in touch, I can collect you from the car hire place after lunch and we'll all go back together. I have no idea what Griffiths is up to so I'm not hanging round for him, but I do need to stay until Pierre gets back."

"How long have you known Pierre, Vic? he is obviously a good friend of yours."

"I've known him for years. When Spike and I ended up at The Stables, Pearson's wife hadn't been long dead. He was lonely, treated us like sons, taught us to sail, taught us all about navigation. We made lots of trips to France and always met up with Pierre. He spoke English fluently; his mother was English you see."

"And his father French?"

There was a pause. "No, he was German. I don't suppose Pierre would mind if I told you. His mother studied French at university in the UK. At the end of her third year she came over to perfect the language. She must have been about twenty-four in 1940. She was working in a village quite a long way from here when the Germans invaded. When the Vichy government took over she decided to go home. She got as far as Fougères, where she had other friends, and got caught up in the Resistance Movement. She was contacted by the SOE, they got a radio transmitter to her and she did very useful work – speaking French as well as she did, and she stayed throughout the war. Then in 1944 she heard the most terrible news from the Haute Vienne where she used to work in a village called Oradour. You may remember the name – it should never be forgotten." Vic stopped and took a gulp of his lager. "In response to the killing of an officer, the Germans stationed there, herded all the villagers into the church, more than six hundred men women and children, and set it alight. They all burned to death. Anyone would have been appalled, but you can imagine how she felt. She had looked after and loved some of those children.

"A few days later, she was spotted by a patrolling soldier – a German. She was in the process of attaching explosives to rail tracks. A train full of troops was on the way to the Normandy coast. He caught her and raped her and – well, she killed him. She picked up a rock and beat his head until it was pulp. All that rage gave her strength. She was covered in blood when she walked away, not sure where she was going. She hadn't gone far when there was a massive explosion. The German had been so determined to get her knickers off that he had forgotten to detach the explosives. The train had had about two hundred soldiers aboard. They didn't all die, of course, but the body of the rapist wouldn't have been far enough away to be anything but one of the passengers.

"The villagers were jubilant, but she – her name was Mary – felt nothing but horror and revulsion. She kind of withdrew after that, didn't talk much, and certainly didn't claim responsibility. When she realised that she was pregnant she was determined to keep the baby and bring it up to respect life. Conflict turns people into monsters she told Pierre. The villagers of course took a different view. They knew who was responsible for the train and although they never knew who the father of her baby was, from that moment on, mother and baby wanted for nothing. It wasn't long before France was liberated. Mary did her best to forget it. Pierre grew up to be a happy little boy with a village full of friends.

"Before she died she told him about it. She knew he had to be told who his father had been. He said he'd guessed anyway, there were so many rumours about that night and the fact that she never spoke of it was the most significant clue. He adored her and he is one of the best people I know."

Kate and Jake were silent for some time. "What an incredibly moving story," said Jake, "and thanks for telling us, Vic. I think it's something we needed to know. Now we had better go and keep our appointment with Charlotte. Look forward to seeing you and Pierre tomorrow."

*****

Charlotte was just closing up when they arrived and invited them into her home through a door towards the rear of the shop. It was surprisingly bright and cheerful. A window looked out into a well-kept garden with a huge old grapevine clinging to a mellow brick wall and a small lawn with a circular bed full of pink and scarlet peonies. There was a basket chair and matching table set with three glasses and a bottle of the wine that had excited Jake so much, with a box of bonbons beside it. They were invited to call her Charlotte and Kate was quite amused when the old lady lit a cheroot.

Once again Jake did the translating to save time. Charlotte began by producing with a flourish a yellowing newspaper open at the page which showed the picture of a young man who looked as if he was in his teens sporting a pad over one eye and a bandaged wrist. A woman who could have been anything between twenty and forty had her arm round his shoulders.

Man arrested in Fougères following vicious attack on son. Neighbours called police after hearing screams coming from the home of Jaques Tellier, who was later charged with grievous bodily harm and remains in custody.

Jake read and then asked, "Would you be able to recognize him from that, maybe twenty years later?"

"No but Spike might. Ask if she knows what happened to the aunt."

Charlotte was speaking quickly and enjoying every moment of this moment of celebrity.

"He had beaten the son because he wouldn't tell him where his mother was. The thing is, Francois had no idea where his mother was, neither did his aunt. In fact, the mother was so fed up with being abused that she had left. I think Francois blamed her for his beating. She got in touch a few days later and said she had gone back to England. She wanted Francois to join her. He did go for a while, but the father, after he was discharged from prison, went over to England and found them. By then his sister, Francois' aunt had moved away to Fougerolles and I lost touch with her. I did hear though

that his father had died some years later and his

mother too, poor soul. I have no idea what happened to Francois. He was a strange boy and didn't have the best start in life."

Am I beginning to feel sorry for him, thought Kate? No! Like father like son. Pray that he didn't spread his seed in places that might result in another generation. "Hey, Jake was saying, "Kate look at this. This was a photograph of a group of young men, which had been taken in black and white. The boy on the bench, right in the middle is Francois. Charlotte is certain of that, she remembers it. They were being rowdy, look one is kicking a tin around and you can tell they're shouting. The guy next door was going to complain and took this as evidence."

"He isn't shouting."

"No he's not really part of the group, is he? Looks unhappy, but it's a good clear shot. Gaunt face, dark eyes, big nose. I'll get an expert to age it, and we'll know exactly what we're looking for. I'll ask for photo-fits with and without beard etc."

"That's so good, Jake. We're on the way. I've a good feeling about this now. Ask if she remembers Aunty's name. She hasn't mentioned it yet."

Charlotte put back her head and closed her eyes for a moment and then, "Edith – her name was Edith Tellier."

They stayed for a while, chatting and finishing the bottle of wine and then rose to leave. "Thank you, Charlotte. You have been so helpful. We will certainly keep in touch; we have your phone number and address now. Goodbye and thank you again."

Jake kissed her on both cheeks and she seemed to expect the same from Kate, who gave her a hug. They paid cash for the case of wine and left with promises to call again on their next visit.

"God I'm tired," said Jake, rubbing the back of his neck. "It seems like days since we left home. Let's go back to the hotel, open a bottle in our room and I'll give them Edith's name. With a bit of luck we'll have an address in the morning."

It was in fact near midnight when a text came through: *Rue de les Fermes, Fougerolles du Plessis. No numbers available. She lives alone age seventy-six.*

"Bugger – I'm too excited to sleep now. Why don't we go and have a look?"

"Are you quite mad? We've had half a bottle of wine each. Go to sleep."

And they did.

*****

If ever there was a typically boring French village this was it. Nothing to distinguish it at all, unless you happened upon the chateau which was a bit like a film set: lawns, lake, luxury and loneliness. Not a person in sight. They left it sleeping in the sunlight and found Rue des Fermes close by. The street seemed to be uninhabited.

"The only bloody life in this place is the minimarket

car park," remarked Jake. "And that's because half the cars had UK number plates."

"And you think I'm a Philistine! This isn't Paris. It's the way they live. I expect all the women are indoors slaving over daubes and the husbands are out seducing under-age girls singing, 'Every little breeze seems to whisper Louise' and pretending to be Maurice Chevalier."

"Who the hell is he?"

"I think he's dead. Perhaps I mean Thierry Henri."

"Look! This must be the place. Rue des Fermes. Go and ask somebody."

"Like who? There's no one in sight."

"Well knock on a door. Look there's one."

"One what?"

"A door."

"This is getting silly."

Jake climbed out of the car and made his way to a blue wooden door, which opened onto the pavement. It opened promptly and there was a brief discussion. Kate saw the inhabitant point up the road and Jake beckoned to her. He was smiling broadly.

"Madame Tellier lives up the road three doors away. Let's move the car up and say hello."

"I wonder if she speaks English. I'm rather tired of waiting for you to translate and I think you're probably leaving out all the good bits."

"You know three days ago, the sun shone out of my backside and now everything I say is suspect. Suddenly

I'm a second-rate tour guide, without whom, I would like to point out, you would still be trying to find your way around Rennes Airport."

She laughed and put her arms around him. "I appreciate everything you've done. I would be lost without you. You know I love you, Jake."

"Yes I know. Come on. This next bit is the thing that will make all this worthwhile."

It was with some trepidation that Kate knocked on the door of Mme Tellier's home. What if it's wrong, a false trail, suddenly it all seemed too easy. What if he answers?

This terrifying thought was dispelled when a well-preserved, elderly lady opened the door and looked at her enquiringly. Jake stepped forward quickly sensing that Kate was searching desperately for the right words.

"Madame Teller? Oui? Bonjour je suis Jake Scott et voici Madmoiselle Meredith. Nous venons d'Angleterre pour chercher des informations de Monsieur Francois Tellier, votre neveu? Pouvez vous nous aider?"

"Why are you looking for my nephew? Is he in trouble? He's not here anyway."

"Ah! You speak English very well, madam, that is a relief. It saves me translating for the benefit of my friend. May we come in?"

Edith Tellier could have been anything between sixty and seventy, frail with greying hair and pale blue eyes. She stared at them for a while and then stepped aside and motioned for them to enter. When they were seated in her small living room, she sat silently waiting for them to speak.

Kate began. "I'm going to be perfectly honest with you, madam, I see no point in beating around the bush."

"Please, my English is basic. Please get to the point."

"May I ask, when did you last see Francois?"

"You may not. Not until you tell me why you are here."

Jake looked at Kate. "May I explain?" She nodded.

"Madam, we believe that ten years ago, Francois was managing a home for boys; boys who had no family. He may have been a priest – or he may have been posing as a priest."

"He was a priest. He was ordained in Great Britain, and worked there for a while. His mother told me this. He only contacted me when he was in trouble, and then only to ask for money."

"So when did you see him last?"

"You still have not told me why you want to know. What has he done?"

"I'm afraid that it is possible that he hurt a child, but we don't know. That is why we need to speak to him, but it is something that happened some years ago. It is possible that we are pre-judging him."

"Nothing would surprise me. He had no love for children. When he was a child himself, he had no friends. To be fair to him, he had a bad start in life. He was unlucky enough to have been born the child of my brother. There was something wrong with him. I have to say it. My brother was a vile cruel man. He had no love or pity for anyone. The terrible thing was that he knew how to be good, how to charm people, to get what he wanted. That poor simple English woman, he took everything from her and left her damaged. Not only that but he gave her a son who was an echo of himself."

"When did you last see him – his son?"

"When he last needed money. He just turns up. When I came here I thought I had escaped but somehow he found me. I have told the police but they aren't interested. They have bigger fish to fry than a troublesome nephew. All the records of his bad behaviour are years old and threats are hollow are they not until they are manifest. I have a phone but he sometimes uses it when he's here. He never stays long. Never overnight. He comes when the banks are open so that if I have no cash here, I can get some. He comes to the bank with me and stands close all the time."

"Do you have a mobile phone?"

"No I don't think I could use it. They are so complicated. Modern technology confuses me. You are staying here in France?"

"No but I know people who can help you and I am going to give you a mobile phone," said Jake taking one out of his pocket. "You needn't try to use it, just leave it on the table. Say someone gave it to you and you don't like it. Give it to him or let him take it, which I'm sure he will, even if it is just to sell."

Kate looked at him puzzled then understood.

"Now we must go," she said. "This is my number. Call me whenever you want to on your landline and I will call you sometimes. If he is there when I call, don't answer, or if you do just say 'I'm sorry I don't want insurance', and put the phone down then, I will know he is with you. Take care, Edith."

With that they left.

"As soon as he gets that phone we'll know where he is as soon as he turns it on."

"Assuming he takes it and we might not be around anyway."

"Yes but I know a man who will be – three in fact. They'll be tracking."

"Are these guys that Griffiths happens to know as well?"

"Yes, he's here on other business, rather more serious. I think he'll be keeping a close eye on Pierre right now. When he comes back we should be able to tell him that it's unlikely that Pierre was involved in something nasty."

"Please don't tell me that Vic is involved in something illegal."

"Kate, if I tell you, it will feel like a betrayal. It's a rule you see, and my telling you this is a breach. I know you wouldn't risk telling anyone else for my sake, but by telling you I will start the rot. You might just 'have' to tell someone that you trust absolutely and so it goes on. It may sound melodramatic, but lives depend on it."

"Yes I do understand and I promise not to ask again – just tell me that Vic is a goodie."

"Vic is definitely a goodie."

"And Pierre?"

"Pierre like Vic and Spike is a good man involved in good things. The trouble is, Pierre's pickups have been noted by the bad guys. There is a Syrian. Let's call him Ali Baba for now. You know we get intelligence from all over Europe and beyond. We think that Ali will soft talk Pierre into picking him up from Cherbourg and dropping him round here somewhere.

"We think when the time comes he will persuade Pierre to get him onto Vic's boat. There is a specific bomb plot, Kate, and the target is in London. Ali is the bomb maker and planner. He has connections at home that we need to trace. We can't possibly tell Spike and Pippa. We know that the child smuggling has ceased while the hunt is on for the priest, but it would help us if Vic did let Ali on board, and we can't work out how to go about it. Vic will certainly not agree to do it, so there might be force involved, which could be dangerous for Vic. It would be better if I was there as a friend who has no idea what is going on – just to see that things go smoothly."

"Two friends would be better and I'm certainly not flying home alone."

"I can't risk taking you, Kate."

"You won't be taking me – what do you think I am – a pet poodle. I will be going with you. Don't even try to stop me. Do you have a gun?"

"Don't be so dramatic."

"Do you have a gun?"

"I might have."

Chapter Twenty-two

Richards Griffiths was travelling half a mile behind Pierre's van. He had planted the tracking device when the van had been parked outside the hotel just before it had left. It was held in place underneath the wheel arch by a strong magnet. He had hoped that Pierre would go in and join them for a drink before he set off on his journey to Cherbourg, but no such luck, and Griffiths had had leave his drink and make his excuses. He didn't want Pierre to get too far ahead. He knew the route that he would take so it was just a matter of keeping him in range until they got to Cherbourg.

He was confident that Vic was not involved in getting the Syrian to the UK, not at this stage anyway. Vic and his friends chanced their arms by reuniting families and refugee children, and good luck to them. No one with a heart could challenge their motives but there could be heavy penalties if they were caught. That, however, was not part of his remit. His job was to enable the Syrian to join up with his fellow conspirators in the UK so that they could catch the whole cabal in circumstances which would put them away for good and probably others too. If that worked out, he would certainly suggest in his report that there should be no interference in the activities at The

Stables. Their ventures could be a useful asset to the service.

How to do it this time without Vic being knowingly involved was not going to be simple. He knew that the Syrian intended to get aboard Vic's boat. He didn't know how he planned to do that. By force would mean that Vic and the crew would be in significant danger. They would go straight to the police once ashore if released and the Syrian could not let that happen. By persuasion? Well that would be it – what the story would be he had no idea. If Vic asked permission from Spike, he wouldn't get it. Spike's mission precluded any adults. The rot would set in and he would have no part in that. By hiding on the boat – not a chance. There was nowhere to hide. Or was there?

The only way, he decided, was to take Vic into his confidence and explain what he needed to do. He would also persuade him not to tell Spike which wouldn't go down well. They could drop off the Syrian in the south of England and forewarn his colleagues who would be waiting with a team to follow the guy wherever he went. The boat could then go on to its mooring at The Stables, clear and clean, job done.

He had confided all this to Jake, of course. He had to. He hoped that Jake would persuade the delectable Jane Meredith to fly back on her own. He suspected that Jake might have talked to her about the mission, hoped not, but Jake was only human and he guessed she could be pretty persuasive. She was a cop after all. With Jake on board they could stay in control. They would both be armed, both praying that they needn't reveal the fact.

He was now on the outskirts of Cherbourg and Pierre's van had turned left. It was early evening. Griffiths followed him to a service station where the Frenchman filled up and then sauntered towards the café alongside. Once in there, Pierre was hailed by a man who was very obviously French. He was accompanied by a young, good-looking, dark-haired, dark-eyed man whom Griffiths immediately recognised as his target.

The exchange between the two Frenchmen was fast and guttural with lots of laughs. Hands were shaken and the third man was introduced. He spoke French well as do most educated Syrians. Griffiths, who had donned a baseball cap and sunglasses and a shabby donkey jacket got up as close as he could at a table directly behind Pierre. The conversation continued in French with all the local patois, which was no problem for Griffiths but he realised that the Syrian was just a little unsure of himself.

"So, Mustafa, Pierre was saying, "you want a lift down to Le Mont-Saint-Michel, yes? I can do that but you need to be ready to go. I have to pick up some cargo locally, but if you are here in half an hour, I will give you a lift. Do you know people there? Will you be okay? I can do no more than drop you off because I'm collecting three English people who are sailing back to England tomorrow. I'm taking them back to their boat, so there will be no more room in my van. Do you understand?"

The Syrian nodded. "Yes, yes of course. I will just stay here till you get back."

The two Frenchmen got up to leave. Griffiths buried his head in a paper as they went past. The Syrian stayed looking out of the window, then there was the sound of a mobile phone ringing and he took one out of his pocket. The language switched to Arabic.

"Yes, all okay. I have been introduced to the chap who ferries the kids. He's picking me up in half an hour. No not yet. I have to persuade him. How are things over there? Did you get hold of the stuff on the list? Okay. Keep it safe and keep it dry. Is there any unusual activity? New people moving in next door? Different cars parked outside? Anything like that? Okay, we have six days. Make sure you keep in touch with the others. Change the password every day. Don't call me again on this phone. I'll call you. Hopefully the day after tomorrow. Bravo."

"Six days, thought Griffiths, that was cutting it fine. The only consolation was that if the Syrian didn't make it, if he realised they were on to him, and they had to act before he met up with the others, at least they would have him in the bag, but that wouldn't stop the plotters, and even Guantanamo Bay tactics wouldn't persuade the Syrian to talk. Now that he knew the timespan, he could at least head back to Fougères, drive slowly and wait for Pierre to overtake him.

He'd heard from Jake that the couple had planned to meet up with Vic in Fougères and travel with him to the boat after their meeting with the priest's aunt the next morning. They had her address. He hoped it had gone well.

There were two kinds of evil, he thought. The priest used children in the most sickening way for his own benefit. The Syrian would slaughter randomly, in the name of Allah, in a desire to rid the world of infidels, no personal gain on earth, but perhaps a place in paradise. Both twisted cruel bastards, he thought, and hoped Allah would be on the side of the angels. How on earth had religion become so terrifyingly disparate? The cause of so much conflict on this beautiful planet?

Travelling along the A84 nearly two hours later he began to feel uneasy. Pierre's van should have caught up by now. If he lost him he was stuffed but unless the tracker device had come adrift, he shouldn't lose him. He put his foot down and decided to park just outside of town to wait. It was getting late. He knew where Vic usually stayed for the night. Maybe Pierre would get in touch with him. There was no signal from the device now. What the hell had happened? By midnight when there was sign of Pierre or Vic he decided to check into a small hotel and pray that Pierre and the Syrian would show up sometime the next morning. By noon the next day he had no choice but to go to the rendezvous where Vic was to meet the others and pray that there was news of Pierre.

Jake greeted him as soon as he walked into the Café de Paris. Griffiths ushered him outside. "Problem," he said. Pierre is with the Syrian somewhere but I lost them.

He had promised him a lift to Fougères. I'm pretty sure that the guy intended to find a way onto the boat but somewhere between Cherbourg and here, I lost the track. Is Vic about? What time are you due to meet?"

"He was here when we arrived. He's inside with Kate. Pierre is due in about fifteen minutes. Take it easy. I don't think Pierre knows where the boat is moored, come to that neither do I so they can't go without us."

"What you again, Mr Griffiths? Is there no escape? I thought you had business in Cherbourg," exclaimed Vic when they walked inside.

"Yeah well you know how it is. I'm back and have to get home soon. I've also lost my baggage with my passport so I may have to throw myself on your mercy and cadge a lift."

"Really! Well I'll have to check with Spike but I think it'll be okay."

"That's great thanks. Any news of Pierre?"

"No! He usually checks in I but haven't heard from him today He's overdue here anyway. Kate was just telling me that they met up with the priest's aunty this morning."

"Really," said Griffiths, looking out of the window. How was she?"

"Well if it hadn't been for the neck brace and dislocated shoulder," replied Kate, aware that Griffiths wasn't listening, "it would have been fine, then of course when she pointed the shotgun at us we decided to leave."

"Excellent," said Griffiths, standing up as a battered

van drove into the car park. "I'll be right back."

Vic also got up to leave and Jake put his hand on Kate's shoulder. "I think one or two problems have arisen," he said. "I'm going to have a word with Griff. Going to tell him that you know what's going on. It'll make life a bit easier for him. We'll probably have to bring Vic in from the cold as well."

"Okay, but please remember what we are here for. I'm not a spy catcher."

"How would you feel about staying here on your own? I'll sail back with the others and fly back here ASAP. You can eat French food and do a bit of shopping."

"No chance."

"Well I'm sorry, you might have to. The boat is going to be overloaded. Just hang fire and I'll explain later."

The van that had arrived was not Pierre's. Griffiths was becoming extremely worried and was pacing up and down. Vic came back inside. "Dunno what's the matter with Griffiths. He seems very edgy. I've told him to ring the embassy in Paris and report it. How can a grown man lose something as vital as a passport when he's abroad, I can't imagine?"

An hour later Vic saw the familiar shape and plate of his friend's van. "At last," he announced. "He's here."

"Is he alone?" Griffiths stood up and made for the door following Vic. They arrived at the van together. Pierre slid out holding his hand over his face. He was alone.

"Mon dieu, Pierre, qu'est ce que se passé?"

Pierre was clearly unsteady on his feet. "Bloody British drivers. Sorry I'm late had to make a detour through Villedieu-les-Poêles yesterday. We then stopped at a parking spot off the motorway, and as we drove out, some idiot with GB plates came round a corner on the wrong side straight into me. I smacked into the wheel. No airbags on this car. The Brits were shaken but okay. Police had to attend and they insisted I went to accident and emergency. That's why I'm late, sorry I couldn't call because they whisked me away and I left my phone in the van which thank goodness is still driveable, just a bit bent."

"You said we," interrupted Griffiths quickly. "Did you have a passenger?"

"Yes a young Syrian. He disappeared as soon as the police were mentioned. No sign of him when I got back to the car. Not a problem really. He'll be okay. He speaks French fairly well."

"Gosh," said Jake, "did he tell you where he was going or anything?"

"He never stopped asking questions. He's mad keen on boats and water sports. Wanted to know the best places for mooring boats. Wanted to know where the people I was meeting would go to get back to their boat. I'd mentioned that I was picking you up. I said I had no idea. Which is the truth of course. I said it might be in several places on this coast." So where is it, Vic, where are we heading this time L'Aberwrach? Sablon? We should get going."

"L'Aberwrach this time. The crew of one decided that was best today, and with twenty knots behind us once we're aboard we should be home in no time at all."

"Did you happen to mention that particular place to him?" asked Griffiths.

"Yes that and two others: St Malo and Sablon. Is that a problem and if so why?"

Griffiths got up, took out his phone and walked outside.

"Vic looked puzzled and shook his head. "There's something going on here, Jake. What should I know?"

Jake raised his eyebrows. "I think you are going to be told, mate. Just stay cool."

Griffiths came back looking less anxious and sat down. "I've told Pierre to get himself home. He's had enough for today. I'm hiring a large car to get us where we want to go." He turned to Vic. "Vic," he said, "please listen carefully, I need to explain things to you. There is something going on which could have very serious implications for our country. I work for the government. My frequent visits to The Stables have absolutely nothing to do with that. I am genuinely buying a boat, which will in fact belong to Her Majesty although she'll never know it. What goes on there is of no interest to me, I promise. I am in fact able to protect you. I have cottoned on to what you Spike and Pippa get up to and I see no reason to interfere. Good luck with it." Vic waited for more.

"The young man Pierre picked up in Cherbourg is known to us through our intelligence sources. He has plans, Vic, that could result in a significant degree of carnage back home. He has to get to England and meet up with a group of like-minded individuals who are planning a bomb attack at a time and a place where maximum damage can be done. Somehow he knows what you do. He will try to get aboard the boat and that is precisely what we want him to do. We need to know where he is and who he is meeting with, so that we can take the whole group of them."

Vic was silent, staring at Griffiths and trying to take it all in.

"He seemed to be such a nice kid. I can hardly believe this. Tell me what you expect me to do. I can't think straight."

"Well to begin with, resist telling Spike. I know that is difficult but we don't know how he would react. There's nothing he can do to help. Tell him when it's all over if you like. That's up to you. I suggest not. As I have said you face no interference from me and I meant it."

"All right. Okay, but what do we do now?"

"We wait. I have put people on the alert. Those three possible places will be watched carefully. As soon as he shows, we'll be back on his trail again. We've made it difficult for him. Is there any way he could identify the boat?"

"He knows the name Sophia and he knows the colour

stripe and he'll look for a Union Jack."

"Okay, well all we can do is wait for news. As soon as he's spotted he'll be tracked. If he goes to St Malo and Sablon first, then we know he'll be on the way to L'Aberwrach and we can get there before him. Is the skipper likely to stay on board? Could you get in touch and ask him to go ashore at some point. Give the Syrian a chance to get on?"

"Er yes. He will have re-fuelled already but I could ask him to go to a tabac and pick up some fags for a lady I know who loves Gitanes. That's no lie. I daren't go back without them. I'll tell him I forgot to pick them up and don't want to stop again."

"Good. Now assuming he gets aboard, where would he hide?"

"There's a hidden compartment below decks but he'd never find it. I suppose he would hide in the shower until we got going but he's bound to be found at some stage. He must know that."

"My guess is that he'll have some sob story and beg us not to take him back. People want to kill him etc. and couldn't we just drop him off somewhere, which of course we will agree to. We can moor offshore and let him swim for it once we know security is in place. Do not mention Pierre. As far as he knows Pierre is still tied up with the police after the accident."

Griffiths turned to Kate. "Jake tells me he's spilt the beans and that you are happy to come aboard. Would you prefer to stay here and get a plane home?"

"I could go off you, Griffiths. What kind of a wimp do you think I am? The only thing that would stop me going with you is an appearance on the scene of Francois Tellier and I suspect he is just as dangerous as Ali Baba, if not more."

"Ali Baba?" enquired Griffiths.

"It's the name I dubbed your Syrian, when I gave her the rundown," said Jake.

"Ah you mean Mustafa. I dare say he has more names, but let's stick to Mustafa for now. If Tellier shows up, Kate, I guess he is far more dangerous to you as an individual. I'm sure Vic and his crew of one and myself can cope without him but at the same time it would be good to have him aboard. He's a better actor than I am. The only other option is for me to ask the contacts I have here to keep an eye out for Tellier and keep you informed. It's up to you."

"Well I have to get back really by whatever means. I think Tellier's visits to his aunt are sporadic. It could be weeks before he shows his face again. I'm waiting for the enhanced images which might give some indication of what he looks like now, but until we have something to match them with, the case is on hold. We did make progress though and I'm pleased with that."

"Yes indeed. He's another poisonous threat to mankind. Once this thing is over, I will be happy to take some leave and help you, if you would let me."

"Thank you, Griff."

"Dick"

"Griff – Dick sounds derogatory."

"Okay. I'll tell my mum." They both laughed.

Chapter Twenty-three

Back in England Pippa's article had been published and was getting results. Two letters had been sent anonymously to the paper commenting on the home and the suspicions that had been aroused during the years and months before it had closed.

One reader who had not identified himself reported that a teenager who had done gardening for him, had seen strangers in the place late evening and through a window had seen a man holding one of the smaller boys by the back of the neck, propelling him along a corridor. The boy was crying. The older boy had hammered on the window and the man had hurried away. The following day the teenager had been reprimanded and put in what they called the glasshouse, by the priest for two days. There was food and water but no books, TV or visits from friends. No views from the windows. The only light came through the glass roof. Solitary confinement was not nice.

Another message came in from one young man, now twenty-eight, to say that he was willing to talk, for a reasonable payment. He suggested one thousand pounds. The paper refused the offer. Making payment was too risky. For any sum at all, people on tight budgets might just remember things that didn't actually happen. The recollections had to be genuine and voiced for the right reasons, to punish the perpetrators and to exorcize the guilt and misery that the survivors had had to bear. Should a prosecution result from the information received, appropriate payment would be considered.

The day after Jake and Kate had left for France Pippa received a call from the editor. "We have something. It sounds genuine. Can you come in after lunch?"

"I'll be there at two."

The Gazette offices were as usual busy with clerks and contributors tapping furiously in front of computers, abandoned coffee cups and papers all around them. Thankfully it was no longer a smoke-filled hell. Smokers were personae non grata and the few that were left huddled from time to time just inside the open back door when it was raining or sat on the surrounding wall when it was not. The dustbins were surrounded by cigarette ends, which had just missed the opening that gaped between the rim and the misplaced lid.

When she arrived, the editor, Grubby Ted (a nickname due to his insatiable lust for printable scandal) told her to take a seat and thrust a printout of an email at her. "Cop a load of that. It'll make the nationals if we give them a chance."

She read

My name is Curtis Reynolds. I live in Australia but became aware of your report when my father brought back the newspaper after a visit to the UK.

I was born in England. I was taken away from my mother when I was ten years old. I did not know my father. My mother was a drug addict. I was a resident at The Sanctuary for four years until a couple of months before it closed.

I was regularly abused by the priest, and other men who visited the home in the evening. I was not the only one. It was something we learned to live with but, looking back now, I am filled with revulsion. After the home closed, I was adopted by my uncle. He had left for Australia to work before I was born but came to England to find his sister. She told him about me, and with the help of several agencies, he found me. I could not have been luckier. He has been father and friend to me. I studied at the university in Adelaide and I am now a qualified oceanographer. I love my work and I am proud of what I have achieved. Recently my father visited England again and brought back the newspaper, which featured your latest article. It brought back so many memories. I remember them so well, those men who used us and hurt us. I will never forget the face of the priest. I do not remember Joey. I must have left before he arrived.

In his memory I would be glad to come to England and assist with your enquiries. While I consider myself to be a lucky survivor and am proud of what I have achieved, there must be young men, not as lucky as me. They should receive help. They deserve support and compensation. I would like to see programmes put in place which would

*make it impossible for such horrors to occur again. I have
no hesitation in giving you permission to print this letter.*

Pippa sat back in silence after she had finished reading. "We need to publish this in its entirety. He doesn't mention any names, except Joey's so we should be safe enough. If that doesn't persuade them to come forward nothing will."

"Better run it past the police first, I suppose. And tell him we will pay his fare."

"Yes, I'll call Knowles right now and hopefully it'll run tomorrow. But he has a point you know. Could we launch a programme, a mission so that it could never happen again? Make all homes, which are responsible for the health and welfare of these children, publish the measures they take. Make sure there are regular, unannounced inspections. Why are there not already such measures in place? There's even a Minister for Children, isn't there?"

"The Minister of State for Children and Families, yeah, responsible for protection of children from sexual exploitation amongst other things. It's been in place since 2010. It may have been introduced as a result of stuff like this. Stuff that was kept very hush at the time. When, if, we publish this letter we can challenge its efficacy. Keep the buggers on their toes. I suppose the comforting thing is that most of what is crawling out of the woodwork now is historical. Nowadays it's vulnerable immigrants that are being exploited – girls. Maybe we should do something on

249

that."

"Yes, well we can't put the entire world to rights," said Pippa shortly and left to call Knowles.

The man himself was considering an email he had just received from the chief superintendent.

"With regards to the investigation into The Sanctuary case which you have seen fit to resurrect. I have no recollection of making any payment to the home or any members of staff. I can only assume it was for a good cause. If at any time you unearth evidence that might jog my memory, I would be grateful if you could contact me immediately. I think, however, that after all this time that would be unlikely

Since I am not in good health, I have decided to take early retirement. I will be leaving my post at the end of this month. Should I find any documentation in my records which might assist you, I will get in touch.

You know that I know all about you, you slimy bastard, thought Knowles. You're going to slink away and keep a low profile and hope to God this will die a death. You think I have absolutely no evidence that might point to you, and dammit you're right. But it's not over yet.

Just then his mobile phone vibrated. He didn't recognise the number. "Yes," he said shortly.

"Hello – DCI Knowles? It's Philippa Hilton. I think we have a witness."

"Philippa!" He sat down. "Tell me more please. I need some good news right now."

Philippa read the email from Australia. "Read the bit about never forgetting the faces please. Read it twice out loud and then forward the email to my address. Have you heard anything from Kate?"

"She's made progress. She's met his aunt. He visits her from time to time. Auntie doesn't have a very high opinion of him and will contact Kate when she hears from him again. I think they have plans to track him but I have no idea how. She sounded confident though. I'm not sure whether she'll be flying or sailing back."

"Oh well, no doubt she'll remember to tell me at some stage. Thanks again, Philippa, for the good news. Best thing that's happened all week. You'll pay for his airfare I hope, but please get him over here as soon as, okay?"

This deserves a celebration he thought to himself after he had received the forwarded email, and I know just who to celebrate it with. He called Jill Irving. "Fancy a pie and pint, darlin'?" he said in his best cockney.

"Honestly, Charlie, I'd much rather have smoked salmon and crusty brown bread. Pies and pints are so bad for the waistline. Pick me up at seven and I'll give you a good time."

"Will that involve removing my underwear?"

She laughed. "Not till we get back to my place."

They had been out a couple of times without so much as a peck on the cheek, but they laughed a lot and he could tell she enjoyed his company. He had lost weight and was feeling much better for it. Jill was auditioning for a part in a new TV cop series and picking his brains about policing, although from what he had seen of TV police dramas, they bore little comparison to the real thing. To begin with, the females in his squad, with the exception of Kate who was stunning, had thick ankles and moustaches. Some of the guys were prettier.

It was while he was getting ready for his night out that he had a call from Ava Blakey. She had been in touch from time to time just to keep him posted. There had been little in the way of information about other names on the list. One is managing a football team in Peru and the MP had died. Others had been traced but were reluctant to help.

"Hi, it's Ava. Just a bit of news. The coroner at the time is now living in Edinburgh. He called me. He is willing to come down, seemed eager actually, but not till next week."

"Ava – this is turning into my lucky day. Things are progressing. The super is claiming to have lost his memory but I have a feeling that soon I will be able to jog it in a big, big way. He's leaving by the way."

"Yes, I just heard. Good riddance. His successor is a really nice guy. Good cop too."

"Excellent! Keep in touch. Why don't you move down here? We need girls like you."

"I'll think about it. Byeee."

The letter from Australia was published the following day, with the name of the priest redacted. Too soon to risk legal action for libel, but the response was immediate. Not a flurry of letters and phone calls from victims, but letters of outrage from the public who demanded to know how such appalling acts had been carried out on their own doorstep culminating in the death of a child. It was the spontaneous reaction of a lynch mob. Local television featured it too and sales of *The Gazette* peaked.

The following day, another article, in an effort to calm things down suggested that it was hoped that victims would come forward but that hysteria would not encourage them. Even Curtis might think twice if he thought he was going to be mobbed by enthusiastic supporters as soon as he set foot in the country.

He would of course be ushered in secretly until the time was right for him to appear on TV, before being whisked away to avoid reporters. With a potential witness like him, it was not simply a matter of arranging photographs. It was something that had to be arranged very carefully and Knowles would work on it as soon as Curtis was in the country. Faces could change in ten years and at this stage, he had no idea of what the priest looked like, and maybe would never find out. They were a long way from a successful prosecution of anyone at this moment in time, and maybe at the end of the day, all that they would manage to do was to put the wind up the miscreants and deter potential ones. That, he thought, was significantly better than nothing.

Kate called later that day and gave him a detailed report of the progress she had made. To have even a lead on Pious was good and he congratulated her. He was delighted to hear about the old photo and urged her to send a copy without delay. They had their own experts who would produce images of the face twenty years on.

She could not of course acquaint him with the details of their current dilemma and was unsure of whether she ever would be. She trusted him absolutely of course but as Jake had pointed out, if everyone passed on information only to their trusted friends everyone would know everything in no time at all. At the moment it was a case of divided loyalties but the Griffiths' affair was nothing to do with Knowles right now and she knew he would understand that.

*****

Dinner with Jill was followed by a return to her house in Grebe Avenue. He paused as they passed Wellstead's house. No, For Sale, signs yet but they would come. Jill had been appointed his executor and was diligently pursuing all leads that might lead to relatives. The sister, who was disappointed not to be mentioned in the will, had paid a brief visit and found nothing worth keeping in the house. A children's charity of Jill's choice would benefit and she looked forward to selecting one that Wellstead would have chosen. She also fully intended to pay regular visits to make sure the money was used in an appropriate way. She now knew the details of Wellstead's previous life and judged him simply as a man who had erred and repented.

His spiritual presence, however, was not conducive to a wonderful sexual romp and Knowles vowed to take Jill to his flat next time. It might feel a bit strange but he knew that Harriet would wish him well. He could almost hear her saying 'about bloody time, darling, I promise not to watch!'

The old black and white photo of the young Francois Tellier arrived and he looked at the young unsmiling face. It had an almost haunted expression as if he was considering something disturbing and unpleasant. Nature or nurture? Knowles wondered, having heard something of his history from Kate. Whatever had happened in his past could never excuse this man's conduct in his lifetime. He thought also of the accomplices, the men who had paid for the destruction of young lives, and vowed to find them.

He took out his phone. "Research Department please – get me everything you can on that ginger-haired bloke that's just gone out to Peru. Football coach I think – on TV sometimes – thinks he's funny. No not just his sports career – his life.

Chapter Twenty-four

By mid-afternoon it was reported that Mustafa had been to both sites south of Le Mont-Saint-Michel and had then hitched a lift north. They decided that it was time to head for Alberwich. Kate had insisted on going with them as the sea trip should get her within sight of London in less than twenty-four hours. Flying would be almost as time-consuming by the time she caught the early flight next morning. When they reached the small port they decided to keep watch for the Syrian from a small café by the side of the road that led to the moorings. It should only mean waiting for a couple of hours at the most if he managed to get lifts. Speaking fluent French would help him.

In fact, it was two and a half hours before they saw a dishevelled figure climb down from the back of a truck transporting three skinny sheep. He was scratching furiously. "That's him," said Griffiths.

"Fleas," remarked Kate. "The boat is going to be full of bloody fleas. I wish I'd opted for a plane."

"Don't be such a wimp," laughed Jake.

"Look! Guns I can handle, even crazy Syrians but the thought of my back and belly being covered in flea bites is more than I can stand."

"Enough you two," interrupted Griffiths. "Vic, are

you in touch with the crew?"

"Yes, in fact I'm about to go and meet him. He is ashore and I need to put him in the picture. It would be unfair not to. I've told him to leave everything unlocked, which he failed to understand. He is an intelligent, adventurous young man and I know he'll love this, when he knows what's happening, but I have to warn him to act naturally and follow my lead when it comes to any discussion about getting this guy ashore. We're breaking boundaries now. This is something he will not understand, unless I give him some sort of explanation."

"I understand and accept that, but there are things they must not be told. Once we've found him on board, we will 'interview' him alone. I'm sure he will come up with some persuasive story, which we will swallow whole and agree to help him. If he gets nasty, Jake and I will deal but I'm pretty sure that won't happen. He already has his story ready and rehearsed for anyone who'll listen. As far as we are concerned he is a genuine asylum seeker who needs to get to UK quickly. We will sympathize and agree to drop him off somewhere near Poole – where, is up to you Vic. We will then sail into

Poole Harbour and unload Kate and Jake. While he's here we must all treat this guy with sympathy and respect like gullible mutts, apart from when we first find him aboard of course when we will display righteous indignation. You meet the crew, Vic, and we will keep watch to see when he makes his move from here. I'm guessing he'll wait until it's getting dark. As soon as he's on board I'll signal and you can come back. We will all go aboard together. We will be laughing and chatting and talking about the trip home. Okay everyone?"

Everyone meekly agreed and Vic went off to meet with the crew and have a quick meal.

What on earth have I got myself into, thought Kate. Jake is in his element and I have to admit it's quite exciting – but this guy is planning to kill as many of my countrymen as he possibly can. Will it be easy to put that out of my mind and treat him with sympathy and respect when my instinct will be to push him overboard mid channel? Jill Irving wouldn't have a problem. She'd just adopt one of her character acts.

Griffiths took a stroll along the lines of boats. The signal would be when he saw Mustafa, then he'd light a cigarette. The others watched him carefully. Time seemed to pass very slowly. It was nearly ten o'clock when Griffiths lit up and leaned against the rail, looking everywhere except at the boat Sophie. She was an impressive sight, dwarfing the boats alongside. Nice life, thought Kate, sailing to and fro in a mini gin palace.

Not much gin on board though apparently. Beer and wine only, but hey! That could be good. She saw Griffiths light up.

"Time to go Jake!" she yelled. Let's go aboard, I'm dying for a shower and a drink."

"Yep I'm right here. Hey, Dick, are you coming

aboard now?"

"Just waiting for Vic," called back Griffiths. "Hang on he's on the way. He has the keys."

Vic appeared a few minutes later with a young man, a student from The Stables, and an experienced sailor. Introductions were made and Kate wondered if Vic had actually told him anything because he was relaxed and looking completely unfazed. She grinned at him.

"Hi, what happens if I'm desperately seasick?"

"We chuck you overboard or lock you in the boiler room with a mop and bucket, depending on the weather. Hi, I'm Tom."

The group sauntered to the boat and Jake helped Kate across the plank, Vic going ahead with the keys. "Hey, Tom, you forgot to lock up."

"I never do that, insisted Tom. "I'm so sorry. I could swear I did."

Impressive, thought Kate, he must have been told. "Look just let's get aboard I'm going to have a shower."

"Let me go first, please," said Jake, blocking her way and frowning at her. "You stay here and pour us all a drink. Please allow me to pay for some really good booze, Vic. I know you have some."

"Sure – and yes you can pay, I'll see what I can find in the storeroom." He winked and disappeared. Shortly afterwards they heard, "Hey! What the hell! What are you doing here? Who are you? Stand up."

Griffiths headed out to go to Vic's aid. Jake followed

and Kate motioned Tom to stay where he was. "Just look astonished but don't overdo it. Pretend this is an audition for The Old Vic," she whispered.

Vic came in pushing the Syrian ahead of him with Jake behind them. "Look what I found hiding in the store space. Sit down while I call the police and don't move."

"Please, please no police," begged Mustafa. "Please listen to me. My mother is dying. She lives in London. I want to see her before… I have tried so hard to get papers. It takes so long. I have a little brother. He is just thirteen. He has telephone me for help. They live in London. I am not lying. I know you are good people. You have helped people like me. Please just take me over the water. I am a good swimmer, when we are close I can jump and swim ashore."

"What makes you think we help people like you? What's your name?"

"My name is Mustafa. I speak to a man in Cherbourg. He say you with this boat, help people."

Griffiths wondered if Pierre had in fact broadcast the fact that Vic and his friends did such favours and could see that Vic was considering the same thing. You just never knew whom you could trust, but it was quite possible that the news had come from elsewhere. However much they stressed to the families that they must never divulge details of their journeys, they must sometimes be tempted to spread the news. Give hope to others. Pierre had always been discreet and was well paid for his trouble. It was unfair to doubt him now.

Kate was playing her part now.

"Oh, Mustafa, that's terrible. How old is your mother? When did she come to England? That poor little boy at home." She looked appealingly at Vic. "Couldn't we help him Vic? No one would know."

"Do you know just how much trouble I could be in if we were stopped. And the owners of this boat. I could be ruined. I just daren't risk it."

"When did you last have something to eat?" Kate asked Mustafa.

"Yesterday but I don't want to take your food."

Griffiths scratched his head. "How long would it take to get the police here, Vic? I really have to get back for that meeting. If you decide to do that I think I'll have to go ashore and catch a plane."

"Please, please, Mr Vic… no police. I just want to go and see my mother before she dies."

There was a long silence, everyone looking at Vic.

"Tom, go get ready for cast off," said Vic at last. "I don't like this at all, but I'll drop you off on the other side. In the meantime, sit down and keep out of my way. Get him some bread and cheese, Kate, and keep an eye on him."

"Good," said Griffiths. "You're a lucky chap, Mustafa, so just keep quiet. Get some sleep if you need to and I'll wake you when Vic is ready to unload you."

"Do you think he will tell the police in England and

they wait for me?"

"Not a chance. Too many questions he'd have to answer. Just keep a low profile. We're on the way."

He left the cabin to speak to Vic and Jake and Kate was left alone with the bomber. "So where do you come from, Mustafa? Do you have a passport or papers?"

"I did have. Someone took them and all my money. If I get to London where my mother lives in Lambeth, I try to get a job. I have a degree in science."

"What kind of science?"

"Chemistry."

"Well that's interesting. How do you apply it?"

Jake interrupted. "Leave the boy alone, this is no time to interrogate him. Anyone would think you were a policewoman. Go and have your shower and I'll put some supper together."

He propelled Kate out of the room as Griffiths came back. "You just can't resist digging, can you?"

"I was only having the kind of conversation I would have in normal circumstances."

"Normality is not the prevailing feature of this situation. Anyway, just don't get too close. Shower and galley in that order. Go."

Mustafa was clearly very hungry and enjoyed the goats cheese with crusty bread, tomatoes and fruit. He refused wine but drank almost a pint of milk. The boat was well under way and he seemed quite relaxed now that he had succeeded in his mission to hitch a lift to England. He told them that he lived in Damascus with his uncle who sold cars. They had a big house with gardens and his uncle had wanted him to stay. His mother had been married to his uncle's brother. She had not been popular with his relatives who thought she was too educated. Not what a wife and mother should be. She had applied for a job at an English university, he couldn't remember which, and had taken his young brother with her. From then on the family had disowned her and only Mustafa had loved her and missed her.

Griffiths who had listened to this story with one eyebrow slightly raised told them later that it was a load of rubbish. Mustafa was totally embedded with Isis. The only grain of truth was that he had studied chemistry, and developed his knowledge with the sole purpose of assembling explosive devices. At this he excelled. His mother had died in northern Syria and he had no siblings.

Griffiths had disappeared on deck to update the team in UK. They were on the way to pinpointing an area off Studland where they could let the Syrian leave the boat and be tracked by those ashore. It was vital that they didn't lose him.

"When we drop you off, Mustafa, you have two options: you can get to the mainland via Swanage; it's quite a long journey that way and there won't be many lifts available at this time of night. The alternative is to bed down somewhere and go as a foot passenger across to Poole when the ferry starts the next morning. I think it starts at about seven a.m. It takes about five minutes to cross. Once there just follow the road into Poole town centre."

"Just five minutes? It must be a short distance. I could swim. I'm a very good swimmer."

"Yes you could – no sharks there, but you would be very cold and wet which may arouse suspicions. Maybe we could persuade Vic to give you a sleeping bag. If we zip it into a waterproof case with your other belongings, when you go ashore, you could snuggle in somewhere and set off the next morning looking almost normal. From then on it's up to you. We can't help you any more."

"Absolutely not," added Vic, "and quite honestly I would prefer never to see you again."

"Yes, I know you hate me. I'm used to that," said Mustafa. You have not had a life like mine. You are lucky. but have no fear. I will leave your life tomorrow. Do you live in London? Maybe you should visit and find out what people like me are really like. There are lots of us there. Comrades in arms, always fighting to survive, we will succeed. Inshallah!"

"Yeah well, good luck, mate," said Vic and disappeared to the cockpit. There was an uncomfortable silence but, Griffiths thought, things could not have gone better. Just the right amount of doubt, hostility and acceptance, he couldn't have written a better script.

Mustafa had decided to accept the offer of a sleeping bag. They found him an old T-shirt and shorts, which he rolled up inside the sleeping bag and the whole thing was sealed inside a large plastic bag. They got in as close to the shore as they could and Griffiths gave him a torch. He slipped down the ladder and they saw him strike out for the shore, the plastic bag bobbing along behind him.

Griffiths texted the compass points to the men waiting at Studland, men with details of the torch which had a device inside it. Kate and Jake made ready to go ashore at Poole and Griffiths arranged for a car to take the three of them to London. Vic would make for The Stables and insisted that he was given regular bulletins. He didn't know how or what he was going to tell Spike, but Griffiths promised to get there before him and give him all necessary support. He was quite sure that in his place, Spike would have done the same.

Chapter Twenty-five

The clean white lines of Sophie looked beautiful against the clear blue sky. Vic had often thought how fantastic it would be, just to pile everything he had into the copious storage on this boat and take off. He'd have no problem making a living. They'd be lining up to charter this glorious lady for months at a time. He could take a crew with him, see the world – what more could a man want – well a wife would be nice, or at least a long-term girlfriend, someone like Pippa. This thought he put straight out of his mind. Lovely, but off limits. She was devoted to Spike anyway.

The time had come when he had to tell Spike what had happened in France. He felt sick at the thought. Spike may not forgive him. Time to face the music. He strolled up to the house. It looked good in the sunlight too. Pippa always had a beautiful display of flowers, not only in the window boxes but in huge wooden tubs on the old paving outside. He stopped to nip the dead head from a pink rambling rose and with no further excuse to delay matters went inside and headed for the kitchen.

"Vic. Hi," said Pippa giving him a hug. "We missed you. Come and tell us all about it. School has just started so there'll be no interruptions. Have you eaten? Let me pour you a coffee."

"Where's Spike?"

"He's taking the RYA skipper class today, they have practical exams soon. They'll need a lot of instruction from you, Vic. Especially the shoreline stuff."

"Yeah I know. Look, Pippa, things happened while I was away. I need to tell you both about it – do you want to wait for Spike or shall I give you a rough outline first. It's not good but I found myself in a situation which I couldn't handle. I wasn't really in control anyway."

"Tell me," said Pippa, sitting down.

"Well it started with Pierre's contact in Cherbourg. I'd stake my life on Pierre's loyalty, he would never knowingly betray us – in any case he has too much to lose himself, but it seems that what we do is no longer a secret." He detailed what had happened in Cherbourg and how they had eventually found themselves in L'Aberwrach. All four of them together with an extra passenger.

"So Griffiths has known all along and now a detective inspector and her boyfriend know too."

"Griffiths is no danger to us. He hunts much bigger game. He likes what you do and has no intention of stopping you. Kate and Jake feel exactly the same, but as Griffiths said, once one person discovers a secret, you may as well put it on Facebook."

"Where are they now?"

"They jumped ship at Poole and were going to drive to London. We have the advantage of knowing Griffiths' secret now. All he cares about is stopping this imminent attack and I hope he succeeds. It's a nightmare what these terrorists plan to do. He will stop them and I think he couldn't have done it without us, Pippa. Actually, he promised to be here before me. Any news of him?"

"Couldn't have done what?" asked Spike plonking himself on a chair and grabbing an apple from the fruit laden bowl on the table.

*****

It was half an hour later that they all sat in silence contemplating the implications of what they now knew. Spike had been unexpectedly sanguine about the turn of events and certainly had not held Vic responsible at all.

"This is my venture, Vic, and you have been a willing participant for which I will always be grateful. We knew what we were doing, and it may be a good thing if we stop for a while. Pippa's already giving me grief for not including girls here anyway so we might have to consider a totally new strategy. I hope Griffiths will be in touch soon so that we know whether or not we're looking at immediate arrest. From what you tell me, Vic, I think that's unlikely. I think he's on our side and I think Kate and Jake are too. You never know they might give us a few tips. Nobody likes to see kids suffer. As for the information leak, as you say, it could be anyone, and I simply refuse to believe that the folks we associate with would have done it out of malice. Trouble is, too many have got wind of it. Maybe we could find a less risky way to help. Bring 'em over lawfully and house them somewhere decent until the paperwork is done. Get lawyers onto it. Some of them may just work for free."

He gave Vic a friendly hug and said, "What you did, Vic, was spot on. I would have done the same myself and I'm proud to be your mate."

"Group hug," said Pippa and they did.

"You know what! It's exciting I can't wait for Griffiths to get in touch. Just think, we've had a spy in our midst for months. I wish I'd known. At least we know it's not drugs or diamonds now."

"Yeah! I quite liked the diamond theory though. There's no way he can just abandon the boat build either. He'll have to go through with it or pay massive compensation to keep us quiet."

*****

At that moment, Spike's mobile signalled a call. It was Kate.

"Hi, Spike. Just keeping in touch. Is Vic back safely?"

"Yea, we're all here in the kitchen discussing the rather strange turn of events. No of course we're not angry with Vic. He handled things perfectly. Hopefully we have nothing to fear from you." A pause and then he laughed.

"What?" said Pippa.

"Kate is saying that the only thing we have to fear from them is a serious assault on the wine store when they next come up. They're home now."

"Anything on the latest situation?"

"Nothing that she can talk about on this line but as I understand it, all did not go according to plan. Griffiths will be up tomorrow if things are back on track but it seems like the fox evaded the hounds."

"Oh, no. That's serious."

"Well Kate seemed to think they have eyes everywhere. She said Griffiths didn't seem as devastated as she felt.

"All he said was that she must take on board the fact that they have stopped countless plots like this before, that nobody even knew about, and they knew enough about this to have things in hand. Whatever he's up to, he ain't sharing it."

"Why would he be coming up here though?"

"We'll just have to wait and see, won't we?"

"Did you ask her about Pious?"

"Oh God. What will she think? We've been totally distracted from the whole point of the trip. Did they make any progress, Vic?"

"Well I saw them off and on. To tell you the truth, I was so surprised when Griffiths turned up, I thought of little else. They disappeared the day I arrived and were going to an address that someone had given them. They were quite excited, and then the next morning we all met up to go to the boat, and they said they had been to see an aunt I think –not their aunt, Pious's. We didn't talk about it on the boat what with this Mustafa bloke getting on board. I don't think we talked about anything else. It was weird. We were all acting our parts and trying not to put our feet in it. After he went ashore and we headed into Poole harbour we were still just discussing that. Griffiths didn't say much because he was waiting for reports from ashore. Quite honestly, I was glad to see the back of them when they went ashore. All I could think of was what I was going to say to you two."

"I'll give Kate a call later when they've had time to settle in. I expect she'll spend most of today telling Knowles all about it."

And so she was. Information was flying back and forth across Knowles's desk. Put it all together and progress had been made. Contact with Curtis had resulted in a booked flight the following week, which would coincide with the attendance of the retired coroner who seemed to be looking forward to the meeting with a mixture of dread and relief.

"There are things I need to get off my chest," he told Knowles, "things that are going to upset at least one high ranking officer but I'm naming no names right now."

"Very wise," agreed Knowles. "We will proceed with caution, trust me."

Kate had given a word for word report of the meetings in France but was vague as to how much the local force had assisted. They had not, in fact, at all. Griffiths' contacts and Jake's fluent French had been all that was needed but if the French Special Forces came up with the whereabouts of their target, she might just have to take Knowles into her confidence and she couldn't do that without implicating Jake.

"You seem to have achieved so much," he was saying." We might just have a success story here. You bring back the priest and I'll line up the witnesses. That would be so bloody good, Kate. What a partnership."

"Never mind all that, more importantly, how's your love life?"

"It's fine. She's really clever you know. I had a call the other night and a woman told me I had won a trip to Las Vegas. My name had been selected by an American company. She sounded just like a Yank. They would give me a thousand dollars and pay all expenses. All I had to agree to was one thing. I was so excited, I would have agreed to almost anything until she said I had to play the tables stark naked, then she giggled and I realised what was going on. She said if I had agreed, she would dump me immediately."

"Sounds just your type. I'd love to meet her again. We should arrange a foursome."

At that point, Kate felt her mobile vibrate in her jacket pocket and she found Griff displayed on the screen. Hell, I can't talk to him now, she thought. I'll give him a clue.

"Hello! Detective Inspector Meredith here." There

was a silence then a voice, which was not Griffiths' but one, accented, and sounding familiar said, "You police bitch." There was silence, then there was the sound of a muffled shot and then again silence.

Kate, too stunned to speak sat frozen on her chair.

"Kate, Kate, for heaven's sake, Kate, what is it?"

"I'm sorry I have to go. I have to get Jake."

"What? What's wrong I forbid you to leave until you tell me what's wrong."

But Kate was already in the corridor phone in her hand calling Jake as she headed for her car.

He answered immediately – "Kate?"

"Jake are you in touch with Griff? I think he's been – hurt. You need to get in touch with whoever he works with. I'm on the way home. Just do it." The line was cancelled and she knew Jake was immediately doing whatever they do when one of their kind was in trouble. The traffic was heavy but she did everything to get back quickly. Jake was talking on his phone as she entered.

"Hold on," he said to it. "Look I'll call you back directly. You know where I am."

He looked at her. "Okay. Tell me." It didn't take long. "Have you told Knowles anything about this?"

"No I just left."

"Well maybe it's time to. We might need him."

"He saw I was shocked. He might turn up."

"If he does – leave him to me, please."

"What do you know, Jake?"

"I know that Mustafa got to London Waterloo long before we did but they were waiting and he was spotted and tailed. You already know they lost him in London but they know what they're doing they have various systems in place. There would have been five or six of them following and changing places. They have cars and mopeds and whatever they need. He headed for Oxford Street by tube and then dived into John Lewis. He went up to men's clothing and that's where they lost him. Probably grabbed a different coloured jacket and went into a changing cubicle. They weren't too bothered because they have tabs on some of his associates and knew he would make contact with them at some stage. They were all watched and of course facial recognition cameras were placed up and down the street anyway. Griff had called in to say he had picked up the trail, the others all got that and were converging. They know where he is right now – at least they know where his phone is, but now they also know about your call. It may be 'man down.' I pray that it isn't. All you and I can do now is wait."

Kate went and sat down in the garden. She had sat in the car on the way to London from Poole, sleeping for a while and then considering the two men in the front seats of the car: Jake with his tousled hair and intense blue eyes, and Griff, with his athletic frame, short hair and face that reminded her of Rudolf Nureyev. Straight nose, brown eyes and sensual lips. Quite pretty really, she thought, and wondered, "Could I?" and then, "Yes I think I could – but wouldn't – probably." She had got to know and like Griffiths and hearing that shot had shocked her to the core. She had been incredulous when he had reported that Mustafa had slipped the net in London.

"After all that bloody pantomime on the boat, you go and lose him?" Jake had turned and glared at her. Is that how they lived, these real-life James Bonds? Could she deal with that whenever Jake disappeared for a few days. He said he spent most of his time in front of a computer, but having seen him with Griff, the way they interacted, she realised that Jake had not been entirely truthful, for her sake.

Jake came outside. "Well his phone is somewhere in the middle of the Thames I expect. There's no signal from it. Hopefully he isn't with it. Easy to dispose of a phone, but I think someone would have been in touch with the police if they'd seen anyone heave a body in. Someone is coming over to collect yours by the way to see if there's any way we can trace the call to you. We can get an area and possibly tie it in with the people we know are involved. I'm not giving up hope, Kate, but now that he knows you're a DI it's not going to help Griff. They'll know it was all a set up."

"Oh God, Jake. I was sitting there with Knowles. How could I know I was speaking to one of them.? I just did it to warn Griff that I couldn't say too much."

"Of course you couldn't. Don't fret. What we need to work out is why they chose your name to call. Think –

what could the reason be?"

"I can't think. I was slightly more sympathetic than the others. He knew I lived in London, he asked where. I was telling him about the garden. Then I realised that I really didn't want him knowing where he could get hold of me so I told him it was in Lambeth. He seemed to know the area. He asked if it was near the War Museum. And I said it was closer to the Palace – Lambeth Palace, and he said, that's not too far from the Houses of Parliament. He seemed to like that idea."

"Interesting – this from a man who has never been to England before. He seems all too familiar with the area. I need to call this in. We have about four days left to pinpoint the target. Do you think he would pick up the fact that you recognised his voice?"

"How could I know? I'm not even sure now, but it was my immediate thought. Even before the shot. It was the way he pronounced the P in police, more like a B. But I wouldn't bet my life on it."

Minutes later Jake came back. "The area fits in with what we know. If you look on the aerial view on the computer it shows those two buildings, south of the river with Parliament buildings to the north. Did you mention any road?"

No, I haven't a clue about the road names."

"Okay, well there'll be surveillance all round there. He'll definitely want to go and take a look. Maps don't give you the right details. I suspect he'll be looking at

Westminster."

"What about the Abbey? Four days takes us to Sunday. There's always a huge congregation. What better target than a Christian church full of infidels. Wait a minute, he asked me about it."

"About what?"

"The Abbey. What was so special about it. Was it not just a big church? So I told him about the coronations and weddings and everything I knew. He got bored after a while and changed the subject to football."

"Look, Kate, I have to go out. Will you be OK?"

"Can I come with you?"

"No, but I promise to call in every half hour. If Knowles turns up, you're going to have to make something up. I'll let him know all he needs to know when I come back."

"I don't want to lie to him."

"Well don't. Tell him you've discovered something highly confidential about a colleague of mine that you are not able to divulge at this stage. He'll respect you for that. You can promise him that it is not police business, which is true."

"Is this what my life is going to be like with you Jake?"

"Yes. Get used to it or go and marry an accountant." And with that he left.

·

Chapter Twenty-six

When Knowles did arrive he was full of concern for her, but accepted her reason for not explaining fully. He had studied her face intently and then changed the subject.

They discussed the situation in France. Kate was suitably vague about the source of their information and inferred that she was waiting for updates.

"Well unless you have successfully seduced the entire Gendarmerie, we seem to have had some extraordinary strokes of luck," he remarked. "To have stumbled upon the address within twenty-four hours was remarkable in itself, and then to meet the aunt. Well! good luck indeed. Tell you what, Kate, you stop treating me like an idiot, and I'll promise not to ask any more difficult questions. I wasn't born yesterday and I'm guessing that young Jake has access to intelligence that is denied to us at this stage in the investigation."

Kate sighed. "He'll be back soon. It's up to him to explain. Most of the time I'm as much in the dark as you are. In the last few days I've learned just how difficult it is not to reveal sources even, without having my fingernails pulled out with pliers."

"Don't worry. I do understand and I admire the fact that you're sticking to your guns. That's not to say I'm not mortally offended by your lack of trust. Just kidding," he added hastily

There was no news from Jake for the next four hours. Knowles had had to leave, promising to return to see Jake the same evening "But if you see your way to telling me on the scale of ten, assuming the pointer is now at five, whether it is going up or down. Up being more serious, I would appreciate it."

"Yes, but I'd put the pointer up to seven right now, not five."

"Oh dear! I wish I'd kept that gas mask. See you later, love."

When Jake did get back. He had nothing much to report, except that one of the known contacts did live in a basement flat in Lambeth. According to an aerial survey, there was a garden at the back, with a gate that opened into a narrow lane. The gate was padlocked. The garden had walls at the side and back and was quite secluded. Just inside the wall at the end of a neglected lawn was a substantial wooden shed with water and electricity. The adjacent terraced houses were occupied, but enquiries had already been made to see if it would be possible to place agents with cameras, upstairs in one of them. People seldom refused this kind of request, excited by the thought of being involved in a police investigation, especially if they were sworn to secrecy. In no time at all a couple of 'students' with large rucksacks were greeted at the front door, and were ensconced immediately behind lace curtains in a back bedroom with very expensive cameras. Nothing to report yet except that the occupants of the basement flat next door were not inclined to be friendly with their neighbours and had gone out of their way to avoid any contact with them at all.

By the time Jake came home Knowles had returned and was enjoying a beer in the garden. They were about to go out and join him when Jake took a call. Kate waited expectantly.

"They have just bundled someone in from the lane," he reported. "They were able to park just a yard or two away, he was in a wheelchair and they had a struggle getting it, and him, through the back gate. They had to hold him up as if he was unconscious, or… The neighbours say, they have seen deliveries being made at night from the lane but they thought they were bags of logs or coal. There's no easy way of getting heavy stuff through the front door so they thought nothing of it."

"Do you think it's Griff?"

"I don't know," he snapped.

"Well for heaven's sake get in there and find out," said Kate. "Just do it. You do realise that if anything bad happens to him, it's my fault and I'm going to have to live with that for the rest of my life?"

Jake was silent. for a while deep in thought. "Hell! I wish I still smoked. The worst part of this job is waiting. Losing touch with colleagues. Knowing that at some point, you could have gone in and pulled them out. Against that is the choice of saving all kinds of people from being blown up by terrorists: burglars, rapists, paedophiles, fraudsters, mothers, fathers, children, angels, demons, who knows? But when you sign up to do this job, you accept that it's not for you to judge. Most people, Kate, are decent. Just like you and me, it is for them, that we do what we have to do. If Griffiths is dead, then that simply is a product of this enterprise. He would accept that. At the same time to, I have to tell you that I am longing to get into the car, drive to Lambeth and get him out. Right now."

"So let's do it, Jake. He's our friend. I'll come with you. If we go in with enough support, they'll have to abandon their plans."

"They'd kill him straight away. That way at least they would have achieved something, we'd take out some, but others would take their place. All we can do is hunt them down and then wait. Each time we bag a few we gain a little more information, which just might help to prevent the next one. It's like a bloody production line. These people are like Pious on a massive scale. They destroy not one child, but as many as they can in one go. Their motivation is incomprehensible to us. Don't worry, this group will be stopped, even if some get through the net. We've stopped them time after time. That's all we can do, but it never ends."

He paused. and clapped his hand to his head. "Oh dear, Kate, I'm sorry I didn't tell you immediately, but I do have good news for you, about France. He's been spotted – Pious. They told me earlier and I was so worried about Griff that I forgot. He's been seen at Le Mont-Saint-Michel. He got a job looking after the horses. They have horses ferrying people from the coach station to the island. He looks different. Short hair, with beard, smelly and dirty."

"So life isn't all bad – gosh, I've gone all weak at the knees. I've got to tell Spike; in fact I'll go up there tomorrow. Knowles is in the garden. Go and talk to him while I get in touch with Pippa. Jake, please please, keep in touch with me while I'm away. All this is horrific. I thought some of the things I've had to deal with are pretty upsetting. My colleagues get hurt from time to time, but not like this."

"Look, give me half an hour to talk to Charlie…"

"Call him that and you might regret it."

"Tough – I always think of him as Charlie – he'll have to get used to it or I'll insist that he addresses me as Mr Scott."

Kate sat in the kitchen and scrolled through her numbers until she found The Stables. Spike answered and she told him the latest news about Pious, not mentioning Griffiths.

"At last. This is amazing, Kate, I can hardly believe it. Are they sure it's him – sorry! Silly question. I'll fly over tomorrow. Vic will come with me. What about you?"

"I'll meet you there. I'll fly from London City. We need to plan the approach. I need to sort out an arrest warrant and hope to arrange for it to be executed over there. The timing is difficult and we may have to wait a while before we move in on him, but at least we know where he is and we can keep tabs on him. Evidence is in short supply but we have two potential witnesses lined up for interviews in a day or two."

"I know, I know all about that and it's encouraging, but I don't want him to give us the slip."

"He will have no idea we're on to him, don't worry, but I understand how you feel. I'm as anxious as you are to get this in the bag. I'm about to book my flight. Hopefully we'll meet up tomorrow. Will Pippa be with you?"

"No someone has to keep things under control here."

"Sure well I might not be on my own. Knowles is insisting I take a plain-clothes with me. I have met her. She's bright and capable and from your neck of the woods. I'll be booking two singles at the Castle in Fougères, and it would be good if we're all in the same place. Vic knows it, so see you tomorrow. Keep in touch."

Kate went into her bedroom to pack and then went out to find both men looking serious.

"Anything new?"

"No. Your boss in concerned about you though and wishes you weren't so involved with my stuff."

"Well I am. Nothing will change that. It's quite exciting in a horrible sort of way. You know what? I found myself saying my prayers just now. Remember DC Petrus, when we thought he'd been shot. I prayed then and don't think I've done so since."

"Did it work?" asked Jake.

"No," she said shortly. "Well, yes in a way. Turned out he hadn't been shot at all. The gun was fired and he fell and didn't move. The shooter ran off and by the time we got to Petrus he was sitting up mopping his brow. Not a scratch. I could have slapped him. We were so worried about him, that the perp got clean away and as far as we know is still armed, dangerous and laughing."

"Really, Kate, that is simply not true. We got him the next day and he was in the Scrubs within the month as you know full well."

"Yes, well there's nothing like a bit of embroidery. Has he told you about Lambeth?"

"Yep and we're discussing the possibility of putting a van of armed officers in the vicinity. If they decide to go in and rescue this friend of yours, which I think is the right thing to do, we'll have guys picking up the dross."

"If it was my decision I would be on the way, but I have to wait."

"It's Griffiths op, isn't it? Who takes over if he's down?"

"It's a decision taken by the Head of MI6 and a government minister. And yes, it might be me simply because of the degree in which I've been involved so far. I have been trained you know. Look I'm going to the office. They will decide, based on the number and nature of likely casualties. We can't just rush in. If Griff is alive, he's a hostage, so his survival is in the balance anyway. You'll just have to wait for news. I may not be back before you go." He hugged her. "Be careful and call me when you arrive and at every stage later."

"I promise. I can hardly believe that just over a week ago we were sitting in the garden out there without a care in the world."

"Well it could have stayed like that if you hadn't been so bloody curious about me."

"Stop making everything my fault. Go."

"Any more lager going?" said Knowles helping himself from the fridge "You know what, Kate, there's too much bloody secrecy between services. We have to have our chaps patrolling all the hot spots and then when there's a disaster, we find that there was intelligence that pointed to the possibility of exactly that situation. Jake feels the same way. He and I discussed ways in which we could be poised for trouble without causing panic, or pre-warning the terrorists, and I realise how crucial that is, and how careful we must be, but we're not complete idiots."

"Some of us are though. I've met uniforms that wouldn't reach fifty on the IQ scale."

"Yes I know that, and it's up to us to make sure they are the ones that do the dumb stuff. There's a place for them all. In my view, the ones we should concentrate on training, are the ones who have some sort of clue about the reasons for this religious war, because that's what it feels like. I suppose the Crusaders had the same idea and they committed plenty of atrocities. We have quite a few Muslims in the force and they make excellent coppers; if we had a few undercover we might make some progress."

"But that would make them feel like they were spying on their own, wouldn't it? which isn't fair. It sounds like the kind of prejudice the force has been accused of before. I guess we have to set aside any signs of seeing a difference. We're all just coppers."

"Yes and we're all just people but some of us – and please note I say US, are terrorists, and most terrorists these days are Muslims, and while I appreciate that all Muslims are certainly not terrorists, the facts are inescapable."

"Can you imagine what would happen to one of our Muslim copper friends if he was sussed? If they realised he was spying? We'd get a gory picture of them chopping his head off. We're doing the best we can. I just wish we had Griffiths here. I can't bear to think of what might be happening to him. What with his captors and people like Pious, religion rears its ugly head, with different labels. If there is a God, I'm sure he didn't mean it to be like this."

"You know, Kate, when I was a kid, there weren't any Muslims. Everyone was British, Catholic or Protestant. Every Sunday I went to church and sang in the choir. There were only four of us, and admittedly when we weren't singing we were reading rude comics and sometimes there was a competition to see if we could insert a daft word into the hymn. You know like 'Gladly the cross-eyed bear' but the word terrorist only applied to other countries like the Mau Mau in Kenya. There was no knife crime and kids behaved themselves. Mind you I did live in a village which was off the map and everyone was related and the vicar came to tea."

"Yes, well maybe your nice civilised family protected you from real life. I'm not all that much younger than you, and I remember plenty of horror stories. What about Myra Hindley? It's all about diversity these days. Variety is the spice of life and we should embrace everyone. Don't forget, the priest is half British."

"Yeah, well it must be the French half that decides what he does."

Chapter Twenty-seven

By the time Charlesworth and Jake met to discuss what was known, unknown and the possible developments of the situation in Lambeth, Kate and Ava were on their way across the Channel, having caught an early plane to Dinard. They were to pick up a car at the airport.

Jake was waiting at the North gate of the Abbey where there is wheelchair access when Charlesworth approached with a uniformed officer.

"Jake this is a member of the Westminster Police Department. He is fully aware of what goes on here and will be happy to help you any way he can. I've given him brief details. I'll leave the rest to you."

The men shook hands.

"This may be theory. We are working with what we know. Can you tell me this: how many visitors come to the services in wheelchairs, and do you or your chaps recognize the regulars?"

"There are usually two or three. Getting here with a wheelchair is complicated and I think regular churchgoers prefer other venues. Give me time and I'll get what information I can from the other officers."

"As soon as you can please. We only have three days. What I suspect may happen is that a chair will arrive with someone who may appear to be asleep. He'll be well bundled up. Can you forewarn your team, that if that should happen, find an excuse to detain them. One of my chaps will be hanging around at every wheelchair entrance."

"This the only one."

"Okay I thought so. How many services will there be on Sunday? If my theory is right we should be able to give you the wink when they're on the way, but just in case, be prepared for trouble at any time."

"If you know as much as you seem to, why don't you move now."

"Because one of my men is probably being held captive by them and I really would like to make sure he survives if I can."

"Understood – that must be awful."

"It is. We've had our eyes on this bunch for some time. Intelligence indicates that there is something likely to happen on Sunday and this is the likely venue. If my colleague hadn't got himself nabbed, I think we'd have enough to arrest about nine of a group right now, but somehow he was rumbled. I think he may be the one in the wheelchair. He may already be dead, hopefully not, but he is almost certainly needing medical attention. They've probably kept him drugged, but alive. I think a corpse would be smelly by Sunday!

"If they succeed in what they plan, a lot of people are going to be blown to bits. I guess one of them has been chosen to go to Paradise. He'll be the one pushing the chair. One thing I promise you is that they will not even get close to the Abbey itself. That's a risk I wouldn't consider for a second. We will move before they get close, whatever the cost. What I'm trying to do is to make sure there is nothing that might suggest that we're expecting them but there are so many ifs.

"IF they use my colleague by putting him in a wheelchair with a bomb round his waist and chest. IF they park in a place where we can pull up behind and in front of their vehicle. IF we can identify the vehicle they're going to use. IF whoever is going to press the remote button can be disabled before he has the chance. The list goes on."

"Right. What I'm going to do now is contact all of this division. There are about forty of us, and if anything significant comes to light you'll have it within an hour. Let me show you the room I use as an office here, when necessary, and we can meet there."

"Can I speak to whoever is on duty right now? Just to get a feel of what it's like at the busiest times, who if anybody they search and so on."

"Yes, well as you know, we don't allow suitcases or rucksacks in. We sometimes search handbags, but not all of them. You do get a feeling about people, but you can be so wrong. Better safe than sorry though.

"Most people are understanding, especially after some of the incidents we've had in this country lately. Come with me and you can talk to the two inside the door right now."

By the time Jake had spoken to the policemen on duty, a plan was taking shape in his head. He had to create a diversion to draw the crowds away from the Abbey entrance, and for what he had in mind, he first needed approval and then he had to source some unusual participants.

What he had learned from the staff was, that apart from the familiar wheelchair visitors, there had been one last Sunday, who had been unloaded from a van with a ramp, in a temporary parking area close by.

He had entered through the North door and the van had been driven away. From the description it was clearly not Griff, and in any case last Sunday he had been miles away. It was a man, awake and conscious, wrapped up in a rug over a puffer jacket, which seemed strange as it was a hot day. One of the attendants had asked if he would like to leave his jacket. He had looked confused, apparently not understanding, and his companion had explained that he always wore it outside, hot or cold, had shrugged, grinned and made a gesture to indicate that the wheelchair-bound person was a bit loopy.

He loved this building, the carer had explained, and he wanted to hear the singing. The staff had seen him parked at the end of an isle and given him a hymn book. Strangely, after about ten minutes and before the hymns had started, he was pushed out again, and as they emerged, the van drew up again.

"Could they have phoned for it, do you think?"

"No one is allowed to use mobiles in the Abbey during a service. It is strictly forbidden and as far as I know, no one did, but I'll ask the others."

A trial run thought Jake. The van as far as staff remembered had been dark red. It looked as if it had once had a different coloured flash down the side but that had been painted over with a similar, but not quite the same colour. Useful stuff. He contacted the team and instructed them to watch for it and report any sighting in the vicinity of Lambeth Road. Then he headed for London Zoo.

*****

Kate had met Ava Blakey at London Airport and they had landed safely at Dinard and picked up the car. They had already established that Spike and Vic were at the Castle Hotel and arranged to meet for a late lunch. Of the group it was quite possible that Pious would recognize Spike and Vic, even after such a long period of time, so the exploratory trip to Le Mont, would be made by the girls alone. Having made the introductions, Kate took Spike aside to tell him about the latest developments back home. He had been horrified to hear about Griffiths and agreed with Kate that not knowing what had happened to him made everything so much worse.

"He could be suffering as we speak, or dead

somewhere. Do you think they would dump him in a place where he was likely to be found, or just keep us guessing?"

"Depends how their minds work. On the one hand, if he remains missing they must know we'd go all out to find him which might cause us to reveal ourselves. That could be useful to them. On the other hand, if they dumped his body somewhere, we'd be tempted to go in all guns blazing and take out all the bastards we know about. I don't think they'd risk that. It would be my choice but I do tend to be impulsive. I didn't like Griff much at first but after a while I realised what a nice guy he is, and brave. When we were travelling home from Poole and he received the message that Mustafa had given them the slip, I was incredulous. After all that performance on the boat, all that planning, but he just took it in his stride. He absolutely trusts his team and won't accept any criticism. Sure enough they picked up the trail and I think they have him in their sights again. I'm going out of my mind because I'm the one gave the game away. They had his phone, dialled my number and I promptly disclosed that I was a cop. I thought it was Griff calling."

"How could you possibly have known? Don't beat yourself up, Kate."

"That gunshot is still ringing in my ears."

"Look – put it out of your mind for now. Easy to say I know, but we have to concentrate on our target. What's the plan?"

Ava and I are going over there this afternoon. It gets

pretty crowded and it's a good time to go. We have to locate the stables and make a big fuss of the horses. We're going to say we are journalists from an English Country magazine who are preparing a holiday supplement and Le Mont-Saint-Michel is a big feature. How to get there, where to park, how much it costs, the walk to the Castle from the car parks, the alternative horse and cart trip, how the horses are treated, the fact that they have to walk backwards and forwards all day, poor things, and what their conditions are like at the end of the day. We have our ID badges and an impressive camera. Hopefully Ava likes horses. They terrify me, but I suppose I'll have to put on an act. They have such bloody great teeth."

"Take some carrots and they'll bite them instead. Wear gloves. Come on let's see how Vic and Ava are getting on. I think he fancies her!"

"Hey that's good She's unattached at the moment and Vic is just her type."

"Really, how do you know that?"

"He's a man, he's attractive and he's funny. I wouldn't mind myself if it wasn't for Jake."

"So the scars wouldn't put you off? I think he's a little self-conscious about them."

They make him look more interesting. Tough. Although I know he's not – he's a softie, but no – the scars are okay. Women don't like pretty boys, Spike. They like real men and there's nothing wrong with battle scars."

When they did find the other two, they were arguing

about the merits of the tenor sax over the alto and hardly noticed the arrival of Spike and Jane.

"We have to go, Ava, we need to get there at about six when the horses go home."

"See you later," smiled Vic and suddenly anything seemed possible.

*****

Predictably on a sunny Friday Le Mont was seething. They parked in one of the designated parks and took a ticket from the machine. "So where do we pay this 6.50 euros when we want to get out? There's no machine."

"Later," said Kate. "Come on, let's catch a horse They're over there, look, and they're just moving off."

"Stop. Attendez Deux autre passagers." They ran across the grass and the carriage stopped Two more passengers meant another 15 euros in the pot. They climbed aboard, and clutched the seat in front as the horses jerked into motion.

"Tell you what," said Kate, "I'm no horse whisperer, but if I was, I'd advise these poor beasts to make a run for it at the earliest. They look so unhappy and tired, and just a little bit thin."

"I don't think the French are known for their love of animals. They shoot garden birds. We'll take pictures and have the animal welfare people check them out as soon as we have what we need. If we do strike lucky and find

Francois we can try to get him in one of the snaps. Proof that he is here, for Spike. Mind you, we'd have to tie him down to prevent him tearing across here to wreak revenge. That mustn't happen. It has to be done properly. Arrest and trial with lots of publicity and then a long, long prison sentence preferably in a prison where they'll make his life hell."

"Actually, he'd have to be kept apart, I think. nonces get a rough time that's why they are 'Not On Normal Courtyard Exercise'- it's an acronym."

The trip took twenty minutes and they climbed out close to the stone steps into the battlements.

"It's pretty impressive," said Ava, "and quite beautiful really. I'd love to see it without all these people. Imagine it, empty and quiet. It's lovely."

"Never mind that go and make a fuss of the horses. Ask what time they stop and I'll find out where they're stabled. Here, take this carrot."

Ava approached the horse drawn carriage and spoke to a tour guide who was standing nearby and accepting tips from his audience with a smile and a handshake. "Excuse me, but do you speak English?"

"Like a native, I'm from Clapham. How can I help?"

"You're hired! Stay right there while I grab my friend."

She motioned to Kate who was busy taking shots with her camera. Nothing significant. Just trying to look the part.

"Kate, this is er…?"

"Simon Oakley," he said. "Welcome to the Mount. Is this your first time?"

"You mean, some people come more than once?"

"Mostly staff. What are you up to?"

"We work for a magazine and we're doing a 'Visiting France' edition, so it's just useful info really."

"Great! which magazine? *Horse and Hounds.*"

"Countryfile," replied the two simultaneously.

"Shall we start again, after you've sorted yourselves out?" He grinned.

"What time do you go off duty?" asked Kate.

"About now. I'm about to take the last ride home."

"Right! Can we come with you? Where do you live?"

"I have digs in the village at the end of the causeway. This is a holiday job. I'm reading French at uni and we're expected to spend summers working over here to perfect out language skills."

"Sounds like you're doing okay. Can we buy you dinner? I noticed a selection of hotels as we came in."

"That would be nice. I usually just buy stuff to take home but a good dinner would be very welcome. They do a nice steak and chips with salad."

"How very normal," observed Kate "Nothing exciting then. Nothing that might persuade me that the French reputation for fine cuisine is merited."

"Nah. You have to go to Paris for that. Let's go I'm starving."

They sat in the bar of a nondescript hotel, and explained as far as they could, what their mission was.

"We believe that a witness to a pretty nasty crime that happened more than ten years ago in the UK, is working over here. He is French but was working in England at the time. He does speak English very well. When the offence occurred, he disappeared. Probably frightened that he'd seen something that would make him a target. Someone might want to shut him up. Hence the subterfuge. We didn't want to frighten him off. Recently we've obtained evidence that has caused us to reopen the case. If I show you an enhanced picture, can you tell me if you recognise him?"

"Sure, of course."

Kate had three enhanced photos; she produced the clean shaven one first. He looked for a while and then shook his head. The second photo showed a man about fifty to sixty with a beard and glasses. Simon looked longer this time. "Have you one without the glasses?"

"Yes here."

"Well he does look familiar, but the guy I'm thinking of certainly doesn't speak English. He's a raggy old tramp who looks after the horses. There's a stable near my digs in the village. It's over an old wine cellar. I think he squats there. I see him sitting on the ground outside smoking fags. He's a miserable sod. I always say Bonjour or Bonsoir – the French always do, but he never responds."

Kate felt her heart pounding in her chest and saw that

Ava was trying to suppress her excitement.

"Well look," said Kate. "We're all starving, let's eat. At least we tried, and maybe if we walk home with you, we might take a look at him just in case."

"On her lap, Kate pulled out her mobile and sent a text to Spike, *'Bingo'*.

Chapter Twenty-eight

All Griff could feel was pain. Every part of his body felt as if it had been beaten. He could smell urine but didn't care if it was his own. He felt wet and cold from the waist down, and knew he was lying on a hard-cold surface. There was no light, although sometimes there was light, bright light. He was drifting in and out of consciousness. From time to time cold water was poured into his mouth. He half choked but some went down. He would gladly have died, but sensed that someone was making sure he didn't – not just yet anyway. He didn't bother to wonder why he was there or how he'd got there. All he could think about was the pain.

He became aware of some man sitting near him. "Are you okay, Mr Griffiths? Comfortable? Probably not, but don't worry, it won't be much longer, then you can go and meet the angels. We have such plans for you. We would like some of your friends to see you go. Detective Inspector Meredith would enjoy it, I'm sure. Seeing you go out in a blaze of glory, and Victor too, but I'm afraid we can't send out invitations, just photos, later perhaps. Here let me give you something to ease the pain and then you can enjoy the story more."

Griff felt a sharp pain in his arm and then all the pain

faded away. He tried to sit up but couldn't move at all. He was paralysed, hopefully by some drug or other. Now that the pain had abated, he desperately wanted to live. How the hell did he get here? He knew this man, he thought. Concentrate – he tried to clear his mind.

"Let's see how much you remember," went on the man. "Do you remember the boat the other night? Not so long ago. There was you, and Vic, and Jake and the woman. The woman who said she lived in Lambeth. The woman who was a police officer? – a liar. You were all good at lying, Mr Griffiths, I was completely fooled, but Allah enlightened me and now I am here, you are my prisoner, and I am telling you the truth."

Griffiths closed his eyes and tried to make sense of what he was hearing. The names. Spike his colleague, was he captured too, and Kate, Jake's girl? Was she hurt? He tried to ask, to form words but couldn't even his face seemed to be paralysed.

"The boat, remember the boat, the voice went on. We crossed over to Poole and you let me swim ashore. You made sure I got ashore. Why was that, Mister Griffiths? You knew who I was, why did you let me go? I think I know now. When I was on that train to London, a man came into my carriage. He took no notice of me, until we got to a station, Winchester I think it was. When I got off he did too. And when I got again, just before the train moved, he did too. He didn't look at me, but I know the tricks you see, so I was very careful when I got off. He didn't follow me of course, but another man did, then he stopped and another one took up the chase. I am so used to the tricks you see. All I did was to look relaxed and happy, until I darted in a shop, grabbed a bright red jacket and hood and darted out again having changed in the gents' toilets. I stayed in there for twenty minutes. This is the story of my life, Mr Griffiths, always dodging, and I always get away."

Griffiths managed a nod. Feelings were coming back and so was the pain, but slowly.

"At that time, I thought the woman was genuine, gullible. When I took your phone I saw her name. It was Kate, wasn't it? She told me she lived in Lambeth. I thought she might be useful. She seemed to like me. I thought her place might be a useful bolthole, but that was very stupid of me. Easy to be wise after the event, isn't it, Mr Griffiths? She identified herself when she answered your phone. She thinks you're dead now. She would have recognised the sound of a silenced gunshot. That muffled thump. Maybe I'll get her one day, but only idiots waste time on revenge, don't you think, Mr Griffiths?

"Do you remember how I seized you? That was so satisfying. Perfect. There you were in Lambeth Palace Gardens. I was following you. I knew where you would go. You had no idea I was there. You were following one of my men, dressed to look like me, wearing the tracker you hid inside the sleeping bag you gave me when I left the boat. I found it and discarded the bag in Poole. I know how to disable those things, Mr Griffiths, and how to enable them again. You were following him and I was following you. Isn't that just brilliant? Your face when I tapped you on the shoulder, you looked so surprised. I felt great having bamboozled one of MI6's best spies.

"So now we're even, you must agree, but you're out of the game now, Mr Griffiths. It'll soon be over. They must be looking for you but we're laying a false trail. They won't realise that until they pick up the pieces."

Very slowly, Griffiths was beginning to understand what was going on. The pain was subsiding and his memory was coming back. He knew there was little he could do and the chances are that he would not see his friends again. But there must be some part he was intended to play otherwise why keep him alive. His head throbbed and he tried to concentrate on what he could remember. Anything useful he had heard or seen since the confrontation in the gardens. They had been under one of the arches under the railway when Mustafa had taken his phone. He hadn't heard the conversation but remembered the bomber taking out a pistol with a silencer and firing it into the ground. The pistol had been pointed at him first, the man's face full of fury, but he had turned away at the last minute. From then on nothing was clear. He had been bundled into a car parked nearby and after that it was hazy. Why was he still alive?

He remembered that his team had established Lambeth as the meeting place. As far as he knew they were still there. His recollection of a short drive before he was half carried into this place indicated that they hadn't been wrong about Lambeth. He knew there must be people out there watching and trying to work out what was going on, probably from next door.

He realised that his phone would no longer be giving out a signal but thought it possible that they'd know where he was, and would be doing everything to save him; he also that knew that if the worst came to the worst, he would be expendable. He hoped not to die but he had loved his life and regretted nothing. He thought of Kate Meredith and how attractive she was. She must have said something that gave her away when they had called her number. She must have thought it was him. Why wouldn't it be, then the shot. He would have loved to call her and say, 'Hey! I'm fine. Don't worry.'

No time for such things now. He had trained for situations like this. What could he do? What could he use? Why were they letting him recover from the drug? They must be expecting him to do something. Had they left a phone? Nothing like that in sight. Was the door locked? He pulled himself toward the door and could just reach the handle – locked! Window? Painted over with white paint. Could he scratch a message in the paint? If so what? He knew bugger all that might help and if they noticed they would realise they were being watched by someone close. He hoped they were. They were laying a false trail, why had he been told that? Was it because they wanted to taunt him, knowing he was helpless, or did they expect him to pass the message on – confuse everyone? He wished he could think straight. The best and only thing he could do now was to recover as much as possible. He began to move his limbs, loosen his joints and clear his head.

*****

Not too far away, Jake was facing am equally difficult dilemma and discussing the situation with a colleague. "Let's assume they have very little knowledge of what we actually know. All they do know is that we clocked Mustafa, but the fact that we were waiting for him in France gives them some idea of how we work."

"I don't think they know we have people next door to them. They would expect us to go in hard and fast, but they must know that we have some idea of why he came and who is likely to help him."

"I think we must assume that they suspect that we've worked out their target or at least the area that they're likely to hit because the last signal from Griff's phone came from somewhere near here and a bomb in or near the Houses of Parliament or Big Ben would be such a coup."

"Griff is their trump card. They might not understand it, but they have learned that we put a higher value on human life than they do. You're right, as soon as they have achieved their goal, he will be of no further value to them. Hopefully they'll take him with them as a bargaining chip if things go wrong. Then we'll have a chance."

"If they think we know their target, surely they'll abandon it?"

"Only if they absolutely have to. If they think they can fool us they will go ahead."

"They know enough to realise that they can't just pack up and go home. We'd simply wheel them in. They will assume we know where they all hide out. The only thing they can do is what they're here for or lose face. They will blow something up and hope to get away with it in the furore. I still think the original target is the one that they'll go for. The Abbey is an international symbol. I suspect the bomber will try to get away. He's useful alive. The others are just fodder. We need to take them alive of course if we can."

"To begin with, we will ostensibly focus all our efforts in the wrong places. Visible defences round the Eye. Close the Visitors' Gallery in the H of P," he said to his team. "Security around the Abbey will seem to be as normal – uniformed officers outside, and undercover guys just inside the door. The public will be there in droves on a Sunday. Once they're in we must have teams to usher them straight out of another door if there's any risk. They'll have to keep the organ playing so things outside seem normal."

"Just to stop people gathering round the entrance I'm arranging a diversion, something that will draw them all away, but not look at all like a security measure."

"What's the diversion?"

"If I told you, you would never believe it."

"A naked woman doing a Salome dance?"

"Close! I'll tell you. I know a guy who was at uni with me. He was a great traveller and worked with David Attenborough for a time. He was mad about animals, got involved with all sorts of crusades. A few years ago he was in Turkey. At the time they used to have dancing bears in the street markets. I think it's against the law now. Anyway, he rescued a young bear and got him back to England. There was a problem because it was so tame other bears wouldn't accept him. They had to put him in a cage on his own for a while, and every time they gave him some food, he would do this little dance round and round. His keeper absolutely loved him and couldn't resist training him to do more steps, side-to-side and so on. He was clearly happy and healthy too. His coat became shiny and its eyes clear – a perfect bear.

"Anyway, it's something that you never see here, but with the permission of the RSPCA and as a charitable event, Bruno is going to do a little dance on the green outside the Abbey, well away from the entrance. He'll be on the end of a strong silver chain just to be on the safe side. There will be posters up the day before, an RSPCA van in attendance, and of course three keepers. The kids will love it and it will draw the crowds away from the danger area. There'll also be an ambulance, and that's where you'll be, waiting for Griff with a bit of luck. There will be armed officers in the RSPCA van. They will only make themselves known if there is a serious problem and the public are at risk.

"Here's a list of things I want you to do. With as little fuss as possible. Get onto BBC and get them to broadcast the following: The London Eye and the Houses of Parliament will be closed on Sunday for repairs. All tube stations in the vicinity of Westminster to be warned of a possible threat. Close the end of Lambeth Road at the first set of lights but leave the end leading to Vauxhall Bridge open. None of that till Sunday morning. If they're watching TV that might fool them. Everything round the Abbey must look normal and the dancing bear will make it look even more normal if you see what I mean. No Brit would risk the life of a wild animal if there was any risk even to its fur!

"Now we need to go and get some rest. Keep me apprised of any changes or problems."

*****

Griff was beginning to feel stronger when the door to the shed was opened and two unfamiliar figures came in and pulled him to his feet. He was dragged and half carried into the house where he was placed into an armchair and given some coffee. They didn't speak. There was no sign of the Syrian.

More comfortable now he lay back and thought of what he knew about Mustafa. Born to a middle-class family, he had gone to study sciences in Saudi Arabia at the King Abdulaziz University. In Riyadh, Osama bin Laden, whose mother was also Syrian and was a distant relative, had also studied there. He had made a great impression on Mustafa who had followed his career in Afghanistan with great interest. He too believed that Sharia Law was the only thing that could put the world to rights and destroy the ways of the western world. He too believed that all citizens from western countries, including women and children, were legitimate targets for Jihadists. When Bin Laden was captured by the Americans, and killed, Mustafa was outraged and swore that he would spend his life, avenging that death. Violent Islamic extremism was his reason for living. While he was an expert in providing the right kind of bombs and planning the best targets, he went to great lengths to avoid capture. He needed to survive to carry on his work. He tended to stand aside and watch the mayhem and carnage that resulted from his skill and planning.

This as far as Griff knew was his first UK venture. Following two different incidents in Germany and France they had miles of footage which was scrupulously analysed and had revealed one man at both scenes. Information gained from various other captured suspects, who were not as enthusiastic about an early Paradise, had helped them to build up a picture of this man, and there had been various other sightings since. Griff had studied that face so many times that when he had turned up at

Calais and was believed to be heading for Cherbourg, it was just a matter of getting there first.

Griff had discovered the venture at The Stables months before and decided that it could be used to his advantage. He had chartered a boat a few times making trips that he just as easily made by other means, and found it a very useful way to get about quietly and relatively quickly. The boat that was being built on his behalf would be completed and paid for. The firm was aware of the ferrying of children, and quietly made sure they were legally in the UK with as little delay as possible, a fact of which Spike and Pippa were completely unaware.

Now he was stuck here without a chance of getting out and he knew that an incident was planned for the next day. He just hoped that Jake and the team would be on to it. They would know where he had been caught. Westminster just up the road would provide so many targets. This latest concern for his welfare had an ominous feel about it and he expected that Mustafa's plan would provide him with a bird's eye view, but at least it meant that they'd take him out of here.

He tried to work out what Jake would do. How he would contain it. He thought of all the likely targets and how the threat could be contained. Would they close the whole area down? Almost impossible. Jake would try to make things look as normal as he could with various contingency plans. He cursed himself for being caught. If it hadn't been for my capture, he thought, it would probably have been over by now with the plotters in the bag. He was almost certainly going to die anyway, so why risk other children's lives?

As he considered the option, the Syrian came back into the room.

"Hello Mustafa," he said as calmly as he could.

"Mr Griffiths – how are you feeling?"

"Just a little curious about what you have planned for me, and I'm quite hungry."

Mustafa laughed. "Whose idea was it to call me Mustafa? You must know that it's not my real name."

"Haven't a clue," lied Griff. "We call all terrorists Mustafa till we find out more about them. Makes life confusing sometimes 'cos you all look the same – skinny, ugly and grubby. We call the fat ones Ali, just to differentiate."

The bomber just smiled calmly. "Looks like you'll have to stay hungry," he said. "This time tomorrow you'll be in little pieces all over the pews." He glared and left.

The pews, thought Griff, the pews. Oh God the Abbey. I'm going to have to stop this somehow.

Chapter Twenty-nine

Unaware of the threat to one of the most iconic buildings in his home-town, Knowles was gearing up for the interviews he would be conducting with three men claiming to have been abused at The Sanctuary. Not one of them had described sexual abuse, but certainly physical. Knowles took the view that any form of abuse needed to be investigated and it was always possible that shame held them back. Those who had suffered not only as children, but throughout their lives since, because they couldn't bear the humiliation of revealing that they had been victims of this form of cruelty.

What he had to do was to make them feel that they were his guiding light, the ones who were part of an investigation that could result in serious criminals being put away. Give them back their dignity and self-esteem by making them feel like heroes, and at the same time, shining a light on nasty secrets, might make them feel that something beastly had erupted and gone.

Am I good enough to do that? he thought. I'm not the most tactful man in the world. Do I have it in me to be gentle and persuasive. Will I find the right words or will I forget and say, 'Oh for heaven's sake, man, grow up, show a bit of backbone', that would be no good at all. They'd just walk out. He needed Kate to be there, but she wouldn't be back till Tuesday, and even that depended on him.

In France, a court would only give authority for a European Arrest Warrant if a National Warrant had been issued and was based on sufficient evidence to charge. At the moment Kate was kicking her heels in Fougères waiting for him to provide her with what she needed to get a warrant issued over there. She was worried that Tellier might just move on. Now that they had found him, speed was of the essence but international warrants were something new for him so he needed to do a bit of homework. He had two chances to get things moving today, with these two guys. The coroner wasn't due till Tuesday, and he was more likely to land the super in it than provide the evidence that Knowles wanted. The guy from Australia wasn't due till Wednesday, Kate couldn't wait that long. If he had nothing today, he would tell her to come back. It was up to Spike whether he stayed or not but Knowles was seriously worried that Spike might take matters into his own hands. Vic had more sense he thought. Hopefully, he'll keep the lid on things. How, he wondered, am I so convinced that the priest is guilty? I have the recorded deathbed statement of Wellstead, which at best is persuasive. I have the evidence of Gambler which didn't amount to much, and that's about it. The letter from Curtis was hearsay at this stage, but he could come up with the goods when he arrived.

Ideally, what he wanted was for someone to come in

sit down and say, 'It was about ten or eleven years ago, the priest at The Sanctuary whose name was Francois Tellier, (he was the only priest there) on several occasions took me to a room pulled down my trousers and raped me. I kept struggling and saying no no stop I do not want this.' Actually, just once would be enough although several times would increase the sentence. Getting a witness to state that without prompting or suggestion was difficult but not impossible assuming it or something like it, was true of course.

What he needed was a night out with Jill Irving who always managed to put things into perspective, but he had the coroner to see first. Sam Cartwright had spent hours of overtime tracing and interviewing men now aged seventeen or more, and had come up with two locals who had reluctantly agreed to be interviewed as long as their names were not made public. Knowles would be interviewing Mr Smith and Mr Jones.

"They're pretty reticent," Sam said. "It's clear something happened but they don't want to talk about it. It was only when I said to them both, 'You have kids. What would you think if they'd been hurt in any way? Wouldn't you want to get the offender punished? How would you feel if you were told that someone knew about it and didn't want to talk?'

"'I'd find the bastard that did it and kill him with my own hands', had been the response.

"'Well that would be pretty silly but I can tell you feel

314

strongly about it. Look, we can get him sent to prison for years if your evidence can convince a court that he – well I'm not going to put words into your mouth. You need to tell me what happened to you, or what you know happened to others and you can only know it, if you saw it. What others have told you won't help – that would be hearsay – we need to find victims, so they can come to court and tell it for themselves. The more witnesses we have the better. If we can find them and if they talk, he'll go down. And believe me, he won't be happy there. He'll have a very hard time'."

"Oh dear," interrupted Knowles. "That is a tactic which we try to avoid. All we are concerned with is getting suspects to court. After that it's up to the jury and judge, and then the prison service. Promising them gory retribution just might persuade a witness to exaggerate. If they're seen to do that in court it destroys their credibility. Don't think I'm not grateful to you for your efforts. I really am – it's just a word of advice."

"Yes, Guv, sorry. I know what you're saying it's just that I'm still sore about Crowther. I accept that the crash probably was an unfortunate accident. I've spoken to the accident investigation officers and I accept that it was a genuine accident, but it wouldn't have happened without that phone call and he was a good mate."

"Yes I know, and talking of that phone call from his secretary, the coroner she assisted, is due down from Edinburgh Tuesday and your two guys should be here any minute. I promise to keep you in the loop, now go and take a break."

"Yes will do. I'm meeting Simon's wife this evening, which will be nice. She's understandably interested in this investigation and well, we enjoy each other's company." He smiled and left.

It would be nice to think that something good would come out of this situation, he thought. His relationship with Jill was promising but nothing was guaranteed and the private lives of cops often suffered because of the pressures they were under these days. Twice as many police on the streets would halve the number of offences committed.

The interviews of the two potential witnesses had been timed so that they didn't have the chance to sit in the waiting room and compare notes. The first came in looking very apprehensive and then after the usual handshakes, sat down and fidgeted with his glasses.

"This is so difficult. I'd never spoken of these things ever, before your sergeant came to see me. It brought it all back, the feeling of disgust for myself. Why did I let him? I could have punched him, bitten him done anything to stop it."

"How old were you?"

"About eight."

"Do you have children – boys?"

"A nine-year-old."

"Imagine an eight-year-old; a little boy with no dad to

run to. No one to protect him."

"My lad knows I would beat anyone who hurt him, black and blue."

"And who did you have to protect you then?'

"No one."

"Exactly! From what I have learned about the regime there, it was without warmth or any kind of love – any kind of concern for the children – an absolute disgrace."

"Matron cared about us, she was kind, but she was scared of Pious. He was evil. She was meant to sleep there to look after us at night but sometimes he used to tell her to go home, that he would take over. We all dreaded that. We knew that it was going to happen."

"How often did it happen – every night?

"No no, sometimes there would be weeks between. We used to hope it was all over."

"Did it happen to all the boys?"

"No there were always about three of us. Some of the others were bullies, horrible boys. We used to hope that they would be chosen but I think they would have made a huge fuss. They were quite strong. It was only the timid boys."

"Can you tell me when you're ready, what used to happen, at those times to you?"

The man breathed deeply and put his head in his hands. His voice was muffled when he spoke but Knowles did nothing to interrupt. "Some nights, the priest would come into the dorm and tell one of us that we would be sleeping in a room next door to the sickbay. There was only one bed in the room. I remember him coming in, and holding my breath, praying it wouldn't be me. Sometimes it was of course. He would take me to the room and tell me to go to bed, then he would disappear. He locked the door. After a while I would hear the key being turned in the lock and a man would come in. Not always the same man, and then it would happen."

"Was the priest with him?"

"No never. The men used to lock the door then."

What was described to Knowles, was rape or serious sexual abuse. It varied from time to time. At the end of the description the man was in tears and Knowles had no idea how to comfort him, but offered him a large scotch from a bottle in his desk. He had one himself.

"Thank you," he said "that was so helpful and I can't tell you how desperately sorry I am that it happened to you. Rest assured, I will do my level best to trace these visitors and make sure they themselves feel the disgust and humiliation that they inflicted upon you. All I can say to you now, is that you have survived with courage and dignity and you should be proud of yourself for having the strength to come here today. I am in your debt."

The man took a deep breath and shook Knowles's hand. He managed a smile. "You know what?" he said. "I feel better than I have done for years. It's like I've recovered from a sickness. I'm glad I came and if you need me to give evidence, I think I will." After he'd gone,

Knowles stared at the wall and considered whether there was enough there to charge the priest. Not yet he thought. Hopefully the next one would be better, but if it was the same he'd have to rely on the coroner. Bloody hell, he thought, even Curtis might be a let-down if the same sort of thing happened to him, but he did mention never forgetting the priest's face. There must be a reason for that.

The second man's story was almost a duplicate of the first but there was just one detail that the first lacked. The second man had sneaked out of the dorm one night, when the first had been taken to the single room. He had seen the priest lock the door, and leave. The key was in the lock. He was about to dive over to unlock it when he heard footsteps on the stairs. He saw a man and the priest approaching and dived back into the dorm just in time. He heard the door being unlocked and then locked again as the priest went downstairs.

It's all beginning to look like something decidedly unpleasant, thought Knowles, as he accompanied the second man to the door and strolled with him into the car park. They stopped to make sure that Knowles had all necessary details for future contact when a large black car drove up and the superintendent climbed out. The second man has just turned to walk towards his own car when he stopped short. The Super had strolled past and was opening the office door. The man's face had paled. He stood still and clasped Knowles's arm as if for support. "Did you know he was here? Did you do this on purpose?"

Suddenly Knowles understood. "No I didn't. Are you saying you recognise him?"

"It was him? A policeman? A policeman who did that to me? I can't believe it. I would know him anywhere. He hasn't changed. He looks just the same apart from his clothes. He used to wear jeans and a jumper. I need to get away from here please."

"Calm down."

"But he might recognise me."

"I'm sure he didn't. He hasn't changed but you have, you're a man now. He didn't even look at you." Knowles looked at the camera over the door. They were well within range. That had been the best kind of confrontational recognition – spontaneous, unplanned. Hopefully the speech would have been recorded too. Things were definitely looking up, but was it enough for a warrant for the arrest of the priest. Not yet. But it was worth a try. He had the dying declaration of Wellstead, which just might pass as evidence rather than hearsay, which without any doubt pointed the finger at the priest. He had the statement of the second witness today who had seen the priest show a man to the room where the first man had been locked. That together with the first man's evidence would surely be enough for a warrant. He certainly had enough to charge the superintendent but that could wait for a while. That was something he wanted to savour once he had made it watertight. Perhaps another interview.

He took out his phone to bring Kate up to date. She

agreed that there was enough to issue a warrant for the priest's arrest and he promised to fax it over with all the primary evidence so far. "Have you heard from Jake?" she asked. "Have they found Griff? I just can't get through to him."

"I've not heard a thing. I guess if there was any good news about Griff you'd be the first to know," he replied. "But I do know that Jake is up to his eyes at the moment. He'll be in touch as soon as he can I'm sure. For the time being, he's doing his job and we must just get on with ours. How did you get on with Ava?"

"She's great, good company and an astute detective. I couldn't have got this far without her. She must be back by now though. By the way, could you get all the stuff on the priest translated into French please? Without Jake I'm struggling with the language."

"Will do. Keep in touch."

"You can rely on it," she replied and the connection was broken. Knowles decided to go and have another chat with the Super. If he could just perhaps persuade him to assist, even if it meant letting him off a large hook and hanging him on a slightly smaller hook it would do for now. If he revealed the fact that Jones had recognised him as an abuser, chances are that the slimy git would come up with some story, or point out that his face must be familiar to countless people because of his public appearances. The inescapable fact that the force would do anything to avoid this kind of publicity was unfortunate but inevitable. He must make sure that he preserved that piece of film, even if he only got to use it to apply pressure on the bastard. Give him a few sleepless nights. He knocked on the Super's office door and entered when invited with a smile on his face, and was the first to speak. "Hello, sir, I just thought I'd pop in and thank you for lending me Ava Blakey. The London aspect of this case has me running round like a headless chicken. I hope this will be my last visit. Did you notice me as you came in just now? I was talking to a witness. He seemed to recognise you."

"Really, well that's hardly surprising, is it? My face is well known in this area."

"Yes I realise that, but this guy has only just come back from Kuwait," he lied. "He has been working away, since you were a sergeant I imagine. He's done very well, got all sorts of engineering qualifications. Coincidentally enough, he was one of the boys from The Sanctuary. You remember Sam Cartwright? He's been doing some research for me. Actually traced two of the boys who were there. I interviewed them both this morning. They were very helpful."

There was a long silence.

"What are trying to do, Knowles? You seem to be intent on smearing my name. Whatever went on at The Sanctuary, I had nothing to do with it. Whatever you have planned, you'll never make it stick. I visited the place a couple of times when the boys were troublesome. I knew the chap who ran it – Wellstead, who was a useless, timid man who was singularly unwholesome, I had the distinct impression that he had a guilty secret. The priest ran the place and I spoke to him once or twice – that's all. I probably made a contribution to some fund or other."

"Yes, sir, expect you're right, but there's no denying that bad things went on there. Children were most certainly abused, time after time, and that probably went on for years. Don't you think that anyone involved should be named and shamed, because it was shameful? Those children had no one to turn to, no one to protect them. Most of them had lost their parents or been abandoned by them. What kind of start in life is that? Who could blame them if they turned into criminals or abusers themselves? I lied about that boy in the yard, sir, he's been in trouble most of his life. Trouble he's brought on himself. Who's to say that little Joey would have lived the same sort of life if he had survived. After all, the priest sent his brother away just so that he would be deprived of any protection. Doesn't that make you feel sick with shame? In fact, his brother has made it his mission in life to expose what went on there, and at the same time to make sure boys in his town never experience that kind of 'care' and I'm doing everything I can to help him."

Another long pause. "And this man, in the yard?"

"Come and look at what the video caught, sir. Watch his face when he sees you. We'll look at it alone, and then you can tell me what you want me to do with it." They watched together in silence and then Knowles played back the interviews of Messrs Smith and Jones.

"It wouldn't stand up in court," said Britten defiantly.

"Do you have children, sir?"

"No. I'm not married."

"Are you prepared to help me to get the priest convicted?"

"I fail to see that I can do that without…"

"Without implicating yourself. Yes, I realise that. Don't you feel any shame at all?"

"I have no reason to."

"Very well, sir, I shall just have to do everything I can without your help. I think I have enough anyway. When were you thinking of going abroad, sir?"

There was no reply the superintendent had left the room and moments later his car left the car park at speed. Ava Blakey was back in her office and greeted him with a happy smile. You seem to have put the wind up my boss. He nearly knocked me over in his haste to leave.

"Yes. I imagine he'll be going away for a long holiday."

"He's booked a flight to Jamaica. Leaves this afternoon."

"Oh well. No witness – no cry. It would have created such a storm when the newspapers got hold of it. The entire force would be tainted. Good riddance. He'd have got support from on high. Wriggled out of it somehow. How was it in France? Tell me all about it."

Chapter Thirty

Armed with the text in French of the evidence against Tellier so far, together with a copy of the warrant in English, Kate had enlisted the aid of a French lawyer.

"So this statement from the retired headmaster, Wellstead is written evidence, but he is dead yes?"

"Yes. That is effectively a dying declaration. Shortly after that recording was made, he was dead. But in the UK that should be admissible. He knew he was dying. There was no point in lying."

"And this statement from Gambler doesn't really say much, just that there were visitors to the home at night."

"Yes, but there was no one for them to visit except children and Tellier."

"What does that prove?"

"Well there are the two statements from Smith and Jones?"

"Are those their names. These statements aren't signed."

"They weren't happy about having to talk about such awful things and they wanted their identities to be kept secret at this stage."

"So you do not know whether they will come to court."

"I'm sure they will. Look, Claude. A little boy died because of what went on in that home. He was nine. His parents were killed in a crash; he was so vulnerable. Surely you want to do everything you can to bring this man to justice, he was selling little children for sex."

"Yes I know I know. It makes me feel sick, but I need to know that the court will be satisfied that the warrant, issues on convincing grounds. This is a French citizen, a total bastard if what you are telling me is true, but I have to be convinced because if I'm not, neither will the court be."

"Actually I think he has dual nationality. Okay give me time. I'll call you again later."

This is so bloody frustrating, thought Kate. Another two days before we have the evidence from the Australian guy and the coroner. Spike was getting very impatient although Vic was doing his best to keep him calm and make him see sense. He had insisted that she and Ava moved to a measly chain hotel at the edge of Le Mont-Saint-Michel, against her advice, and he was expecting them to take evening walks around the village where the horses were stabled, in an effort to catch a glimpse of Tellier. To make matters worse there had been no sign of him for the last twenty-four hours. She had tried to contact Jake but his phone seemed to be switched off. It was Sunday morning and already the place was crowded.

*****

In England it was early Sunday and Jake was aware that Kate was trying to get in touch. He daren't even think about her. There had been activity on Lambeth Road. A man had arrived with a young girl and gone into the house. Outside in a parking area was a black taxi modified to take a wheelchair. One of the back doors was extra wide and a ramp enabled a chair to be loaded with the passenger in it. The taxi made sense, but the girl? He told the team to keep him up to date with every move. An entirely redundant order, he knew they would anyway.

He was positioned in the RSPCA van to the left of the North door. Inside was the most realistic bear costume he had ever seen and half inside that was his friend who actually had rescued a bear from an Istanbul street fair. It had cost him around two hundred pounds, but the bear was now well looked after and residing at Whipsnade. He had studied it for so long that his dance was so convincingly bear-like that he had terrified Jake when 'the animal' had lunged at him with a convincing growl waving sharp looking, brown claws. "I'm sorry, Jake, but we can't possibly risk taking a live bear out amongst the public, but tell you what, we can put on a very convincing show."

*****

In the house in Lambeth Road, Griff had been allowed to sleep on the sofa, and had been given a breakfast of toast and tea, which he forced himself to drink although it made him feel quite sick.

At approximately ten o'clock Mustafa came in holding a young girl by the arm. She looked frightened. There was another man, not seen before, with them.

"Mr Griffiths, meet Mira," Mustafa announced. "She will be helping to look after you. Now it's time to get you ready." He took a large bag from the hall and carefully pulled out a length of cream linen about a metre long and fifty centimetres deep which appeared to have a series of long pockets, bulging with what Griff immediately took to be explosives. There was a small timing device attached.

"Stand up please, I want to see if your corset fits."

"Do you really expect me to cooperate?"

"Then we'll have to help you!" he shouted and the two who had been at the house throughout Griff's stay, came in. Griff knew exactly who they were and where they lived and had the small satisfaction of knowing that one way or the other, they would be seized and interrogated when this show was over.

They manhandled him into a standing position and the belt was secured around his waist, gingerly fastened by one of the men.

"Don't worry. It's safe. I have the control in my pocket, it's disabled right now. The timer will be set when we go, a secondary measure, just in case anything goes wrong. I will be waiting outside, and Mira will walk with you all the way into the church. Do not try to escape or shout for help, because if you do I will press the remote button and Mira will go to heaven with you. That would be a shame, don't you think? – a young girl dying because of you. You would die with her, of course, so you would have company in heaven, if that's where you go."

"You absolute bastard," said Griff. "She's just a child."

"She'll be fine if you behave. Her father will take her away, when the time comes. Her fate is in your hands. Right, time to go." He looked at the two men. "You know what you have to do. The others will be back here within an hour to help you to clean up here. Leave no clues. The van will pick you up as soon as you signal you're ready."

Outside the taxi was ready to load. Once in, they handcuffed Mira to the handle of the chair. Griff took some comfort in the thought that his colleagues in the office would not have been idle these last few days. They must be doing something and the fact that there was absolutely no sign of help meant nothing.

They travelled along Millbank and as they approached the Abbey, he saw crowds of people congregating near an RSPCA van. He couldn't see what was going on, but whatever it was had certainly drawn the crowds. Thank God, thought Griff, they're on it.

The taxi stopped in the parking area and the wheelchair was unloaded. The man was behind him to the left and Mira, handcuffed to the handle on the right. They headed slowly towards the North door. Griff was unable see what was happening behind him but he was sure there would be something.

As soon as the wheelchair was out a bus full of noisy students pulled up close behind the taxi and a battered blue Volkswagon parked in front. A duty sergeant went up to the front of the VW and was apparently signalling for it to park elsewhere. The driver who had climbed out, argued and then shrugged and climbed back in. The policeman waved it forward again, and it promptly shot backwards into the taxi. The policeman raised his eyes to heaven and went to the driver's door of the taxi and smiling and shrugging politely asked the taxi driver to get out so they could have a look at the damage. "It'll just take a minute, sir, we can look at the damage and then hopefully you'll be able to move on as soon as we get rid of this lunatic driver."

By this time the wheelchair was halfway to the door. The bomber furiously opened the taxi door and began to climb out, right hand on the door frame, left on the dashboard. At the same moment one of the noisy students approached, and firmly grasped his right hand. The 'policeman' took his left and in a second both wrists of the bomber were pulled behind his back. The two passengers also were pulled out of the vehicle and marched immediately to the bus behind. Jake approached and carefully put his hands in to the pockets of the bomber's jacket. He removed a device and placed it into a metal box.

By now the wheelchair was going through the North

door. As soon as they were through two men stepped forward. The man to the left of the chair was disabled and handcuffed. A bomb disposal officer came from the right. "Hi, Sid, what kept you? You'll need bolt croppers to get this girl out of danger, Sid, and there's a timing device on this belt. I think we have about ten minutes."

"Okay, no problem, bomb first though, just sit still and lift your arms up." It took seven minutes to disable the bomb by which time the girl was hysterical. Finally, the bomb was removed from around Griff's waist and taken outside. He stood up.

"Is that your father?" he said, nodding towards the man who was cuffed and waiting by the door. She nodded. Griff walked over and punched the man in the guts with as much force as he could muster. "Whoops sorry about that," he said. "It should have been harder but I haven't had much to eat lately." He took the girl's arm and although he felt quite weak, walked with her into the sunlight. The bus drove away as did the Volkswagen. Only an empty taxi remained. The public were completely unaware that a disaster had been avoided

Crowds were now surging back into the Abbey. The whole episode had taken no more than twenty minutes. It wasn't long before the sounds of the glorious choir drifted across the green and Sunday went on as before.

Griff left the girl with one of his officers with strict instructions to be kind to her and then walked to the ambulance to be checked over and was whisked away for blood tests.

The house in Lambeth Road was searched, items seized, three men arrested and the watchers in the house next door went home for a well-earned sleep.

It was with a massive sense of relief that Jake sent a text to Kate to tell her that Griff was safe and undergoing tests for any drugs they had used on him. No lasting harm was the result. If it hadn't been for Kate suggesting that the target might be the Abbey, they might not have been able to tie it all up so neatly. The sight of Mustafa furious and defeated filled him with pleasure. I don't care what happens to evil men like him. Waterboard him all you want if it prevents his planned indiscriminate slaughter and that goes for all of them.

He thought of Kate, away in France, trying to find and arrest another evil man. He hadn't dared to think of her over the last three days. He had had to concentrate, on his own situation, but now all he wanted was to see her.

Later that evening they had a long chat. She was waiting for reports from Charlesworth to reinforce her case for getting an EAW and struggling a bit with the language. She was worried about Spike and quite concerned that the priest may have moved on. He promised to fly over as soon as he possibly could, tomorrow if not this evening, but he did have things to do first.

Griff had discharged himself from hospital against all advice but was eager to be present at the interrogation of Mustafa. Up till now the bomber had refused to speak but there was always the hope that in order to protect others like him, he would attempt to send them off on a wild goose chase. It was amazing just how much truth could be detected from lies. Most of the other captives had been singing and comparing stories was quite illuminating.

The young girl was sixteen. She had been an unwilling associate of the bomber crew but had been promised a marriage to a man she loved if she assisted rather than to the ugly seventy-year-old who had offered a huge dowry for her. Thoroughly disillusioned by her experience, and the knowledge that she was expendable as far as her father was concerned, she was quite happy, almost eager to tell the Secret Service all she knew, and she knew quite a lot. A number of addresses were raided following her interview, and she was offered a new identity and an education which could lead to a university degree and a whole new life although she may have to forget the man to whom she had been attracted until he had been vetted. The service would be keeping a close eye on her for some time.

The conspirators had revealed little that the service didn't know but they would be out of the way for the foreseeable future. It was quite difficult for the team involved in dealing with the plot. They had little sympathy for detainees who would have destroyed life and limb and history. Given the chance they would have set up their own interrogation techniques which would have made Guantanamo look like Butlins and they had to supress their fury when the Americans were criticized.

Interrogation techniques such as the ones reviled in this country had prevented unspeakable carnage on a number of occasions. If some of those smug politicians had lost their wives and children to an indiscriminating killer, they might just feel differently. No we could not sink to the level of these religious fanatics, at least not deliberately. Civilian casualties during wars, when we have been on the offensive, have never been deliberate or calculated but certainly foreseeable.

Jake managed to see Griff before he packed a bag and left for London City Airport. Griff was battered and bruised but in good spirits.

"I took a few beatings," he said, "but I couldn't tell them much even if I'd been weak enough to cave in. They injected me with something which made me ramble on a bit, I'm not sure what I said, but I think it was some story we learned during training. I must have been a great disappointment, but they were at least glad to have me as ammunition. I was a bit worried towards the end that I might end up spattered all over the pews but when I saw that something was going on over on the green, I guessed, well hoped it was some sort of diversion. What the hell was going on?"

"Ha! Some of the team still think it was a real bear dancing, I honestly thought we could do that, but couldn't get it approved, not even to save your skin. After all, weigh your safety against that of a bloody bear and there's no competition."

"Quite and it would have ruined the turf. But hey Jake – thanks. Give my love to Kate. I wish I could come with you but there's the long debrief and you can't get decent sausage egg and chips in France, they're always frozen."

"I'll give your sincere affection to Kate, love might get her too excited. See you soon. I'll keep you in the loop."

Chapter Thirty-one

Knowles had no idea of what to expect when the coroner arrived but it certainly was not someone who looked like Father Christmas in civvies. The man must have weighed twenty-two stone and when he sat in the armed upright chair on the other side of the desk, the problem of how he was going to extract himself from between the slender wooden arms, did flit through the inspector's mind. There had been a noticeable wriggle to get in there. Nonetheless, it must have been a regular problem because there was no visible concern on the white-whiskered face with the matching eyebrows and beard.

"Err... jolly good of you to come all this way, Mr Morrissey. Are you comfortable in that chair?"

"Nigel... please... perfectly. Thank you, and I'm glad to be here. I can't say that I have dwelt on this matter consistently over the last ten years or so, but now and again it does keep me awake at nights. I think it would be best if you go first. Why, tell me, after all this time have you decided to probe?"

"Well, it all began with a corpse in London. There were things about it that caused us to look into his past, and that, in fact, led us to The Sanctuary, which you probably recall was a care home for children in this area.

"Our body was that of a man who, it transpired, actually died naturally. Although, where he was found and certain items found beside his body aroused my suspicions, and while I'm satisfied as to how and why he died, I'm like a dog with a bone really. I can't close the case until I tie up some loose ends. And honestly, it definitely is getting under the skin of Chief Superintendent Britten."

"Ah! I thought as much, he and I had a few arguments when I was here. He always wanted to take the easy way out and when he realised that the little boy had no one to make a fuss about it, he suggested quite forcefully that I tie it up without delay."

"Could you not have done something about that?" Knowles asked.

"Like what? He was right to a certain extent. The evidence indeed pointed to an accidental death or suicide. Suicide would have created one hell of a rumpus. A ten-year-old boy, it was desperately sad. I stood my ground at first and wanted to declare an open verdict, but he made such a hell of a fuss, declaring that there would be government officials down and heaven knows what, so it was marked 'accidental' and the body was released.

"The funeral was quick and quiet. They didn't even have time to locate the boy's brother who was on the run, apparently."

"Okay. Tell me all about it – right from your first knowledge of it, until the inquest."

"Right. I've brought my notes and I'll get in touch with the medical examiner for his." Saying that, he shuffled through the pages in an embossed leather-bound book. "It's all online now, I suppose, but I'm too old for all that stuff.

"The police were called out very early in the morning on the day and the cop who found him is now sadly dead but I have his statement here somewhere."

"Yes, we have been in touch with his colleague who has been very helpful. When did you become involved?"

"I was notified of course and my secretary took the call. Over the next few days, details came in until finally, we received the forensic report which I have here. Statements were taken from just about everyone at the home, including staff, children, matron, gardener, cleaners, everyone except the one person I suspect would have had the most to tell."

"The priest?"

"Yes, I didn't get anything from him at all. Apparently, he had gone to France before it all happened or so I was told at the time."

"By?"

"The chief superintendent – he said the priest had left the evening before."

"Well, that was a bold assumption because it seems that nobody knows when or how the priest left. I think it was probably wishful thinking. Did he give you any clues as to the mode of travel?"

"No, I was waiting for more information. Matron made a statement to the effect that she had been sent home by the priest because she had told him that she was tired. She insisted that she would be quite happy to stay but he made her go."

"Did you ever take a statement from Britten?"

"No, didn't feel the need. He wasn't involved in the actual case."

"But, tell me, at some stage, was he the one who told you that the priest had gone the evening before?"

"Yes, and I didn't think anything of it at the time, it was only when I was considering all the evidence that I recalled it. Listen, I'm not a detective, I had to work with what I got. I knew there was no statement from the priest but I knew he had gone. And it was only when I got all the evidence together that I realised something was odd about it."

"Sadly, the matron is no longer able to help us, she has dementia, but she clearly gets very upset when this business is mentioned. Nothing adds up."

"Exactly what I thought myself, at the time." The coroner was in agreement. "But days went by and it wasn't until I had the reports from the forensic pathologist that I actually began to feel very uncomfortable. You can read them in your own time, but they effectively described a young underdeveloped child's body that had suffered consistent abuse, brutal abuse. My assistant cried when she read them."

"But apart from the signs of regular abuse, there were some very fresh grab marks, as if he'd put up a fight and been grabbed by the arms, but more significantly there was fresh skin, under his nails… very fresh. He had dug his nails into somebody, and his nails were not cut short. To be fair, no members of staff had scratches, nor any of the kids except one and he was cleared, when we did a DNA test on him. Anyway, I phoned Britten and asked him to come around."

"And he did?"

"Yes. He read the stuff. We were in the inner office. He categorically asked me not to open an inquest. Just to issue the death certificate. He asked me not to mention the skin under the nails. He explained, there was no point, it would just upset people and all the staff had been cleared. I pointed out then that if no one had been in charge, anything could have happened. And that's when he said he wasn't sure when the priest had gone. But apparently, he had not gone the night before, he stayed because Matron had gone home feeling ill. It was one hell of a mess. He said he would take care of the statement and if further evidence turned up he would reopen the case. When eventually I got the papers back, that statement had been redacted. And there was no mention of the skin under his nails."

"So you didn't argue. You let him get away with it?"

"Yes, I did argue at first. In fact, I pointed out that I am not obliged to follow his advice or instructions." He tried to explain. "I am as you know completely independent, but I suppose he had a point. There was no suspect. It was probably accidental death. There was no indication that it was murder. The children in the vicinity of the scene had heard nothing unusual, according to their statements and there was a responsible member of staff on the premises. With hindsight, of course, we know that the priest never came forward to confirm that all was well that night and we could not possibly have known that ten years later he would still be missing. At the time the bishop's staff reported that his hasty return to France was absolutely justified." He sighed. "But I do, from time to time look back and wish I had been more thorough. I made too many assumptions and that case comes back to haunt me. If that child had had parents or relatives, I doubt that they would have accepted it."

"He did have a family; his brother is moving heaven and earth now to get justice for him. We have people over in France looking for the priest and they've made progress. Watch this space."

"And the chief superintendent? If you solve this mystery he'll have egg all over his face, and come to think of it, so will I. Well, I suppose I deserve everything I get."

"I think the Super will be keeping a very low profile now. He fell far short of his duty at the time but I can say no more than that just now. You know that you were wrong at the time although your finding on the basis of what you knew was probably correct. We both know that.

Nevertheless, if you had insisted on an inquest, the spotlight would have been on the priest and within a couple of weeks, his failure to return would have looked suspicious. I reckon the French police then would have done their best to trace him. But today, ten years later they won't lift a finger unless I manage to get enough evidence for a European Arrest Warrant and even then, they won't do a thing until I can persuade them that we have a case to answer.

"Anyway," he stood up, "I know what it's like to have to make decisions under pressure. You're here now and thank you for that. You may need to come back, but as a witness. Albeit, some others I could name might not be so lucky. I'll keep you informed."

The two shook hands after Morrissey had levered himself out of the chair and Knowles went down to tell Ava the latest.

"Are you telling me that Britten deliberately misled the coroner?"

"It seems to me that Britten did what he could to deflect attention from the priest at the time when the trail was fresh. Therefore, he had something to hide. He has yet to come up with a reason for his name being on that list. Yes, he has made vague references to a donation. I know it sounds unlikely because it is so revolting, but I think the priest was not only abusing children but hiring them out as well and there is a possibility that Britten was one of his clients."

There was a long pause as Ava put her elbows on the desk and her head in her hands.

"Oh my God. I can't think straight. If this gets out, what will that do to our reputation? It's unthinkable... we'd all be tainted by it. I feel sick."

"Yes, I know how you feel, and I may be wrong which is why I'm keeping my powder dry for the time being. He's out of range now anyway."

"Do you think he'll come back?" Ava asked curiously.

"Not if he's guilty. We need to check his bank accounts. See if he's taken everything with him, but we'll need permission to do that and I'm not yet ready. What we really need is, in fact, an admission from the priest. What we do have however is a vestige of hope. Come and look at this security video."

They played it through twice. It had been a sunny day and the range of the camera took in most of the parking area and was directly over the door. There was a clear picture of Jones and the back of Knowles' head. He was facing out and Jones was speaking to him. But he turned his head as he heard footsteps approach. Britten appeared and the expression on Jones' face changed from a smile to puzzlement and then shock. He seized Knowles' arm and his words were clear: *'Did you know he was here? Did you do this on purpose?' And then: 'Was it him? A policeman who did that to me. I can't believe it. I would know him anywhere.'*

Ava watched and listened, concentrating. Then announced, "Well, three things are quite clear to me – one, that was clearly not a setup. No one could have arranged that, and two, his reaction was absolutely genuine. That poor bloke."

"And three?"

"The man who has been my guv for five years and who expected me to bow and scrape and make him tea is nothing but a vile lying pervert. I want him caught and punished. I want him to have to serve at least fifteen years in prison as an identified nonce. Is his laptop here? Let's go and look."

She was out of the office before Knowles could get to his feet. He caught up with her at the door of the immediate past Chief Superintendent's office, which had been cleaned out thoroughly. Nothing there that could help.

Knowles had the distinct impression that Ava had the bit between her teeth and wouldn't rest until she had found something, even if it meant breaking a few rules.

"Look," he said – we could find ways of getting into his bank. We could go straight to the Police Complaints Authority, they may be able to get him back here, but calm down and let's try to be rational. What exactly have we got? That recording is not enough. I believe Britten can be identified as an abuser, but it wouldn't be enough. Not ten years after the event. Not enough to get him back here to answer questions. We need a cast iron case and we'll work on it. I'm going to ask your new boss if you can have a temporary transfer to my patch so that if you need to go to France again, there'll be no holdups. Okay?"

"Brilliant! I'll go and pack. Let's take that recording with us just in case he has any mates here."

"Good thinking, now let's have a coffee and you can tell me all about the French trip. I've heard from Kate; it would be good to know your side of the story."

Chapter Thirty-two

Knowles drove to Heathrow alone and in good time to meet the overnight flight from Melbourne. Curtis Taylor, he realised would be stiff and tired after the long flight, unless of course he was rich enough to travel first class – he had no idea, but had booked him into a classy London hotel at the expense of the force. No one, thought Knowles, could deserve a bit of comfort more than a chap who was prepared to travel all this way to help in such an important investigation.

He had decided that of all the people involved in this sickening affair, and at this stage he had no idea how many were, the two prime movers were the priest and the superintendent. He would wind them in if it was the last thing he did. The evidence of this man just might support a case against both wherever they were. If the guy was too tired for an interview this morning, Knowles was quite prepared to wait until this evening and then either get him picked up and brought to the station, or go to the hotel and interview him there.

Trouble is he needed to video record everything. Just in case Curtis was not able to come back. Defence solicitors were entitled to demand his attendance for cross examination of course, but right now – well no collars –

no solicitors, but when the time came, he would at least be able to show them the strength of the prosecutor's case

If he could just get so much compelling evidence together that the defendants would realise that their only option was to plead, that would be best for everybody. Right now identification would be the main problem. Neither suspect was available to stand in a line up and they had no photograph of the priest anyway. He could and would show Curtis a series of photos amongst which would feature Britten. He had found one of him in civvies and although he had no reason to believe their paths had ever crossed, there was always a chance. If the case was strong enough, he hoped that both his targets would avoid the embarrassment of a trial and the sickening disclosures that would hit the headlines

The flight was on time. Knowles held up a card with Taylor's name on it and hadn't long to wait before a tall, tanned young man in jeans and a denim jacket approached. "It's me," he grinned, "are you a mere lackey or the chief inspector himself?"

They shook hands. "I think lackeys died out with Queen Victoria, we have oily rags and skivvies now, but I am the chief inspector and I am so pleased to greet you. How was the flight?"

"Not bad at all, I slept well, but I did have a very comfortable reclining seat and breakfast was excellent."

"Good. When do you think you'll be ready to talk? I don't want to rush you. How long are you expecting to stay?"

"Well it would be pretty daft to travel all this way and not see the sights, maybe look up old acquaintances although there weren't many, and do some shopping. I expect to be here for at least two weeks. I'm a bit of an art freak too, so the Tate Galleries will definitely be on the list."

"Okay, let's grab a coffee. I could do with one, and a bacon sandwich would go down well although I'm on a diet."

Half an hour later they were on the way back to town and heading straight to the interview room in Whitehall. Knowles gave a brief summary of what he knew up to now, not revealing of course the fact that a high-ranking police officer was on the list of suspects.

"So you see, we think that there was a degree of abuse involved at the home, and that the abusers were, with one exception, from outside. Without giving you too much information or trying to influence you in any way, I would like you to give me any details you can which might help me to understand what went on, and who was involved. I believe you gave some details in the letter to *The Gazette* and I recall that you indicated that you would never forget a particular face. My problem is that I have never seen that face and we have no photographs of it. Furthermore, the owner of that face has been lying low for ten years – you see the difficulty?"

"You have no idea where he is?"

"Where who is?"

"The priest – Pious the terrible."

"Please say no more just now. I need to formally record your evidence without saying anything that might influence you just like any other witness statement." He explained the procedure on the way to the interview room. "When we've finished, there'll be a transcript for you to sign. I'm going to switch on the recorder now. Please identify yourself."

"I am Curtis Taylor. I live in Australia and I am in England for the purpose of this investigation."

"And I am Detective Chief Inspector Charles Knowles of the Metropolitan Police. Also present is DI Oakley. You have told us that you were living at The Sanctuary home twelve or thirteen years ago."

"Yes."

"And you are aware that evidence has come to light which may relate to offences against children at that home when you resided there?"

"Yes that is why I have travelled from Australia to assist in your enquiries."

"How old were you when you were placed there?"

"Seven."

"Do you recall the names of any staff members?"

"Only the priest."

"What was his name?"

"Pious."

"Any others?"

"No just him."

"Is there anything about him that causes you to remember him in particular?"

"Yes he was a vile cruel bastard and if you ever find him, just let me know where he is."

Curtis's anger was tangible and Knowles tried to calm him down. "Taking a short break at 12.05." He switched off the recorder.

"I can't tell you why, but this is one of the most important cases in my career and I don't intend to give any defence lawyer the chance to pick holes in it. Your evidence has to be spontaneous and convincing. I cannot lead you in any way. Are you ready to go on?" Curtis nodded and the machine was switched on again.

"Sorry. I was upset. I'm okay now. Right let me try to give you all the details. I think I was about six when I went there, it was quite small then, not all that many boys. The carers and teachers were mainly men but there were a couple of nuns too. It wasn't bad really. The food seemed good to me and we had lessons and play times. After a couple of years, the building was extended, they built another wing, and older boys came in. The nuns disappeared and it became less comfortable: there was a bit of bullying. The big boys picked on the little ones and made them act like servants, like it used to be in public schools." He stopped and asked for a drink of water.

"Then suddenly we had a new head. The priest came. I'll never forget that day, because it was if a light had been switched off. We assembled in the hall and he stood on the platform and addressed us. He never smiled. He just said things were going to change. He segregated the little boys completely, which at first we were really pleased about because the bullying stopped, well by the big boys anyway, but day to day life became a miserable routine. No shouting in the playground, no playing games unless they were board games or quizzes, no running, no answering back, we daren't even laugh out loud."

"What were the sleeping arrangements?"

"Our dormitories were upstairs, four beds in each and we had a matron to look after us, make sure we cleaned our teeth and so on. She was nice. When he was out or away, we were allowed to behave like normal children. If he came back Matron would rush in and say he's coming, go to sleep, and we'd pretend to be asleep." He paused.

"You say 'he'."

"Pious the priest."

"Do you need a break before you go on?"

"No I'm okay but it's not easy to go back to that place."

"I understand. Take your time."

"I suppose he'd been there for about three or four months. He came into the dorm one night and shook my shoulder. I wasn't asleep but I tried to pretend I was, until he shook me roughly, and I turned and looked at him. He stared at me and said, 'Get up' and pulled me out of bed. He said 'come with me', and I had to. We went to an adjoining room, next to the sick bay. I was so frightened. He told me to take my clothes off. I wanted to say no, but the best I could do was to shake my head, and then he came at me with his hand raised as if to hit me, so… I did what I was told. He told me it was a routine medical examination." He paused and gazed out of the window. "I don't think I can go on."

'No? let's stop for a break," said Knowles. "This is difficult for both of us. Tape off for comfort break," he said and switched off the machine.

Curtis was trembling. "Funny," he said. "I have avoided thinking about that for so many years. I thought I would be able to do it, and I will, but remembering the details makes me feel sick."

"Do you ever drink spirits?" asked Knowles, taking a bottle of single malt from the cupboard under his desk.

"Christmas and birthdays and er… what day is it today?"

"Friday."

"And certain Fridays. Make mine a double."

Fifteen minutes later after Cutis had given a detailed account of what had followed that evening, with the recorder switched on, they had another drink.

In all his years as a detective, Knowles had never before been moved almost to tears. What kind of man, he thought, and he has the audacity to call himself a priest. Does he attend for confession, I wonder? Surely God there are times when you want to strike them dead, and then remembering that he was not a believer, he concentrated on the vision of Pious being left to the mercy of a group of thugs in prison.

"That bastard deserves to spend the rest of his life in there," remarked Knowles. "I'm going to leave it for today. I think you need a break. We may continue tomorrow and concentrate on anything that you can remember that might have involved other people. I don't mean similar details, I'm sure you wouldn't have been a witness to anything like that. But anything you were aware of that was out of the ordinary."

"Yes I'll apply my mind as soon as I've recovered from this little exercise. You say you have no photographs of him?"

"No but hang on, I think I may be wrong there. Just a minute." He took out his mobile and called Kate.

"Kate, a few days ago, you'd had been to see someone who worked in a shop near Tellier's original address, and you said you had been given a newspaper cutting with a picture of a group of kids. Do you still have it?"

"Yes of course. I sent a copy back so that they could do an ageing but I still have the original."

"Could you fax it through to the station – now. Are you near a computer?"

"Yes there's one here at the hotel. Stand by."

It felt like an hour before the fax machine whirred into action. He called her back. "Which one is he?"

"The one on the bench."

Knowles handed the black and white picture to Curtis. "Have a look, is there anyone in that group of six kids that you recognise. Just say yes or no."

He studied the picture for no more than thirty seconds then turned and looked solemnly at Knowles. "Yes."

There was another whirr from the machine and a face which had been aged by facial experts came through. They didn't look at it at that stage.

"You said you were an art freak. Can you draw?"

"Fairly well, yes."

"Okay from memory could you possibly produce a likeness of the priest, as he was when you were there, without looking at anyone in this photo again, and then another one, only try to age it, so that he's about fifty."

"Yeah, okay."

It took half an hour with Curtis closing his eyes and concentrating hard on what he was doing. He produced two pictures, which Knowles compared to the paper cutting and the experts' 'aged' picture. Then he spoke into the recorder, which had not been turned off. "I am looking at two exhibits. Both drawings by Curtis Taylor, they will be produced in evidence by the prosecution."

The two drawings were in pencil. The first bore a strong resemblance to the boy on the bench. The second was very similar to that of the art expert who had produced what he thought the boy would look like as an older man. The only difference was that Curtis had given him a beard.

"And lastly for today, Curtis," said Knowles, "did I do

anything which might have influenced your decision to select any one of the group of six boys in the photograph I showed you?"

"No nothing. Actually you didn't have to. I recognised him straight away – the boy on the bench."

Curtis was delivered back to his hotel by police car. The driver had no time to linger as he had urgent business to attend to, and to Curtis's delight, used his siren and blue lights, switching off only as they approached the hotel.

"Hey thanks, that almost makes up for this morning."

He had given Knowles his mobile number with a promise to keep in touch. Knowles in turn promised to keep him in the loop as far as he could. Hopefully he would be back to give evidence at the trial if they ever caught up with the priest, but he hadn't been able to help with any evidence that might support a case against Britten.

Knowles toyed with idea of bargaining with Tellier, if he would give evidence against Britten, but then dismissed the idea, Curtis Taylor needed to see a full and fair trial of that hideous parasite and he would make sure that happened. No doubt if he did come before a court he was malicious enough to take all his clients with him when he went down. What he needed right now was an encouraging update from Kate.

Chapter Thirty-three

Kate took the call from Knowles as she and Ava were heading back to the hotel.

"Hi, Kate, Just an update really. You okay? Any developments?"

"No, I'm just sitting here twiddling my thumbs waiting for you to issue that warrant. I have a solicitor here giving me a hard time. He doesn't think we've enough. What we claim happened amounts to child exploitation, but what we can prove is sadly lacking."

"Aha but things have changed a bit. Correct me if I'm wrong because this is foreign territory for me – pardon the pun. We can only get a European Arrest Warrant, if a court here in UK issues one. Then it can be executed by a member state, France in this case, but only if it was issued by a judge. Yeah? A police warrant is not enough. Then the French court will look at the evidence on which we have based our decision, to make sure it's an offence in their country. I don't think that would be a problem, but to make matters more complicated, there are time limits. I think sixty days for the French court to agree to do it, and then ten further days after issue, to execute it. Knowing the French, they'll take as long as they can. Although how they could possibly doubt the offence when it comes to the exploitation of children I don't know.

"I'm faxing through a transcript of Curtis Taylor's interview. If that doesn't make them weep into their café au lait I don't know what will. It nearly had me reaching for my handkerchief. We need to move fast, Kate, I really think that once they see this stuff they won't waste time. The problem will be getting the hearing fixed in the first place. That could take weeks. Is your chap good? Is Tellier still in place?"

"My chap is okay, he just wants to make sure we do have a strong case, and by the sound of it, Curtis Taylor's evidence should do it. I can understand Claud's reluctance to rush things. He's horrified at what we suspect, especially if it was one of his countrymen organising it. He does keep pointing out that Tellier is half English, but most of what we did have was surmise. The fact that there wasn't a huge rumpus about Joey didn't help. I'll see him this afternoon with the transcript and I'll let you know when we have a date."

"Good girl and good luck. How is Ava?"

"She's fine, really enjoying it. We should recruit her. She's managing to keep Spike and Vic calm too. Gotta go, things to do. Bye, Guv."

Kate immediately dialled the number of the French solicitor and explained that more evidence was on its way and asked if they could meet up. She asked how long it might take to get a hearing.

"It's infuriating, getting an appointment with his

secretary is difficult enough, but I had an idea."

"Tell me."

"Well if we could just drop a hint to the press. They will make a huge headline out of almost anything. Something like *'French Priest accused of Child Exploitation in the UK. Scotland Yard seeking warrant'*. If the judiciary thinks the press are going to make a huge meal of it, they'll get their skates on."

"The trouble with that is that Tellier might see it and then he'd get his skates on. We'd never find him again."

"Hmmm. Okay, let me toy with the idea. A headline that would mean nothing to him but would excite the judges. Maybe... *'Procrastination by the French Courts is allowing Foreign Criminals time to settle here'*, followed by something like, 'Does this country want to be a haven for foreign crooks bla bla – We have enough of our own. The EAW gives us the chance to send them back to be dealt with in their own countries, but by the time our judiciary gets around to agreeing, suspects have disappeared'."

"Better but the papers would be screaming for examples and short of making one up."

Okay I'll try to find an example. See you at three o'clock with your new evidence... au revoir."

"See you."

Kate herself dwelt on the headlines she would like to see but knew they would be unlikely to go to print. *'High ranking English police officer colludes with Anglo-French priest. Both now face charges of child exploitation'.*

Please please let that happen, she thought, and let me be the one who gets to charge them.

Now that Griff was safe and she was in touch again with Jake, she was impatient for things to progress. Jake was due to arrive first thing tomorrow and she was waiting for a message from Simon to re-assure her that Tellier was still living in the cellar. No call so far. Spike was biting his nails and insisting that they went back to pick up the trail, which she felt was a bad idea. She was just about to call Simon when her phone vibrated in her pocket. She grabbed it. "Hi, it's me," came Simon's unmistakable Clapham tones. "Look he has disappeared but I found an excuse to go down to the basement and most of his stuff is still here – rolled up sleeping bag, and some personal stuff inside. Did you know he had a British passport?"

"Well I knew he might have. Is a French one there?"

"No. The English one was stuffed in a welly."

"Okay, thanks, Simon, can you make sure everything is back exactly where you found it? We don't want him to get the wind up."

"Trust me. I looked for booby traps but nothing there so he must feel fairly secure. Are you coming over soon?"

"Yes definitely tomorrow. I'll watch out for you. Bye for now."

Kate decided not to tell Spike that Tellier was temporarily missing. He was very stressed. Everything that had happened in the last couple of weeks had brought back all the horror to Spike. She was worried that he would snap any day soon and vent his anger and sorrow in such a way that his own future would be ruined. She decided that she would drag Ava away from Vic and go to Fougerolles to ask the aunt if she had heard from the priest. She had two hours to kill before her appointment with Claud. Half an hour later they were on the way, in the hired car, admiring the French countryside.

"It's funny, but all these little villages are exactly the same, one long street with white and cream single storey bungalows, a bar/tabac, a church and a little grocery shop which sells mostly wine, garlic and onions. No sign of life at all."

"They've probably all died of boredom," observed Kate whose respect for France had been only partly restored by the superb food at the Castle Hotel. "There's not much life outside Paris unless you go south. Everything improves then especially the weather."

"Well you're right about the food. This reputation they have for 'cuisine superb' must have originated before we could buy garlic and decent wine at home. We were just overwhelmed by the unfamiliar flavour. I don't think my mum ever used wine in cooking, and garlic was something that 'made weirdos smell funny'."

Kate laughed. "Right and it still makes weirdos smell funny. Jake puts it in everything, and he's the biggest weirdo I've ever met."

"He's lovely though, isn't he? and quite mysterious. I

love his hair – definitely the gypsy look."

"He thinks it makes him look younger. He's going to have to cut it when he goes grey. Old hippies don't really cut it these days."

"He can always dye it."

"Heaven forbid – although I most certainly will dye mine. Look – I'm going to park here and we'll walk to her house. I don't want to upset her, and in any case, it's just possible that he has a visitor."

"You mean…? Oh God, Kate! He might recognise us from our visit."

"I don't think so. We didn't see him, did we? so he can't have seen us."

"I hope you're right. But we can't go knocking on the door, can we? Just in case."

"No, I'm going to call her. She speaks English very well, and she's not daft. She'll know it's me and if he's there she'll find a way of letting me know."

The number rang and Edith answered, "Oui, bonjour?"

"Are you alone?"

A pause.

"Desole, je ne veux pas l'assurance. Moment attendez." There was the sound of a door closing. "Allo, Jane. He was here. He has just gone. Where are you?"

"Too close. Just around the corner in the square."

"Mon Dieu. He is going to get my car. It's down the road from me but he may leave that way."

"What make of car is it and the number?"

"It's a big old Citroen DS. I haven't used it for months. I can't remember the number but you can't mistake it. It is a black car with one blue door. I had an accident and someone had a spare door. They were going to spray it. Never mind that. If he doesn't come back in five minutes he must have gone. Then you can come and see me."

"Kate pulled Ava up the steps, into the patisserie and away from the window. "Keep a look out for an old black Citroen. One like Maigret had."

"Who? There's a beaten up one just gone past with a blue door."

"Whew! Come on. A quick visit to Edith and then we need to hurry."

The aunt answered the door immediately and kissed Jane on both cheeks. "I am so pleased to see you. I was frightened when he came. He has taken money and my car. It was only when you called that I remembered what I had to say. I think he is planning to travel. Do you want to follow him? I don't want to hold you up."

"Don't worry. I think I know where he will be going right now, and if he does move on, we know what the car looks like which is very useful. Thank you. We must go now but I promise to let you know when we find him. I think it will be soon."

They left leaving the old lady reassured but rather sad. "It would have been so nice to have a nephew who cared about me," she said wistfully. "How is Jake?"

"He's fine. He was in London but he's coming back tomorrow and he will come and see you – I promise."

Once outside they ran for the car. Ava drove while Kate rang Simon in Mont-Saint-Michel to ask him to keep an eye open for a strange looking Citroen.

"Well there's only one car park in the village so if he's on the way here, I'll find him. I asked the carriage drivers if they were looking for a new stable lad and they promised to let me know if a vacancy arose."

Kate reported the conversation word for word to Ava and then they joined the main road back to Fougères, keeping an eye open for the Citroen. From a road map on the back seat, Kate could see that there were two routes he could have taken, the quickest was through the town of Saint-Hilaire because the roads were better, but she chose the windier route on the basis that he would have little confidence in the car he was driving and wouldn't want to have to stop anywhere public. She was pretty confident that he would head for the village to pick up his passport anyway and possibly needed time to plan and pack the rest of his miserable belongings. Nevertheless, it was a relief to see the Citroen ahead and follow a good distance behind until they saw it take the turn off for Le Mont-Saint-Michel.

After that, it was simply a matter of dropping Ava back at the hotel and going on to meet Claud at the solicitor's office, the new evidence folder in her hand.

Claud looked very thoughtful as he handed the folder to his assistant to take copies of everything. He had spent almost half an hour reading and re-reading the statement of Curtis and then going back to the statements of Smith and Jones.

"I think it would help if we had the video-tape. I know it isn't related directly to Tellier, but the whole thing stinks. I think the judge I have in mind will feel very strongly about the entire set up, especially as a member of the police force appears to be involved and all the details will help. He will want to be satisfied that the Frenchman isn't going to be a scapegoat for all the others."

"Absolutely not. If you want me to meet him I will let him know as much as we do and assure him that we are working on that. My boss is one of the most highly respected at the Yard and he has the bit between his teeth. How long do you think it will be before it goes before a court?"

"Stay there a few minutes. I have some calls to make. In fact, would you mind waiting outside? I need to speak to my mother." Kate raised her eyebrows and went out.

After fifteen minutes she was getting impatient. For heaven's sake, she thought, there's something very wrong with his priorities. Then the door opened and he beckoned her in.

"Sorry about that but it was important. I'm waiting for a call back now. Would you like a coffee, or would you prefer to wait and we can go and have a glass of wine?"

She was about to make a sarcastic remark about having waited for an hour already but was interrupted by Claud's desk phone ringing. Another bloody delay!

Claud was listening carefully and uttering the occasional 'oui' or 'bien', 'sure' and then with a "Fantastique! merci beaucoup, Monsieur," he put the phone down and smiled at her.

"We have a hearing in three days. We must be there before ten a.m."

Kate gave a huge sigh of relief. "Well done, Claud. That's amazing. How on earth did you manage that?"

"There is one judge who specialises in this kind of case, and it just so happens that he had an affair with my mother. That's why I spoke to her first, and then she spoke to him. You of course do not know this so please keep quiet about it."

Kate laughed. "Honestly you French."

"What do you mean? Did your mother not have affairs? You English are so boring."

"Well actually, my mother married three times so maybe affairs are okay. More interesting in fact. At least you're not stuck with the wrong partner until the divorce. Enough of this, where will the hearing be? Will it be in a closed court?"

"Closed court yes and we'll have to go to Rennes. I guess it will take a couple of hours. I'll make sure there are copies for him to keep for the records, maybe two.

"Now shall we have that drink?"

Chapter Thirty-four

There was a group hug when Jake and Griff arrived from Rennes. Griff looked a little pale and had lost weight but was in very high spirits.

"I can't imagine what you must have felt like," said Kate. "It must have been like being on death row. You couldn't have been sure that they were poised to intervene."

"I must admit my pulse was racing, but when I saw Jake stroll past with his camera and that daft baseball cap and dark glasses, I knew they had it under control. I had to suppress the impulse to yell, 'Get a fucking move on – my corset's killing me'."

"It can't have been much of a disguise if you recognised him."

"It was the cap. I've seen it before. It has 'I'M FIVE' on the front believe it or not, with two boss eyes underneath. He keeps it on his desk."

"Would you have let them blow up the girl?" Vic asked Griff.

"There was bugger all I could do about it to stop them. If it was a choice, between her, me and a group of churchgoers I suppose it would have been her and me. To be quite honest I don't know what I would have done if there had been no sign of help. There wasn't much time to think about it. I suppose I would have waited till the very last minute, and if I knew that innocent people would die with me unless I exploded outside, I think yes, I would have done, but it didn't come to that. I knew that if our guys were there, everything would be okay. The worst thing was not being able to see behind me because of the two pushing the wheelchair. It wasn't until we were inside the door and security guards stepped forward that I began to breath normally."

"That girl has been a huge help since," said Jake. "I think it was because she felt so betrayed. The fact that she was handcuffed to the chair and her father wasn't! He could have got away in time. There didn't seem to be much love there. She came to see me in hospital. I don't know whether she is in touch with her mum. I think not. Western clothes, make-up, she looked great. Her boyfriend was with her. He's a Muslim. A very nice chap. She looked so happy and she's singing like a canary. I reckon that information from her has resulted in fifteen more suspects."

"How can you be sure she'll be safe?"

"We've persuaded her and boyfriend to move to a safe house for the time being. She should be okay, but they'll probably move out of area anyway. We'll do everything we can to help. So bring me up to date, what's happening over here?"

Kate gave the details in sequence. "So you see, if all

goes to plan," she concluded, "they should be able to execute the warrant as early as the day after tomorrow – Friday. If he moves on in the meantime he'll be in such a recognizable car, they'll be able to grab him anywhere."

"And what makes you think he will stick to such an obvious mode of transport?" interrupted Spike. "I think Jake and I need to go to Mont-Saint-Michel today and check him out if that's okay with you, Jake. We've come this far. If we lost him now, I think I'd blow myself up. Let's have the number of your student spy. He could be a useful guide, and we'll get going."

They stayed long enough to enjoy an extremely good lunch and left.

*****

At home Knowles could do nothing but wait. He didn't want to jump the gun, but rather than sit and twiddle his thumbs he decided at least to take some advice from the Police Complaints Authority. He made an appointment with a representative the same afternoon.

Officer Nathan Clissold met him at the door, shook hands and invited him to sit down. Before Knowles could launch into his prepared statement, Clissold got in first.

"Correct me if I'm wrong, but are you here to talk about Chief Superintendent Britten?"

Knowles raised his eyebrows. "First, would you tell me why you have come to that conclusion?"

"Because, as it happens, he also has been in touch with us. Apparently, his name features on a list of names recovered from the computer of a priest who it seems is a suspect in an historical child abuse case." There was a period of silence. "Well?"

"Well what? You clearly have knowledge of this and I'm not saying another word until you reveal what you know. If that's not possible, I have other things to deal with in my office."

"I know very little, but Britten has been in contact because he thinks you are concocting a case against him with very little evidence. He contributed sums of money into some charitable scheme at a children's home years ago and because of that you are lumping him together with a bunch of child abusers who seem to have paid for services. He thinks your case may be reinforced by the fact that someone recognised him as a visitor there."

"And did he tell you that the someone was a victim?"

"Who saw him for a matter of seconds after ten years."

Knowles stood up. "Well I'm clearly wasting my time – if you'll excuse me…"

"Sit down please, Chief Inspector. Do you really think we would dismiss such a serious allegation without a thorough investigation? I know we are not very popular with the force, but please give us a chance. Now tell me everything you know. I'm going to record it."

So Knowles told him, beginning with Joey, the

inadequate investigation, the evidence of the medical officer which had been suppressed, the evidence of the coroner's secretary, the recently obtained coroner's statement, the list of names, the evidence of Gambler and Smith and Jones and finally the video tape.

"Do you think Jones or whatever his real name is will give live evidence?"

"Yes I do, especially if we have the priest. Hopefully a European Arrest Warrant will be executed within a week. I have an officer over there who has done fantastic work in tracing him."

"We need to get Britten in. Is he still in Jamaica?"

"I think he's gone for good."

"No I don't think so, that wouldn't assist his defence. I think he mentioned being over there for a month. Wants to study the life of Bob Marley so… Don't worry 'bout a thing – every little thing is gonna be all right."

"He actually sang it," Knowles told Kate later. "So! Some of them do have a sense of humour."

When Knowles had left they had shaken hands again. Maybe every little thing WAS going to be all right.

*****

Ava came back on Thursday and was thrilled with the news.

"They're keeping an eye on incoming flights from Jamaica for the week after next," Knowles told her. "You do realise that it will all be taken out of our hands now. I have to send copies of all the evidence to Clissold, including whatever new stuff comes in. Wouldn't it be superb if Pious was shipped over and was in custody here when they brought Britten in for questioning?"

"Well I won't be there to see it I'll be back on my own patch, but I have a feeling that they will keep them entirely separate and somewhere where we can't possibly interfere. They'll almost certainly release Britten on bail and confiscate his passport. Although I suppose I might bump into him if he has to report daily. God I hope not."

"They'll probably just impose a curfew. We'll have to wait and see. I'm reaching the stage when I would like this whole damn thing to be over, as long as it has an appropriate ending. I need to get back to my desk in London and deal with some refreshingly clean stuff, you know – money laundering or a nice healthy murder, this has all been so smutty and convoluted. Not my kind of stuff at all."

"I still find it hard to believe that he would take such risks. It is smutty. Did he ever think of the risks or consider what might happen if he was found out?"

"I think they're driven. As Wellstead said when he was talking to Spike before he died, paedophiles are born and not made. And that word does mean lover of children. He was quite sure, in the beginning that he had never hurt a child, and maybe he didn't at the time, but it was later when they were old enough to know what sex should be all about, that sense of shame and disgust at themselves resulted. But Britten is an entirely different case. He must have been able to see those kids were terrified. There was no love there. Britten and the priest were monsters."

"Do they have crocodiles in Jamaica? That's the kind of ending Britten deserves. I can imagine his bare feet sticking out from between a croc's jaws."

"He'd be wearing socks."

"Now you've ruined it."

He said goodbye to Ava and headed for his car. He could be home in four hours. A quick shower and he could call Jill Irving. For the first time in weeks, he felt as if they were getting somewhere with this case and to top it all he was losing weight and feeling much better for it. The Westminster incident had caused little more than a ripple, thanks to the way Jake and his crew had handled it, and Tellier was almost in the bag. He had to be very careful how much he did tell Jill, but with edited versions of the two matters, which had exercised his brain for the last couple of weeks, he could keep her entertained. For the first time in months, thinking about Jill had not caused him to feel that little frisson of guilt. Harriet had let him go and wished him well. He would never part with her pots, but maybe the flat could do with a coat of paint. New curtains and a couple of new sofas might be a good idea too.

Before he left for the evening out, He went to the office and updated the teams, who in turn gave him all the information on the latest cases. With a bit of luck he would be able to concentrate on a new set of problems, and resolve them. That was what he was good at. He was on his own turf and he loved it.

*****

Griff and Jake were also recovering from what could have been world news and a staggering disaster in every sense. Not only dead and mutilated bodies, but the partial destruction of a thousand-year-old building. Sometimes Griff chided himself for not arresting the bomber as soon as they were within sight of England. It could have gone so wrong but the group would have found some other way. As it was, a cell of serious terrorists had been put out of action. Sadly, there would be others.

It was a beautiful day when Griff and Jake arrived at Le Mont-Saint-Michel. Simon Oakley met them in the restaurant of one of the hotels. "The car is parked near the cellar where the horses are kept. There are a couple of parking bays opposite for the use of people in the street. There are two notes under the wiper telling him to move but he never did care about annoying people. Oh and the door is still blue."

"Where is he right now, do you know?"

"Haven't a clue. I actually have a job to do so I can't watch him all day. I did get the wind up when the car disappeared yesterday – I checked at lunch time. I was just about to text Kate when he rolled back. Still with a blue door."

"Where are the nearest shops? I mean where he might be able to buy spray paint?"

"Not sure. Saint-Hilaire probably."

"Well the main thing us he's still here. Hopefully he'll stay for a couple of days. There should be a warrant in force from lunchtime Friday and if Kate is keeping the heat on, they should be poised to make an arrest then. Is there a police station here?"

"Just a tiny office – one cop."

"Hmm one won't be enough. Look, Simon, I'll happily pay for your time but could you take a sicky. I mean are there plenty of other guides?"

"More than enough. As long as you pay me enough to buy a few sandwiches and then a huge dinner at the end of the day, I'd be glad to help."

"You're on, and when this is over we will buy you a veritable feast – as long as it includes frogs' legs. I need to see if anyone really eats stuff like that. Right he has never seen either of us before so I think it'll be safe enough to stroll past his place. I would so like to get at the car and put a tracker in place but he mustn't see and the car is in a public road, right?"

"It's a quiet road, but yes. Anyone fiddling with a car would stick out like a sore thumb."

"Could you distract him – if we started kicking up a rumpus?"

"No but you have cameras. We could create a

diversion."

"Let's go there now and perhaps we can think of something on the way. Is he likely to be at home now?"

He was in fact leaning against the door-frame smoking a Gaulloise. Jake tried hard not to stare. Griff looked straight ahead. "Just chat normally," he muttered.

"Okay, if you think you're so clever," he said looking at Jake. "Who wrote Plato's Symposium?"

"Is the clue in the title?"

"It might be"

"Must have been Plato then."

"Wrong! It was Cicero. They thought Cicero's Symposium had too many sss in it. Sounded like a bag of snakes."

"I've never heard such rubbish. Wow! Look at that classic car. Isn't it beautiful?"

"Well I wouldn't want to drive it. The door doesn't match. That would be easy to fix though, wouldn't it? I wonder if it's for sale?"

The priest wandered over. "You want to buy my car?"

"Hello, sir. Are you English?"

The priest didn't answer but repeated, "You want to buy the car?"

"Well I don't know. How much would you want?"

"It's hard to sell with an odd door and I have nowhere to park it. It was my aunt's. Maybe 800 euros?"

"Gosh that is cheap. Could I take it for a test drive?"

The priest shrugged. "I'll come with you." He took the

key from his pocket and handed it to Jake. They both got in. Jake looked at Griff who had the tracker in his pocket. He gave a wry smile and climbed in beside the priest, who looked very little like a man of the church and was so malodorous that Jake was tempted to climb straight out again. They took a short ride. The car had been idle for months and sounded terrible. Jake pretended to be impressed and raved about Citroens until he ran out of technical details and they drove back. Griff and Simon were leaning against the wall when they returned after about ten minutes.

"Would it be possible to meet you here at about midday tomorrow, sir? I'd need the registration book of course and I need to see if I can get the money transferred. Could we settle on 750?"

It's worth more than 800."

"Yes okay. Till tomorrow then."

The priest nodded and went back to his cellar. The three returned to the hotel for lunch.

"Pity about that," said Jake.

"What?"

"Well even if I'd had the tracker I wouldn't have had the chance to fix it."

"Yeah shame. Never mind though eh. It'll work just as well in his rucksack. I split a seam with my penknife and shoved it in while Simon kept watch."

"That is absolutely brilliant. He might abandon the car but not his rucksack. I should have guessed. Anyway,

376

talking of the Symposium, I need to go and call my other half. She'll be itching to know what's going on. There's not much point in staying here any longer. We have our trusty spy in place. I wanted to go and have a chat with Pierre, I want to warn him to be careful who he picks up. No one older than fifteen should be safe."

"I don't think they'll be doing any immigrant trafficking for a while," said Griff. "I haven't let them know we have been on to it for weeks. It just happened to work for us and while it was children there was absolutely no problem. As I told you, we saw to it that the paperwork went through as quickly as possible. Nevertheless, they are going to resent the fact that we were using them for our own purposes. They are good people. I admire them."

"Look, Griff, once Pious is in the bag, Spike will forgive you anything, I'm sure he'll understand. Choose your time and tell him the truth."

Chapter Thirty-five

Kate slept badly on Thursday night. She had spoken to Claude the night before and felt that he was still edgy about the evidence. Surely, she thought, the copy of the signed statement of Curtis should be enough to prove the offence, but was the identification sufficient. The statements of Smith and Jones supported what he had said. The weak link was the time that had elapsed, but his drawings presented a definite similarity to the art- work of the expert.

Her thoughts were interrupted by the vibration of her mobile phone. It was Simon. There was no text, just a picture of a dirty-looking, skinny tramp, standing by an old car, shaking his fist at the camera. Some text followed.

'I went to look at the car which Jake was 'considering buying'. I wanted to make sure it was still there. The owner was standing by it and I asked him to move, hoping he would ignore the request, as he was the picture I really wanted – he did. I think that you'll find that this car is registered to a Mme Tellier, in Fougerolles, and that this picture is of her nephew Francois.'

Absolutely brilliant, Simon, thought Kate, a bonus for you my friend. Several attempts had been made to take a picture of him had failed over the last few days as he always seemed camera shy. This time when he thought the car had been the object of the exercise, he had fallen neatly into the trap. That should clinch it. She looked at the face in the picture. "Well done, Curtis, he is sporting a beard and looks just like your drawing!"

She leapt out of bed, showered and dressed. Jake and Griff had stayed overnight at the Mount and would be home by lunch time, assuming the warrant was issued. She had to keep her appointment with Claude at the court and wanted to get there in time to show him the additional evidence. They had spent hours filling out the required form in French for the benefit of the court and Claude had made sure everything was correct. He told her that if the court required more details, it had a duty to make sure the suspect didn't disappear, by making him surrender his passport, stay at a registered address or by imposing reporting conditions which Kate was sure he would ignore. "Make sure the court is aware that he has dual nationality," she insisted. "He definitely has two passports."

With the additional evidence, Claude was confident that they were in a strong position, and the nature of the alleged offence itself was so serious that they should succeed today, nevertheless he spent the entire journey describing applications that had failed. "There are so many technicalities, so many exceptions, so much case law," he said. "It's a bit of a nightmare."

The court itself was imposing and Kate's heart was thumping as they were ushered in to a closed courtroom, before a judge who was not in robes, but in a smart suit. He smiled and invited them to sit down His assistant was making notes and also present was a uniformed officer.

"I have read your application," he said, "but before I make a decision, perhaps I can ask a few questions, Miss Meredith." Kate stood up.

"Please sit down, Miss Meredith. I am curious to know how it is that a member of the... he looked down at the papers, The Metropolitan Police Force, should be making this application, when the alleged offence, took place a long distance from London."

"Yes, sir, I can see why this is confusing." Kate then proceeded to describe the finding of Wellstead in a London Borough and the links with the children's home in Yorkshire, and the investigations that followed. "We felt we could not close the case involving a suspicious death until we had all the details. As far as the Met is concerned, once this warrant is issued, the local police will deal with the prosecution of Tellier."

"I see, so this Englishman with the French father has questions to answer."

"We prefer to consider him to be a Frenchman with an English mother," Kate replied with a smile. "I think his father had a tendency to be violent."

"Hmm. Yes. I have his history. Well, Miss Meredith, it seems from a recent statement attached to the file that you have managed to locate Francois Tellier. Is he aware of that?"

"No, sir, we have been careful. We have spoken to his aunt. She had nothing to contribute to this investigation but she is nervous. If you agree that the warrant should be executed I would be grateful if among any conditions you impose, one not to contact the aunt would be appropriate."

"I think the warrant should be executed immediately and he should be kept in custody until arrangements can be made to extradite him. He's escaped a fair trial for long enough."

"I'm grateful, sir."

"There are just one or two things I would like the French police to check for me." He addressed the police officer and charged him with checking the ownership of the car and its owner's current address, which would effectively confirm Tellier's identity. The notes concerning the information from the aunt were detailed on the form. "Once these details have been checked the warrant can be executed. I will leave the rest to the officer here who will arrange the arrest. It should be possible tomorrow. In the meantime, he can arrange for local officers to keep an eye on him."

The judge nodded smiled and wished them a safe trip back and left the court. It had taken just over an hour.

"Thank you so much, Claude, you have been a tremendous help. I'll probably see you tomorrow to arrange for your firm to be paid and if you're ever in London, please look us up."

"I will do. It's been a very interesting experience and

a pleasure working with you." They hugged and kissed in the French manner and went their separate ways.

Kate immediately took out her phone and called Spike, who, she knew, was very anxious for news. Pippa answered, the landline phone.

"Kate, I've been biting my nails. Do you have good news? Spike is on his way over – I couldn't hold him back."

"There should be an arrest tomorrow. We know where he is and Jake is over there keeping an eye on him. You might find yourselves in possession of a shabby old French car, I'm afraid. Jake is negotiating a deal with the priest himself. It was a delaying tactic. We knew he needed money to help him disappear. The car was too obtrusive for him to stay in the shadows, but the negotiations have meant that Jake and Griff could keep tabs on him. We honestly didn't expect things to go so smoothly here. Is Spike flying over?"

"Yes, he's on the way to Dinard. He has his mobile with him, it's probably switched off now, but he'll be in touch when he lands. He hasn't arranged a car. Any chance of you picking him up?"

"Give me his flight number and I'll see what I can do."

The next call was to Jake – no reply. Griff answered on the second ring. "Just tell me you have good news," he muttered. "Jake is counting out notes to that revolting monk, for this hideous car. I managed to sneak here and let one of the tyres down late last night, which should delay the transaction. Jake is pretending not to notice it right now. When can we expect some action?"

"The warrant will be executed tomorrow although the local cops are supposed to keep an eye on him until then. Any sign of them?"

"Not even a whistle but they may be heavily disguised as milk churns or something."

"Or not, but they should be there soon. I hope they do keep a low profile because if he gets wind of what's going on he'll be off."

"Don't worry. We won't let that happen. Are you coming over?"

"I have to go and pick Spike up at Dinard, so I will be there this evening. I'm going to persuade Spike to stay at the hotel with Vic until we're done."

"He'll probably argue, but I don't like the idea of him being here. Jake said he's quite volatile right now. I think he's managed to keep his emotions in check for all this time but now that the priest is an immediate live presence, the urge to attack him must be almost overwhelming. I was tempted to smash him in the face myself. But in my job instincts and emotions have to be strictly controlled."

"Is that why you've never hugged me?" laughed Kate.

"Don't flirt it's dangerous, and I value my skin. If Jake saw me grab you and hug you he'd put something nasty in my coffee. Looking forward to seeing you tonight – although first thing tomorrow would be better so that you can monitor Spike."

"Yes. Right. A demain!"

Griff put his phone in his pocket, and walked over to where Jake and the priest were discussing the flat tyre.

"It was looking a bit soft yesterday. I did notice that. You must have a slow puncture. What's the spare tyre like?" The priest without speaking opened the boot.

"Well let's change it. Where's the Jack?"

"The what?"

"The jack, the jack. The thing that lifts the car up so you can take the wheel off."

The Priest looked confused and answered in French. "Je ne comprends pas ce que vous voulez dire. Je peux conduire je ne suis pas mechanique!" Then in English. "I can't fix this. If you don't want the car leave it. Go." He walked away and disappeared into his cellar.

Jake beckoned Griff. "Was that Kate? How did she do?"

"She did everything she had to do. The warrant can be executed tomorrow. The local police should have been informed by now but they can't act yet. Just a few things to complete the process. Spike is on his way and Kate is collecting him from Dinard about now. I've told her not to let him come here until tomorrow. He can watch the finale."

"That will be just the end of the beginning. I don't think there's any more we can do here. He's sulking. Let's go and catch up with Simon. We can do a couple of discreet checks between now and tomorrow."

"Well according to Kate, the locals should be watching him until they get the signal to go go go tomorrow."

"They will have been told about the car; they probably think watching the road will be enough."

"Do you think differently?"

"I don't believe in taking chances, but unless he's found it, we've got the tracker in place. Keep your laptop handy. Right now I fancy a beer."

*****

Spike looked relieved when he saw Kate in the Arrivals Hall and was excited by the developments. "It's been such a strange few weeks, Kate, although I was determined to do something about that terrible episode in my life, deep down I didn't think for a minute that I'd succeed. When Vic and I drove away from the embankment that night, I had visions of Wellstead just rotting away, undiscovered, or being eaten by foxes. I had nightmares. But now it's all happening. We have him, and he will be getting the punishment he deserves. I can't tell you what that means."

"Not only him, Spike. There is at least one more to bag, and that seems to be reaching a climax. Those guys who used the service are equally guilty. There's a rather unpleasant police officer, who must be having nightmares too. I don't think we'll get any more but you never know. There's a sports personality who shall remain nameless for now, and an MP from one of those 'jolly hockey sticks and cocktail party' constituencies, but it all depends on witnesses coming forward. If we only get these two it'll be a victory for justice and the others will always be afraid that the past will creep up on them."

"Yeah! When this is done I want a rest. I want to take it easy with Vic and Pippa. She is more or less insisting that I expand the school to take girls, but I can foresee all sorts of complications there. Lovers' tiffs, jealousy, pregnancies – nightmare! What do you think?"

"You could always limit it to fat ugly ones."

"What a devious mind you have. Anyway I couldn't do it. Pippa's like a tiger when she sees injustice. Pity you live so far away, we could employ you as an agony aunt."

"Thanks but no thanks. I love my job and can't wait to get back to London I promise though, that I'll be a frequent visitor. I love your place and so does Jake. We could also help and advise any of your kids who might need it, not that you seem to have any difficult ones."

"Well I'd like to take credit for that, but to be honest, I have turned away a couple of kids that I thought might bring trouble. I've felt guilty ever since, but I think in some cases, so much damage is done from birth to teenage years that the rot has set in. That may sound defeatist, but it's one thing that I did learn from my short stay at the home. One or two of those lads were irrevocably evil. They seemed to thrive on the misery of others, feed it, sustain it, never let the victim see any hope of escape. I would have thought they were the very ones that the priest should have tried to deal with, but he never did. If they blamed someone else for their own misdeeds, he didn't question them. He just acted on that information. It will be those bully boys who leave and become violent crooks and their victims will always be victims who have lost hope. Why should anyone believe them or stand up for them? I've had one or two victims at the school. Vic and I taught them how to stand up for themselves physically and verbally. It's amazing how one can use eloquence as a weapon especially if you follow up with a skilful throw. Can we stop for a coffee do you think? The stuff on the plane was disgusting."

"Sure. I could do with one myself."

Over a drink they discussed the plans for the day and Spike reluctantly agree to wait until the next day before going to the Mount. Kate told him about the efforts Jake and Griff had made to keep him in place until the warrant was sanctioned

"He might just recognise you, Spike."

"Okay but I want to speak to him before the police arrive. I need to hear him tell me what happened. I'm sure when it gets to court he won't speak. He's entitled to remain silent. He'll hope there isn't enough evidence."

"Well I'm sure there is enough evidence now. The most difficult thing is going to be getting him to talk about his customers. As far as I'm concerned, there's a police officer who is just as guilty as he is, even more so."

"Don't be daft. He's going to love taking them down with him. That's the kind of bastard he is. He'll probably make up some story about them twisting his arm and saying they were just investigating some petty crime and wanted the boys to be witnesses. I don't know. He is cunning. Has he any idea the police are about to arrest him?"

"We think not."

"Just give me a few minutes then."

"Well let's see what the others think."

"Is this your case or not?"

"All right all right, but we need to get over there first thing tomorrow, before the police turn up."

"Why not now?" said Spike, and he took a left turn and headed in the direction of Le Mont-Saint-Michel."

Chapter Thirty-six

The news that Superintendent Britten was coming home a week earlier than expected had Knowles on edge. "I can't leave here right now, Ava, there's been enough fuss because I haven't been at my desk recently and right now I have some very serious matters to deal with. Can you give me daily updates?"

"I don't think the PCA will be keeping me up to date, Charlie, they're more likely to contact you, but bearing in mind the fact that he is retiring early on the grounds of ill health they're going to be especially careful. If they besmirched his character after his long years of service, and then prove nothing against him, he could sue them for millions. If they do contact me, I'll let you know of course. What's happening in France?"

"They're on the point of picking up Tellier on a European Arrest Warrant but there's no way of knowing if he will cooperate. If only we could get them in a room together and tape the conversation. Hang on a minute, I have an idea."

He called Nathan Clissold. "I understand that Reginald Britten is cutting short his stay in Jamaica. Would you kindly let him know when and if you meet, that the French police arrested the priest, Francois Tellier, this morning and will be obtaining a statement from him within the next few hours. I'll fax you a copy. I don't think the superintendent has any idea that we have managed to trace the chap or even tried. The *Jamaican Times* can't have been following this story, otherwise, Mr Britten would have thought twice about coming home. However, if he thinks Tellier is talking, it might just persuade him to get his story in first."

"Er... Yes. Thank you. I will bear that in mind. Goodbye."

"Hm. Don't mention it – or anything else, miserable sod."

Knowles turned his mind to the papers on his desk, which involved various drugs being smuggled through Amsterdam to Lowestoft by boat and then to Ipswich and beyond.

*****

Kate and Spike had arrived late at the Mount Hotel. Jake and Griff had already retired and set alarms to be up early the next morning. Simon was still up, having a drink at the bar and watching a football game on a large television screen. Kate introduced the two men and headed off to Jake's room.

The two chatted briefly about anything that wasn't the matter in hand, and then Spike said, "Do you fancy a short walk, just a short trip so that I can sleep easy, knowing he's still there."

Simon hesitated. "Yeah. Okay! How could I refuse? I've heard a little of what you've been through. It must be good knowing it's nearly over."

Spike smiled in response and stood up. They were both wearing trainers and made no sound as they walked. The Citroen was still there, still with a soft tyre. There was no street lighting but a warm glow came from some of the houses on either side of the stables. The horses were moving inside and disturbing the straw. Spike sidled up to the window and peered inside. He could see the opening in the stone wall at the back. There was clearly a light shining up from the cellar below.

Spike looked round and beckoned to Simon. "Listen, Simon, you know nothing about me apart from what you've been told by my friends but I sense that you are sympathetic." He spoke very quietly. "I'm going in."

"Please, Spike, don't go in. The others will be furious with me."

"Why should they be? I only want to talk to the man who killed my little brother. Wouldn't you want to do the same?"

"I'd want to do more than that, and that's what I'm afraid of."

"I want you to come in with me. Stay at the top of the stairs and listen. You can intervene if the talking turns into violent action but I promise you that it won't. We can get through this window; the horses are making movements anyway."

"Yes, okay, but please make it quick."

"As quick as I can. Now take this. It's a powerful recorder. It will pick up everything we say from up here." He handed over the device, which was switched on and showed a dim red light.

Spike went carefully down the stairs and looked at the unkempt figure crouching in the corner of the cellar. The priest looked up and froze when Spike appeared.

"Vous etes' qui? Qu'est ce que vous voulez?"

"So, Pious or Frances which would you prefer?" The man looked puzzled and shook his head. "Je ne comprend pas."

"Let's not begin this session with lies. I know you speak English perfectly well. Don't worry, I'm not going to hurt you. I'm not a bully, Frances, I'm bigger than you and I live my life by civilised rules, something you may not understand. I know who you are and what you have done. I just want you to tell me yourself, if you have the decency, but I doubt it. Why not confess, monk. Tell me what happened to my brother, Joey. I'm Spike, remember me? I believe you were the last person to see him alive."

The man got to his feet. He was actually taller than Spike expected but frail. His eyes were red rimmed and his skin wrinkled and set in with dirt. He had a rancid smell about him.

"We can continue the conversation in French if you like. I have someone outside who can translate. It's up to you."

"So what do you intend to do to me? You think I'm going to confess all. You think you can make me pay. Retribution? Save your breath. I'm not going to tell you about my life. You can go to hell."

"Ah. Jolly good. Spoken like a true half Brit, but let's not be too hasty. The way you live now. Not very pleasant, is it? You stink and you must be hungry. Is that where you sleep?" He pointed to a heap of soiled blankets in the corner.

"It does for me. The weather is clement and I don't care if I stink. It keeps people away. That's just what I want."

"Is there no one who matters to you at all, Frances? What about your mother?"

Frances recoiled. "Leave my mother out of it. She's dead. Her life was a nightmare. The bitch is better off where she is." He put his head in his hands.

"And what did you do to make things better for her, Frances? Did you try to help? Did you do anything for her? Did you protect her from your rotten bullying father?"

"Shut up, shut up, you bastard. I'll bloody kill you." He came at Jake with fists up, his rheumy eyes blazing with anger.

Spike took a step toward him and pushed with one hand. Frances staggered back and then fell to the floor.

"You left her, didn't you? You left her to it when your father was attacking her. He broke her leg and you did nothing you slimy coward."

Frances was crying now and Spike felt nothing but contempt for him. He would carry on provoking him, and every verbal thrust would be a score for Joey.

"When did you decide to make a living selling young boys? Your customers are all talking now. Their sentences will be reduced if they inform on you. They're singing like blackbirds, can't wait to tell all."

"They won't get anywhere. No one will believe them. It'll never get to court. I have insurance."

'You mean the superintendent," laughed Spike. "He's the one with insurance. He's giving everyone up in return for immunity from prosecution," he lied. "Superintendent Britten won't help you."

"He can't give anyone up. He didn't know about the others. I told him he was the only one. He insisted on that."

"So the list we recovered from your computer with names and dates and money paid will be useless you think? They were sums of money, weren't they? Payment for sex with little boys."

There was silence.

"And then there was the gardener," went on Spike, "the odd job man – Gambler."

"He didn't…"

"Didn't what?" asked Spike. "Didn't pay for sex. No we know that, but he did know what was going on. He kept quiet while you were blackmailing him, but he's telling all now. He saw some of your visitors. Recognised a couple, and as we speak, they are being interviewed."

"And you think they're going to admit shagging little boys. I don't think so."

"So are you saying that's what they did, Frances? That's what you arranged and took money for?"

He was silent.

"The evidence is piling up, Frances. Please explain what happened. Look I have no recording machine, no notepad. My little brother died because of some arrangement like that. There are no witnesses here. I need to know. Tell me now and I'll just go away. You can run. They'll probably catch up with you one day, but that's your problem. Tell me about Joey and I promise I'll leave."

The priest leant back against the wall, and closed his eyes.

"Joey was special," he said. "He was new. One of them, the Britten, had him once, and wanted to come back for more. I arranged for him to call and went to get Joey who was in the sick bay. He was hiding under the bed. I had to drag him out. He was like a little tiger then. He kicked and scratched me. My face was bleeding. He pulled away and ran toward the window and started to climb out. I tried to stop him, I tried to grab him but he fell. I didn't want him to fall." He paused and something that could have been a sob sounded in his throat.

"I left then, grabbed my stuff, told the bishop that my mother was dying and went straight down to the ferry. I've kept a low profile ever since. I've lived like a beggar. If you want to know that I've suffered, I have suffered. Is that any comfort to you? I thought I was safe here. How the hell did you find me?"

"Did you go to see if he was alive?"

'What?"

"My brother, did you go and see if he was alive?"

"No time."

"Did you care?"

"No."

Spike was silent and then left the cellar. "Did you get all that?"

"Yes," said Simon.

'I'll leave it to you and Jake and Kate. I need to go for a long walk. Would you look after that tape? Give it to Kate and tell her I'm taking the car back to Fougères. She'll be able to come back with the others."

It was very early when Spike arrived back to Fougères. He found a morning café and stopped for a coffee and croissant. He didn't know how long he sat there thinking. It wasn't until she handed him some folded paper napkins that he realised someone was sitting opposite. Tears had been pouring down his cheeks. He dried them and thanked her.

"Are you going to eat that croissant?' she asked. He pushed it over to her and she wolfed it down. He looked at he: straggly hair, no make-up, no nail varnish – no handbag! He was curious and glad to think of something else.

"You spoke to me in English – with an accent."

"I'm Polish. I'm trying to get to England for work because I do speak the language – but some men…" She stopped and bit her lip.

"Some men?"

"I paid them a lot of money. We stopped here a few days ago. We stay in house. I don't like what happens there."

"Well I'm not going to ask you to tell me what happens there. Do they have your bag? Your papers?"

"Yes, they won't give back."

"Is it near here?"

"Not far."

"Come on." He stood up.

"What are you going to do?"

"I'm going to get your bag and your papers and money. Do you have a passport?"

"Yes they have it?"

"How much did they charge to get you this far?"

"Two thousand euros. That's how much I agreed to pay, because my passport was out of date and I had to leave quickly but I had more. I had three thousand in my bag. They said they would give me some back if I…"

"And did you?"

"No no. I ran away to here."

"What's your name?"

"Josephine, you can call me Jo."

"Right come on, Jo Josephine, you guide me. My car is here. Jump in. I promise you can trust me," he said as she hesitated.

She pointed out a shabby house on the outskirts of town. The curtains were drawn but it was nigh on seven o'clock so he knocked on the door. It took several knocks before the door opened and an array of blue tattoos adorning the upper half of an overfed man with a moustache opened the door.

Before he could speak Spike said briskly, "I have a young lady in my car. You can see her there. She accidently left without her belongings. Would you get them for her please, make sure her money and passport are there?" The man tried to close the door but Spike's foot was in the way. "Quickly please or this young lady will be making a statement to the police and this house will be raided. Get her things now and we will go away."

All the fury from the night before was consuming Spike and it must have been clear, because within a few minutes, the belongings were thrown onto the footpath. Before he took his foot from the door, Spike beckoned Josephine over to check it.

"Yes," she said.

They left. And once out of earshot, she began to laugh almost hysterically. "You are so brave."

"Am I? Most days I would have been terrified, but today is special."

They drove to the Castle Hotel where Spike marched her in beside him. The concierge bustled forward immediately. "I'm sorry, sir, but we don't allow…"

"I have a reservation here. My name is Spike Jacobson. This young lady is going to my room to have a shower, and to change and then we will be having breakfast. Would you show her to my room please without delay?"

Spike went to Vic's room and explained about some of the events of the night before and his recent meeting with Josephine "So it looks as if Pippa's wish will be granted. I'm going to ask Pierre if he'll look after her for a day or two. We can't take her with us because her passport is out of date. We'll have to sort that. She'll be our very first girl."

"I thought we were stopping all this boat stuff?"

"We are for the time being, but I had to step in here, Vic. The girl was being traded. She was just going to end up as a sex slave. I saw the bastard that had tricked her. She thought she was paying for a passage to the UK. Well we're going to make sure she gets there safely. At least we can look after her at The Stables. It was fate, Vic. Her name is Josephine. I had to do it."

Vic grinned. "I like it, boss. We should be hearing from Kate soon. It'll be good to tie things up here and go home."

What they did hear from Kate, however, was staggering. The police had arrived in two cars. The priest and his Citroen had disappeared.

Chapter Thirty-seven

Five days after Kate returned to England, the body of the priest was found just a couple of miles from his cellar. It was in the ruins of an ancient farmhouse and he would have remained undisturbed had it not been for an old Citroen parked outside, only just visible from the road. It had a flat tyre. The police arrived on the scene and the body was taken away. There was no indication that it had been subjected to any kind of violence. A postmortem was carried out and the contents of the stomach did not suggest any form of poisoning. It appeared to have been a heart attack.

There was an investigation. Spike and Vic were still in France. They had things to arrange and they needed a couple of days' rest. When the news broke Spike immediately contacted the police to let them know he was available for questioning if necessary.

They did ask him to attend the police station in Saint-Hilaire, where a plain-clothes officer asked him when he had last seen Francois Tellier. Spike appeared quite willing to tell him precisely what had happened. He also provided him with details of the history of the case. The officer had remained quiet and thoughtful for some time while he digested the information. He had of course been aware of the search for the priest which had been headlines for days, but he had not appreciated fully the distressing facts behind the search. He had young children of his own.

"So, Monsieur, you were probably the last person to see him alive, and you had very good reason to hate him."

"Almost certainly, yes. And yes I hated him."

"And when you left, his car was still there with a puncture. Yes?"

"Yes, but still drivable I imagine."

"How did you leave?"

"I drove back to Fougères. My friend who had brought me here stayed with her boyfriend at the hotel but I wanted to leave. I was upset. I had just heard terrible things about my young brother – how he died."

"Yes, Monsieur. I was not aware of the details until this morning. Did anyone see you leave? What time would it have been?"

"One of the tour guides at Le Mont-Saint-Michel was with me when I spoke to Tellier. We left together and walked to the hotel. He saw me set off back to Fougères. He had the recording to give to the British detective. I'm not sure of the time but before midnight."

"Well, thank you for your time. I am so sorry about what happened to your brother. It was a terrible thing. It is a pity that Tellier escaped justice but he can't hurt anyone now."

"No indeed. You must go and speak the tour guide now. He will confirm my story."

Simon did in detail.

"Yes," he said, "the Citroen did have a flat, it must have been difficult, but not impossible to drive. It was certainly there when Spike – Monsieur Jacobson left."

No enquiries were also made at the Castle Hotel. Had he been asked, the receptionist would have been discreet about the time of M Jacobson's return with a female companion. The hotel looked after its clients.

Miss Meredith and Mr Scott were on the way to the airport to return to England. Mr Jacobson gave the police their contact details. No one in the lane where the stables were located had seen anything, although one resident thought he may have heard the engine of the Citroen firing up sometime after midnight and was delighted to see that it had disappeared when he went out the next morning. After these brief enquiries, the police decided that there had been no crime committed in connection with the death of Francois Tellier. Why he had gone to the cottage remained a mystery, but not one that exercised the minds of anyone for long.

If a young lady called Josephine had been interviewed, she may have said that it was seven o'clock in the morning when she first met Jacobson in the café or she might have just said she couldn't remember. In any case she was staying with Pierre and nobody knew about her.

If Vic had been questioned he would have said he'd gone to bed early and had no idea when Spike had come back. He had been so tired that night that he had gone to sleep leaving the television on. When he woke next morning Spike was in the shower, in his room, at least he assumed it was Spike, who was still in there when he went down for breakfast.

If they had thought to interview two crooks, who were desperately packing up and vacating the run-down house on the outskirts of the town before the police arrived, they would have told countless lies. Josephine at Spike's insistence had phoned the police in an attempt to rescue the other girls but by the time a squad arrived they were long gone. Traces of heroin were found in the kitchen and nearby ports were alerted.

During the two days that he remained available for questioning, Spike was calm. He had frequent discussions with Pippa and a boat was on the way to pick the three of them up. Pippa had spent two days planning and shopping and the decorators had finished Josephine's room which looked 'amazing' in duck egg blue, parchment and white, with a new bed and curtains and a TV. They would go out and buy her clothes as soon as she had settled in.

"Is she very pretty?" she had asked.

"Nah – ugly as sin," lied Spike. "I nearly left her where she was. I expect the boys will be fighting over her though even if she is a few years older than most of them. We're going to have problems, Pips. I hope you're up to it.

"Well we can always start a nursery if things get out

of hand. I think I might have its first occupant within a few months anyway."

"What? Are you serious?"

"Yes – do you mind?"

Spike was struck dumb. With everything that had happened in the last few weeks, this was something he didn't feel ready for. In fact, he didn't know how he felt?

"Spike?"

"Yes I'm here, just digesting the news. It's great. I'm delighted. Honestly, I'm thrilled. Just take care of yourself. No climbing ladders to hang curtains. I can't wait to get home. When is it due?"

"Tomorrow."

"What!"

"The boat. I won't be on it but I can't wait to see you all."

Spike sat down to weigh up the direction of the rest of his life. And as the news sank in, he smiled, and suddenly felt very happy. This child would be so well protected that no one would ever be able to hurt him – or her, but him would be nice.

By the time the boat arrived he, Vic and Josephine were waiting at Alberwich. Pierre had taken them there and waved goodbye. They didn't expect to see him for some time but he was a good friend and they promised to keep in touch.

Knowles had the news of the discovery of Tellier early that morning. Spike had called him, knowing that the

French police may take their time. Kate had flown back and was on the way back from Hackney where at Knowles' request she had been studying the access to a certain warehouse, which she believed was being used by the drug traffickers. It was difficult to see how they could set up an Obs. Post, as the nearest buildings were some distance away and there was a high wire fence all round it. She had already ascertained that the lease was held by a Kurdish chap who was rumoured to be planning to establish a car wash and polish business. There was a very successful one a quarter of a mile away which would seem to render this one unnecessary. She took a number of shots from various angles, hoping she wasn't being observed and headed back to the office.

"Guess who's dead. That bloody priest," Knowles greeted her when she arrived.

"Really? How?"

"They don't know and I don't care."

"Have you told Police Complaints – this is going to damage the case against Britten."

"Do you know what – I just can't get through. I'll try again later."

"You haven't tried, have you? You're waiting until they have played the recording of that conversation with Spike, haven't you? So that he will assume the priest is still alive and might give evidence in court about his customers."

"Okay, you call and tell them."

"I will, after I've had a coffee, maybe two. Do you know what time they're seeing him?"

"About eleven this morning. I hope it's over but they did tell me they would ring with an update. Can you get a coffee for me too, my nerves are in shreds?"

They were just considering the second cup when the call came. "Yes DCI Knowles here. Ah. Officer Clissold. Nice of you to call. How are things?"

Kate listened anxiously as Knowles nodded, said, "Hmm," scribbled a note on his desk pad. And finally said, "Thank you so much for letting me know."

He leaned back on his chair, heaved a deep sigh and shook his head. He looked at her and grinned. "He's put his hands up. Admitted his involvement, tried to say he was investigating the matter at first then must have realised that wouldn't wash. He couldn't get away with it. It's all on tape. Enough to charge him at least with being involved in the exploitation of children. He's been remanded in custody for a month. Bail refused. He's looking for a solicitor to take his case. No one seems keen. Dear oh dear what a shame."

"Well done, Guv."

"Well done all of us, Spike included. Oh dear I forgot to tell Clissold about the priest. Never mind. Makes no difference now. No trial for either of them. Think of the money saved. Shame though, one dead and one due for a long holiday behind bars. All's well that ends well, eh. Pub?"

"Pub yeah. I just need to let Spike know."

"Give him my kindest regards and tell him we might need to charter one of his boats and arrange for a cheque for that tour guide."

"Will do."

The following weekend Kate and Jake drove up to The Stables for a celebratory dinner and some sailing lessons. Ava was there too, and Griff.

Josephine took Kate upstairs to show her a beautiful room with views over the garden at the back. It had its own small shower room. She also had a wardrobe with a selection of casual clothes. A teddy bear sat smiling on a pillow. "It's not mine," she said, "but Pippa said to keep it till the baby came."

"You're pregnant," gasped Kate.

"No not me. Pippa is."

"That's brilliant," she said. "It's just what Spike needs. I'd better not say anything until they tell me."

It was a happy relaxed crowd that sat down to dinner. The food was lovely, the boys, who were always included (because they're family Spike had explained) were happy that everything was back to normal. Spike had proposed a toast to the new member of the family, due in about five months' time and it was not until much later, when the boys and Josephine had left to play table tennis that the conversation moved to the happenings of the last few weeks.

"You know, sometimes it feels like only a day or two

away, when you two first came here," said Pippa. "Before that, well, The Sanctuary was never mentioned. It was a dirty word."

"It's still a dirty word," said Spike, "but it doesn't make me feel sick any more. It wasn't until Vic and I decided somehow to restore the balance, to try to expose all the bad stuff that I was able to think of Joey. Before that I couldn't stand the pain. But when I realised it was ten years since Mum and Dad were killed, I thought I would never rest unless I did something. Suppose they were watching and waiting for me to act. They were lovely kind people. Retribution was not in their psyche. Anything like torture or any kind of aggression was alien to them. I had to bear that in mind all the time. I needed to get the right kind of civilised justice."

"And in the end he got away. Never had to answer for it," said Jake.

"Well," said Spike, 'it wasn't quite like that." He got up to bring another bottle of wine to the table. "I went back after Simon had gone. He saw me drive away but I stopped in a layby and walked back."

"Oh my goodness, Spike, why? Whatever you did, we don't want to know. We really don't, do we?" said Pippa looking at the others.

"Spike if you're going to make any admissions, please remember I'm a police officer. Right now, as far as I'm concerned, Tellier died of a heart attack and I'm happy to leave it at that."

"Civilised justice," I said. "Do you think I would go back and throttle him or something? Ten years ago I might have done, but then I'd be no better than he was or Mustafa or any other uncivilised thug."

"I saw him. I didn't touch him. I went back because I couldn't clear my mind. I couldn't go through the rest of my life with the vision of Joey lying there, possibly injured, and that swine just didn't care. He wasn't really surprised to see me. I took hold of his arm and pulled him out of that cellar and up the steps. I pushed him into the back seat of the car and drove it, bumping along till I saw the empty shell of the cottage and drove through an opening and parked. I pulled him into the house and he sat down leaning against a wall. Then I moved. I sat opposite a few feet away, and made him talk about his childhood, his mother, his father, why he became a priest.

"I think he thought I was going to kill him so he talked a lot to postpone my final move. I even felt quite sorry for him at times, although he was probably laying it on thick. He said once his father had tied him to a chair and made him watch him rape his mother. I heard all about his rotten dad and how he felt ashamed for not protecting her. I asked him if he felt shame about what he did at The Sanctuary – stupid question really. If there had been shame, he wouldn't have done it."

"But what did he say?"

"I think he hated his own childhood. He despised himself for enduring it. He obviously felt shame because he hadn't challenged his father. When he went to get Joey that night, when Joey struggled and fought him," Spike paused, "he told me that he actually admired his spirit, he respected him for it. His cheeks still have the faint scars. He touched them when he was talking to me. When Joey began to climb out of the window, he really did try to stop him. He might have tried to help him – I don't know. I may be wrong, but he did go down, he said, and Joey was dead. There was no pulse. He said at that point he felt remorse. A dead child! He had whispered to him that he was sorry. He may have been lying but it didn't seem so. Then he knew he had to get away."

"Did you believe him?"

"Yes. I think I did. I think it was all the truth. I made him talk about everything wicked in his life. How he manipulated Wellstead. How he had blackmailed Matron who'd had an affair with her sister's husband. How he'd attracted his customers most of whom had just turned up professing a desire to help the children. There hadn't been many, but yes, the Superintendent was one of them. He referred to him as that police pig but he knew his name. What he did after he came back to France, – he hadn't had much of a life, living like a beggar, hiding, because he thought they would be bound to come after him. I just made him talk but I didn't go near him again. I was there for hours. Whenever he stopped talking I made him start again. I think I made him talk himself to death, because he did stop in the end, then gripped his chest. It reminded me of Wellstead, and I realised he was having a heart attack. It went on for what seemed like half an hour. There was pain, he was groaning. I just watched until he died, he stopped breathing. It was over. I found myself looking at the corpse of the man who'd killed my brother – or caused his death, and realised that he had probably never in his life been loved or cared for except perhaps by a weak mother who ran out on him. I wasn't sorry. He made choices."

"So!" he looked at Kate, "do you want to arrest me?"

"I have no reason to. I think you used commendable restraint, and I hope that seeing him die, released you from the misery of those memories," said Kate. "Did he by any chance give you any other names?"

'No, just the ones on the list. Thanks, Kate. Yes, I know I will get over it now although it still gets me sometimes, but Pippa and I have work to do and a baby to look forward to. You must be two of the first people to come and see her when she's born."

"Or he," added Pippa.

"After that, they sat in the evening sun, with glasses of wine, and talked about boats and smugglers, dancing bears, Ava and Vic's engagement party and all the good things in life and when they were all likely to meet again.

It was sooner that any of them expected.

Epilogue

The following report by Phillipa Hilton was on the front page of *The Gazette* the day after the trial.

JUSTICE DELAYED NOT JUSTICE DENIED

TEN YEARS AND THIRTY-SIX DAYS AGO A TEN-YEAR-OLD BOY WAS FOUND DEAD IN THE GROUNDS OF A CHIDREN'S HOME IN OUR COUNTY, JUST A FEW MILES FROM THIS OFFICE.

Yesterday in London a man was found guilty of an offence, which was instrumental in causing the death of this little boy. He was sent to prison for fifteen years. This was a man to whom the Home Office had given the responsibility, amongst other things, for keeping our citizens safe, from torture, abuse and cruelty. This man himself was guilty of all three and more. He was not alone. He was just one of a group of men, who, in exchange for varying sums of money, bought the 'services' of little boys at the home. The boys had no choice. They were paraded, chosen and raped. It is difficult to imagine the living nightmare those children had to wake to each morning and anticipate each night.

The rules of the home precluded any attempts to cry

412

for help. Everything was strictly controlled. Few visits were permitted and the children were never allowed out unaccompanied. They must so often have cried. No one heard.

The man to whom they should have been able to turn for help, was Pious the priest, who was appointed by the Catholic church to run the home. He, the very man responsible for their welfare, arranged the 'appointments', took the money and fled to France the night the boy died. He left no address, no clues as to where he was, only a note to say that his mother was seriously ill, and that he must return in haste to France. This lie, was accepted without question, by the church authorities. His mother had died years before, but he was 'above suspicion'.

He didn't come back. There was an investigation into the death of the child, which was patently inadequate. No one attempted to find the priest, although it should have become clear, as the days and weeks went by and there was no word from him, that something was amiss. It was only ten years later that the hunt for the priest, Francois Tellier, began. It was headed by an officer from the Metropolitan Police Force. His suspicions were immediately triggered by the apparent lack of diligence of some of the original investigators. No one had asked the right questions. Officers who had tried were blocked.

Who was in charge of that original investigation? It was the then Detective Chief Inspector Britten and it was he, who yesterday, was sent to prison for fifteen years. He is lucky it was not for life. His name was at the top of the list of 'customers', found on the hard drive of a computer that had belonged to the priest.

Several weeks ago there was an appeal in this newspaper directed towards victims of such unimaginable cruelty. Victims and witnesses did respond and told their stories with courage and dignity. It is thanks to them and the relentless efforts of DCI Knowles from London whose determination to solve the original case finally brought to justice some of the criminals involved.

His team finally located the errant priest living in a cellar Near Le Mont-Saint-Michel in France, but he disappeared hours before the police arrived with a European Arrest Warrant. He was found dead days later in the ruins of a farmhouse close by. There was no inquest and he is believed to have died from natural causes. A lucky escape! Other names on the list will not be released, but further investigations will follow in due course. This paper feels it appropriate to urge once again anyone with information, to contact the local police. We have complete confidence in this division today. More and more evidence of similar historical abuse is being reported countrywide. If you have been a victim, do not hesitate to come forward, wherever you are. Only you and others like you can help prevent a story like this hitting the headlines again.